Mavericks

by

Rhonda Nelson
Tawny Weber

Two all-new, sinfully sexy soldier stories
from two favourite authors!

Military
Mavericks

RHONDA
NELSON

TAWNY
WEBER

MILLS
BOON

Mills & Boon, an imprint of Harlequin (UK) Limited, Eton House, 18-24 Paradise Road, Richmond, Surrey TW9 1SR

MILITARY MAVERICKS
© Harlequin Enterprises II B.V./S.à.r.l. 2012

The Rebel © Rhonda Nelson 2011
Breaking the Rules © Tawny Weber 2011

ISBN: 978 0 263 89748 7

024-0312

Printed and bound in Spain
by Blackprint CPI, Barcelona

THE REBEL

RHONDA
NELSON

A Waldenbooks best-selling author, two-time RITA® nominee and *Romantic Times* Reviewers Choice nominee, **Rhonda Nelson** writes hot romantic comedy for Blaze® and other Mills & Boon® imprints. With more than twenty-five published books to her credit and many more coming down the pike, she's thrilled with her career and enjoys dreaming up her characters and manipulating the worlds they live in. In addition to a writing career she has a husband, two adorable kids, a black lab, and a beautiful bichon frisé. She and her family make their chaotic but happy home in a small town in northern Alabama. She loves to hear from her readers, so be sure and check her out at www.readRhondaNelson.com.

For my father, who was a Navy man.
Love you, Daddy.

1

MAJOR FINN O'CONNER knew his last vacation before shipping off to the Middle East again—this would mark his third damned tour—was off to a terrible start when he felt something warm and wet cascading down his bare left calf to pool in his leather sandals.

Much to his horror, it was dog urine, being delivered quite unrepentantly by a massive English Bulldog with a mouth full of crooked teeth and a black, silver-studded leather collar.

"What the fu—" he grunted, and jumped out of the way. He shook his leg, kicking off his sandal in the process, and looked around for the dog's owner. Why the hell wasn't this animal on a leash, he wondered, muttering under his breath about irresponsible pet owners. When the search proved futile, he tackled the next order of business, which was cleaning the piss off his leg.

Though he'd crawled through worse and witnessed firsthand the ravages of war, he nonetheless found this revolting. He'd gone into the service by choice. The dog, damn its admittedly beautiful hide, hadn't given him one. Still cursing under his breath, he rummaged through the back of the SUV—where he'd been in the process of unloading his suitcase when the dog had nailed him—and grabbed the first thing he could find to wash his leg off with. A shame, he thought, grimacing as he unscrewed the bottle's lid and tilted the contents onto his leg.

"Interesting," an amused feminine voice announced, startling him. "I usually sip my JD, but to each his own I guess."

Finn looked up into a pair of familiar pale-green eyes and felt a smile inexplicably slide across his lips. Unexpected delight seasoned with a startling amount of lust wound its way though him, settling warmly around his heart and loins.

The heat in his loins he was accustomed to.

The feeling in his heart, however, was another matter altogether. He hadn't had that unsettling sensation since the last time he'd looked at her.

"Sunny," he said, surprised. He'd asked her parents—the owners of the Sandpiper Inn—if she was still around when he'd booked his stay. Her father had told him that she'd moved to Savannah, some thirty minutes away. He'd been unreasonably disappointed over that news, he remembered now, and had secretly planned to see her again.

Like her parents, Sunny had been a constant at the Sandpiper here on Tybee Island, Georgia, just a short bridge and a stone's throw from Savannah. His family had started coming to the intimate motor inn when he was a toddler and they'd vacationed here for a week every summer until he'd turned eighteen. He loved the scent of the ocean, the crash of the waves, roasting hot dogs over a driftwood fire, badminton, volleyball and fishing. The whole environment here was laid-back and fun. A beachside Mayberry, complete with a no-gun sheriff (Sunny's father), Aunt Bea (her mother) and Barney Fyfe (Tug Timmons, their slightly accident-prone handyman with more enthusiasm than ability). Was Tug still around? he wondered and made a mental note to ask.

Built in the early fifties, this little motel was positioned on a prime, unspoiled stretch of beach and had stayed true to its family-friendly atmosphere. Audie and Janine Ledbetter had updated it over the years—replaced worn-out furniture and appliances— but had resisted the temptation to level the structure and replace it with a row of trendy condominiums that would have undoubtedly earned them more money.

It was a shame to think that it might happen anyway, Finn thought, soaking up the familiar atmosphere. Seagulls squawked overhead and a salty breeze slid through his hair and into his lungs. Something loosened in his chest, expanded, making him feel...lighter.

Thank God. He'd felt as though he had lead in his shoes for the past six months.

According to Audie, he and Janine were ready to get out of the hospitality business, only Sunny hadn't shown any interest in taking it on in their stead. He'd jokingly asked if Finn was interested, and though he'd initially refused, Finn had to admit that the more he'd thought about it, the less insane the idea seemed. He hadn't been able to get the possibility out of his head.

Nostalgia, he thought, batting the ridiculous notion away again. He was a soldier. He'd been through the ROTC program in college—the University of Georgia—and had logged almost eight years in service to his country.

Duty, honor and courage, those were the traits that he admired, that he could be proud of. He'd always had a keen interest in American history and particularly admired the Founding Fathers. Were they perfect? No. They were human. But their dedication to the greater good, their sheer devotion to building a better country for their children, had left an impression on him that had shaped a career. A life. He was proud of his service and, though he would admit to some strange stirrings of discontent over the past few months, he'd never once regretted the path he'd chosen.

Or he hadn't, until his parents had suddenly died in a car accident last fall.

Finn swallowed as their dear faces suddenly surfaced in his mind, his mom's kind eyes, his father's crooked grin. It was funny the things one truly missed, he thought now. He missed the smell of his mother's perfume—light and floral—and the way she used to sing tunelessly as she painted. He missed the sound of his father tinkering in the garage, the way he cocked his head when he was considering something, his laugh.

He regretted the time he'd missed with them and that regret seemed to intensify every day. The holidays and vacations he'd never managed to come home for. Their passing had put a big gaping hole in his life and had left him feeling alone and out of sorts. Uprooted. Though there were plenty of beachfront properties on Tybee Island—ones that would have been more fortuitous for a single guy with a healthy libido—Finn had purposely chosen the Sandpiper with its individual cottages and retro charm. There were good memories here, he thought, and, irrationally, he knew he'd feel closer to his parents here. It was a tribute of sorts, one that he knew they would appreciate. His gaze slid to Sunny and he took a cautious breath.

Whether she appreciated him being here remained to be seen. The last time he'd seen Sunny had been the summer before he'd left for college.

And she'd been naked.

He'd been a typical horny eighteen-year-old with a certain amount of charm, a known quantity to her because he'd been visiting every summer, and, though it had taken the better part of the week, he'd finally succeeded in charming her yellow, polka-dotted bikini bottoms off.

He remembered soft skin, moonlight and tan lines, the sound of the surf hitting the beach, making promises he'd had good intentions of keeping… and the exact moment when he'd realized he was her first. He'd felt the strangest combination of masculine victory and shame. And, though he hadn't talked to her since that night, he'd never been with a woman when he hadn't thought about her. The combination of innocence and sensuality, the sleepy reverent way she'd looked at him when she'd welcomed him into her body. The slip of her fingers along his spine. It was all indelibly imprinted in his memory.

Other lovers had come and gone—they always went, at his prompting (he wasn't called the Teflon Don Juan for nothing)—but none had ever quite touched him the way she had.

Quite honestly, she'd terrified him. He'd looked into those soft green eyes, felt his chest expand with an emotion so intense it couldn't possibly be named and, though his future had been painstakingly mapped out for years, in that moment he saw a completely different one unfurl in front of him.

One that had included her.

He'd bolted, determined to stick with his predetermined course. Though it had been extremely difficult, he'd cut off all contact, making a clean break.

Later, Finn had chalked his extraordinary feelings for her up to his idealistic teenage mentality; life then had been a lot less complicated and the world was his oyster. But looking at her now, feeling the instant stirring of desire in his loins, he wasn't quite so sure.

She was his same old Sunny—blond curls hanging to her shoulders, a golden tan, the same dimpled smile. But time had added a fullness to her figure that made her all the more attractive. She wore a lime-green T-shirt with the Sandpiper logo screen-printed over her left breast, white shorts which showcased a first-class set of legs and a pair of funky-looking flip-flops with little fuzzy balls, lots of ribbon and pink flamingoes. The shoes made him smile. Her breasts were ripe, her ass was lush and the waist between them was small enough to make her look like a pin-up girl.

The sensuality he remembered was there in spades, but the innocence was gone. *Pity, that,* he thought, and wondered how much of it he was to blame for. There was a tightness around her eyes, a harder edge to her smile. Less open and more guarded.

"I usually sip my Jack Daniel's, too," Finn finally managed to say, his lips twisted. "But I needed something to rinse the dog piss off my leg."

She snickered and mild sense of satisfaction clung briefly to her smile. Her amused gaze strayed to the animal still sitting at his feet. "You've met Atticus, have you?"

He grunted. Atticus. That's right, he remembered. She'd loved *To Kill a Mockingbird*. "In a manner of speaking. Shouldn't you tell the owner to put him on a leash?"

"You just did."

His felt his eyes widen. "He's yours?" he asked incredulously. He would have pegged her as having one of those toy breeds that could be carried in a purse or under the crook of an arm, not this monstrous muscled lump of a dog.

Sunny nodded and patted her thigh. The dog gave him one last look, as though he were contemplating peeing on his other leg, then lumbered up and waddled over to her. "He usually doesn't go off the deck," she remarked. "The sand irritates his paws. He must have been very curious about you." She said it as though it were a compliment, as though he should be honored.

As if.

Finn smiled drolly and passed a hand over his face. "I'm having a hard time feeling flattered."

Atticus suddenly emitted a loud, rumbling stream of gas that would have done an elephant proud.

Startled, Finn frowned down at the dog and a grim note entered his voice. "Er...if he's your Welcome Wagon, sunshine, then business must be pretty slow."

Sunny's lips twitched, then a soft chuckle slipped past her lips. "Come on," she said, jerking her head toward the office. "You're going to want to be upwind from that."

2

SHE COULDN'T HAVE ORCHESTRATED a better passive-aggressive payback if she'd tried, Sunny Ledbetter thought with a small, satisfied smile as she led Finn O'Conner around to the so-shabby-it-was-considered-chic office to get him checked in. She made a mental note to reward Atticus with a special treat this evening. She'd fill his Kong with peanut butter and cheese, she decided, and give him one of her old shoes to rip apart.

In her opinion, her dog using Finn's leg as a fire hydrant and the loss of a little whiskey was a small price to pay for taking her virginity and breaking her fragile sixteen-year-old heart. It was water under the bridge now—it had been twelve years ago, after all—but the first couple of years after he'd left and hadn't come back had been pretty damned hard.

Every summer she'd eagerly anticipate seeing him again—there'd been no reason to think that she wouldn't, since his family had been coming to the Sandpiper for years—only to be bitterly disappointed when his parents arrived without him.

She'd *ached*.

Sunny had read somewhere that first loves almost imprint on your heart, forging a special sort of bond to the memories. Aware that he was watching her—that his gaze lingered on her ass, specifically—she walked behind the desk and nudged the computer out of suspend mode, taking a covert peek at him in the process. Her heart, which up to this point had been racing in her chest, skipped a beat and a low hum of desire pinged her middle. *Uh-oh.* The sensation felt like a portent of doom and she determinedly shrugged it off.

Been there, done that, bought the T-shirt.

She didn't know whether the imprinting theory was correct, but Finn O'Conner had certainly had a lasting impact on her. Because she'd seen him every summer since she was a child, it hadn't taken her long to develop a crush on the bronze-haired funny boy with a penchant for pranks. But that crush had morphed into something much more powerful that last summer, and she'd loved him with all the fervor, passion and innocence her young heart could manufacture.

Though he'd never kept his promise to "keep in touch" after he went off to college, Sunny nevertheless didn't regret that he'd been her first. He was the first guy she'd ever truly loved, after all, and it only seemed fitting. The only thing that spoiled the memory of that night was the goodbye that came at the end of it. The rest—the resulting heartbreak—ultimately didn't signify.

Besides, she'd learned a valuable lesson as the result of his desertion, one that had held true with every guy she'd dated since.

Guys, on the whole, were an untrustworthy lot.

An image of her most recent ex, Heath Townsend, rose in her mind's eye, making her grimace. Because she made a habit of being the dump*er* instead of the dump*ee,* Sunny had been planning to cut Heath loose anyway. She'd known after a few dates that there was no permanent future with the real estate developer, but had avoided breaking things off with him when she should have because she tended to avoid things that were unpleasant. Heath was a salesman, and she instinctively knew that the idea of not closing the deal with her wasn't going to sit well with him.

But when she'd found out—via a message she'd heard on his answering machine—that he was more interested in the Sandpiper, or more specifically the land it stood on, instead of her, she'd coolly and succinctly ended the relationship. She should have known what he'd wanted when he'd kept wanting to spend time with her parents, even going so far as to drop in on her father. He'd been an opportunistic asshole, Sunny thought now. She heaved an inward sigh.

Unfortunately, dumping him hadn't stopped him from repeatedly calling her and dropping by her place in Savannah. The first few calls and visits had showcased a repentant, cajoling Heath who'd declared his love and intentions, but when those had been kindly rebuffed, he'd gotten increasingly more irritating.

In addition to bothering her, he'd actually had the gall to bring a couple of business "friends" by her parents' place to "show them around." He'd acted as though they were still together and the property, by association with her, would soon be his. She didn't fear him exactly, but there was something decidedly strange about his continued inability to take no for an answer.

As much as she hated to admit it, being here this week could actually be a good thing. Perhaps her absence from Savannah over the next few days would prompt an official retreat on Heath's part. One could hope, anyway.

Honestly, when her mother and father had asked her to step in for them and run the inn while they took an unexpected cruise to the Caribbean—her mother had won the trip through her local supermarket and "She'd only gone in for a Polish sausage!"—the blanket of dread that had settled over her shoulders had just about smothered her. She'd barely restrained a scream.

This place, while seemingly an ideal place to grow up, had stolen her childhood and the bulk of her teen years. It wasn't until she'd gone away to college that she'd felt truly...free. *Number Eight needs ice. Take these batteries down to Three. Six needs cleaning. Nine wants a babysitter, etc....* It was a never-ending list of chores and, as the only child, the bulk of the gophering and menial tasks fell to Sunny.

Even now, just being here invoked the strangest feelings in her. An odd sense of peace and belonging combined with the strangest urge to flee, to escape before something happened that would change her forever, keep her here forever. People came to this place to run away from their lives—to vacate their reality—and the irony? Growing up, she'd wanted nothing more than to escape from here to have a life of her own.

And she had.

Using her business degree, she'd morphed one of

her hobbies into a very lucrative business she was proud of. She'd started Funky Feet in the spare bedroom of her apartment in Savannah—close enough to maintain a relationship with her parents but far enough away to preserve her independence—and now she had a brick-and-mortar store and contracts with many of the local upscale boutiques.

Nothing gave her more pleasure than seeing a pair of her extravagantly decorated flip-flops on a stranger's feet. Knowing that it was her creation and her expertise that had put them there gave her a sense of pride that was virtually indescribable. She'd hired two new staff members who worked to fulfill orders in the back and another full-time clerk to man the front of the store, leaving her free to design and negotiate new sale venues.

She counted herself as one of those increasingly rare individuals who genuinely loved what they did, and, though she knew it was a disappointment to her parents, she had absolutely no intention of coming back here and taking over the inn. A prick of regret surfaced with the admission—she missed living right on the beach, missed the laid-back atmosphere—but she knew it was the right course for her. Her parents could sell this place for a tidy sum and retire to their own vacation community where someone would wait on them for a change.

The fly in the ointment of that plan? Her parents weren't going to sell to anyone who wouldn't agree to keep the Sandpiper as it was. Meaning, no leveling the building and putting a more lucrative multilevel set of condominiums in its place. Furthermore, as thanks for years of service, her parents had given Tug Timmons, their longtime handyman, his own unit, so he would come with the place, as well. It was fitting, Sunny thought. Though she could easily see her parents enjoying an active retirement community, she couldn't see Tug anywhere but here. The beach had gotten into his bones, he liked to say, and he spent most of his time near the water. Rather than hire a replacement for him, her parents employed Clint Marsden, a local college kid, to cover the busier summer season. He came in a couple of days a week and the arrangement seemed to be working out nicely.

Though she knew there were probably other people out there like her parents who appreciated the old style of the Sandpiper—a single strip of small cottages with kitchenettes and individual decks, the nostalgic family feel to it—finding them was going to be difficult. It was going to take the right buyer. And waiting for him or her to come along just eked more time away from their retirement years.

Finn released a long breath and smiled at her. "Man, this place hasn't changed a bit."

For perverse reasons she didn't wish to explore, she booked him into Number One, which was the closest to the house. And to her. Clearly she was a glutton for punishment. Why should she keep him close when she fully intended to avoid him? She didn't know what sort of plans Finn had in mind, but if he had any intention of including her in them then he needed to think again. She was hardly the doe-eyed virgin of her youth and, though he still looked the part of her hero, there was a sadness around his eyes that hadn't been there the last time she'd seen him. War? she wondered. Or the death of his parents?

"Evidently, it's part of its charm," she said, handing him his key. Their fingers brushed and that briefest contact made her breath catch. *Oh, hell,* she thought, as her knees wobbled. That wasn't good. "You're in Number One," she managed to say, trying to steel herself against him.

"A real key," he said, shaking his head.

"No newfangled plastic system around here," she told him. "Words of wisdom from Audie Ledbetter— if it ain't broke, don't fix it."

Finn chuckled, the sound deep and sexy and woefully familiar. "Can't fault the logic there, can you?"

He hadn't changed much either, Sunny realized.

Certainly the boy had become a man. He was bigger, harder. The lean, rangy build of his teens she'd found so beautiful had grown into the broader, muscled body of a professional soldier. There was an inherent confidence in the way he moved; the set of his shoulders and his jaw suggested a sense of strength without trying. She smiled inwardly. He didn't have to beat his impressive chest like a gorilla to show the world he was a badass.

He simply was.

Just like grass was green and the sky was blue, Finn was lethal. Definitely somebody you'd want as an ally instead of an adversary.

Because her sense of self-preservation had obviously malfunctioned the instant she'd seen him again, she found that incredibly—stupidly—thrilling.

Laugh lines bracketed those hauntingly familiar blue eyes—a clear aqua ringed in turquoise, utterly unmatched in beauty—but a new knowledge lurked in their depths, suggesting he'd seen some of the worst the world had had to offer and wasn't all the better for it. To her regret, the evidence of war had left its mark on his face, a series of fading jagged scars across his cheek. Her heart inexplicably squeezed.

And those were just the scars she could see.

But even with as much change as he'd been through, she still recognized her Finn. The line of his jaw, the smooth slope of his brow, those wavy bronze locks and, most tellingly, his smile. Slightly crooked, unwittingly sensual, endearingly playful.

And damned dangerous, she knew from experience.

He looked up and his gaze tangled with hers, momentarily leaving her breathless. Heat sizzled through her, concentrating in her breasts. "I wasn't expecting you to be here," he said. "When I called to make my reservation your dad told me that you'd moved to Savannah."

Had he asked first? she wondered, unreasonably paranoid. Would he have chosen another place to stay if her father had told him that she was still here? Disappointment pricked her heart. "Er, yeah, I'm over in Savannah," she said. "I'm just filling in this week for Mom and Dad." And it couldn't end soon enough. She felt weird here, like an old version of herself, not the Sunny she'd become.

He arched a brow. "Nothing wrong, I hope."

She chuckled and rolled her eyes. "Only if taking a Caribbean cruise is wrong."

He laughed softly under his breath. "Definitely nothing wrong with that."

Speaking of parents…

Sunny winced. "I was sorry to hear about your mom and dad, Finn. They were good people." And they had been. Like many of the families who'd come to the Sandpiper over the years, the O'Conners had felt like family, an indulgent aunt and uncle who always had a ready smile and a kind word.

She watched the muscle play in his throat as he swallowed and a flash of anguish wrinkled his forehead. A shadow slid behind his gaze. "Thank you." He gazed out at the window toward the ocean, as if seeing something very different from her. "They certainly loved it here."

"Number Four, second week of June," she said with a sigh, looking inward. "Your mother brought me a new journal every summer. She'd said it was good therapy and I would appreciate it later." She nodded once. "She was right on both counts." She still kept a diary, usually snagging a few minutes in the early morning to jot down her thoughts. Occasionally she'd pick up one at random and thumb through it, seeing what her younger self had been doing on any given day. A window into her past, one that never failed to make her smile.

"She usually was," Finn admitted with a fond grin.

"And I could always score some Smarties from your dad. It was like Halloween every day."

Another chuckle rumbled up his throat. "I actually slipped a couple of boxes into his coat pocket before the funeral," Finn confessed, shooting her a look. "Crazy, huh?"

She swallowed the instant lump that rose in her throat. "Nope. I think *thoughtful* is a better word." She paused. "So what's going to happen to the guy that hit them?" Her father had told her the circumstances of the accident, how the driver had run a red light and broadsided them.

"Nothing," Finn said, straightening away from the counter. He exhaled a small breath. "He's just a kid and a good one at that." He tapped the key against his large palm. "He had a newly minted license and too little experience. I think living with what he's done is going to be punishment enough. I damned sure don't envy him that."

Mercy was an underappreciated virtue, Sunny thought, her throat suddenly tight. She hoped that boy recognized it enough to be able to pay it forward one day. He was probably too young to fully appreciate the gift that Finn had given him, but with maturity would come wisdom and possibly gratitude.

She merely nodded, not sure what to say. Thankfully, they both heard Atticus break the increasing silence in his usual way—by breaking wind—and they chuckled.

Finn's eyes widened and his face crumpled in disgust as the scent rose. "Geez, dog. Is this a chronic problem?"

She shushed him with a feigned frown and, out of habit, squirted some lemon-scented freshener into the air. "He can't help it."

Finn aimed a skeptical look at Atticus. "Does he try?"

"Probably not," she admitted with a smile. "But he's mine and I love him."

His gaze bumped into hers and the atmosphere instantly changed between them. Became charged, almost static. The air in her lungs thinned and a snake of heat wound through her limbs. "Lucky dog," he murmured, his eyes dropping to her lips, making them tingle.

Sunny inhaled a shaky breath. And on that note, it was time for her to go. She needed to clean the pool or check the ice machine or something. The last damned thing she needed to do was get involved on any level with Finn O'Conner. He was a walking expiration date, as fleeting as smoke. A hit-and-run-romance waiting to happen.

A more progressive-thinking woman might simply take advantage of that, adopt the enjoy-it-while-it-lasts mentality. And if it were any other guy but Finn, who was to say she wouldn't? It wasn't like she'd never had the occasional one-night stand. But it *was*

Finn and Sunny didn't trust herself enough to not let her heart get involved. This guy, for whatever reason, was her Achilles' heel. Her gaze moved over him once again, taking in the unequalled magnificence of the man he'd grown into and she felt a bolt of sheer lust land in her belly and drift south, warming parts of her that were better left alone. Just looking at his mouth made a vision of those talented lips slipping down her throat suddenly surface in her mind's eye, causing her heart to skip a beat in her chest.

She grimly suspected she was going to have to trade in her feisty flip-flops for a pair of combat boots.

An irrational surge of terror speared through her, jolting her into action. Honestly, between being here at the inn and seeing Finn again, she was feeling increasingly out of sorts.

"So you're here until Friday?" she asked, coming around the desk. She inwardly winced at the sound of her voice. It was too high, too happy. Shrill even.

Something shifted behind those too-perceptive eyes. "I am."

"Well, we're pleased you chose the Sandpiper for your vacation stay," she said briskly, the official spiel they routinely gave the newcomers. Not that they had many. Once people stayed here, they typically came back, just like Finn and his family and the various other tenants here at the moment. She felt an especially bright smile stretch across her face, but couldn't seem to stop it. "If you need anything, just let me know."

Recognizing the dismissal for what it was, Finn stilled and gave her a curious look—one that was eerily discerning. He'd always been able to do that, damn him. Peer right into her brain and pluck out her thoughts. When they were younger, she'd thought it romantic. She'd fancied that he was the only guy who could open a window to her soul.

Time to close the shutters.

Sunny turned and stepped to the door. She was almost through it when Finn said, "It's really good to see you again, Sunny. Can we catch up later?" She could hear the grin she loved in his voice—the slow, sexy, playful one. The one that made her want to kiss the corner of his mouth. "I'll share what's left of my Jack."

Swearing emphatically under her breath, she squeezed her eyes shut, pasted a smile back on her face and reluctantly turned around. If she said no it would look bad. Like she was still angry at him for what had happened, which would make her look pathetic for holding on to a grudge for a dozen years.

But if she said yes, he might perceive it as the green light for another vacation tryst. She wasn't blind. She'd seen the interest flare in those mesmerizing eyes and, while it was more gratifying than she could have ever imagined, she'd be a fool to respond to it.

Finn O'Conner was a slippery slope. And, while the idea of slipping and sliding all over him might hold vast physical appeal—she inwardly shivered at the thought—it was a very bad idea.

An idea of *epically* bad proportions.

She hesitated, torn.

"Come on, Sunny," he cajoled, adding an additional dose of charm to his smile. As if it wasn't lethal enough already. "It'll be good to catch up."

"Sure," she finally agreed, not seeing a way out of it. But beyond tonight he was on his own. She couldn't afford to get tangled up with Finn O'Conner again. He was every bit as temporary now as he'd been at eighteen. And she grimly suspected her heart wouldn't fare any better than it had the last time.

What was that old saying? Fool me once, shame on you. Fool me twice, shame on me.

She'd already been his fool once. She hadn't regretted it then, but something told her it would be a different story this time around.

"Morning, Martha Ann," Tug Timmons said with a deferential nod. "How are you on this glorious summer day?"

Martha Ann Bradford looked up from the romance novel she was reading and, silently cursing the rush of pleasure merely hearing his voice brought, sent him a look and smiled sweetly. "I'd be a lot better, Tug, if you weren't standing on my foot."

He blinked, then leaped back. A red flush crept beneath his tanned skin and those bright-blue eyes—the exact shade of the sky this morning, she noted—darkened with chagrin. "Sorry," he murmured. "Are you okay?"

She'd be a helluva lot better if he'd quit being so nice. How the heck was she supposed to fall gracefully into her dotage and enjoy her retirement if he was making her feel like a schoolgirl again, complete with her first crush. She'd spent entirely too much time in front of the mirror this morning and had been pretty heavy-handed with the anti-wrinkle cream. Such foolishness at her age.

Martha Ann didn't want to like Tug. In the first place, she'd only been widowed a year and in the second place, she was certain her kids wouldn't approve. They wanted her to plant flowers and make sugar cookies and dust the picture of their father on the mantel. She was sixty-eight—a youthful sixty-eight, she would admit—but the time for romance had past.

Unfortunately, her libido didn't agree.

In fact, she'd suspected her libido had died long before her husband and it was quite disconcerting to discover otherwise.

"I'm grilling steaks this evening," he told her, his voice low and smooth. "I thought you might like to come down for dinner."

Martha Ann smiled, unable to help herself. "Don't you grill steaks every evening, Tug?" she asked. He'd proffered the same question every morning since she'd arrived two weeks ago. She and her late husband, Sheldon, had been coming to the Sandpiper every summer for the past ten years. She'd noticed Tug, of course. He was fit from working at the inn, he had a smile that was warm and genuine and he never failed to make some positive comment about her hair, her outfit, her pedicure, whatever.

After years of being practically invisible and listening to constant criticism from her husband, she'd be lying if she said she hadn't preened a little when he paid her a compliment. But she'd been safely married then and hadn't allowed herself any unseemly thoughts.

But she wasn't married anymore. And the unseemly thoughts were beginning to get the better of her. She heaved a mental sigh.

It would be so much easier if he'd stop being nice to her.

Tug chuckled, the sound welcome and curiously intimate against her ears. "Not every night, no," he said. "Just the nights I invite you to dinner. What do you say, Martha Ann?" He frowned as a thought struck. "You're not a vegetarian, are you?"

She felt her lips twitch. "No."

"Are you off red meat?"

"No."

"Then come to dinner," he said. "I'll take care of everything."

She suspected he would. And she would like it. Too much. Martha Ann sighed again. "I'd better not," she told him. "I'm working on something." A puzzle. How exciting. Maybe after she'd completed it, she'd do something really thrilling like a crossword or a paint-by-number kit.

Though she knew he was disappointed, he was too much of a gentleman to let it show. He merely nodded and smiled at her, almost knowingly, as though he knew what she was afraid of. "Maybe another time, then," he said.

And with that parting comment, he moved on, ambling along the beach, his bare feet in the surf.

Martha Ann ignored the regret that weighted her middle and determinedly settled in with her book once more. She was widowed, she was retired and, like it or not, this was what was expected of her.

Pity that she hated it.

3

IT WAS A RELUCTANT YES, but a yes all the same, Finn thought as he watched Sunny disappear around the side of the building, Atticus a big wad of furry muscle on her heels. He shook his head, the sight of them together making him smile. Though it was difficult, he resisted the irrational urge to follow her, to go ahead and tender the apology he owed her now rather than waiting until later.

Though he had a reputation for being a little reck-less—he had a hair-trigger temper and an affinity for doing things his own way, conventional or not—Finn didn't function without an agenda. He always had a purpose and, though one would think that he'd go into a vacation without one, one would think *wrong*. While the locale of his retreat had been decided when he'd been flipping through old family photographs after his parents' death, it was the only impromptu decision he'd made, one that had immediately felt right.

Finn had good instincts—it was no small part of what had made him a good soldier—and he'd learned to listen to his gut. Some of the happiest memories of his childhood had been spent here with his family—fishing with his dad, picking up shells with his mother, hanging out with Sunny. He'd ripped and romped from one end of this beach to the other and had enjoyed every single minute of it.

Furthermore, though it might sound a bit bizarre, Finn had always had a thing for water. He loved the crash of the surf, the smell of the ocean, the sound of it hitting the beach. It soothed him in a way that was hard to describe, to put into mere words. When he was a kid he used to stand in the surf and draw a direct imaginary line from where he was to beyond the horizon, then would run and look at the globe to see what body of land that line would encounter next and marvel at the expanse. He chuckled, remembering.

Coming here had been a no-brainer.

But coming here didn't change what he was supposed to do. He'd soon be starting his third tour of duty in five years—this time to Afghanistan—and getting his head ready for war was his first priority.

An Army Ranger did *not* go into enemy territory

without preparation, particularly not one like himself who often found himself on covert ops.

With that in mind, his second order of business was to try and figure out what had brought on this burgeoning sense of discontent. It would be easy to see his parents' death as the reason behind this pressing urge to reevaluate his life, to step back and reassess, to see if his priorities needed to shift, but ultimately, he knew that wasn't true. He'd felt this coming on now for some time. Seeing fellow soldiers moon over a picture of their wife and kids had never bothered him before, but now he found himself turning away, unable to look at their happiness without a strange pang echoing in the empty pit of his stomach.

Overhearing the occasional intimate conversation—the I love yous and I miss yous, a father reading a story over the phone to his kid five thousand miles away, the soft intimate chuckle of a guy talking to the woman he loved... None of that had ever mattered to him. It was part of the scenery and par for the course. Honestly, he'd always been above it, for a lack of better description, operating on a less complicated playing field than the rest of them. In some sense, he'd even pitied them. He'd been solely focused on the job, utterly intent on being a soldier, doing his absolute best.

And those things were still important—Finn O'Conner didn't do anything half-assed and never would. It was all or nothing.

But he had to admit that there was an ever-expanding hole in his gut that was making him feel emptier by the minute. Whether he was experiencing a really early midlife crisis that would pass or a genuine sense of discontent that wouldn't be remedied without action remained to be seen. Whether the idea of owning the Sandpiper and carving out a new life—one that would better accommodate a family, if that ended up being what he wanted—was simply a product of essentially being orphaned or of a sense of nostalgia, he wasn't sure.

But, one way or another, he would know by the end of the week.

In all honesty, other than that one night all those years ago on the beach with Sunny, Finn had never imagined that he'd ever tick anything but "single" on his tax return. He'd wanted to be a soldier since he was old enough to play with the little plastic kind, and that desire had only grown as he'd gotten older. By the time he'd been ready to start college, it had hit fever pitch. He'd determinedly resisted the urge to contact Sunny after he'd left and had quickly leaped into the dating scene at the U of G. It was there that he'd earned the "Teflon Don Jaun" moniker and the nickname had been with him since.

Nothing ever stuck to him, most certainly not a woman.

Going the whole family route had never held any appeal for him. And, while he wasn't certain it was more palatable now, he also couldn't deny that the idea had been slowly circling in the back of his brain. As his father had always been quick to point out, he was the last of their O'Conner line. There was something unaccountably sad about that, Finn thought, and if he had children now, they'd never know their grandparents. The thought made his throat constrict, forcing him to swallow. That the O'Conners had lasted for centuries—through famine and disease, in wealth and in hardship—and would ultimately end with him.

By choice?

Furthermore, when he'd decided to come back to the Sandpiper, he'd also put another thing on his to-do list. He'd resolved to man-up and apologize to Sunny. It was a long time coming, he knew, but better late than never, he'd hoped. When he'd found out that she wouldn't be here, Finn had realized just how important righting that old wrong had become to him. So much so that he'd planned on getting her address from her parents and making the short drive over to Savannah.

How fortuitous that she was here.

His blood quickened and the telltale burn of desire seared through his veins, but Finn determinedly beat it back, grimly noting that it was more difficult to do that than usual. He had plenty to occupy his mind this week—readying for war and evaluating potentially life-changing decisions.

Seducing Sunny Ledbetter was nowhere on the list.

He'd do well to remember that.

Resolved to that course, he made quick work of unloading his gear and moved everything into his room. This one had a double bed, covered with a pale blue spread. A love seat with two shell-shaped pillows sat in front of an entertainment center and various watercolor beach scenes decorated the walls. He was particularly drawn to one. It depicted a young boy and a girl—the boy bronze-haired, the girl blond— holding hands on the beach, their backs to the artist, feet in the surf. They looked strangely familiar. Upon closer inspection, he realized why and the knowledge made another knot form in his throat.

The artist was his mother and the subjects? Him and Sunny. He couldn't have been more than ten, probably younger, he thought, leaning forward to get a better look. Had Sunny put him in here on purpose? Finn wondered. So he would see the painting? If so, he appreciated it. It was nice to know that a part of his parents remained here, in a place they'd cared so much about. He could remember them dancing on the deck, his dad giving his mom a slow twirl. His mother's smile when she wound up back in his father's arms. He remembered his mother cooking breakfast at the stove, his dad kissing her cheek. They'd always been an affectionate couple, never afraid to demonstrate their feelings.

It was only as an adult that he could appreciate just how rare that was, how happy they'd truly been.

Finn passed a hand over his face and looked around, noting some of the other changes. The old Formica countertops in the kitchen had been replaced with a modern shiny black laminate and the appliances were relatively new. The familiar scents of lemon cleaner and salty air triggered a sense of homecoming he hadn't expected, making a smile crawl across his lips.

Strangely energized, he made quick work of settling in. Within minutes his clothes were on hangers, his shoes in the closet and everything else was packed away in the drawers. He'd stopped on the way in at a little grocery store, stocking up on drinks, snacks and different things to grill. Finn was of the opinion that any meat was better when it was cooked over an open flame. He'd bought a new beach chair and a cooler and soon had both on the sand, his feet in the surf. Armed with a packet of peanuts and a cold beer, Finn sighed and rested more firmly into his seat.

Now *this* was what he called a vacation.

He watched a sailboat bob around in the distance, a boy paddle out on a surfboard. Down the beach, a couple of kids were building a sand castle, being overseen by what he imagined were their grandparents. He drummed his fingers on the chair and looked in the other direction.

More of the same.

He sighed and took a mouthful of beer. Popped a few peanuts into his mouth. Watched the water shift the little bits of shell around his feet, the rhythmic move of the ocean as it returned over and over, eroding the sand beneath his heels. He looked over his shoulder, hoping to catch a glimpse of Sunny, or even her horrid farting dog.

He saw neither.

Yes, he was officially on vacation, Finn thought. And with a dawning sense of dread, he realized… he was bored to death.

Shit.

THOUGH SHE WAS TRYING not to be too aware of him—quite futilely, of course—Sunny found herself looking out the window at Finn for the rest of the afternoon. She'd seen him take his chair and cooler down to the beach and had expected him to sit in the sun for several hours until it was time for them to "catch up" as he'd put it.

Interestingly, he hadn't.

He'd gone for a walk, stopped and talked to fellow vacationers, taken surfing lessons from Jamie, a kid from South Carolina whose family was staying in Number Nine and, most recently, she'd watched him help the Morrison twins—more guests of the inn—build a moat around their sand castle.

He had no idea how to be still, Sunny realized and wondered exactly when he'd forgotten how. In summers past, he would have spent hours with his toes in the water, simply…being.

Clearly, she wasn't the only one who'd changed.

But the inn certainly hadn't, she thought, watching the activity on the decks in front of the cottages, the families playing on the sand and in the ocean. Teenagers played volleyball and tossed Frisbees, children toted buckets of water to their sand castles and played in the surf. Laughter and music floated to her on the salty breeze, inexplicably pushing a smile over her lips.

A man suddenly poked his head into the office. "Mrs. Ledbetter?"

She wasn't expecting anyone else and, as usual, they were fully booked. "I'm Ms. actually. The Mrs. is on a cruise. Can I help you?"

"Ah, it's nice to finally meet you. I'm Victor Henniger," he said, as if she should know the name. He smiled a bit bashfully. "I hope that I'm not being too presumptuous, but was hoping I could take a look around."

For whatever reason, an alarm bell sounded in the back of Sunny's mind. She winced regretfully. "I'm afraid that we're full," she said. "But I'd be happy to take your number in the event of a cancellation."

His own smile turned uncertain. "Oh, I don't need a room. I just wanted to check out the property out before the surveyors arrived."

"Surveyors?" she said. "Who did you say you were again?" Her parents hadn't mentioned scheduling a survey. Furthermore, a survey for what?

"I'm Victor Henniger," he told her again. "Your fiancé is coordinating the sale of the property between myself and your parents."

Her fiancé? She blinked and gave her head a shake. "Er, I'm not engaged and my parents aren't selling the Sandpiper."

He frowned and raised a brow. "You're not engaged to Heath Townsend?"

Sunny felt her expression blacken. "No, I'm not, Mr. Henniger. And I don't know exactly what he's told you about the inn, but it's not for sale. Even if it were, he certainly wouldn't be brokering a deal on behalf of my parents."

Honestly, the nerve of the man! She'd like to literally squeeze his head right off his shoulders. He'd ordered a survey? Had he lost his mind? She knew he'd been behaving bizarrely, but this… This took the cake.

Mr. Henniger grew thoughtful for a moment, seemingly as perplexed as she'd been a moment ago and he smiled an apology, then gave a helpless shrug. "I'm very sorry for bothering you. Clearly, I've been misinformed."

That was a nice way of saying he'd been lied to, Sunny thought as she watched the man leave. Damned Heath. Did the truth even know how to come out of his mouth?

Satisfied that all her arrivals were in for the day, Sunny closed up the office and hurried over to the house to freshen up a bit before she met Finn. Though she hadn't lived here in years, the house still smelled familiar, like cinnamon buns and furniture polish. The tongue-and-groove ceilings had a new coat of white paint and the gleaming hardwood floors were covered in various rugs. Her mother had been collecting sea glass for years—bits that had washed ashore—and she'd displayed them in clear jars on the windowsill in the kitchen. Her father had the same affinity for old globes, which lined the bookcases on either side of the fireplace in the living room.

Everywhere she looked she saw her parents, bits of their personalities, a lifetime of living, loving and laughing in this old house. She breathed in the familiar sounds and smells and felt a little bit of her soul sigh. She'd moved away ten years ago and was utterly content with her apartment in Savannah, the life she'd carved out for herself. But she had to admit it was nice to come home. Nice that she could think of it that way now.

Because this place, no matter where she lived, was always going to be home.

That probably wasn't a good thing, since she had no intention of ever moving back. She'd made her life and she was happy. She loved her business, loved having her independence. *You could have that here, too,* a little voice whispered in the back of her brain. *You'd be happy.* Determinedly ignoring the wayward thoughts, she sighed and hurried upstairs to her old room.

Though she didn't want to encourage Finn in any

way, Sunny was just vain enough to want to look good. She resisted the urge to change into something more flattering—too obvious—but tidied her hair and makeup and spritzed on a bit of cologne. Atticus promptly sneezed, sending peanut-butter-scented slobber all over her leg.

Oh, goody.

Used to his excessive spit and to having it routinely wiped and spewed upon her, Sunny merely heaved a beleaguered sigh and washed it off. She clipped the leash onto the dog collar, grabbed his water bowl and a flip-flop for him to chew on, then made her way back over to the inn.

The sun was sinking low on the horizon, casting orange sparkles over the waves. Tug was playing Otis again—"(Sittin' On) The Dock of the Bay"—and was sitting outside on his deck tying fishing lures. She waved at him, but he didn't see her. The beach was alive with guests going about their evening activities. The sizzle of meat hitting a hot grill, the smell of shrimp boiling in spicy water, children flying kites and laughing, the occasional admonition from a parent. Though she wouldn't have believed it even a day ago, Sunny had to admit that she'd missed this. The beach, the way of life, was in her blood. Though she liked to be busy, she appreciated the pace of life around here and had carried it with her to Savannah.

Finn was waiting for her on the deck, a smile on his sinfully sculpted lips. That little smile sent a dart of heat straight to her womb. He wasn't sitting, of course—he seemed incapable of that now—but rather leaning against the railing. Good Lord, he looked good. Not just good, but absolutely freaking fantastic. A coil of heat tightened in her middle and she had the inexplicable urge to walk up to him and kiss the living hell out of him, to taste him and breathe him in. He'd already gotten a bit of sun and it gleamed on his nose and cheeks.

Despite the military cut, his hair still had a bit of wave to it and she loved the way it curled at the nape of his neck and around his ears. He wore a pair of khaki shorts that clung dangerously low on his lean hips and a navy blue T-shirt. His feet were bare, which she found ridiculously sexy. He'd showered before she'd come over and the scent of some musky fragrance rose off his skin. It was intoxicating and made her want to lick him all over. While he was naked.

It was criminally unfair.

He glanced at Atticus and raised a brow. "You're not expecting me to fill that bowl with Jack, are you?

Given his digestion problems, I can tell you that I wouldn't recommend it."

"He prefers champagne," Sunny quipped, mounting the steps. She let go a shaky breath and fastened the leash to the deck, then tossed the dog the shoe. Atticus immediately snatched the hot-pink flip-flop up and began tearing it into bits. She rolled her eyes, a wave of affection running through her. "It's for his water," she said. "He's always thirsty."

He shot her animal a skeptical glance. "He sure looks like a high-maintenance dog."

Determinedly ignoring the sizzle of awareness that tingled along her nerve endings, she slipped inside and quickly filled the bowl, then rejoined him on the deck. He had a tumbler waiting on her when she returned, and his fingers brushed hers when he handed it to her. Deliberately, she thought.

Eek. This was going to be harder than she thought.

"He *is* a high-maintenance dog," she said. Did that strangled voice belong to her? Sheesh. "His previous owners couldn't handle the stress."

He settled into one of the Adirondack chairs and kicked his feet out. His legs were longer than she remembered. Had more muscle definition. Her mouth suddenly went dry. "You haven't had him since he was a puppy?"

Sunny struggled to focus, tried to forget the bed mere feet away. "He was still a puppy when I got him, a very gassy one," she said, laughing.

"So you found him at a shelter?"

"I did," she confirmed with a nod. "I'd actually picked out a little poodle mix—chocolate with sweet brown eyes—from the website. A good dog for apartment living. Small, relatively inexpensive to feed. I'd considered all the options, determined to make the right choice." She took a sip of her drink, appreciating the burn. "I walked in to get a little dog and came out with Atticus. He's a purebred, you know," she added. "But he gnaws on everything, slobbers even worse and could win an international farting contest hands down."

Finn chuckled, the sound smooth and sexy. Intimate. *Damn.* Want, need and pure sexual desire swirled through her, settling hotly in her sex. "In other words, no one was lining up to take him home."

She swallowed. "He was a misfit and he was lonely. I couldn't leave him there."

"And the poodle mix?"

"Was adopted before I finished the paperwork for Atticus," she told him. She took another sip, savoring the flavor. "The cute dogs never lack for homes. It's the ugly ones that get passed over."

Finn reached down and slid a large hand over Atticus's wrinkled head. She found herself unreasonably jealous of her dog and imagined that big hand skimming down her back. "He's got some personality issues, but he's sure as hell not ugly."

Pleased, she smiled. Heath had hated her dog to the point that he couldn't appreciate anything about him. Atticus hadn't cared for him either, which should have been a clue to his true character.

He leaned back and released a big breath. "So your mom and dad are cruising the Caribbean and you're here?"

"That about sums it up, yes."

"So what do you do when you're not here?"

She shrugged. "Hook mostly. I've been working a corner downtown for years."

Finn choked on his drink and a wheezing laugh rattled up his throat. She'd missed that sound, Sunny realized, chuckling, too.

"That was evil," he told her, seemingly impressed, his eyes watering.

"Sorry." She shrugged. "Couldn't resist."

She loved the way his eyes crinkled around the corners when he smiled. "So when you're not hooking, what do you do?"

She held her feet up and wiggled them significantly. "I design flip-flops."

He stared at her, his expression blank. "You're yanking my chain again."

"I'm not," she insisted, laughing. "I started playing around with them when I was still in high school, actually sold them from the front office here in the beginning. More and more people started calling me, asking for designs to go with specific outfits—the bridal ones were particularly good sellers—and the rest is history." She pushed her hair away from her face. "I got my business degree, started a web business first, then went brick and mortar. I've got a store in Savannah." And if she sounded proud of herself, it was because she was. She loved her business and knew she was good at it.

"That's incredible, Sunny," he said with a wondering shake of his head. A slow grin slid across his lips. "And sort of ironic coming from a girl who never wore shoes."

Too true, she knew. "Ah, but if you remember, when I did wear shoes, I wore flip-flops. They were always my first choice."

He laughed. "Only because you could get in and out of them so quickly."

"And the sand didn't collect in them the way they did sneakers."

"I'm happy for you," he said, sincerity ringing in

his voice. "That's awesome. No wonder you don't want to come back and run this place."

She stilled. "What?"

"Your dad mentioned they were thinking about selling when I called to make my reservation. He said you weren't interested in continuing in the hospitality business."

"He mentioned selling to you? Seriously?" She knew they'd been talking about it, but she hadn't realized until right this very minute that they were seriously ready to leave. Funny, Sunny thought. Before she'd come back to step in the idea of them selling the place had seemed like the best plan, but now... Oh, hell, now she didn't know how she felt. The idea of another owner, another family here...

It was Finn's turn to pause and he regarded her steadily. She resisted the urge to squirm beneath that direct scrutiny. "Was he not supposed to?"

She gave her head a small shake. "No, it's just that he must finally be coming around. They've been talking about it for months, but have very specific ideas about the buyer. I wonder if they've talked to a Realtor," Sunny mused aloud, a strange sense of panic in her chest. It was ridiculous. She didn't want this place; in fact, she had built her own life away from it. Her parents were ready—quite rightfully—to retire. And yet... She knew they hadn't talked to

Heath about it, though. Heath had certainly brought it up to her parents often enough. His eagerness had annoyed her father and frankly, neither one of her parents had been too keen on him.

"What do you mean exactly by 'specific ideas'?" Finn asked.

Sunny looked down the row of rooms, saw families sitting outside, much as they were, enjoying the cooler dusk temperatures. The scent of hamburgers on the grill flavored the air and the hum of an ice cream maker sounded somewhere close by. The Sandpiper was cozy, intimate and, because her parents had always been concerned with making sure the families who stayed here would come back, affordable.

She released a small sigh and her rueful gaze tangled with his. "They don't want it to change," Sunny confided. "The land the Sandpiper is sitting on is worth more than the business. When they put it on the market, developers are going to be circling like sharks. Mom and Dad are going to insist on a buyer who won't raze the place, but will continue to run it the way that they have, to preserve the family-friendly laid-back feel of the place. And then there's Tug, of course." She jerked her head toward the last unit.

Finn blinked and his head swiveled in the direction she'd indicated. "He's still here?"

"Yes," she said. "He's retired, though. Mom and Dad gave him Number Fifteen."

He sipped his whiskey. "That was generous."

"True," she agreed. "But he earned it."

Finn seemed to be mulling that over. He stared thoughtfully down at his Jack, swirling the remainder in the bottom of the glass. "It would be a shame for it to change," he said. "Some of my very best memories are of this place. That's why I came back."

There was an odd undercurrent in that statement, Sunny thought, giving him a closer look.

Feeling her scrutiny, he glanced up at her. "And if they can't find the right buyer? What do you think will happen then?"

"They'll stay. They'll have to hire help—much as he'd never admit it, Dad's getting too old to handle the bigger repairs—which will mean raising the rates, but it can't be helped." Feeling unreasonably defensive, Sunny shot him a look. "I bet you think I'm being incredibly unreasonable and selfish, don't you?"

His eyes widened in surprise. "Why the hell would I?"

"Because I don't want to stay here. Because I like my life the way it is. Because I spent the bulk of my childhood as an unpaid maid, babysitter and gopher." Feeling unaccountably antsy, she handed him her glass. "Top me off, would you?"

Finn chuckled, but obliged. "I don't think you're being selfish at all, Sunny," he told her. "It's not selfish to want to blaze your own trail. This—" he gestured to the inn "—is the life *they* chose. You are free to choose, as well." He relaxed more fully into his seat, impossibly taking up more room and his leg brushed hers, the innocent contact making her melt inside. "It would be unreasonable for anyone to think otherwise."

She'd need to hear that more than she realized, Sunny thought. Heath had certainly had a different take on the idea, that was for sure. He'd wanted her to "claim her rightful inheritance" and had told her that she'd be a fool not to do so. That she'd worked her butt off here and she deserved it. Of course, given that he'd been telling people that they were engaged—her blood boiled anew—and had basically promised the property to this Mr. Henniger, she was hardly surprised that he would take that stance. *Asshole,* she thought now. The next time he called—and there would definitely be a next time, particularly after what had happened today—she was going to give him a dressing-down he was never going to forget.

Finn hesitated, then turned to face her. "Listen, Sunny, there's something I need to say."

Oh, shit. She'd hoped to avoid this, had hoped that he'd just leave it be. She had no desire to rehash the past and honestly didn't care to hear any excuses. It made her feel pathetic that she even cared. She should be over it. Over him. And yet seeing him again made it all come rushing back. The keen affection, the aching desire, the inability to look at anything but him. He'd been her world twelve years ago and she'd practically orbited around him. But then he'd left, leaving a black hole where her heart had been.

"No, you don't," Sunny told him, her voice too bright. She hated that, but couldn't seem to control it. The more nervous she became, the higher her voice climbed.

"Yes, I do," he insisted, leaning forward, an earnest expression on his too-dear, too-handsome face.

Her mouth went dry and her heart kicked into a faster rhythm. "It's water under the bridge, Finn."

"Maybe so," he admitted, his voice low. "But I still have to tell you that I'm sorry. I'm not going to offer an excuse, because I don't have one that justifies my behavior. But I do regret that I didn't keep my promise to you. I—I need you to know that."

It would have been so much better if he hadn't apologized, Sunny thought despairingly. She could have left tonight, fulfilling her obligatory "catching-up" session so as not to appear rude, and then avoided him for the rest of the week. It wouldn't have been easy, particularly where her libido was concerned, but she could have done it. The apology—which she *did* deserve—didn't wipe the slate clean, but it showed her another facet of his character. It would have been easier to ignore him if she knew he didn't have any regret.

She swallowed. "Thank you," she said, touched. Her voice shook. "I appreciate that."

Her cell phone went off, sending Bill Withers's soulful "Ain't No Sunshine" into the warm night air.

"I like your ring tone," Finn said, chuckling softly. "Ironic for a girl named Sunny."

She grunted. "It was better than Shelly or Sandy," she said, checking the display. Sunny frowned and sent the call to voice mail. She had every intention of blasting Heath with the brunt of her considerable anger, but she wasn't going to do it in front of Finn.

Naturally, his keen gaze missed nothing and she watched the curiosity form in his eyes. "Telemarketer?" he asked, his tone deceptively light.

The devil poked her with his pitchfork. "Worse. Ex-boyfriend." Damned Heath. Miserable rotten bastard. But as an exit, this worked beautifully. There, she thought with a tiny bit of smugness. Finn could stew on that for a while. And, from the slightly irritated look on his face, that's exactly what he was doing. She handed him her glass and stood, then gathered Atticus's things.

His brows winged up his forehead in surprise, transforming his expression into something less readable. Panic maybe? "You're leaving?"

She steeled herself against him, against the pull to stay, the raw need hammering in her veins. "It's been great talking to you, Finn, but I've got an early morning."

"I thought you might want to have dinner. I've got a couple of steaks marinating. I could toss them on the grill real quick."

That certainly sounded better than the ham sandwich she'd be eating tonight, but being here with him felt too familiar. Too many walks down memory lane would weaken her resolve and land her right back in his bed. With little to no effort, she knew, thanks to her own traitorous libido. Finn hadn't made the first pass—he didn't have to. She could feel the energy humming between them, the ever-present current of desire that was only going to strengthen according to the amount of time she spent with him.

He was leaving again—off to war this time—and though her sixteen-year-old heart had ultimately recovered, she wasn't sure her twenty-eight-year-old one would be able to muster the wherewithal to bounce back.

A flash of loneliness and panic raced across his face so fast she was inclined to believe she'd imagined it. That hint of vulnerability pricked at her heart. It wasn't an expression she'd never seen on Finn's face before and it didn't fit at all. He'd always been so confident, so self-assured. That was part of what had drawn her to him in the first place. Even when they were children he'd been fearless. He'd never dreamed that he *couldn't* do something. He'd been her rebel with a cause, she thought fondly, remembering.

What was Finn afraid of now? she wondered. What was it specifically that he was either avoiding or not willing to face? Had he become so accustomed to being busy and surrounded by people—she imagined there wasn't much privacy in the military—that he didn't know how to be alone? To be still? Her gaze slid over him once more and she repressed a shudder of pure desire.

"Did you bring a kite?" she asked suddenly. If she didn't make her exit scene now, she was going to be incapable of it.

His brow furrowed at the abrupt subject change. "No. I didn't think about it."

"You should get one. And some books," she added as she hurriedly descended the deck stairs to the boardwalk that connected the rooms.

He frowned. "Why?"

"Because you've forgotten how to be still," she called as she started off. She breathed a silent sigh of relief, resisting the urge to look back and see what he thought about that little insight.

Intuition told her he probably wasn't going to like it.

TUG TIMMONS TIED OFF the fly he'd been working on, then sat back and rolled his shoulders. It was hell getting old, he thought. Determined to be the eternal beach bum, he'd spent the better part of thirty years here on this piece of sand. Though he would never say that he'd wasted his life, he had to admit that he did have a few regrets. He'd never married, never had children.

Of course, he'd never wanted to do either of those things until Martha Ann Bradford turned up ten years ago and upended his world. He could remember it like it was yesterday. He'd been working on the pool pump, muttering and cussing under his breath when he'd heard her laugh.

That was all.

She'd laughed and it had been so intriguing, so delightful, so beautiful that he'd stopped what he was doing and looked up. A siren's song, he realized now. And then, of course, he was done for.

Martha Ann had sleek blond hair—the kind that

merely looked lighter as the gray came in—and it had been cut into a style that brushed the nape of her neck and hung in a wave around her face, curling along her jaw. She had intelligent bright blue eyes and a soft smile that made a man think she was always enjoying a private joke. She hadn't uttered a word, hadn't actually looked in his direction, but none of that had mattered. It was as if a lightning bolt had struck when he'd looked at her, and he'd wanted her to be his with every fiber of his being.

He'd wanted to hold her hand, to hear her laugh again. He'd wanted to mine her mind for her thoughts and figure out what made her tick. He'd wanted to make her breakfast and rub her shoulders and watch the sun go up and down with her. He'd wanted to show her his beach, walk along the hard-packed sand and tell her why every grain was so special.

He'd just wanted her…and she'd been taken.

Then. But not anymore.

Tug knew it was bad form to speak ill of the dead, but he'd never cared much for Martha Ann's husband. Still, considering he'd fallen in love with the man's wife, it wasn't likely he'd ever genuinely like the guy, anyway. In the ten years that they'd been coming here, Tug had never once heard Sheldon Bradford say a single complimentary thing to or about his wife. He'd treated her as if she'd been put on the earth to serve him and as though any good qualities she had were merely a reflection of his own influence in her life.

He'd been a self-important, condescending ass. Tug grinned to himself. Not that he had an opinion on the subject or anything.

When Martha Ann had arrived a couple of weeks ago without Sheldon in tow and had conveyed her newly widowed status, the joy that had bolted through Tug had just about sent him to his knees.

She was free. Finally.

And he fully intended to make her his.

Of course, that would be a lot easier if she'd agree to spend some time with him. But he hadn't waited ten years for her to give up just because she was a little resistant. He knew that she was interested, whether she'd admit it or not. She watched him when she thought he wasn't looking, and she was bad to fidget when he came around. He made her nervous.

That was a start.

4

HE'D FORGOTTEN HOW TO BE still? Finn thought. What the hell was she talking about? He'd been sitting here with her for the better part of an hour and hadn't moved off the deck. He'd had to fight the impulse to move closer to her, certainly, and had been silently congratulating himself on his restraint. But he could be still, dammit. He could. If he wanted to.

Though he'd like to blame his desire to be nearer to her on the monumental sexual attraction—which, unbelievably, had only worsened since the last time he'd seen her—he knew something else was at work here, as well. He was drawn to her, for lack of a better description. He had to physically fight the compulsion to lessen the distance between them all the time.

Furthermore, though he'd been continually distracted by her mouth—specifically the way it moved—and the tanned expanse of bare leg only inches from his own thigh, Finn had to admit that it had been a long time since he'd felt so settled in his own skin. She was a restful kind of company, his Sunny, and while he was getting the impression that she'd like to keep some distance between them… Finn had no intention of letting that happen.

The small noble part of his character knew he should respect her wishes—especially after what had happened last time—but the more substantial selfish part wanted to make her change her mind.

And the confident, observant part of him knew he could.

Because she was every bit as attracted to him as he was to her. *That* part of their relationship, despite time and his bad behavior, hadn't changed. He could read it in the slow curve of her lips, the lingering feel of her gaze as it slid over his body. She'd unwittingly moved closer, tilted her head in toward him, a soft hitch in her breathing. Little tells that signaled that her body was going through a similar meltdown of desire. Hell, he'd gone hard when she'd bent over to set the dog dish down, and he had been fighting the erection ever since.

He snorted. Didn't know how to be still, his ass. He could be still.

He purposely threw himself back into his chair,

then popped back up as another thought surfaced. A dark one.

Okay, so maybe he couldn't be still when he was thinking about the ex-boyfriend. If the guy was an ex, then why was he calling her? Had they just broken up? Had they been living together and he was merely calling to coordinate getting some of his stuff back? Or was he an unwilling ex? Finn wondered grimly. One who wanted her back?

Little red spots danced behind his lids at the thought and he suddenly felt as if he'd eaten something that hadn't agreed with him. His fingers tightened on the deck rail and he pried them loose to toss back the rest of his whiskey. It took a moment for him to label the emotion swirling in the pit of his stomach and when he did, shock momentarily jolted through him.

Jealousy? He was jealous? Of the ex-boyfriend of a former lover he hadn't seen in twelve years?

Nah, Finn told himself, shaking his head. He was not jealous. He couldn't be. Certainly he was fond of Sunny and she'd been the only girl he'd ever imagined a future with, the only one who'd ever scared the hell out of him, and he definitely wanted her with an intensity that bordered on manic, but…jealous? He wasn't that invested, he told himself. He was simply outraged on her behalf. He'd seen her frown when she'd checked the caller ID. Clearly the guy was bothering her.

He would make him stop.

Glad that he had a purpose, Finn easily hopped over the deck railing and made his way down to Sunny's house. He'd always loved that the main home was just separate from the rest of the inn. Close enough to still be a part of things, but detached for a bit of privacy. It was a two-story shingled cottage with a small widow's walk. For as long he could remember, the house had been painted a pale moss-green accented with white trim and shutters.

White and hot-pink oleander bloomed against the structure, splashes of happy color along the front. Two swings were at either end of the long front porch and a small table and chairs sat to the right of the front door, a comfy place to sit and take in the view. He'd seen Audie and Janine enjoy their morning coffee there many times.

Before he could stop and ask himself what the hell he was doing, he mounted the steps and rapped on her door.

From inside the house he heard an ominous growling bark and the telltale sound of toenails scrambling on a hardwood floor. Atticus skidded around the corner and hurtled toward the screen. He drew up short when he reached it, left a trail of spit against the door and then greeted Finn in the usual form—by farting.

Finn knew there was a doorbell outside the main office that would ring here at the house, alerting the Ledbetters that a guest needed assistance, so Sunny had to be wondering who was at her door.

She peered out into the hall from the kitchen and her eyes widened with something more than recognition when she saw him. Relief, maybe? She'd pulled her hair into a ponytail and donned a white sleeveless shirt and men's boxer shorts. The ex-boyfriend's? he wondered, gritting his teeth.

Her gaze turned wary. "Finn? Did you need something?"

Yes, he thought. *A lobotomy.* Because clearly he was losing his freakin' mind. Over the mere idea of an ex-boyfriend.

"I wondered if I could borrow a book," he said, improvising quickly. He patted himself on the back for sounding almost normal. Though he could presently chew nails into scrap metal, his voice sounded strangely calm.

She blinked, still startled at seeing him on her porch evidently. She unlatched the screen door. "Er, I'm not sure that I'm going to have anything that you would find of interest, but you're welcome to go through what I've still got here."

He stepped inside and took a moment to bend down and rub one of Atticus's velvety ears. "You're a decent guard dog, old boy, and the gas?" He gave a thumbs-up. "That's an excellent deterrent."

Sunny chuckled. "That's the only benefit to it, believe me." Her gaze slid to him. "So, a book? Right." She nodded once. "Follow me."

He sniffed the air and smelled something sweet. "Are you making cinnamon rolls?"

She shot him a look over her shoulder and smiled. "No, but Mom often makes them and the scent lingers."

Indeed. It was mouthwatering. "I'm not interrupting you, am I?" he asked as he trailed behind her to the stairs. Her heart-shaped rear end swung back and forth in a mesmerizing fashion that left him curiously light-headed. He grunted under his breath. Probably because most of his blood was rushing from one head to the other.

"Nothing that can't wait."

Was she being purposely vague to torment him? he wondered. Why couldn't she just say what she was doing? Better still, why in sweet hell did he think it was any of his business?

Though he'd been to her house many times, he'd only been in her bedroom a handful of them. She had the same white spindly furniture she'd had when she was a teenager. A colorful quilt covered her bed and half a dozen pillows littered the surface. Framed photos from her childhood hung on the walls, various trophies—mostly for softball—sat on her chest of drawers and a small pink jewelry box with a single ballerina that didn't twirl held a place of honor on her dresser.

She led him over to a bookcase and said, "Take your pick."

"I'm surprised your parents didn't turn your room into a bigger bathroom or a guest bedroom when you moved out," he remarked, looking at the titles. Romance, romance and more romance. He was beginning to see a theme here. "Mine sure didn't waste any time," Finn said, laughing softly.

"I don't know if you've noticed this or not, but my parents tend to resist change," she said, a droll smile in her voice. She stubbed her big toe into the carpet and shifted nervously. So she didn't like him in here, did she? Too close to the bed to suit her? His lips twisted with masculine satisfaction.

"Have you read all of these?" he asked, trying to keep the grin under control.

"Of course. Why else would I have them?"

He shot her a smile over his shoulder. "Do you have anything that doesn't have a man and woman embracing on the cover?"

With a put-upon sigh she shouldered him out of the way, squatted down and selected a book from the shelf, then handed it to him.

He glanced at the title and raised a skeptical brow. *"Harry Potter and the Sorcerer's Stone?* Are you serious? Isn't it a kid's book?"

She lifted her chin. "Read the first fifty pages. If you're not hooked, I'll—"

"Have dinner with me," he interjected before she could finish. He had to seize the opportunities when she presented them, after all. He was only here four more days, then it was back to his reality. Orphaned soldier, no home, no family. His chest tightened and a bizarre sort of panic punched him in the gut. He shook the unsettling sensation off. Geez, Lord. What the hell was wrong with him?

She grinned, recognizing the ploy for what it was. "I was going to say—"

But whatever she was going to say was interrupted by the ringing of her cell phone again. She made another ominous face, growled low in her throat and bolted downstairs. After a second's hesitation, Finn followed her.

She'd just looked at the display when he caught up with her in the kitchen. "Dammit," she muttered, obviously irritated. "I'm going to have to take this. Excuse me a minute."

She left him standing in the kitchen and walked into the dining room, presumably for some privacy. He noted sandwich fixings on the counter and tried not to be annoyed, then edged closer to the door so that he could listen to her. Yes, it was rude. Yes, his mother had taught him better. Yes, he was still going to do it.

He was curious, dammit. And if she was in some sort of trouble or needed assistance with anything, then he intended to help her.

"Listen, Heath," he heard her say through clenched teeth. "It's over, you understand? We're not dating anymore. Ever. Period. I don't want to see you anymore. I thought I made that clear. I—"

Masculine pleasure bloomed in his chest, pushing a smile across his lips.

"I'm sorry that you feel that way, but you are going to have to leave me alone. Stop calling me. Stop coming by my apartment. Stop dropping by my store. And for the love of all that's holy, don't ever tell another person that I'm your fiancée. Let it go," she said, her voice so hard it should have shattered Heath's balls. "If you don't, I'm going to have to contact the authorities."

An alarm sounded in the back of Finn's mind. If she was threatening to call the cops, in all likelihood she probably already should have. That's the way it usually worked.

He *was* going to have to make the jackass go away, Finn thought, familiar adrenaline—his fix—hitting his system.

A course of action quickly came to mind. Finn abruptly walked into the dining room and in loud, carrying tones said, "Baby, this massage oil is going to get cold if you don't come back to bed."

Sunny inhaled with shock, her eyes widened in horror and then narrowed into tiny little slits that were shooting a very convincing death ray at him.

Oh, hell, Finn thought. That didn't exactly look like gratitude to him.

"WHO'S THAT?" Heath demanded, his voice throbbing with anger. "You're seeing someone else? *Already?* I can't believe you, Sunny. I thought we had something special. I thought—"

"Whatever we had is *over,* Heath. For the last time, stop calling me." She abruptly closed the phone before he could say anything else and made a mental note to call her cell company and have his number blocked. She released a huge breath, hoping to ease a bit of the tension gathering rapidly in her shoulders.

It didn't work.

She glared at Finn. *"This massage oil is going to*

get cold?" she repeated, each word coming out more mangled than the last. "Have you lost your *freaking* mind?" she practically screamed at him. Anger had replaced the initial shock and she could literally feel the top of her head vibrating, ready to blow. "Where in the hell do you get off interfering in my personal business? What makes you think you have the right?" Her gaze narrowed. "I don't know what world you've been living in, Rambo, but that *wasn't* cool."

He retreated a step, and, though she imagined her vision was wobbly due to the fact she was literally quaking with irritation, she thought she saw his lips twitch. "Rambo?"

He *was* laughing at her, the wretch. "Finn, I am not amused."

He tried unsuccessfully to flatten his lips. "I can see that. I can't believe you s-stomped your f-foot. I've never seen a girl do that b-before." He didn't just laugh, he roared. She'd never wanted to whack another person more, Sunny realized.

She crossed her arms over her chest to keep from doing just that. "I did *not* stomp my foot." At least, she didn't think she had, though she supposed it was possible.

"You did," he wheezed, his big shoulders quaking. "God, that was priceless. The next time I need a laugh, I'm pulling that memory out."

She flushed, mortified, then bared her teeth in a smile. "Not if I knock your head off your shoulders first."

He stilled and studied her thoughtfully for a moment. His eyes widened in surprise. "You're really pissed."

"You think?" she asked sarcastically. "You should probably brush up on those deductive reasoning skills while you're here. Maybe work a few crosswords or something."

"I was only trying to help, Sunny. I—"

She almost stomped her foot again, but resisted the impulse and tossed her cell phone into the nearest chair instead. "I didn't ask for your help, Finn."

He lifted his chin and something shifted in his gaze. Grew harder and more intuitive. "Maybe not, but you need it."

A finger of unease nudged her middle. "What makes you say that?"

"Those deductive reasoning skills you seem to think I need to work on," he said, his lips curving into a grim smile. That barb had struck a nerve. "He phoned while you were down at my place and you ignored the call. Less than an hour later, he's made contact again and, from the sounds of your end of the conversation, it's been going on for a while."

"It's rude to eavesdrop," she muttered, plopping down on the sofa with a dejected thump.

He sat down next to her, entirely too close for comfort. A current of heat snaked through her, irritating her all the more. She was too aware of him for comfort, too sensitive to every breath that went in and out of his lungs, the fine hair on his arms brushing hers. "I would have heard you even if I hadn't been trying."

Spent, she managed a weak laugh. "You're not even going to try to deny it, are you?"

She felt him shrug and knew that he had moved closer. Again. She smothered an inevitable sigh. "I don't see the point. Besides, you baited me with the ex-boyfriend comment before you left."

She feigned offense. "I didn't bait you!"

He chuckled. "Liar."

Sunny harrumphed and rolled her eyes. "Being a soldier has obviously made you paranoid."

"Being a soldier has made me extremely observant. I saw that smug little smile when you turned to leave."

Damn. And she thought she'd been so cool. "You do get regular physical exams in the army, right? I think you might need to get your eyes checked."

"And I think you need a restraining order. Heath

doesn't sound like the kind of guy who's going to give up."

She grimly suspected he was right, but didn't want to admit it to him. "Oh, I'm sure he'll stop now that he knows that I'm getting rubbed down with heated massage oil by another guy," she said, purposely injecting a huge load of sarcasm into her voice. "I still can't believe you said that. Moron," she complained.

A sexy chuckle rumbled up Finn's throat. "I'm sure he's only sorry that he didn't think of it first."

She turned to look at him. "And what makes you think he didn't?"

A comical amount of confidence faded from his smile. "Did he?"

She turned away and sniffed primly. "I don't see where that's any of your business."

Finn sighed happily, the self-assured smile back on his face. "That's a no then."

"Sandwalwood is my favorite," Sunny said thoughtfully. "It's warm with a touch of spice and a hint of rose, the perfect combination of sensual and romantic. I also like lemon verbena. So…invigorating." She lingered purposely over that last word and gave a delicate little shudder. She popped up from the couch. "So, you've got your book?"

He blinked stupidly and his beautiful mouth had gone a bit slack. "Come again?"

"Your book," she reminded slowly. "The one you came over here for."

Finn didn't stand. "Oh, yeah."

"Did you leave it upstairs?"

His brooding gaze found hers. "I left it in the kitchen. I'll get it when I leave."

Meaning he wasn't ready to leave yet, despite her quite obvious hint. She exhaled a slow breath. "Finn—"

"How long has this been going on? How long did you and this Heath guy date? How long since you dumped him?"

She shook her head and looked heavenward for divine assistance. How was she supposed to avoid Finn if he barged into her space? How was she supposed to keep from sitting in his lap and kissing his neck and slipping her hands all over his body if he wouldn't leave her alone? "You have no concept of personal boundaries, do you?"

His unwavering stare was dead-serious and unnerving. She felt herself flush. "Your safety is very personal to me."

She'd have to be made of stone not to appreciate his concern and sincerity. She found herself reluctantly softening toward him. "Finn, I'm perfectly safe."

"I don't think you are. How long has he been harassing you?"

"Several weeks," she admitted. She moved to the mantel and adjusted a photograph. "He just doesn't want to accept that I've broken things off." She couldn't tell him the rest. It was too embarrassing.

"How long did you see him?"

Since he wasn't going to leave, she might as well sit back down, Sunny thought, but took a chair instead of joining him on the couch. "A couple of months."

"Intimate?"

Beating that horse to death, wasn't he? she thought, inwardly pleased. "None of your business."

The edge of his mouth tilted. "It could be important."

"I doubt it."

He grimaced. "Why did you break up?"

"Because I knew it was a dead-end relationship and I don't like to waste my time," she said.

That wasn't the only reason, of course, but there was no way in hell she was telling him that Heath had been telling other developers that once the Sandpiper was hers, it was as good as his. It was just too damned galling to admit. She was eternally thankful that she hadn't slept with him.

Sunny had a healthy libido and had had several lovers over the years—some more serious than others—but she was especially selective when deciding who she shared her body with. There was a level of trust that had to be met first and, with Heath, they never gotten to that point. He'd been attentive, courteous and said all the right things…but something inside of her simply hadn't been able to make that leap.

"And how long since you ended it?"

"Three weeks ago."

Finn's expression blackened. "So, long enough for him to recognize that it's a lost cause." His gaze slid to hers. "Something's not right, Sunny. Any man with a grain of self-respect would have backed off by now. He's harassing you and, from the sounds of it, with increasing frequency. You need to report him, get a restraining order."

She'd resisted that idea because she didn't want to overreact, but hearing Finn say it somehow made the idea more credible. And after Mr. Henniger's appearance today, she had to admit that Heath was becoming increasingly erratic and irrational.

She released a shaky breath. "Okay."

He nodded once, seemingly pleased and settled more firmly against her couch. "In the meantime, I'm staying here."

5

FINN KNEW THE MINUTE the words left his mouth that she was going to vehemently resist and he was right. Sunny gasped like a dying fish, then bolted up from her chair. A long curl escaped her ponytail and her cheeks pinkened.

"You are not," she said, a hint of hysteria and desperation in the protest.

He shrugged lazily, confident that this was the right move. "It only makes sense."

And it did.

This Heath guy was definitely a threat and, though Finn had only been trying to help with his massage-oil comment, he grimly suspected that it might have actually made things worse. He'd thought that if Heath had caught the scent of another guy around Sunny, he'd back off and give up the idea of a reconciliation. But he wasn't dealing with the average guy here and had a hunch that his stunt had only painted a bigger target on Sunny's back.

That was *his* fault and he'd be damned if he'd sit idly by and do nothing.

And if he'd learned anything today, it was that he didn't seem to be capable of *doing nothing*.

Sunny looked away, seemingly trying to figure out a way to frame a reply. She looked miserable and desperate and just a smidge hysterical. "Listen, Finn, it's not that I don't appreciate the offer, but it really isn't necessary. I've got Atticus—" she jerked her head in the dog's direction "—and Heath doesn't even know I'm here. I'm perfectly safe."

He shook his head. "All the same, I'd feel better—"

"Well, I wouldn't," she interjected, the wild look back in her eyes. Her pulse fluttered rapidly at the base of her throat, and suddenly her panicked reluctance made sense. He'd already noted that she was still attracted to him, that the desire hammering away at him was taking a mallet to her, as well. Too much temptation then? he wondered. Didn't trust herself around him?

Finn felt a slow-dawning smile drift across his lips. It was all he could do not to preen. "Why wouldn't you? It's not like you don't know me."

Her own gaze grew mistrustful as she noted his grin. "I haven't seen you in *twelve* years, Finn. I knew the boy. The man is still a mystery."

"I'm the same guy," he told her.

She lifted her chin. "Then that's disappointing. I was hoping you'd matured a bit."

That dart penetrated because it was accurate and well-deserved. He swallowed. Well, while they were being truthful… He laughed softly and shook his head. "I know why you don't want me to stay."

"Yes, because I just told you," she bit out, evidently irritated by the innuendo in his tone.

A bark of laughter erupted from his throat. "That's not why."

She blinked in exaggerated confusion. "It's not? Oh, gee, Finn. Then why don't you tell me?"

"Because you want me," he told her. "And if I'm here with you, then I'm too close."

She did the guppy face again and the whites of her eyes kept getting bigger and bigger. "You— I—" She emitted a long, frustrated growl, then pointed to the door. "Out!"

"Sunny—"

She started toward him and picked up the closest thing at hand, a heavy ceramic vase, and drew her arm back.

Startled, he jumped up. "I'm going," he said before she could hurl it at him.

"Not fast enough," she said through gritted teeth.

He swung through the kitchen and snagged his book, then headed for the back door. "Sunny, listen to me. I really think that you need a guy around. I don't think—"

She laughed without humor. "No, you don't, but that still doesn't keep your mouth from working, does it?" She opened the door and shoved him through it, staggering a bit as she did so. "This is not your problem, Finn. You're on vacation. Deal with it."

She abruptly slammed the door.

She was wrong—this *was* his problem.

And she might have gotten mad, considered attacking him and kicked him out of her house because he'd told her that he knew that she wanted him…but not once had she denied it.

This battle was far from over, but if there was ever a time to retreat, this was it. Finn shoved his hands into his pockets and, whistling tunelessly, strolled over to the porch swing and took up his post.

SHE LOOKED LIKE DEATH WARMED OVER, Sunny thought as she met her reflection in the mirror the next morning. The bags under her eyes had their own set of luggage and her head ached from lack of sleep.

Ugh.

Adding another black mark next to Finn's name, she stepped into the shower, hoping to wash some of the irritation away. She'd forgotten just how easily he'd always been able to yank her chain. Her feelings where he was concerned had never been mediocre and the reactions he inspired in her only followed suit.

Of course, it didn't help matters that he was right.

And, more gallingly, that he knew it.

She groaned aloud and pushed her face beneath the spray.

When he'd announced that he was going to stay with her, Sunny had gone into full-blown panic mode. She'd had a hard enough time leaving him when he'd asked her to stay for dinner. In fact, she'd actually felt guilty about it. But she'd left because every second that she spent with him only intensified the attraction. Only made her more hammeringly aware of the exact curve of his smile, his sleepy heavy-lidded gaze, the mesmerizing shape of his hands—big and competent—and how they would feel sliding up her skin.

To be perfectly honest, Sunny wanted him to want

her. Wanted him to burn and ache for her, to make him crazy with desire.

But she wanted to resist him.

The fly in the ointment? She wasn't altogether certain that she *could* resist him. That's why she'd freaked. That's why she'd lost any resemblance to a rational human being when he'd confronted her with the mortifying truth and, like a crazed harpy, had rushed him to the door.

She did want him. Still.

Against all reason and better judgment. It didn't matter that he'd broken her heart, that he'd left her once without so much as a postcard later. It didn't matter that he was leaving again. It only mattered that he was here now, however fleetingly, and that Finn O'Conner still had the ability to melt her heart.

Though she knew she was fighting a losing battle, Sunny nevertheless would continue to fight. She couldn't afford not to. He'd wounded her before, she knew, but something told her that this time around when he left, she'd be obliterated. The life that she'd managed to carve out for herself would lose its luster when he left, and she'd never be able to find her happy place again, because he wouldn't be in it.

Not no, but, hell, no.

Furthermore, she'd taken a cheap shot when she'd said she didn't know him. That she'd known the boy and not the man. True, she hadn't seen him in the last twelve years and there were many things that had happened to him during that time that were a mystery to her...but she did *know* him.

Her Finn was there, more mature, of course, but she still recognized him. He was the merciful guy who gave a pass to the young teenager who'd accidentally killed his parents; he was the sentimental guy who tucked Smarties into his father's pocket at the funeral. He was the humble guy who tendered an apology more than a decade late, just because it was the right thing to do. She swallowed.

He was still her Finn...and that made him all the more lethal.

Sunny rinsed her hair, then shut the water off and reached for her towel. Furthermore, much as she'd like to think that he simply wanted to stay with her to charm his way back into her bed—and she wasn't stupid enough to think he wouldn't try—Sunny believed that he was genuinely worried about her safety. She'd seen the look on his face, the anger and concern when she'd finally admitted how long Heath had been bothering her. And he was right. It was past time for Heath to know that any chance of getting back together was a lost cause. Hadn't she suspected something was off? Hadn't there been a niggle of unease?

Hadn't she noted the panicked note in Heath's voice? The hint of hysteria lurking in his tone?

Clint, their part-time summer help—big on muscle, short on common sense—would be in today at ten and she had every intention of going down to the police department and seeing precisely what she needed to do to make Heath leave her alone. Having Mr. Henniger show up yesterday had really clued her in to how out of touch with reality Heath was.

To ease some of Finn's anxiety, she'd let him know, Sunny decided. And this way, she avoided becoming a project, because she knew damned well he was looking for one. He didn't have a clue how to simply enjoy the moment anymore, to appreciate a sunset or the feel of sand beneath his feet. What was he avoiding? Sunny wondered. What thoughts crept in during the ensuing quiet that he didn't want to deal with? Why didn't he want to be still? Was it the war? The death of his parents? Probably a combination of both, she decided, which would make anyone not want to be in their own head.

But he was going to have to be, Sunny decided, because, as much as she'd like to help him, she didn't think she could risk her own sanity in the process. She was happy, dammit, and wanted to stay that way. Her good life wouldn't be so good anymore if she let him in, if she let him get too close. All the things that she'd told herself that she could do without—a lover, a family of her own—she'd start wanting again, and the contented world she'd built would crumble around her in ruins.

She couldn't let that happen.

Sunny shuffled through her bag until she found something to wear, then made quick work of drying her hair. When she ended up with more frizz than curls, she resignedly pulled it into a ponytail. Her hair had a mind of its own and she didn't know from one day to the next how it was going to look. She'd tried every styling product known to man and nothing had ever made a whit of difference. A couple of swipes of the mascara wand, a bit of blush and lip gloss and she was good to go.

Though her mother used to make a variety of breakfast foods every morning for their guests and put them out in the office, they'd stopped doing that a couple of years ago and instead had an assorted mixture of donuts and danishes delivered from a local bakery. For an extra buck, they'd been bringing a pot of spiced tea, as well. Sunny checked her watch, winced, then quickly put Atticus on the leash and grabbed his bowl and a chew toy. He'd been standing at the back door for the past fifteen minutes and she assumed a potty break was in order.

She'd taken one step onto the porch when she

realized there'd been a different reason the dog had been parked in front of the exit.

She let out a mighty breath.

Finn had been semireclined on the porch swing, but had moved into an upright position when she'd opened the door.

"Morning, sunshine," he said, his voice rusty, as though him being on her porch at 6:00 a.m. was a normal occurrence. His clothes were wrinkled, his hair mussed. Impossibly, he looked even better than he had last night.

She closed her eyes tightly, then opened them again. Nope. He was still there. *Damn.* She hung her head and released a long, dredged-from-the-bottom-of-her-soul sigh. Could she have actually forgotten how stubborn he'd always been?

"Please do not tell me that you've been out here all night."

He stood and stretched, making his muscles bunch and move in ways that made her appreciate the male anatomy. And more specifically, his. "Okay, I won't tell you."

"Did you stay out here all night?" she demanded.

"It's too early in the morning for you to start playing mind games with me, Sunny. I thought you just said you didn't want me to tell you."

"Finn!" she cried, whimpering with frustration. "I told you to go home."

"No, you just kicked me out of the house," he corrected. "The next time you run me off, you're going to have to be more specific." He rubbed his eyes tiredly. "I need coffee."

She needed something stronger, but it was too early to drink. "I can't believe you spent the night on the damned porch swing. Why didn't you go back to your room?"

"We've been over that, remember? You don't want me in the house? That's cool. I'm used to being outside."

She could quite cheerfully throttle him, Sunny thought, descending the stairs. Atticus led her over to a patch of sea oats and hiked his leg, then steered her toward the office. She could feel Finn behind her, trailing along in her wake. "So what? You're just going to follow me around all day?"

"No, there are going to be times when you're going to have to follow me. For instance, I need to shower and change clothes. Since I'm not going to be able to do that at your house, then you'll need to wait on me in my room." He smiled at her. "I'll hurry."

She unlocked the office door and pushed inside, feeling inevitability closing in on her from all sides. Her stomach tightened, an indistinguishable cramp of want and irritation. He'd spent the night on her porch, she thought, softening unwillingly, simply because he wanted to protect her, to keep her safe. Had any man ever done anything for her that could come close to a comparison? No. Still...

"Finn, for the last time, this isn't necessary. I'm going today to get a restraining order. I don't need a bodyguard." Though if she was going to have a bodyguard, a girl could do a helluva lot worse than Finn O'Conner. Geez Lord, he was a beautiful man. Tall and lean, with muscles on muscles and skin that begged for her touch. She smothered another whimper and dragged her gaze away from his distracting mouth. It was a little full for a man, but unbelievably sexy all the same. She wanted to feel it beneath her own lips and gliding along her jaw, feeding at her breasts. Warmth pooled in her center, making her shift.

His gaze narrowed at something over her shoulder. "What does Heath look like?"

"Like a soap-opera star. Blond hair, blue eyes, trendy dresser." She frowned. "Why?"

His brow formed a menacing line and a skitter of unease slid down her spine. "Because a guy matching that description is staring at us through the window."

Sunny gasped and whirled. *Damn.*

6

FINN LOCKED EYES WITH the stranger who he suspected was Sunny's ex and felt the hair on the back of his neck rise. White-hot anger bolted through him, tripping some sort of trigger he'd never disengaged before. *This* was the man who was harassing Sunny. *This* was the man who wouldn't take no for an answer. *This* was the man who she may or may not have slept with.

Sunny's jaw dropped and some of the color leached from her face. "I can't believe this," she said faintly. "What have I done to deserve this?" A thundercloud of irritation worked its way across her previously smooth brow and she started forward.

He caught her arm. "Oh, no," he said, his voice hardening. "I've got this."

"I can fight my own battles, Finn," she all but growled.

"But that's the beauty of it." He flashed her a smile devoid of humor. "You don't have to." He strode forward and opened the door just as Heath was reaching for the handle, blocking him from entering. "Listen, buddy, you and I need to have a little talk."

Heath merely grimaced and made the mistake of trying to go around Finn. "Sunny, I—"

Finn grabbed the back of Heath's neck and squeezed, the way you would control a recalcitrant puppy, then steered him farther away from the office. Heath yelped with pain and tried to wriggle out of Finn's grip. "Get your hands off me! Who the hell do you think you are?"

Why was everyone asking him that? Finn wondered. He gave Heath a harder than necessary shove into the porch railing to make sure he had his full attention. "I'm a friend of Sunny's and I'm here to convey a message." He lowered his voice to a lethal level and speared the man with a straight look. "Leave her alone. Do not ever contact her again. *Ever.* Do you understand?"

Heath's mouth formed a condescending sneer and he made the unfortunate decision to dismiss Finn's threat. "The only thing I understand is that I don't take orders from you. I—"

"Wrong answer." Finn slammed his fist into Heath's jaw and sent him flying backward over the railing. Damn, that felt good. Not as good as the sex he'd like to have with Sunny, but there was a lot to be said for expending some energy this way, too.

Horrified, Sunny rushed outside. "Finn, don't!"

Finn ignored her, easily leaping over the railing and crossing his arms over his chest. "Let's try this again," he said. "Leave. Sunny. Alone." He enunciated each word plainly and succinctly, as though he were speaking to someone of limited intelligence. Which he was. "She does not want to see you ever again. Do you understand?"

Heath spat a wad of blood from his mouth and looked past him. "Sunny?"

"Oh, for heaven's sake," she wailed. "Go, Heath! It's over."

Finn reached down and dragged Heath to his feet. "Come on, Heath. I'll help you to your car," he growled, giving him a shake for good measure.

"I don't want your help. Get your hands off me," Heath said again, struggling to get out of Finn's grip. He'd be lucky if Heath didn't file assault charges against him, Finn thought, but decided it didn't matter. Hitting him had been worth it.

"Which one is yours?"

"The Lexus."

Of course, Finn thought. The guy was wearing a designer shirt, penny loafers and more jewelry than his great-aunt Marge. He was slicker than goose shit and Finn was having a very hard time figuring out just what in the hell Sunny had seen in him in the first place.

He opened the car door and shoved Heath inside. "Have some self-respect, man. She doesn't want you."

Heath looked as though he was considering running Finn over with his car, but ultimately he sped out of the lot. He did not look like a man who was going to give up just because Finn had nailed him in the jaw and sent his ass sprawling into the sand.

When Finn came back around the building, Sunny was waiting for him.

"You dated a guy who wears a pinky ring? Seriously, Sunny?"

She flushed. "Say what you want, but he's handsome."

For whatever reason, that absolutely infuriated him. "He's slick. And he's a wuss. The pansy-ass never even tried to hit me back. What kind of guy takes a punch and doesn't retaliate?"

"Not everyone can be a badass, Finn," she said with a beleaguered eye-roll. She turned and walked back into the office.

Something warm settled in his chest and he smiled. "You think I'm a badass?" he asked, following her.

She snorted. "Don't play coy. You know you're a badass."

He shrugged. "I'm not afraid to throw a punch if I think it's warranted, and I'll come out swinging if I'm backed into a corner. If that makes me a badass, then I guess I am." He paused. "He's not going to back off."

She looked up at him. "Even after what just happened?"

Finn shook his head. "I don't think so. He looked thwarted when he left, but not defeated."

She swore, a line he longed to smooth furrowing her brow. "So you still think I need the restraining order?"

"Definitely." There was something more at play here, something else Heath was after. The eternal question, of course, was what?

Sunny bit her bottom lip and another anxious line wormed across her forehead. The expression bothered him, made him want to chase Heath down and pummel him again.

Finn put a finger under her chin and lifted her face. "Hey, no worries, okay? I've got this." He smiled down at her. "I'll stay on your porch." He jerked his head toward Atticus. "He's not your only guard dog."

"I wonder how long he's been sitting out in the parking lot," she said.

"Long enough for the dew to collect on the hood of his car."

Her stomach rolled. "Do you think he came near the house?"

"I didn't hear him if he did."

"You wouldn't. The ocean," she reminded him.

It had been pretty loud, certainly noisy enough that he could have missed hearing Heath, much as he hated to admit it. Nevertheless, he shuddered to think what might have happened had he *not* been on her porch. Finn would rather go toe to toe with another badass any day than deal with a coward. A badass wasn't afraid to rumble and a guy knew what to expect. But a coward... Cowards were sneaky and unpredictable.

"Did Atticus notice anything?"

"Nothing, and you were on the porch all night." She glared at the dog. "You've got to do better," she scolded.

Predictably, Atticus farted in response to the criticism.

It was possible that Heath had seen him on the porch—he would have approached the house from that direction—and backtracked. After a moment, Finn said as much. "I'll install some motion-sensor lights," he told her. "Your parents need them anyway. It's a good precautionary measure. Anything that gets close enough to set them off near the porch needs to be illuminated, right?"

She nodded. "Thanks, Finn."

He grinned, glad that she seemed to be rallying. "Anytime. So do you need to put a sign on the door or what?"

"What do you mean?"

"The restraining order. We need to go down to the police station."

"I can't leave until Clint gets here."

Another man? Just how many guys were orbiting through her life? he wondered irritably. "Who's Clint?"

"Our part-time help. He comes in during the summer on Tuesdays and Thursdays." She glanced at the clock on the wall. "He'll be here at ten."

Finn nodded once. "We'll go then. What exactly do you do now?"

"Set breakfast out," she said. "It should be here soon. I'll check the weather for the day and post it on the door. Do a sweep of the grounds, pick up any stray trash. I've got people in Number Two and Number Five who are leaving today, so those rooms will have to be cleaned and ready by three because they're booked again."

"I'll help you."

She winced regretfully. "Finn, you're on vacation, you've had no sleep. You do not have to help me. Heath is gone. I seriously doubt he's going to come right back here. Go beach it today. Read your book or—"

"I've already read it," he told her. Her startled look was especially gratifying. "Would you happen to have *The Chamber of Secrets?*"

"You've already read it?" she repeated skeptically.

"I have," he confirmed with a nod. "Last night. You were right. I *did* like it." He made a moue of regret. "Pity, too. I almost wish I hadn't so I could get that dinner you were going to owe me."

She laughed, the sound vibrating something deep inside of him. "If you read that book from cover to cover last night, then I'll make you dinner."

"Do you want to quiz me?"

She was looking at him with the strangest expression, Finn thought. A mixture of helplessness and affection and something else, something he couldn't readily identify. It made his guts tingle and shake.

Still smiling, she shook her head. "I'll take your word for it."

"If you'll do that from now on, we'll argue a lot less."

She stilled, grew more serious. "Finn, thank you. For keeping watch," she clarified. "I have to admit I'm a little spooked."

He was, too, but for an entirely different reason. He felt it again, that tug behind his navel that was drawing him closer and closer to her. A sense of dawning inevitability, of Fate making a play. It was the same sensation that had sent him running last time.

He would not run again.

Unwittingly, he lessened the distance between them, reached up and ran the pad of his thumb over her lower lip. She gasped and her gaze darted up to his. She had the prettiest green eyes, Finn thought, and a lone freckle on her lid. Odd that he should find that so compelling. Adorable even. He brushed his lips over hers once, twice. She tasted like minty toothpaste and cherries, Finn noted vaguely, and the soft sigh that she finally breathed into his mouth as she melted against him held the sweetest flavor of all.

Victory.

SHE WISHED SHE HADN'T SEEN that, Sunny thought, that flash of something sweet and funny and, God help her, *tender* in his gaze. She'd been having a hard enough time dealing with the heat, those charring glances that made her belly knot up and her nipples tingle. The desire she could have potentially—though doubtfully—ignored for a little while longer, anyway.

But that other look? Whatever was left of her will simply crumbled away, weakening her body in the process. She sagged against him and the feel of his big, hard body next to hers, the slide of that incredibly carnal mouth over her lips made her want to weep with joy.

She slid her hands up over his arms, savoring muscle and sleek skin and he deepened the kiss with a groan. His tongue tangled around hers, a mindless seek-and-retreat as he made love to her mouth.

No two ways about it, Finn O'Conner was a damned fine kisser.

Nothing ruined a kiss faster than too much spit or concrete lips or what she liked to call the Dale Earnhardt, the fast kisser bent on lapping her mouth like the Talledega Speedway, then moving on to other things.

If a guy couldn't master the basics, then chances were he was a lousy lover. Sunny didn't have sex often enough to waste her time with someone who didn't know what the hell they were doing, so a bad first kiss was always a deal-breaker.

Finn, however, kept the moisture at that elusive level between too wet and too dry; his lips were masterful, molding *around* hers rather than *against* them, and he'd set the speed dial on Cruise, as though he would be content to kiss her all day long and never tire of it. His hands roamed her body, first bracketing her face, then trailing down over her shoulders and back, his thumbs along her spine.

Sunny slid her hands up and over his neck, into his hair, and the short locks felt smooth against her palm. The low hum of desire that had been thrumming in her womb had expanded to her sex and she could feel a resulting throb with every hurried beat of her heart. The achy heaviness of need weighted her breasts and she felt her nipples pearl behind her bra.

Finn's hands slowly shaped her rump and he gave a low growl of approval in her mouth as he gently squeezed. She felt the long, hard length of him nudge her belly and a thrill of feminine satisfaction whipped through her. Her sex wept, readying for him, and she squirmed against him. Finn lifted her bottom and set her on the desk behind the counter, then sidled in between her legs, applying the pressure she so desperately craved between her thighs.

It was her turn to groan and she felt him smile against her lips.

He rocked forward, snatching the breath from her lungs in a loud gasp that was almost embarrassing. She could feel the tension coiled in his body, the purely masculine energy that was so potent it was practically intoxicating. She felt drugged, primed, desperate.

From a mere kiss.

She was doomed.

"When do you have to fix breakfast?" he murmured against her mouth.

Breakfast? she wondered, trying to make sense of the word. *Breakfast!* Oh, hell. She froze and glanced at the clock. "Shirley will be here with it in a few minutes."

"No problem," he said, dragging her closer to him and flexing determinedly against her. "I only need one."

"Finn—"

He killed her protest with a nuzzle of his nose along her throat and did something with his hips that perfectly aligned their bodies to where he hit her sweet spot. She inhaled sharply and he chose that moment to move her shirt aside and pull her nipple into his mouth through her lacy bra.

The feeling was exquisite, his hot mouth, the damp fabric, the perfect tug as he suckled her. He flexed again, then increased the tempo, bumping her clit with every deliberate thrust. Each hit pushed her further and further to the edge, closer and closer to release. Sunny clamped her feminine muscles, sank her teeth into her bottom lip and listened as her breath ran away from her.

"Don't make me a liar," he murmured, then began to count down. "Five."

Harder.

"Four."

Faster.

"Three."

He licked her throat.

"Two."

He dragged her nipple back into his mouth, sucking deep, and pressed himself more firmly against her.

"One," he breathed, a smile in his voice, as she shattered.

Little colored dots floated behind her closed lids, her sex spasmed over and over, each contraction more powerful than the last, and her limbs felt as though her bones had turned to rubber. Weighted, sated and limp. He didn't move, but stayed against her until every bit of release had pulsed out of her body.

Still breathing heavily, Sunny dropped her head against his chest.

There was no way in hell he was sleeping on her porch after that.

"You can have the guest bedroom," she said.

She felt his chuckle vibrate against her forehead. "You're letting me into the house? That was the key? An orgasm?" He sighed dramatically. "Damn, I wish I'd known that last night." He drew back and looked down at her, a wicked gleam in his eye. "What's it going to take to upgrade from the guest bedroom to yours?"

"A voodoo priestess and a live chicken," Sunny deadpanned because she desperately needed to lighten the moment.

Finn's eyes widened, then deep, rumbling laughter bubbled up his throat. She loved the way he laughed. It was honest and unrestrained, infectious, she realized as she began to chuckle along with him.

She might as well laugh now. No doubt she'd be crying later.

Eyes twinkling with latent humor, Finn merely looked at her and shook his head. "You have a very frightening imagination, you know that?"

She shrugged helplessly. "It entertains me."

"I can see where it would."

What was it going to take for him to upgrade from the guest bedroom to hers? Sunny thought as she stared up at Finn, a sense of inevitability, resignation and anticipation settling around her. She sighed softly.

Very, very damned little, she feared.

7

"Morning, Martha Ann."

Though she knew that she should be expecting it—Tug had greeted her in the exact same way every morning for the past two weeks—she was always a little surprised when he continued to make the effort. Pleasantly so, she would admit.

"Morning, Tug," she responded with a put-upon sigh, feeling a flush of unwanted pleasure move through her chest.

His gaze slid over her body, lingering on her breasts. Impossibly, her nipples tingled and she felt twin flags of color rise on her cheeks. "Still working on your tan, I see."

She resisted the urge to fan herself. Goodness, what was wrong with her? "It's typically what one does when one vacations at the beach."

"How much longer are you going to be here,

Martha Ann? I don't remember you and Sheldon ever staying more than a week at a time."

That's because Sheldon had had fair skin, burned easily and was too vain to use sunblock because he thought it wasn't masculine. He'd invariably burn and then be ready to go long before their vacation was supposed to be over. It had been damned annoying.

"I'm here for another week," she finally answered. And she was considering staying longer, if her room wasn't booked. Her children were grown, her grand-kids in college. She talked to them every few days, but there was nothing pressing for her to go back to, nothing on her calendar that couldn't wait. Why shouldn't she enjoy herself? Martha Ann thought. Why should she rush back to…nothing.

His smile widened, as though he was genuinely pleased. "I'm glad to hear it. The beach is always nicer when there's a pretty woman on it."

She felt a droll smile slide over her lips and re-sisted the urge to fidget. "Does that line usually work for you?"

"It's not a line, Martha Ann. It's a compliment. Try to enjoy it."

And for the first time in two weeks, he continued on his walk without inviting her to dinner. Had he given up? she wondered. Or lost interest?

Either way she'd been a fool.

AS IT HAPPENED, THE GUEST bedroom ended up being just the ticket, Finn thought on Wednesday evening. The lack of sleep the previous night combined with what had ended up being a very full day took its toll. And though he was sure he could have mustered the strength for a little bed sport, Finn knew he needed the rest all the same.

He also wanted to give Sunny some distance. If they became lovers this time, it would be because *she* wanted it, not because he'd forced her hand. Did he want her?

With every fiber of his being.

Tasting her yesterday, feeling her curvy little rump beneath his hands, her breast in his mouth, seeing her come for him…

Perfect torture.

He ached for her, wanted to plant himself inside of her with an urgency and desperation that bordered on insanity. It was completely out of the realm of his experience. Desire he was used to, but this frantic bone-deep need combined with that never-ending tug that only moved him closer to her was not familiar to him. Sunny Ledbetter had that special something, that indefinable special quality that simply set her apart from every other woman. He'd sensed it as a boy, realized it as a teen and was absolutely certain of it as a man.

But he would not charm his way back into her bed. He would wait for the invitation and if it didn't come, then it didn't. And really, could he blame her?

He was leaving again in two days, heading to Afghanistan by way of Fort Stewart. The last time he'd left her, he'd had a choice and he'd made the one he thought was best for his future.

This time he didn't have a choice.

He owed Uncle Sam eleven months overseas and another three after that of contracted service. Though incentives to re-up had already been bandied about, Finn had resisted. The nagging sense of discontent combined with the death of his parents had left him feeling as if he needed to plot a new course. Though he had the odd aunt and distant cousins, Finn was essentially alone now and, while he'd always considered himself an island unto himself, he wasn't so certain anymore.

He wanted…more.

Atticus lay on the front porch of the house, his head resting on his paws, as though surveying all of his domain. The sound of laughter and waves drifted to Finn on the salty breeze and he inhaled deeply, a sense of peace flooding him. Sunny was currently down in Number Six French-braiding the Johnson twins' hair for a family picture and the Wilsons, who were in Number Nine, were roasting hot dogs over

a fire. Number Four had tied a kite to his deck and
the giant butterfly soared overhead, irritating the
seagulls that swarmed around it. Tug was sitting on
his deck, a book in one hand, a glass of wine in the
other. The sun was melting against the horizon in a
grand display of yellow, orange and purple, painting
the clouds with color.

It was beautiful here, Finn realized, and completely understood the Ledbetters' stipulation that
the inn should stay as it was. Once again the idea
of buying the place planted a seed of expectation in
his mind and this time, he didn't try to uproot it, but
rather left it there to germinate.

Pity that Sunny didn't want to stay here, Finn
thought, wincing with regret. He could actually see
them here, running the inn together. Helpmates, lovers, friends…even parents. Was it a cosmic joke that
their timing was always off?

At any rate, he had other things to think about.
Like keeping Heath away from her.

As soon as Clint had arrived yesterday, they'd
made the trip to the police department and put the
restraining order in place. If Heath so much as called
Sunny, they'd pick him up. Finn wished he could get
a handle on what was driving the guy. For reasons
that escaped him, he got the unsettling impression
that Sunny was keeping something from him. When

he'd asked her if she could think of any reason—
any reason at all—that Heath would continue to try
and force a reconciliation, she'd hesitated just long
enough to make him nervous.

Rather than press her, armed with Heath's last
name and the office computer, Finn had done a little
research himself. Within minutes he'd done a com-
prehensive background check that listed everything
from Heath's credit score—the man owed *everybody*
and was several payments behind on that fancy car
he was so proud of—to an outstanding parking ticket
he hadn't paid.

A real-estate developer, albeit a poor one, Heath
lived above his means and was on the verge of
bankruptcy. Via his Facebook page, Finn had noted
several wall posts that boasted about a "big deal coming through," but those had been dated almost three
months ago, and Finn assumed the so-called deal
had gone south because Heath hadn't mentioned it
again.

Finn frowned. That would have been about the
time Heath had met Sunny, he thought, and felt a
tingle across his shoulder blades that told him he'd
made the crucial connection.

Heath was a real-estate developer and Sunny's
family owned the Sandpiper, a prime piece of land
that could be worth millions. If Heath had gotten

wind that the Ledbetters were considering a sale, then, as Sunny's boyfriend, he would have been the logical choice to handle the transaction.

Bingo.

No doubt she knew this, Finn thought as he watched Sunny lope down the Johnsons' deck and start toward him. He'd offered to man the office while she'd donned the role of hairdresser.

Honestly, there weren't many roles a person didn't don when they ran a hospitality business, Finn thought. In addition to cleaning the rooms, answering the phones, booking new arrivals and taking care of the departures, there were countless other things that cropped up throughout the day.

Sunny had dispensed first aid, provided directions to the local grocery store, added chemicals to the pool, inflated a swim toy, supplied Number Two with a tube of toothpaste, given clothing advice to Number Eight—the red bathing suit was more slimming—provided the answer to a crossword puzzle to a guest who was stuck and helped capture a sand crab that had wanted to see what inside the cottage looked like.

She did it all with her trademark smile, without complaint. Though he knew she didn't want to take over the business for her parents, he thought it was a shame. She was a natural at it. The constant onslaught of requests would have worn most people down, but she merely handled each need in stride and moved on to the next.

Meanwhile, she routinely checked in with her store, put out the occasional fire there and last night—while he'd been moving closer and closer to bed—she'd reviewed new designs her team had couriered over earlier in the day.

She was truly remarkable, Finn realized. And very talented. He'd been curious about Funky Feet as well and had checked out her company's website.

For the flip-flop aficionado, her store was the equivalent of shoe heaven. He'd seen flip-flops decorated in feathers, ribbons, beads and shells. Every color, every shape and size, and an entire line devoted to bridal wear—seed pearls, satin, more feathers. Another higher-end line was called "Foot Jewelry" and featured rhinestones and semiprecious stones. Utterly inspired.

She slowed as she drew nearer and regarded him with an uncertain look. "What are you smiling about?" she asked suspiciously. "Should I be worried?"

Finn slung an arm around her shoulder, noting that she was the perfect height and fitted the niche at his side as though it had been specifically designed with her in mind. "Not at all," he said. "I just think you're pretty damned awesome, that's all."

She flushed and lowered her lashes. "Recreational drug use is a bad habit, Finn," she tsked. "You should know better."

He gave her neck a squeeze and laughed. "I tell you you're awesome and you accuse me of being high. Wonderful," he said, looking heavenward. "Hardly the thank-you I would have expected, but…" He sighed as though she'd wounded him and absently scratched his chest.

"Thank you, Finn," she murmured dutifully. "I'm glad you think I'm awesome." From the corner of his eye he saw her lips twitch. "My plan for world domination is working."

"Come on, smart-ass," he chuckled, herding her toward the beach. "Take a walk with me."

FINN LACED HIS FINGERS THROUGH hers, his big cal-loused palm brushing against her smaller one. The sensation was easy and pleasant and, despite what had happened between them yesterday morning, strangely intimate.

Though Sunny had been given many compliments over the years, she didn't think one had ever touched her quite the way Finn's I-think-you're-awesome one just had. The sentiment was simple enough, but it was the look on his face when he'd delivered it that had made it so special. The wondering smile, the genuine awe and affection in his gaze, as though he'd just unwrapped an unexpected present…and she was it.

Her heart gave a little jump and a pleasant warmth settled in her chest. Both rattled an alarm in the back of her head—she was letting him get too close again—but she determinedly ignored the warning.

"Thank you for helping me today," she said, enjoying the wind on her face. Funny how she didn't mind running the inn with Finn there, helping her pick up the slack. She'd actually enjoyed it more than she would have ever thought, and it was hardly the drudgery she remembered from her childhood. Odd… They'd reached the edge of the surf, where the sand sank a bit, but didn't shift and the waves lapped around their ankles.

"You're more than welcome." He shot her a sheepish look. "I, er, like to have something to do."

"Really?" she asked with mock astonishment. "Gosh, I wouldn't have known that. I would have never guessed it given how laid-back you are."

He nudged her shoulder playfully. "Knock if off," he teased. "There's nothing wrong with having an agenda."

She snorted. "There is if you're on vacation. There

is if you've gotten in the habit of staying so busy that you don't know how to be still anymore."

He laughed darkly. "Ah, there it is again. I can be still," he insisted. "I just don't want to be."

"Which begs the question, why?" Sunny drawled. "*Why* don't you want to be still? What happens in the quiet that makes you so unbearably uncomfortable? I have a theory, you know," she mused, letting the comment hang out there, the perfect bait.

Predictably, the curiosity got the better of him.

He heaved an exaggerated sigh. A muscle jumped in his jaw, belying the easy smile. "All right, Dr. Freud," he said. "I'll bite. What's this theory?"

Sunny simply shrugged. "You think too much and you don't want to be inside your own head. Your thoughts are either going in circles or reaching dead ends and it's easier to get up and do something than to sort out the chaos of your mind." She paused. "I'm not condemning you, Finn," she hastened to add, then grimaced. "If I'd seen the things that you've seen, I doubt I'd want to settle down with my thoughts, either." She kept walking, but felt him slow beside her. She purposely looked toward the ocean. "It just breaks my heart though," she continued. "The boy I knew could have spent an entire day in a beach chair, just soaking up the sun and breathing the air.

He wouldn't have jumped up within five minutes, as though a hot poker had hit him in the ass."

Finn stopped, bent down and picked up a shell. He washed it in the surf, then pocketed it. "I'm not a boy anymore, Sunny."

"I know that, Finn." She squeezed his hand. "But when you've got an agenda on your vacation that doesn't include *actually taking a vacation*...then I think you need to see if you can find him again." She took a deep breath. "Let me ask you something."

His lips quirked. "I don't seem to be able to stop you."

"What were your plans for coming here? What did you want to do?"

He smiled, chewed the inside of his cheek. "I'm pleading the Fifth."

"Finn," she admonished. "Come on. Tell me."

He turned to look at her. Orange light from the setting sun backlit him in gold, glinted off his bronze locks. His eyes, that glorious blue she routinely felt herself drowning in, were guarded. Tense.

"All right," he finally said. "I did have a few things I wanted to accomplish."

That was a nice way of saying he'd made a list, Sunny thought. She nodded encouragingly. "Go on."

"I'll leave here Friday, go back to Fort Stewart and

by the end of next week, I'll be in Afghanistan," he said. "This week was supposed to be about getting my head ready for that, for preparing me for what was coming at me for the next eleven months."

Sunny swallowed past the instant panic in her throat. *Eleven months?* She hadn't realized he'd be gone for so long. Her suddenly racing heart constricted in her chest and nausea roiled in her gut. That he'd be—

"This is the first time I'll ship out and won't be able to expect a letter from home, or a care package from my mother. My dad won't keep me updated on college football, how my Dawgs are doing," he said with a mangled laugh. "There will be no one for me to call and no one waiting for me when I get off the plane after it's all over." He shrugged, couldn't meet her gaze anymore. "I never realized how much I counted on that until it wasn't there anymore," he said. "It's all sort of left me feeling…off. Without a tether." Another weak laugh that tore at her heart. "So the next thing on my list was to figure out why. The career has always come first, you know? Next assignment, next promotion, next mission." He shook his head. "In light of what's happened, it all just seems so…insignificant. I feel like I've missed the point of an important lesson and I still don't know what it is."

Sunny couldn't speak past the lump in her throat and she blinked back tears, determined not to let him see them. He would mistake them for pity. He hadn't told her any of this to garner sympathy, but had shared it all in a glib, hollow tone that only seemed to make it worse.

He squeezed her hand. "I came back here because some of the happiest memories of my childhood—of my parents—are here," Finn told her.

He came to be closer to them, she realized.

"And I want you to know something else. Even if you hadn't been here, Sunny, I'd planned on tracking you down in Savannah."

She blinked, startled, and looked up at him.

"To apologize," he said at her blank look. "That's weighed on me much more heavily than you'll ever know."

In light of everything else he had going on, his broken promise made a dozen years ago hardly signified. Hell, no wonder he didn't want to be in his own head, Sunny thought. He'd just given her a tiny peek into it and she was ready to bolt into action, to do something to make her forget about it, as well.

Finn looked up at the sky, where the sun was just resting on the ocean and a smile she wouldn't have imagined him capable of at the moment spread across his lips. He sighed and pulled her more firmly against his side. "Would you look at that sunset," he said, marvel and wonder in his voice. "I bet you don't ever get tired of that, do you?"

She swallowed and shook her head. No, she didn't, it was true. The close of the day happened the same way every day. The sun made its usual descent, going to illuminate the other side of the world. But there was nothing common or even ordinary about the unique way the colors changed, the way the clouds moved through the fading light.

Sunny rested her head against him, slid an arm around his waist. She swallowed tightly. "Finn?"

"Yeah?"

"I'll write."

8

I'LL WRITE.

Hours later, Finn still felt those two words buoying him up and, though he'd merely responded with an inarticulate grunt, Sunny would probably never understand just how much the too casually uttered promise meant to him.

That someone would think about him while he was gone; that at some point during her day, Sunny would sit down and, with him in mind, jot a note and let him know what was going on in her life, was suddenly very important to him. It was a little thing, but it was those little things that people seemed to always take for granted.

He resolved to stop taking *anything* for granted. To appreciate everything. Every minute spent with a friend, every laugh, every beautiful minute of every blessed day. Life was too short not to, Finn thought, and he probably knew that better than a lot of people.

After that somewhat awkward yet strangely therapeutic conversation, he and Sunny had continued their leisurely stroll, then had made the return trek to her house, and he'd thrown those steaks he'd had on the grill. When Sunny wasn't looking, he'd tossed a couple of bites to Atticus and the dog had rewarded him by bathing his foot in spit.

Currently, Sunny was reviewing more work that had come over from Funky Feet and he'd taken a seat on the other end of the couch, *Harry Potter and the Chamber of Secrets* in hand. The book was fabulous—incredibly addictive. It had been a long time since he'd fallen into a good book; he'd forgotten just how much he loved to read.

"All right," he heard Sunny say with an irritated huff.

Finn looked up, not certain what he could have done, then realized that Atticus was doing his I-need-to-mark-my-territory march back and forth from Sunny to the back door.

Before Sunny could rearrange her paperwork, Finn set the book aside and hopped up. "I'll take him," he told her.

"You don't have to do that."

"I don't mind," Finn said.

Honestly, despite the fact she'd told him he could have the guest bedroom, he'd half expected her to try and send him back to his own cottage, based on the argument that she had the restraining order now.

She hadn't, and he didn't want to give her any reason to suggest it.

Finn was determined to stay with her, both for her protection and because… Well, because he wanted to. He wanted to be with Sunny. He felt right, for lack of better description, when he was with her. She plugged the hole, made him feel complete again. The desire was there, of course, ever-present and never-ending, but his need went beyond that.

Take now, for instance. She'd showered after dinner and donned a pink tank top and matching drawstring bottoms. Oink was screened across the front of the top, and the pants were covered in happy pigs rolling in mud. They were hysterical and, though there was nothing piglike about Sunny, the pajamas suited her.

At some point she'd changed her toenail polish from hot pink to bright green and the scent of coconut and pineapple clung to her dewy skin. Her nose was so squeaky clean it glowed and her hair lay in long damp curls around her face. There was nothing overtly sexy or seductive about the way she looked

right now—Victoria's Secret would certainly pass—
but to Finn, whose loins had been consigned to the
fiery pit of the damned since the moment she came
back downstairs, she looked *mouthwatering*.

In the first place, she wasn't wearing a bra. The
pert globes of her breasts sat on her chest like plump,
ripened pears just waiting to be picked. He wanted
to lick them and suck them and rub his face between
them. He wanted to watch them bounce on her chest
as he plunged into her.

In the second place, he'd seen the single strand of
elastic ride up the top of her hip above the pajama
bottoms when she'd sat down—yes, he'd been trying
to look at her ass—and was familiar enough with
women's underwear to recognize a thong when he
saw one. That meant her wonderful, lush ass was
virtually naked and the patch of fabric that covered
her front? Insignificant.

Hell, she could have been wearing a garbage bag
and he'd have wanted her. Because he found *her* sexy.
Just Sunny. *She* was what did it for him.

"Thanks, Finn," she said, smiling gratefully up at
him. "His leash is by the door."

Struggling to pull his thoughts back into focus,
Finn nodded and called the dog. Atticus hurried
ahead of him, pressing his slobbery face against
the screen. He clipped the lead into place and then

followed along in the dog's wake. To Finn's disgust, Atticus didn't just need to mark his territory, he needed to make a deposit as well, a big steaming pile of it that he ultimately covered up with a few paw-fulls of sand.

"Your dog is having an identity crisis," Finn called upon their return. "He thinks he's a cat."

He heard Sunny chuckle, but the laugh didn't come from where he expected. It came from upstairs. He frowned. "Oh? How's that?"

Was she turning in already? Finn wondered, unreasonably disappointed. He'd been going to suggest a movie.

"He covers his—" Finn struggled to find the least offensive term.

"Oh," she said knowingly, laughing. "Yeah, he's always done that." A pause then. "Would you lock up? I'm in bed."

Damn. "Yeah, sure."

Though he wasn't exactly tired yet, Finn didn't see the point of staying up without her. It felt weird. He'd shower, then pass the rest of the evening with his book. He made quick work of securing the house, then made the journey upstairs. He'd brought a change of clothes and his toiletries over earlier in the afternoon and put them in the guest bedroom. Sunny's door was closed as he passed, which he found surprising. He was under the impression that, while he produced too much spit to actually sleep in the bed with her, Atticus slept in her room.

With a mental shrug, he walked into the guest bedroom and drew up short.

Sunny *was* in bed.

His.

And she was naked.

He felt a long, slow smile slide over his lips. "What happened to the voodoo priestess and the live chicken?"

"That was to get you into *my* bed," she clarified. "You didn't ask what it would take to get me into yours."

"Damn," he said with feigned regret. "I never ask the right questions." He grinned and quirked a brow. "Can you give me five minutes? I need to take the fastest shower in the history of the world."

It only took three and it still felt like an eternity. Miracle of miracles, Sunny was still waiting for him when he walked back into the room. He hadn't bothered with underwear, but had just secured the towel around his waist. Her eyes widened appreciatively when she saw him.

"When did you get the tattoo?" she asked.

Finn bent over and snagged a few condoms from

his toiletry bag and set them on the nightstand. "Right after Jump School."

"Why not a four-leaf clover?" she asked. "Why the three?"

"Because luck didn't have a damned thing to do with me getting through that," Finn said. "It was nerve, skill and determination." He shrugged, grinned. "And I'm Irish, so…"

She sat up and the sheet slipped down, baring her to the waist, revealing the prettiest pair of breasts he'd ever seen. She slid a finger over the clover positioned on the front of his hip, then leaned forward and traced the outline of the tattoo with the tip of her tongue.

He shuddered.

"Clover is edible," she breathed against his skin, kissing his hip. "Did you know that?"

"I—"

She gave the towel a gentle tug, sending it to the floor, then wrapped her hand around his shaft and licked slowly down the side of his penis. "Though I prefer this," she murmured in foggy tones, and took the whole of him into her mouth.

Sweet mother of—

Finn locked his legs and his jaw, then groaned loudly against the onslaught of sensation. That beautiful mouth wrapped around his dick, her facile tongue lapping at him… He fisted his hands at his sides because he knew it would be bad form to fist them into her hair and wondered how in the hell he was going to get through this without completely losing control.

Her small hand worked the base of his shaft while her mouth did unspeakable things to the top. She left off and laved his balls, then returned to the sensitive skin just beneath the head of his dick. She licked and sucked and periodically looked up at him, her eyes sleepy and sated, as though tasting him was as satisfying to her as it was to him.

It was that look that simply did it for him, knowing that she wanted him, knowing that she needed him as much as he needed her.

Feeling impending release building in the back of his loins, Finn gently moved her back onto the bed. "Let me, Sunny," he said, gently opening her thighs. He hooked her legs over his shoulders, spreading her before him, then with a hungry moan fastened his mouth between her legs. The taste of woman exploded on his tongue as he laved her clit and he sighed with satisfaction. Her back arched off the bed and she held on to the sheets to keep herself there. His tongue against her clit, he slipped a finger deep inside and began to stroke, and with the other hand, found a nipple and began to roll it rhythmically between his fingers.

He heard her gasp, felt her stomach deflate and smiled against her. "You taste so good," he murmured against her. Stoking, laving, tweaking. He increased the tempo and could hear her labored breathing, music to his ears, affirmation.

"Not without you again," she gasped, grasping his shoulders. "Please. I need—"

He needed, too. He grabbed a condom from the nightstand, pulled it from the foil and swiftly rolled it into place. A second later he was poised between her thighs, nudging her weeping folds.

Hair spread out in a golden halo of curls, cheeks pinkened with desire, lips swollen from tasting him…

Incredible.

With a groan dredged from his soul, he slid into her, and just like before, visions of another path— one that included her and curly-haired children and beachside bonfires and a perpetually farting dog— rolled out in front of him.

Shaken but not surprised, Finn threaded his fingers through hers, stretched her arms above her head, fully aligning their bodies and angled deep, getting as close to her as he possibly could. She clamped her feminine muscles around him and he felt a corresponding contraction in his chest. The same sensation occurred with every greedy squeeze of her body around his.

She was forcing her way into his heart, Finn realized with a start, weakening his resistance with each blissful seek-and-retreat into her body.

And though he'd been taught to fight, never to surrender, Finn grimly feared this was a battle he'd already lost.

IF THERE HAD EVER BEEN anything more wonderful than their joined bodies—the hot, hard slide of him deep within her—then Sunny didn't have the presence of mind to recall it. Sleek muscle, sculpted bone, that sinfully carnal mouth. He was poetry in motion, masculine beauty incarnate. She could feel him in every cell of her body, moving through her blood, winding around her senses.

Why had she ever thought she'd be able to resist him? Sunny wondered. Why had she even tried? He wasn't just her Achilles' heel, he was her Achilles'… *everything*. There wasn't a part of her that hadn't ever been vulnerable to him.

Finn O'Conner owned her…and always had.

Yes, he was leaving. Yes, he wasn't permanent, the expiration date still applied. But ultimately, in the end—when he could walk out of her life and potentially *never* return—none of that mattered. She'd realized that today, when he'd bared his soul on the beach, when she'd promised to write. Ultimately, the only thing that mattered was making the most of the time she had left with him, savoring every moment and, for the time being, simply forgetting all the rest.

Finn bent his head and kissed her, his tongue plunging in and out of her mouth, mimicking a more intimate act farther south.

And he was so damned good at making her forget...

Palm to palm, the desperation in his touch, her nipples abrading his chest as he pushed repeatedly into her...

It was too much, too wonderful, too exquisite for her to bear. She felt the first flash of orgasm kindle in her womb, igniting a frenzy of sensation in the heart of her sex. The pleasant burn in her veins turned into an inferno scorching through her, sucking all the oxygen from her lungs, making her buck frantically beneath him.

She squeezed his hands, wrapped her legs more firmly around his waist and tightened around him as he withdrew, trying to hold him in, to keep him inside her. He was the key, she thought dimly, and any second now he was going to unlock something magical inside of her.

Sunny bent forward and licked his throat, a sleek path from the hollow to the side where neck met shoulder. She suckled, then took a little nip and he groaned and pounded harder.

Aha.

She did it again, coupling the bite with a determined lift of her hips.

The sound that tore from his throat was almost inhuman. "Sunny," he said, her name a warning.

"Finn," she shot back a bit breathlessly, which ruined the effect.

"Do you have any idea how good you feel?" he asked her, punctuating the question with a hard thrust. "How much I've wanted you?"

Sunny smothered a hysterical laugh. Oh, she thought she had a pretty good idea, based on the sheer delight bolting through her. She flexed against him, lifted her hips and felt something shift deep inside of her.

The first tumbler...

She inhaled sharply and bucked beneath him, urging him on. Taking the cue, Finn released one of her hands and slid his arm around her waist, lifting her up to move their bodies impossibly closer. The shift did something amazing and, with every frenzied, methodical journey into her body, he hit the sweet spot nestled at the top of her sex. Another tumbler gave way, then another, and with a final, brutal push the last one fell back, unlocking the most amazing orgasm she'd ever experienced.

She completely lost the ability to breathe, her back arched away from the bed and bright colored lights danced in front of her eyes. The room fell away, shrank until the only thing left was Finn.

Her Finn.

She tightened around him over and over and with each new contraction, the release seemed to intensify instead of decrease, making the sensation go on and on. She felt Finn stiffen above her, then he pressed deep and held, and a long, keening growl of satisfaction roared from his throat. He trembled above her, then bent and pressed a kiss to her forehead. A heartbreakingly tender gesture amid what had been the most primal, elemental sex she'd ever had.

And in that instant, strangely, it became the most significant.

9

TUG WASN'T ALTOGETHER certain changing his tactic was going to work, but Martha Ann had been a whole lot more chatty this morning when he'd spoken to her, so clearly his new not-asking-her-to-dinner method was working.

Foolish female.

Why were these games necessary? Didn't she realize how much time they'd lost already? Didn't she see how much he cared for her? How much he wanted to be a part of her life, to give her everything he was capable of giving? He baited his hook and cast his line again, the symbolism not the least bit lost on him.

The bad news? She was leaving in a week.

The good news? He'd always been one helluva an angler.

"So CLINT WILL BE HERE AT TEN, right?" Finn asked on Thursday as he shook a pillow into a case. He and Sunny were currently in Number Seven, only a bed between them, and though he'd taken her so many times he'd lost count last night, amazingly, he could do it again right now. He was either very virile or very addicted.

Hell, he could be both, Finn decided. The two weren't mutually exclusive, after all.

Sunny looked up. She'd put on a yellow strapless sundress, which had some sort of distractingly stretchy fabric across her breasts, and she was wearing a pair of tricked-out flip-flops. This pair was covered in silk daisies. She looked fresh and wholesome and sexy, a mesmerizing mix.

"Yes," she admitted slowly. "Why?"

"I was hoping we could get out and kick around the island today. Maybe go have lunch, then come back and beach it for a while."

She hesitated.

"No problem," he assured her. He smoothed the spread. "It was just an idea."

"No, we can," she said after a moment. "I was just going through things in my head. Thinking about who was checking out, who was checking in. So long as we're back by three, Clint should be fine. I just don't want him to get overwhelmed."

He grinned. "Are you sure? I could always go get something, bring it back and we could have a little picnic."

Honestly, it didn't matter to him. He just wanted to be with her. He was all too aware of how short their time together was and he wanted to cram as much into it as possible. Already the idea of leaving her was making him anxious inside, making his guts knot with uncomfortable dread. He'd always hated the goodbye part when he was leaving his parents—his mother's worried tears, the proud concern of his father—but this was a different kind of trepidation. It was knowing they weren't going to be breathing the same air, a prelude to an ache he'd never felt before.

Leaving this time was going to hurt.

"I'll have my cell phone," she said, "and can be back here in a few minutes if something big comes up." She brightened and sighed wonderingly. "Wow. I think we're about to have our first date."

Finn chuckled and rubbed the back of his neck. "Done things a bit out of order, haven't we?"

Her gaze dropped to his mouth and lingered, then met his once more. "Oh, I don't know," she murmured, her voice smoky. "I think we've done things in the order of most importance."

If she kept looking at him like that they were going

to have to change the sheets again on this bed, Finn thought. They'd never make it out of this room, much less to a restaurant.

"Come on," she said. "We've still got to stock the towels by the pool."

He blinked drunkenly.

Sunny grinned. "I like it when you look at me like that," she said, rocking back on her heels. "It makes me feel powerful."

He held the door open for her. "Considering your plan for world domination, that should make you happy." She was certainly rapidly dominating his world, Finn thought. The warning bells that should have gone off as that idea slid through his head... didn't. Interesting.

Thirty minutes later, they were tooling around the island in her Jeep. Sunny wore a huge pair of sunglasses and the wind whipped through her hair, sending curls everywhere as they drove around. He'd offered to drive, but since this was her stomping ground and she knew the best ways to avoid the tourist traffic, she'd commandeered the wheel. After pointing out various landmarks—the Pavilion, the Fort and the lighthouse—she finally wheeled the car into a gravel parking lot.

"The island's too small to have any best-kept-secret sort of places," Sunny told him. "It's only two miles long and less than a mile wide," she said. "But if it did have a secret, then Nancy's would be it." She winked at him and jerked her head toward the door. "Come on."

Finn couldn't identify the exact flavor in the air when they entered the little diner, but it was mouth-watering. It was a seat-yourself kind of place, which he liked, and the menus were tucked between the salt and pepper shakers and the napkin holder. Again, another plus. It meant Nancy was more about the food and less about the service. So long as the service wasn't completely lacking, it generally meant he was about to enjoy a good meal.

Sunny didn't even have to consult a menu. "I always get the scallops," she said and gave a little shudder of delight. "They're divine."

With that sort of endorsement, he didn't need a menu, either. The waitress arrived with a basket of hush puppies, quickly took their order and was back with the drinks in record time.

Sunny took a sip of her sweet tea and studied him over the glass. "I'm having a hard time getting used to the hair," she said, surprising him.

He laughed and ran a hand over the top of his head. "It's the classic military high and tight."

"It's still got some wave," she said. "But I miss the curls."

"They'll cut it again as soon as I get back."

Her eyes widened. "What's left to cut?"

"You'd be surprised."

She sighed and shook her head. "Shame."

Finn paused while the waitress brought their plates. "Heath had longish hair," he remarked thoughtfully, spearing a scallop. "Is that what attracted you?"

Her lips twitched and her eyes twinkled as she picked up her own fork. She released a breath. "You are just not going to let that go, are you?"

He wished he'd never laid eyes on the guy, to be perfectly truthful. He didn't understand it. Couldn't wrap his head around Sunny actually going out with that pansy-assed, opportunistic *nut* and the idea that she might have—

His brain seized, refusing to go there.

He shoved the food in his mouth, mildly noting that it was good, and tried to focus on chewing so he wouldn't choke on the rage that had suddenly invaded his throat.

"We didn't, Finn," she said, taking pity on him. "Not that it's any of your business, but…no." She swallowed, then chased a bead of moisture down the side of her glass with her thumb. "The relationship never progressed to that level."

Profound relief poured through him and he went a little slack in his chair. *Thank God*. The idea of another guy... Which was ridiculous, he knew. There'd been other guys. He knew that. Would more than likely be other guys, as abhorrent as the idea was to him.

But he was about to leave for eleven months, almost a year. How could he ask Sunny to wait, knowing that? In a perfect world, he'd do his tour, finish out his contract, then return here and take over the inn. He'd inherited a bit of money from his parents and there'd been a settlement, of course. He could afford it and he wanted it. He'd never been more certain of anything. It had taken some time to work his mind around the idea, but as soon as he had, the discontent, the sense of unease had fled, leaving renewed purpose in its place.

Unfortunately, while he'd been on the wrong track, Sunny had blazed her own trail and he didn't see how the two were ever going to meet.

"You haven't heard any more from him, have you?" Finn asked, struggling to retain the thread of the conversation.

"No. The police must have gotten in touch with him."

It was possible, Finn knew, but something about it still didn't feel right. Like the calm before a storm, he had an eerie premonition Heath wasn't finished yet. He was a cornered man who thought Sunny was the key to his financial solvency. He was desperate and desperate people were dangerous.

"You know he's in debt up to his eyeballs, right? On the brink of bankruptcy?"

Sunny stared at him. "What?"

He leaned back and crossed his arms over his chest, taking a perverse sort of glee in knocking another dent into Heath's tarnished armor. "I don't know how he's hung on to the car. I'm surprised they haven't come and got it yet."

"How do you know this?" she asked faintly.

Finn shrugged. "I ran a background check on him."

She set her fork aside and gave her head a comical shake. "What? When?"

"Yesterday," he admitted. "When I used your computer." He told her about the curious updates on Heath's Facebook page and relayed his suspicions to her. "I think he had designs on more than just you, Sunny. He was working it from a business angle, too, and when you kicked his ass to the curb…"

She glared at him. "That's *why* I kicked his ass to the curb, as you so eloquently put it," she said, her voice throbbing. She flushed and looked away. "Sheesh. I can't believe you did that."

Finn frowned, confused on several different levels. "But if you knew, then why didn't you tell me?"

Her mystifyingly irritated gaze found his once more. "I know this is a very difficult concept for you, Finn, but it was none of your business." She said the last few words slowly and deliberately, as though she were speaking to a half-wit. "Furthermore, it was embarrassing." She stood, tossed her napkin on top of what remained on her plate and mumbled something about the restroom.

Finn sat in shock, not altogether certain what he had done wrong. She'd had an ex who was acting like a potential stalker. He'd investigated. One plus two equals three, right? Where was the misstep? What should have set her off about that? What was embarrassing? He didn't understand.

But he was about to.

Finn tossed enough money on the table to cover the check and added a nice tip, then made his way to the back and knocked on the restroom door.

"Sunny?"

"I'll be out in a minute, Finn."

"Are you in there alone?"

"What? Yes."

"Let me in."

He heard an exasperated sigh. "Finn."

"Open the damned door, Sunny." They didn't have time for her to be pissed off at him, Finn thought. He was going to fix this the best way he knew how.

He heard the lock click and he instantly pushed into the little room, thankful that there was only a single stall. He quickly flipped the lock back into place and in that time Sunny had resumed her spot in front of the mirror. She was staring at him in the reflection.

He walked forward and wrapped his arms around her, enjoying the way they looked in the mirror together. Her curly hair against his neck, his hands over her belly. "I'm sorry," he said, breathing her in.

She gave a helpless laugh. "Do you even know what you're apologizing for?"

He froze. Was this a trick? Did it matter? "Of course. I'm apologizing because you're angry with me."

She chuckled softly and shook her head. "Finn." She sighed again, his name a plea. "What am I going to do with you?"

"Is that a rhetorical question or are you open to suggestions?" he asked, nuzzling the side of her throat with his nose. She smelled wonderful. Like lemons and sugar and sun. She turned her head and found his lips and he took the opportunity to fill his hands with her breasts. No bra, he realized, and that knowledge landed directly in his loins. She reached around and cupped his neck, simultaneously pressing her rump against him.

He was going to take her, Finn thought. Right here in this little bathroom.

With very little effort at all, he dragged the sundress down, revealing her perfect breasts. *Tan lines, pouting pale pink nipples...* She arched against him once more, an unspoken request, but one he was more than ready to answer. Need hammered through his veins and he'd hardened to that sweet point between pleasure and pain.

Mindless with desire, desperate to plant himself between her welcoming thighs, Finn quickly freed himself and lifted her dress. Another thong, which was quickly dealt with. He bent her forward and slid inside, shuddering as hot juices coated him.

It was at that unfortunate point that he realized he didn't have a condom.

Finn swore hotly and met her sleepy, fevered gaze in the mirror. "I don't have any protection."

"I'm clean and covered. The pill. You?"

"Just had a physical." Besides, the last time he'd had unprotected sex had been with her on that beach twelve years ago.

"Then what the hell are you waiting for?" she asked, wiggling closer. "Come inside me."

Finn drew back and then slid home, watching her face the entire time. She winced with pleasure, her eyes fluttered closed and she bit her bottom lip, as though this felt as good to her as it did to him.

Skin to skin, no barriers. Just him. Just her.

Perfect.

He quaked and his knees went weak. She tightened around him, a silent energizer, and Finn suddenly lost all control. "Look at me," Finn told her.

She did.

He bent her forward a little, reached around and stroked her front as he pounded into her from behind. She was hot and tight and wet and he wanted to take her until one or both of them went blind.

In, out, harder and faster, then harder still.

Her breasts bounced on her chest, absorbing the force of his thrusts, and she made soft little mewling noises that did something strange and bizarre to his insides. Finn stroked her faster and she worked herself against his fingers. Her skin was dewy, her mouth slightly open and her curls shook around her face. She was wanton and sexy and that heavy-lidded gaze clung to his, never wavering. She was enjoying the pleasure he was giving her and she wanted him to know it, wasn't ashamed or embarrassed by it.

Vixen.

She'd be the death of him, Finn realized.

She gave a little gasp, a verbal indicator that she was close, and he felt the first contraction grab at his dick. He slid his free hand over her ass, then gently pressed his thumb against the rosebud of her bottom, while his other maintained its position on her clit. Meanwhile, he angled high, deep within her womanly channel and seated himself as far as he could go.

She came for him.

She went rigid, every muscle locked down tight, and her mouth opened in a soundless scream.

She did not close her eyes, but kept them fastened on his.

Had anything ever been more sexy? Finn wondered as he stared at her. Had he ever been more turned on? More connected to another person?

No.

Only her. God help him, it had always been her.

Her violent release abruptly triggered his own, and for the first time in a dozen years, he came inside a woman, spilling his seed deep within her. Though he knew it was impossible—she'd said she was covered, after all—he almost wished she wasn't. That there was a chance it would take root. That they'd make a baby, a little miracle with blond curls and green eyes and her smile.

And with that fleeting but oh-so-telling thought, he knew that he loved her.

10

"AFTERNOON, MARTHA ANN."

Stationed in her usual spot on the beach, Martha Ann looked up with a smile, one that was tinged with as much delight as regret. Her gaze fastened on Tug's blue one. He wore a pale yellow T-shirt and a pair of old denim shorts, and his curly gray hair was pulled back in a low ponytail. She'd never imagined that she'd ever be attracted to a man with more hair than her, but he was living proof that it was true. It gave him a very European flair. Her stupid heart skipped a beat. "Afternoon, Tug."

"Did you have a pleasant evening last night?" he asked. He reached down and washed off a perfect shell, then slipped it into his pocket.

She nodded her lie. She'd watched an episode of *Golden Girls,* then trimmed her cuticles and gone to bed. If her life got any more exciting she was going to have to take some medication to calm her down. "You?"

"Not really," he admitted.

"Oh?" She was more interested than she should be, Martha Ann thought. Furthermore, the more she talked to him the more he'd be encouraged and she had no desire to lead him on. "Anything wrong in particular?" she heard herself ask.

He picked up a broken shell and tossed it into the incoming surf. "Just lonely, I guess. I never used to mind not having someone to talk to. There was always something to do, some repair to be made, a book to read, a movie to watch, someone to share the occasional meal. Everything was fine."

She swallowed. "What changed?"

He smiled down at her, his eyes crinkling around the corners. "I think I did. Doesn't every man when he falls in love?"

Her chest tightened and a green haze of jealousy clouded her mind. "You're in love?" If that was the case, then why the hell had he been flirting with her every damned day since she'd arrived? she wondered furiously. Here she'd been trying to spare his feelings and they were engaged elsewhere.

She was a fool. A romantic old fool.

He nodded, looking away again. "With the same

woman for the past ten years. But she wasn't available so I could tell myself that there was no way things were ever going to work out. I had no choice but to make do, to go on."

Irrational irritation surged through her. She couldn't believe she was counseling him on how to get his girl. Maybe that's all he'd wanted to talk to her about, in which case she could have had a steak last night instead of a pimento cheese sandwich. "You make it sound like she's available now."

"She is."

"Then what's the problem?"

Tug chewed the inside of his cheek and his gaze caught hers again. A knowing twinkle sparkled there, as though he were not only privy to every illogical thought in her head, but to some private joke, as well. "I think she's playing hard to get."

And with that parting remark, he winked at her and strolled away.

Playing hard to get? Martha Ann gasped as understanding dawned and her gaze darted to Tug's retreating figure. He turned then, and shot her a smile over his shoulder.

That image would be indelibly written on her memory.

"Dinner's at six, Martha Ann. I'm partial to your lemon pound cake."

She felt the blood rush to her face, staining her cheeks and she released a breath she didn't realize she'd been holding. Of all the arrogant, egotistical— Her mental tirade came to a screeching halt as another thought struck. He was in love with her? She let the thought settle around her heart and the pleasure that bloomed there pushed a wondering smile over her lips.

He was in love with *her.*

Damn expectations and old age, Martha Ann thought. Steak was definitely on the menu tonight.

WALKING ON SOMEWHAT WOBBLY legs, Sunny exited the bathroom and made her way to the front of the restaurant.

"Man, everyone is staring at us," Finn whispered, sounding pleased. "I bet they know *exactly* what we've been doing." He ran his hand possessively over her ass, just in case there were a few people who didn't realize that they'd been holed up in the women's restroom for the past fifteen minutes.

Her cheeks blazed.

She batted his hand away. "Cut it out," Sunny whispered. "Idiot."

"Ah, you've hurt my feelings," Finn told her. "I'll take my apology in kind."

Unable to help herself, she snickered. He was

absolutely incorrigible and, fool that she was, she loved that about him. Sex in a public restroom, Sunny thought. Clearly she had regressed a decade or she'd lost her mind. Her gaze slid to Finn and she felt her heart give a little squeeze. Probably a combination of both.

He climbed into her car and casually dropped his shades over his eyes. Sunlight glinted off his bronze hair and a smile of pure masculine satisfaction curled his wickedly carnal lips. He was confidently relaxed, the picture of a perfect badass and ridiculously, this gave her a giddy thrill.

Because he was hers. For the moment, anyway.

"You look pretty damned pleased with yourself," Sunny said as she shifted into gear and swung out of the parking lot.

He turned to look at her, his lips twitching. "You weren't complaining just a few minutes ago."

"Who said I was complaining? I'm just making an observation."

"Oh, good," he said. "Then you won't mind if I do. You have a beautiful ass."

Sunny choked on a laugh.

"No, seriously, you do," he insisted. "It's full and heart-shaped and fits in my hands just so and—" he sighed happily "—it's sexy as hell. I love it."

Despite the fact that she'd just lifted her dress

in a public restroom and they'd had wild monkey sex in front of the mirror, his compliment made her blush. Somehow a simple thank-you didn't seem appropriate.

She cleared her throat, wondering when exactly she'd lost her mind. "You've got a decent ass, too," Sunny said, feeling as though a reciprocal compliment was in order.

"Decent?" he asked, sounding disappointed. "I practically write a sonnet about yours and all you're gonna give me is a 'decent?'" He shivered dramatically. "That's cold. I think we need to find another bathroom so you can warm me up."

She rolled her eyes. "You are so full of shit. You know damned well that you're a walking wet dream. You've got the market cornered on sex appeal. You don't need me telling you that I've had fantasies about sinking my teeth into your ass."

Impossibly, the satisfaction that clung to his grin intensified. "You've fantasized about my ass? Seriously? When?" he demanded.

"Most recently? This morning, when you came out of the shower."

"You should have told me," Finn said. "I would have been happy to oblige."

She snorted. "I'm sure you would have."

"I think we should make a pact," Finn said, as though he'd just had an inspired thought.

"I'm afraid to ask."

"I think we should make a pact to tell each other these things every time we think of them. Little pick-me-ups, you know."

She chuckled. "I think you're just looking for a reason to talk about sex."

"You wound," Finn said, with an exaggerated frown. "Your mouth makes me hot."

She blinked, startled.

"See how easy that was?" he asked her, settling more firmly back into his seat. "I'd like to paint your body with chocolate syrup and lick it off, especially the dimples in the small of your back." He sucked his breath through his teeth. "Put a strawberry between your—"

"Finn," she interrupted as a flash of heat blazed through her sex.

He smiled at her, the wretch. His gaze drifted to her legs, which she'd clamped together. "Yes?"

"*Stop.*"

He merely grinned. "Makes you hot, doesn't it?"

More than she would have ever imagined. And he was sitting there, cool as a cucumber.

That would not do.

"I love the way you feel in my mouth," Sunny

said. "Smooth and hard, and at some point before you leave here tomorrow, I want to tie you to the bed and ride you until my eyes roll back in my head and I shiver from the inside out."

She peeked at him from the corner of her eye and, gratifyingly, he'd gone completely still. And judging from the impressive bulge in the front of his shorts, completely hard. She preened.

He was right. This *was* fun.

He put his hand on her thigh and started edging the dress up her leg. She swatted him away, but not before her breathing hitched.

"Are you insane? I'm driving here."

"Pull over."

"No. This is why your pact suggestion is a bad idea. We'll never get anything done."

His smile was truly wicked. "Oh, yes we will."

Her lips twitched. "Well, besides that."

He shrugged unrepentantly. "My argument stands."

"What am I going to do with you?" Sunny asked again, shaking her head.

His eyes widened significantly. "Are you deaf? I've been making suggestions and, for the record, I am wholly on board with that last one of yours."

His eyes went all smoky, and that voice... Mercy. It sure made her quiver.

"Later," Sunny told him as she pulled into the inn parking lot. "I need to check in with Clint and the store, make sure everything is still running smoothly."

"Then we can head to the water? I want to rub oil all over your body. You've got a bikini, right?"

"Forget the pact!" she admonished.

He frowned innocently. "That didn't have anything to do with the pact."

"Oh."

"Are you okay?" he asked, the picture of innocence. "You look a little flushed."

"I'm fine."

"Do you need me to get you something cool to drink?" he continued solicitously, as though he were genuinely concerned instead of simply needling her.

"If I need something to drink, I'll get it myself," she said, glowering at him.

His eyes twinkled. "Self-service isn't necessary when I am here."

"It might be, if you don't shut up," she threatened.

He guffawed. "Sorry," he said. "I got a little carried away."

"I know, and that's so out of character for you," she deadpanned. She climbed out of the car and headed toward the front office. Finn, naturally, followed her. She could so get used to this.

"Any problems?" she asked Clint.

The teenager shook his head. "Smooth sailing, Ms. Ledbetter."

In a nanosecond she went from feeling like a sex goddess to an old hag. Of course she'd be a *Ms.* to Clint. She was practically ancient compared to him. At the ripe old age of twenty-eight. It was so depressing.

"Number Nine needs new batteries for their remote control," Sunny told him. "Can you take care of that please?"

Clint nodded once. "Sure." He started toward the door, then stopped just short of leaving. "Oh, the guy from the grooming service said he'd bring Atticus back by four."

Sunny stilled and her heart rate kicked into high gear. "What?" She looked around and noticed for the first time that her dog wasn't there.

"The guy from the grooming service came and picked up Atticus for his bath," he repeated. "He said he'd have him back by four."

Finn stared at her and as he took in her expression, went on red alert. "He wasn't supposed to go, was he?"

"No," she breathed, her mouth dry. "My vet clinic grooms him. He's used to them there."

"Clint, the man who picked him up... What did he look like?"

Seeming to realize that he'd made a huge mistake with her beloved pet, Clint had turned a bit green around the gills. "Tall, blond, had a spray tan." His panicked gaze swung to Sunny. "I'm sorry, Ms. Led-better. I didn't know, I just assumed that..."

Finn went behind the desk and stroked a few keys on the computer, then motioned for Clint to come around. "Was this him?"

Clint nodded. "Yeah. That's him."

When Sunny's mind caught up with the fact that Heath had taken her dog, something wild and awful snapped inside of her. She picked her purse back up off the desk and headed for the door.

"Sunny, wait!"

"That miserable bastard has taken my dog," she growled. "I've got to get him back."

"Sunny, you've got to call the police first. He's violated the order."

What was wrong with him? she thought wildly. Didn't he understand? "I don't give a damn about the order! I want my dog back!"

"I know," he said, leveling an unreadable look at her. "And I am going to help you get him back. But you have to call the police and let them know what's happened." He glanced at Clint. "They're going to need a statement from you, so you're going to have to hang around."

Still looking as though he might puke, the boy nodded.

"Give me two minutes," Finn promised her. "And I swear to you we'll find your dog."

While Sunny paced and watched the clock, thinking of all the horrible things she was going to do to Heath when she got her hands on him, Finn called the police.

"They're on their way, Clint. You tell them everything." His gaze shot to hers. "Sunny, dial Heath's number and hand me your phone."

"I KNEW YOU'D CALL," Heath said by way of greeting, his voice smug.

"You did?" Finn asked, his voice low and lethal. "How?"

A pause, then, "Where's Sunny?"

"Here's what's going to happen, Heath," Finn told him. "You're going to tell me where you are and I'm going to come and get the dog—"

"Oh, no," Heath replied with an irritating chuckle. Evidently, he was a lot more brave over the phone, safely out of what he presumed was harm's way.

"You're not calling the shots here, Slick. I am and I say—"

"—or," Finn continued as if Heath hadn't spoken, "when I find you, instead of merely putting a bruise or two on your face, I'm going to totally rearrange it for you, you understand? I'm gonna mess you up so much your own mother won't be able to recognize you. Those are your choices. I'll leave it up to you."

"Stop that," he heard Heath say. "Dammit, dog, what are you doing? That's Italian leather!"

Finn chuckled and shot Sunny a smile. "He's using your upholstery as a chew toy, isn't he?"

Heath choked, made a gagging noise. "What the hell—"

"Atticus has a bit of a flatulence problem, too," Finn continued. "Hard to believe you didn't know about that." He paused. "What's it gonna be, Heath? The easy way or the hard way?"

"It's going to be *my* way," Heath said. "I want to talk to Sunny."

"You know who wants to talk to you? The police."

"For taking the dog for a ride?" he asked skeptically. "I don't think so."

Finn tsked. "You violated a protection order, dumb ass. They're going to pick you up. You're going to go to jail. Probably end up as some guy's bitch," Finn added, laughing.

The line went dead.

Guess the moron hadn't thought of that.

"Can we go now?" Sunny asked impatiently.

Finn nodded. "You direct. I'll drive."

Predictably, she mutinied. "No, I want—"

"He'll recognize your car, Sunny. For the love of all that's holy, can you just let me have the lead on this, please? I swear to you we'll get your dog back."

"Before that idiot does something like dump him on the side of the road?" she asked, her voice breaking. "Before he gets hit by a car or someone takes him?"

"Yes," he said, because she needed to hear it. Now he just hoped like hell nothing made a liar out of him.

She nodded, seeming satisfied, and then hurried out to his SUV. She rattled off directions and he shot out of the parking lot.

"I'm going to hurt him," Sunny said. "I've never wanted to physically cause someone pain in my life, but I do him."

"I'll hold him, sunshine, and you can throw as many punches as you want."

Her furious gaze found his. "I'm going to hold

you to that." She paused and her lips trembled with a smile. Unshed tears clung to her lashes. "So Atticus was gnawing on his upholstery, was he?"

Finn nodded, grinning, as well. "And perfuming the air in his customary fashion," he added drolly. Heath must have been watching the place, Finn thought. He must have been waiting for them to leave so that he could make his move. Anyone with half a brain knew that Sunny loved her dog, that she'd do anything to get him back.

A weak laugh echoed up her throat. "Attaboy, Atticus. Way to fight back."

"I'm surprised the dog went with him," Finn remarked.

"He only looks vicious," Sunny replied. "He's not. He'd trot off with Jack the Ripper if he came calling, too. He only gets defensive when we're in the house."

"So he knows to guard you, but not himself."

She rolled her head toward him. "That about sums it up, yes."

"Has he been around Heath much?"

"Enough that he would have gotten into the car with him without a struggle." She looked away, dashed a tear off her cheek. "This is all my fault."

"How so?" Finn asked.

"I should have—"

"What? Taught him to bite Heath?" He shook his head. "You couldn't have foreseen this, Sunny. This is not your fault. You need to put the blame where it belongs—squarely with Heath."

"What kind of person steals someone's pet?" she asked. "What kind of person is capable of something like that?"

A desperate one, Finn thought, but didn't say. Because desperate people did stupid things.

"A crazy one," Finn replied instead. "With a death wish," he added grimly.

"We're here," she said. "He's in Building D."

Anticipation quickened in Finn's blood. He drove down to the right building, shifted into Park and looked at Sunny. "Let's do this."

11

HOURS LATER, AFTER searching everywhere she could possibly think to look, they still hadn't found Heath or, more importantly, her dog. She rubbed her eyes and blinked back tears.

Sunny was quite literally ready to tear her hair out and was getting angrier by the minute. She'd initially thought that she'd only wanted to hurt Heath.

Now she was contemplating murder.

Clint, bless his heart, had cancelled his date and assured Sunny that he would stay at the inn until her return. He'd apologized repeatedly and was desperate to do whatever he could to help.

To be fair, though she'd been initially annoyed, this wasn't Clint's fault any more than it had been hers. He was a kid. Heath was an adult who could be very charming and authoritative when he wanted to be. He'd walked in, known Atticus by name, and when the dog hadn't objected or shown any bit of fear, Clint had let her pet leave with him. It was an honest mistake. She wished he'd called to confirm, but he hadn't, and there was nothing to be done about it now.

Finn, she knew, felt equally helpless. He'd manned the vehicle and had driven for miles without complaint. If she said go back by the apartment, Finn drove to the apartment. When she mentioned Heath's office, he'd immediately pointed the SUV in that direction. She'd checked all of Heath's local haunts and the police had put out an alert on his car. They hadn't seen him, either.

Considering that Heath was in real estate and had the keys to any number of empty homes on and off the island, the frightening truth was...he could be anywhere.

After a moment she said as much to Finn. "This is pointless," she said. "I feel like we're wasting our time."

"We're not," Finn insisted. "People are ultimately creatures of habit and when they're in trouble, they want to be in a place where they feel safe. Usually, that's home."

She hadn't thought about her apartment or missed it once all week, Sunny realized. How odd. She loved her apartment. It was in an old factory that had been converted, with lots of soaring ceilings, exposed brick and hardwood. It was beautiful. But when she thought of home…it was her parents' house that came to mind. Was that normal? she wondered. She'd been gone for ten years now, hadn't used it as an address in a decade. Shouldn't the apartment feel like her home?

"What happened to your parents' place?" Sunny asked suddenly. "Are you keeping it?"

Finn sighed. "No, I sold it. I thought about keeping it," he admitted. "But every time I went back there, I felt like my throat was closing in, you know? It was too hard, being in that house without them."

"I'm so sorry, Finn," she said, reaching over to squeeze his hand.

He tugged her close and slung an arm over her shoulder. "I felt really guilty about it in the beginning, but I think I did the right thing. I've got some things of theirs in storage, keepsakes and such. Dad's chifforobe, Mom's easel. Things like that." He turned to look at her, his concerned gaze tracing her face. "I saw a painting of my mother's in my room," he said. "It's of us."

Sunny laughed softly. "She painted lots of pictures of us," she told him. "There's one in almost every room."

He smiled. "I noticed that."

"She gave one to my mother every year. There are some of just me at the house. Didn't you see them?"

He shook his head. "No."

"You can have some of them if you want," Sunny offered. "The paintings, I mean."

"No," he said. "They were gifts."

"And they can be again. To you." She paused. "I'm sorry this is ruining your last evening here," she said. "I had other plans for you, you know."

Finn lifted her chin with his finger and met her gaze. "I'm with you, Sunny. Nothing is ever ruined when I'm with you."

She swallowed past the lump that welled suddenly in her throat. "What time do you have to leave tomorrow?"

"I thought checkout was at eleven," he teased.

"I think we can bend the rules a little in your case," she told him.

His eyes widened. "You're going to give me special treatment?"

"You've already been getting it, or haven't you noticed?"

He smiled down at her. "Oh, believe me. I've noticed." He paused, turned serious. "I have to be back on base by five tomorrow afternoon."

So he needed to leave by three-thirty, Sunny thought. It was too soon. She wanted more time. She almost told him so, too, but stopped short. What was the point? They couldn't have it. This time he *had* to leave and she was better thinking that he *had* to than thinking that he *wanted* to. If she told him that she didn't want him to go and he didn't say he wished that he could stay, she'd be hurt. Better not to put either one of them through that.

They'd had a wonderful few days together. Rocky at first, admittedly, but they'd come a long way. She'd gone into his bed willingly this time, so she couldn't feel tricked or cheated. He hadn't made any promises and she wasn't expecting any.

Was she in love with him? Most definitely.

Was she going to ache tomorrow when he drove away? Yes, to that, too.

Would she recover? Probably not.

But that was an issue for another night—one when she was alone—and she'd deal with it then.

In the meantime, they were together, not in the way that she'd hoped, of course, but he was here with her now and that was the important thing. She wouldn't let Heath ruin that. She wouldn't let him have that kind of power.

Something Finn said earlier resurfaced. "'People go home when they feel threatened,' you said."

He nodded. "Typically."

If she didn't think of her apartment as home, then maybe Heath didn't think of his condo as home, either. "Do you think he might have gone to his parents' house?" she asked, voicing her thoughts.

Finn gaze sharpened. "It's entirely possible. Do they live on the island?"

"Yes, I think so," she said slowly, her pulse quickening with a new shot of adrenaline.

"You've never been there?"

"No," she said. "But his mother's name is Grace, I believe."

Finn flipped open his cell and dialed directory assistance. In less than a minute he had a phone number and an address. "601 Marion Street," he said. "Do you know where that is?"

"On the other end of the island," she said.

Finn put the SUV in Drive once more and peeled out of the parking lot. Seconds later the phone was back at his ear and he'd called the officer who'd helped her file the restraining order. He gave him Heath's mother's address. "We're on our way there now." A pause, then, "I'll try. I'm not sure about Sunny, though."

After he'd disconnected, Sunny, curious, asked him, "What are you not sure about?"

"He told me to restrain myself. I told him that I would try, but I wasn't sure about you."

She lifted her chin with grim determination. "That's because you're supposed to *restrain* Heath so that I can beat the hell out of him. I hope you haven't forgotten your promise."

Finn grinned. "Of course, not. But do you really think that's something that I needed to pass along to Officer Hancock?"

She grimaced. "I guess not."

"If his car is there, they want us to wait for them."

"Finn!"

"We won't, if you don't want to. I'm just passing along the message."

"I need to get my dog back."

"I told you we would, didn't I? Have a little faith. I've got a good feeling about this."

And his good feeling turned out to be right. Heath had parked his Lexus in his mother's backyard, but it was there all the same. To her delight, Atticus had chewed an enormous hole in the armrest and puked it up onto the floorboard. She was going to give him an entire jar of peanut butter for that, Sunny thought. And the shoes off her feet.

Sunny headed back toward the front porch, but

Finn stopped her with a touch of his hand. "You can't just go up and knock on the door," he whispered.

"Why the hell not?" Atticus was here, dammit. She was going to get him if she had to break down the damned door.

"Because if he's hiding, then she's simply going to cover for him."

Sunny was getting sick of his rational answers. "But—"

"We need to flush him out," Finn said, looking speculatively at Heath's car. Something in his expression intrigued her.

"How?"

Finn grinned. "Come on," he said, towing her around to the backyard once more. "I've got an idea."

And it turned out to be a brilliant one, she had to admit. Finn set Heath's car alarm off. Seconds later, Heath—obviously terrified that the repo man had found him—came hurtling outside. Before he could make sense of what was happening, Finn grabbed him and pinned his arms behind his back.

"Hello, Heath." Sunny drew her arm back and slammed her fist into his jaw, on the same spot Finn had nailed yesterday. "Where the hell is my dog, you rotten bastard?" she asked ominously.

Unbelievably, Heath smiled at her as though she

hadn't just punched him in the face. "Sunny, I need to talk to you about the Sandpiper. I've got investors ready to make your parents a very lucrative offer and I—" Heath winced as Finn tightened his grip on his arms.

"Sunshine, I don't think you've gotten his attention the way you need to. Wanna try again?"

Finn was right. Rather than hit him in the face again, Sunny put her heel straight up into his groin. Heath gave a terrible choking grunt and would have crumpled to the ground if Finn hadn't been holding him up.

"Where's my damned dog, Heath?"

"What are you doing to my son?" an older woman demanded. "Unhand him, you ruffian! Before I call the police!"

At that moment, Officer Hancock arrived on the scene and Finn handed Heath off to him.

Sunny hurried forward. "I'm sorry, Mrs. Townsend, but is my dog inside?" Sunny peered around her, hoping that Atticus was on her heels, desperate to hear him bark or catch a whiff of his scent.

The woman blinked. "Dog? I don't have a dog."

Sunny's gaze shot to Finn and she felt terror bring moisture to her eyes. *Oh, God.* "Your son didn't bring my dog here?"

"No," Heath's mother said, seeming confused. "We don't allow pets in the house."

A sickening sense of dread balling in her belly, Sunny turned and glared at Heath. "What have you done with my dog?" she asked, her voice so tightly controlled she barely recognized it.

For the first time, Heath seemed to fully grasp the trouble he was in. He hung in his head. "The shelter," Heath wheezed brokenly. "I took…him to… the shelter."

Her horrified gaze flew to Finn's. "Come on!"

"REMIND ME NEVER TO GET on your bad side," Finn said after Sunny was reunited with her dog. She'd given Atticus the shoes off her feet as soon as they'd gotten back into his car and she'd piled peanut butter into something she called a Kong the minute they'd gotten home.

Home, Finn thought, startled. At some point this week, this place had become his home. He swallowed tightly. And he was leaving in less than twenty-four hours.

For eleven months, at least.

She looked up at him. "Why is that?"

"That kick below the belt," Finn said. Honestly, his own balls had shriveled up in pain after seeing that blow.

Sunny simply shrugged. "You said I needed to do something else to get his attention."

He chuckled. "True. Is your hand sore?"

"From the punch to the jaw?" she asked. "A bit."

"Let me get some ice for you." He got up from the porch swing and started toward the kitchen.

"I don't need it," she insisted. "It's fine. Thank you for today," she said. "You were great."

"No thanks necessary," he told her. "I was happy to help."

"I felt sorry for Heath's mother," Sunny said. "She didn't have a clue that he was in so much trouble, did she?"

He winced. "Apparently not."

"What will happen now?"

"I think that the trip to jail combined with the humiliation of his mother learning about his horrible behavior will be just the thing to get him off your back."

She shook her head. "I can't believe he'd pulled together investors for this property based on a few dates with me," Sunny said. "Was he out of his mind? This is my parents' place. Whatever they decide to do with it isn't up to me."

"He thought he had an in," Finn said.

She scowled. "He thought wrong."

"You're pressing charges on the dog-napping too, right?" Finn asked.

"You bet your sweet ass I am," she told him, nodding succinctly. She looked down at Atticus. "Nobody messes with my dog and gets away with it."

Atticus farted his approval.

Finn chuckled, unable to help himself. "Are you sure the peanut butter isn't what gives him gas?"

She released a long sigh. "Everything gives him gas. It's part of his charm."

That was one word for it, Finn supposed, but it wasn't the one he would have used.

She cleared her throat. "How long will it take you to pack up tomorrow?"

"Just a few minutes," Finn said, looking out at the ocean. Moonlight painted the silver sparkles on the water and the still of the night seemed to settle around him like a cozy blanket. This was where he belonged, Finn thought. Right here, on this piece of land, with her at his side. "It's thanks to my special training."

"Do you ever get scared?" Sunny asked. She rested her head against his shoulder.

"Will it ruin my status as a badass if I tell you yes?"

She squeezed his hand and chuckled softly.

"Nothing could ruin your status as a badass, Finn O'Conner."

He smiled into the darkness. "Then yes, I get scared. When I have time, that is. But I like it better when I don't have time. When I'm just in the zone, doing what I'm supposed to do."

"Is it everything you thought it would be? Being a Ranger, I mean?"

"Yes," he said, though he was ready to have a new life. It had been everything he'd thought it would be. He'd served his country with honor to the best of his ability. He'd protected democracy, the greater good. It gave him a keen sense of satisfaction, as though he'd done his part to further his country's longevity.

She was quiet for a moment. "So, no regrets then?"

Only one…and she needed to hear it. "I only regret that I didn't keep my promise to you, that I didn't write, that I didn't come back with my parents again."

She tried to pull away, but he held tight. "You don't have to say that," she said. "That's not what I meant."

"It doesn't matter what you meant. It's what you asked and I answered it honestly." He laughed to lighten the moment. "The truth is, you scared the hell out of me, Sunny, and I ran."

She leaned away and peered at him through the darkness. He could feel those expressive green eyes on him, probing for the truth. "I don't understand."

How to explain? "You made me want to stay, you see? I had a plan, I was supposed to be a soldier, I'd already gotten the scholarship. Everything was mapped out, ready to go. And then you and I…" He shrugged helplessly. "And suddenly I was having second thoughts about everything. Second thoughts, second-guessing. It was too late for that. I was eighteen, you were sixteen. It was too soon."

It was quiet save for the waves crashing against the shore. She absorbed his words. "Thank you for telling me that," she finally said, her voice strangely thick. "I needed to hear it."

"I needed you to know the truth. I know you thought that I simply lied to you to—"

"Get me naked," she supplied. "Yes, I did. I thought you'd used me."

"I didn't, Sunny. I meant everything I said. I was just too much of a coward to follow through."

"You were my first."

He nodded. "I know."

"I've never regretted that, Finn. Even when I thought that I'd simply been another notch on your belt, I couldn't regret it." He felt her swallow. "You've always been…very special to me."

"Then I'm honored." He paused. "And for the record, you've always been very special to me, too, sunshine. You make me feel—" he struggled to find the right word "—whole."

That was it, Finn thought. She completely him.

Sunny tugged him up from the swing and pressed a kiss beneath his chin. "Come on, soldier," she said, emotion clogging her voice. "It's time for me to give you a proper send-off."

MORE NERVOUS THAN SHE'D BEEN on her wedding night, Martha Ann, cake in hand, stepped out into the cooler evening air and made her way down to Tug's room. She spied two place settings and a bottle of wine and her mouth went bone dry.

"That confident of me, were you?"

In the process of flipping the steaks on the grill, Tug turned and grinned at her. Her stomach gave a flutter. "You're a smart woman, Martha Ann. I knew you'd come around."

He took the cake from her, then leaned forward and pressed a kiss to her cheek. His lips were soft and warm and she caught the scent of his aftershave, something salty and resinous like a windswept pine. He let out a long breath. "I've been waiting a long time to do that."

She blushed. "You gave me a lot to think about this afternoon," she said.

He set her cake on the table and poured her a glass of wine, then handed it to her. "The subtle approach wasn't working and I only had a week left to work with. I couldn't let you leave and miss my chance." He quirked a brow. "Is it too soon, Martha Ann? Are you still grieving?"

If Tug had been watching her for the past ten years then he knew that it wasn't too soon. She'd loved Sheldon because she believed you could choose to love when you had to. She'd promised to love Sheldon when she'd married him and she thought that she'd done that to the best of her ability. But she hadn't been *in love* with Sheldon in a very long time. Though she'd mourned his passing and even missed him to some degree, his death hadn't left her so bereaved that she didn't know how she was going to carry on.

In truth, she'd been managing on her own for so long—even when he was alive—that his death hadn't required that much of an adjustment. Sadly, just fewer meals, less laundry and less criticism. She'd grieved more because her kids had lost their father, because the grandchildren were in pain.

Martha Ann finally looked up and shook her head

sadly. "It's not too soon, Tug. But it's not going to work, regardless."

He stared at her, his gaze calm and soothing, as though he'd predicted this response, as well. "Why not? You're here, so I'm assuming that you like me well enough."

She chuckled. "I like you well enough," she admitted.

His twinkling blue gaze warmed with pleasure. "Then what's the problem? I'm an adult, you're an adult. We're not in the nursing home yet, you know."

All true, she knew.

"Is it your family? Do you think your kids wouldn't approve?"

A thought struck. "Do you have kids?"

"No," he said. "And that's a regret that I live with every day. But I don't want to live without you any-more and if I don't make you mine, it's just going to be one more thing added to that list."

"Tug," she admonished, looking away.

He slipped a finger under her chin and made her look at him. "I'm serious, woman. We're too old to play games—" he gentled his voice "—but we're not too old for love. Your kids wouldn't begrudge you a little bit of happiness, would they?"

"No. Of course not." She hesitated. "But it would be an adjustment."

He caressed her cheek reverently and she responded to the emotion in his touch. It had been so long since a man had looked at her that way, made her feel like her bones were melting. "Then let them adjust, Martha Ann. Give us a chance, would you? Let me love you."

Let me love you.

She swallowed. "And what of you? Don't you need to be loved?"

His gaze caught and held hers and he gave a little smile. "It'd be nice," he said, making her smile. "But all I truly need is you."

He slid a finger over her bottom lip, then bent his head and kissed her. Heat boiled up beneath her skin and warmth glowed instantly around her heart.

All right, Martha Ann thought. She'd let him love her and she fully expected to love him in return.

12

HER HEART IN HER THROAT, Sunny tugged Finn into the house and paused in the kitchen to get a bottle of chocolate syrup from the cabinet.

Finn saw it and chuckled wickedly. "You were listening earlier then," he said, pleased.

"Who says this is for you to lick off me?" she asked, shooting him a look over her shoulder as she led him upstairs.

His face went comically blank and she laughed as he said, "You mean…?"

"You might have the market cornered on sex appeal, but you don't have it covered on chocolate syrup and sexual fantasies."

"But I thought—"

She shoved him backward onto the bed, then straddled him. "That was your first mistake," she said, licking a path along his neck because she knew he liked it. "You don't need to think."

Sunny tugged her dress over her head and cast it aside, then leaned forward and kissed him, all the while slipping his shirt up over his chest. She loved the way he felt beneath her hands, warm and solid, sleek and muscular. His body was a veritable playground and she was ready to ride. She felt him harden beneath her and smiled against his mouth.

"Get naked."

"You're bossy. Interestingly, I like that."

"Good, because you're about to take a few orders. The first of which is to shut up."

He blinked. "What?"

"You talk too much." She put a breast a hairbreadth from his nose. "There are other things you could be doing with your mouth."

He opened it to say something else and she popped her nipple inside before he could.

He sighed and suckled, slipping his hands up over her back, mapping her spine. His hands were huge and made her feel small and cherished and protected. She loved the way they felt against her skin and told him so.

"I—"

She moved the other breast to his mouth before he could speak again, then reached down and started working his shorts and boxers off. For someone who was used to following orders, he was amazingly slack about doing so with her. "I thought I told you to get naked. You didn't." She tsked. "For that, you will have to be punished."

Finn didn't look the least bit worried. He flattened the crown of her breast deep into his mouth and a reciprocating tug started low in her womb. For a moment she forgot that she was supposed to be in charge, then remembered herself and snagged the chocolate from the nightstand. She put a dollop on his chest and bent forward and licked it slowly off, catching a male nipple in her mouth and giving it a tender bite.

He bucked beneath her, slipping his dick along her nether lips.

The sensation ripped the breath from her lungs and she lost her train of thought all over again. While she was trying to get it back, Finn dabbed some chocolate onto her as well, then began cleaning her up with his tongue.

Determined to keep the upper hand this time, Sunny parlayed this move with one of her own. She leaned forward, then slowly sank back, impaling herself on him one slow inch at a time.

The veins stood out on Finn's neck and he anchored his hands on her hips. "Sunny—"

She gritted her teeth. "Finn, what are you supposed to be doing with your mouth?"

He bent forward and suckled her again, and she began to writhe on top of him, slowly undulating her hips, then quickly finding a faster tempo. She couldn't help herself, she was simply obeying her body. He felt so good, so incredibly perfect. He was big and hard and she could feel him deep inside her, every ridge and vein, moving within her. He flexed his hips, meeting her thrust for thrust, then slipped his fingers into her curls and put a knuckle against her clit.

She rode him harder, tightened around him, creating a delicious draw and drag between their joined bodies. She felt the first quickening of impending orgasm in her sex and raced forward, determined to catch it. Her breathing came in little jagged puffs, her heart raced in her chest, and every cell in her body was focused on rushing headlong into release.

He suckled her again, applied the perfect amount of pressure against her and she came apart. Flew into a thousand little pieces. Sunny straightened on top of Finn, savoring the joy of release, and he continued to slide in and out of her, milking the orgasm for all it was worth. When he'd wrung every last bit of it from her, she collapsed on top of him and tried to catch her breath.

That's when he rolled her over and started the mind-numbing process all over again.

"Finn, I—"

"Now it's your turn to take orders," Finn told her. "Tell me what you want."

"I want you," she said, the simple statement burrowing into his heart.

"You've got me," he told her, and truer words had never been spoken. She absolutely owned him and always would. "Now tell me what you want me to do to you."

A wicked glint entered her gaze. "I want you to slide your hands all over my body. I want you to kiss every part that's white, every part that's pink and every part in between. Then I want you to come inside of me...and come inside of me," she murmured.

Holy hell, Finn thought, releasing a ragged breath. He smiled down at her. "You've got it, sunshine."

He withdrew and took his time, feasted on her breasts, then her belly, her sides and even the backs of her knees. He drizzled chocolate syrup on the small of her back and slowly lapped it up and had the pleasure of watching gooseflesh race down her spine.

"Cold?" he murmured.

"No, I'm not cold," she said, whimpering. "I'm

burning up in my own body. You're killing me, Finn."

He loved the way she said his name. It made him want to beat his chest and roar.

He looked up at her, up the long length of her body. "Do you want me to stop?"

Her green eyes flashed. "Don't you dare. Hurry," she pleaded. "I need you inside me."

How could he resist a request like that? He spread her legs, opening her to him, and slowly, deliberately slid inside.

Heaven, he thought, gritting his teeth against the onslaught of sensation. Had he ever been happier? Had anything ever felt more wonderful?

No.

Never.

And he instinctively knew it never would. Sunny was the only girl for him and always had been. He was more than a decade late and she'd moved on, made a new life, but it didn't change the fact that *she* was the one he wanted, the one he needed.

The one he couldn't have.

He couldn't be that selfish.

Finn pushed the unpleasant truth from his mind and pushed himself back into her, where he told himself he belonged. She wrapped her arms around him and anchored her legs around his waist and held on to him, as if she were clinging to the idea of them as well, as if she never wanted to let him go.

Could he ask her to wait for him? Finn wondered. Could he do that to her?

Eleven months deployed, another three in the service. More than a year. It was too much to ask. He couldn't. Wouldn't do that to her.

"Do you have any idea how wonderful you feel?" she asked him, her voice hoarse with desire. For him.

"I couldn't possibly feel any better to you than you do to me," he said.

Her breathing was ragged, her face flushed. Her curls were tangled around her face, a golden halo. Beautiful. Achingly so. "You're wrong."

"How would you know?"

She tightened around him, slid her hands down his back and settled them over his ass. He quaked. "I…just…know."

"Can we have this argument later?" he asked. "I'm kind of busy right now."

She chuckled. "Really? I hadn't noticed."

"In that case, I'd better work harder to get your attention." He gritted his teeth and hammered more forcefully into her, pistoning in and out, angling deep, getting as far into her as he could without having to be surgically removed. She was wet and tight and her greedy muscles clamped around him, holding him inside her, making him feel loved, needed, wanted.

Less and less alone.

Gratifyingly, her eyes closed and she held on to him, breathing hard, her nipples grazing his chest. He felt his release building quickly in the back of his loins, but wanted her to come again—*needed* her to come again—before he did.

He put both hands under her hips and shifted her until her breathing changed and he knew he'd found the right spot. He pushed harder and harder, in and out, in and out. Fire burned in his lungs and it was all he could do to keep the orgasm at bay. Finally, blessedly, she screamed, a low, keening cry and her feminine muscles fisted around him.

He came then. Hard.

His vision blackened around the edges, the room swam out of focus and everything in his body went still and seemed to explode at the same time.

He shuddered atop her, filling her up with his release. He stayed rooted inside her, didn't move, waiting for the powerful quake to subside.

When it did, he slowly withdrew, then rolled to her side and tucked her against his chest. She fitted perfectly there, as though that niche had been created with her in mind.

"Sunny?" he said, his voice rusty.

"Yeah?"

"I'm going to miss you." *I love you. I don't want to leave you. I want to stay. I want to marry you and have children and grow old together.*

"I'm going to miss you, too, Finn."

He sighed, the weight of everything he wished he could say sitting firmly on his chest. "You don't know how much I wish I didn't have to leave tomorrow." He wasn't making her a promise, Finn told himself, merely stating a fact. He could share that one, right? He could tell her that he'd rather be with her than anywhere else, right? He wasn't asking anything of her, just apprising her of a harmless fact.

He suddenly felt something warm and wet hit his chest and knew it was one of her tears. "Oh, I think I do."

"Don't cry," he told her, giving her a squeeze.

"Don't talk about leaving and I won't," she sniffed. She kissed his chest, then chuckled.

"What's funny?"

"You're sticky."

He hummed under his breath. "Maybe we should take a shower."

She leaned up and peeked at him from beneath

lowered lashes. "That sounds awfully…tame. I had a little something more daring in mind."

Intrigued, he quirked a brow. "You do? What exactly would that be?"

"Skinny-dipping."

In the ocean? Finn thought, a bit shocked. That was daring. And dangerous. He didn't like the idea of using his dick as shark bait. After a minute, while he was in the process of telling her as much, she dissolved into a fit of wheezing laughter that made him pause.

"Not in the ocean, you fool," she gasped. "In the pool."

He paused. "You mean the one in front of the guest rooms?" He felt his smile widen with appreciation. "That *is* daring. How long have you been doing that?"

"For years," she admitted. "If you'd ever ventured outside after midnight when you stayed here before, you would have caught me." She slid a finger down his chest. "I shriveled up many a night waiting on you, you know?"

It was his turn to laugh. "Your parents would have throttled you, you realize that, don't you?"

She grinned at him. "I guess it's a good thing I never got caught then, isn't it?" She sat up and kissed

him. "Come on, Finn. Let's go play Marco Polo…
in the nude."

Well, when she put it like that how could he
refuse?

13

WELL, HERE IT WAS, Sunny thought miserably. The worst day of her life.

Naturally, it was a beautiful one. Fluffy white clouds drifted often enough in front of the sun to keep from making the umbrella a necessity and the surf was high, rolling in on waves that were made for ocean fun. The water was a lovely blue-green and had a clean scent to it that promised rain at some point later in the day. Sunny buried her toes in the sand and let her head fall back against her chair.

Though Fridays were typically busy days for the inn, today had turned out to be relatively calm. Finn had quickly helped her get through the morning chores and they'd brought their chairs down to the water. She'd donned her skimpiest bikini for him and was thankful that her mother and father weren't there.

They'd be appalled.

"I'm proud of you," Sunny remarked, after they'd been sitting there for an hour. She sipped her lemonade and savored the tanginess against her tongue.

He rolled his head toward her and smiled. "Let me guess? It's my stamina, right?"

She laughed. "No."

"My virility? My especially large penis?"

"Would you shut up," she hissed, looking around to make sure no one overheard him. A couple of kids were working on a sand castle nearby and Tug and Martha Ann were only a few feet down the beach, seeming as content as she and Finn were. "There are people around."

He grinned. "Sorry. I'll behave."

She snorted, though affection pushed her lips into a smile. "That's doubtful, but one can hope."

"Why are you proud of me?" Finn asked, seemingly intrigued. "I'm curious now."

She released a slow sigh. "Because we've been sitting here for more than an hour and you haven't jumped up to play in the sand or swim or help someone fly a kite or…anything. You've been content."

"That's because I'm with you," he said, as though it should be obvious. "It's easy to be still when you're around." He slid her a smile that made the top of her thighs catch fire and her belly quake. "Well, except for when I'm licking chocolate sauce off your—"

"Shut up," she said through clenched teeth. "Honestly, Finn. You're incorrigible."

He nodded once, seeming humbled. "Thank you."

She rolled her eyes, exasperated. "It wasn't a compliment."

He blinked. "But you were smiling."

"That's to keep from screaming."

He waggled his brows. "I like it when you scream. Especially my name. It makes me feel like I can conquer the world."

What was she going to do without him? Sunny thought with furious despair. She loved his outrageous sense of humor, the shocking things he said. They made her tingle and glow inside and she knew that light was going to go out again as soon as he left. He was going to have to say it soon, too.

She knew it. Could feel it coming.

He'd already packed everything other than what was right here with him on the sand, but their time together was still closing in on them, circling and circling, getting smaller by the minute.

Tears pricked the back of her lids, but she blinked

them away, determined not to cry. At least until after he left, anyway.

"So when are your parents supposed to be back?" Finn asked.

"Tomorrow," she said, swallowing.

He didn't look at her, but studied the ocean. "And you'll go back to Savannah?" The question was uttered casually, as though her answer was insignificant, but the air suddenly changed around them.

She nodded. How bizarre, Sunny thought. To think of resuming her old life when, for reasons which escaped her, it felt like it belonged to someone else, someone she wasn't anymore. How could that be? Sunny wondered. How could she have changed so much over the past five days? How could everything she'd worked for, everything she'd wanted, shift so dramatically?

But the person she wanted to be—the person she was certain she was *meant* to be—was sitting right here with Finn. If she could have him, she'd want to stay here, Sunny realized, the idea blooming into the perfect dream. She'd want to stay here and build a life with him. Have a family with him. A vision of a bronze-haired little boy with Finn's impish smile rose in her mind's eye and she instantly—irrationally— loved that child, missed him even though he'd never existed.

How was that possible?

Something started to tear inside of her and she wrapped her arms around her chest to keep the pieces together. Swallowed back the sob that rose in her throat.

She couldn't make it hard on him, dammit. It wasn't fair. He was about to go off to war, to fight, possibly never to return—nausea clawed up her throat at the thought—and it wasn't right to make him worry about hurting her, make him feel even more powerless than he already did. It was enough to know that he didn't want to leave her, to know that he would stay this time if he could.

Finn was quiet for a long time, but reached over and threaded his fingers through hers. Seagulls squawked overhead and the sound of the surf pounded against the shore. Kids laughed and parents cautioned and it was all familiar, yet somehow very different.

Finn squeezed her hand and she knew the time had come. "I've got to get on the road," he said, his voice strained and reluctant.

She looked over at him and nodded through misty eyes.

He shook his head when he saw her tears. "Don't do this to me, Sunny. You know I don't have a choice."

She nodded, her throat thick. "I know. I'm all

right." She paused. "It's just been—" she struggled to find the right word, but none were good enough "—wonderful seeing you again. I've missed you," she admitted and gave a little shrug. Her gaze searched his. "You're my Finn."

"And you're my sunshine." He slid a finger over her cheek. "You always have been."

She stood, because she knew she had to. Because she refused to be pathetic in front of him. She'd known from the minute she'd seen his name on the reservation screen that he was checking in and he'd be checking out.

Nothing had changed and yet everything was different.

But that was the way it worked. People came here to vacation then returned to their normal lives. She'd be returning to her normal life as well, as dismal as it all seemed now. She'd go back to Savannah to her business, to her apartment that she loved but still couldn't call home. She'd find her rhythm again. She would. She had to, because she didn't have a choice. She glanced back up at the house, at the inn and her heart gave a squeeze.

Or maybe not, Sunny thought. Maybe she'd stay after all.

Finn gathered up his things and stowed them in the back of his SUV. Though he hated the sand,

Atticus ambled off the porch and came to see him off, as well.

Finn smiled when he saw her dog. "Take care of her for me," he said, and Atticus sneezed and expelled gas simultaneously.

Sunny laughed, which helped keep her from crying. It felt as if her very soul was shattering, as if at any moment it would crumble away inside her. "Listen, Finn. I told you I would write—and I will—but I'm going to need an address." She paused because her throat had tightened painfully. "You'll send me the address right?"

Something shifted in his gaze—regret, maybe? "I will," he said and his gaze tangled with hers. "And that's a promise that I swear to you I will keep. No more broken promises between us. Ever."

She nodded. "Thank you. That means a lot."

He opened his mouth, shut it again and seeing him struggle when he was ordinarily so self-assured made her ache for him. "I really wish that things were different, Sunny," he said, a nuance in his voice she couldn't readily decipher. His gaze tangled with hers. "I wish that I wasn't leaving. And I really wish that our timing wasn't always off."

The lump in her throat swelled. "Me, too."

"I'm going to be gone eleven months," he said,

and there was an undercurrent in his voice that she didn't understand, something that she was missing.

"I know," she told him, nodding miserably. "I'll write, I promise."

He hesitated. "Thank you." He stepped forward and framed her face with his hands, then bent his head and pressed his lips against hers. The kiss was desperate and reverent and held a wealth of unresolved emotion. He tasted like lemonade and maple syrup, home and family, her past, her future, her everything. He molded her to him and groaned and she felt the telltale bulge against her belly.

He couldn't do this to her. They didn't have time.

He tore his mouth away from hers and rested his forehead against hers. "Oh, Sunny," he breathed. "You don't know how much I wish we wanted the same things." He pressed another kiss against her lips, then hastily climbed into his car. "Write, please," he said, his voice slightly thick.

She nodded, wrapped her arms back around her middle, then watched him drive away. Out of her life. Again.

TELLING HIMSELF THAT HE'D DONE the right thing—the noble thing—Finn patted himself on the back for not being selfish and asking her to wait for him, to give up her own life to accommodate his. He knew, at some point, he wouldn't feel quite so gutted as he did now. At some point, he'd be okay again. He wouldn't feel as if his heart had been filleted, his very soul separated from his body.

He sincerely hoped that sensation came sooner rather than later, because frankly, he wasn't sure how long he was going to be able to stand this.

And he hadn't even made it off the island yet.

He wanted to be selfish. He wanted Sunny. He wanted to ask her to wait for him. Ask her to let him buy the inn from her parents so the two of them could run it together and make babies and eat chocolate off one another's bodies from now until death do they part.

That's what he wanted. What he knew was right for him.

But was it right for her? When she'd specifically told him that the inn had stolen her childhood, that it had been her parents' dream and not hers? Hadn't he told her that she was allowed to have different dreams?

Yes.

But he still felt cheated. Because if he'd taken the path with her all those years ago, things would have been different. They would be together. They'd probably already have a family. They would have been happy.

And he wouldn't feel this damned, miserable gaping hole in his chest.

Again.

Yes, he'd gone back to the Sandpiper because it held wonderful memories for him, because he'd wanted to honor his parents in some strange way, but he knew now that it had been more than that.

It had been Sunny.

It had *always* been Sunny.

He'd wanted to get back to her, to the man he was when he was with her. He'd made a huge mistake all those years ago, one he could have righted when she'd been old enough…but he hadn't. The more time had passed, the easier it had been to simply let it go. Had he come back, even two years later, he knew that they would have worked things out. He would have proposed and she would have accepted and their lives would be vastly different now.

But he couldn't rewrite history and he couldn't go back this time, even if he wanted to. Because Sunny had taken the path he'd forced her into and she was happy. Who was he to take that away from her? How arrogant was he to think that he could make her happier than she was now?

His cell phone rang, startling him. He checked the display, but didn't recognize the number. "Hello."

"Pull over."

Sunny? He frowned. "What?"

"Pull over," she repeated impatiently. "I'm behind you."

Finn's gaze darted to his rearview mirror and sure enough, there she was. His heart skipped a beat. Blond hair whipping in the wind, big-ass sunglasses on her face, Atticus in the front seat. What the hell was she doing? Why had she followed him? He inwardly groaned and wondered where he was going to find the strength to tell her goodbye again.

She was making it damned hard for him to be noble, Finn thought.

He quickly pulled his car over to the side of the road, then got out and hurried to the back of his SUV. Sunny had already whipped her Jeep over and was coming toward him.

"What did you mean?" she asked, pushing the hair out of her face.

"I'm sorry?"

She slid her sunglasses up, sliding them atop her head. "What did you mean when you said you wished we wanted the same things? What things? You never told me anything that you wanted. How do you know we don't want the same things? Are you psychic?"

Oh, hell. He'd said too much. He groaned and resisted the urge to move closer to her. To breathe her in. "Sunny, I'm trying really hard not to be selfish."

"Do you know why it's hard?" she asked, glaring at him.

"Because it's the right thing to do?"

"No, because it's out of character for you. What were you talking about?" she repeated, her gaze tangling with his. "And be specific."

All right, then, Finn thought, straightening. She'd asked for it. "I want you," he said simply, his gaze tracing the woefully familiar lines of her face, lingering on the freckle on her eyelid, the shape of her mouth. "I want you to wait for me. I don't want you to so much as look at another guy, much less consider going out with him. I want exclusivity for the rest of your life."

She gasped. "But—"

He shushed her, laying a finger against her lips and her eyes widened. "I'm not finished." His gaze searched hers. "I want to buy the inn from your parents and let them retire. I'll run it myself if you want to keep doing Funky Feet, though admittedly, I'd like it better if we ran it together. Or we can do both. Run the inn together and you keep Funky Feet." He shrugged as if it didn't signify. "Doesn't matter to me, so long as we're together."

"But I—"

He put his finger back over her lips. "Stop inter-rupting. It's rude," he admonished her, then contin-ued. "I want to live in your parents' house and make a family. I want two kids—a boy and a girl—and another dog, a black Lab we can name Scout, and I want to buy stock in chocolate syrup and lick it off you anytime I want. I want to marry you the instant I get home." He was on a roll now, Finn thought. In for a penny, in for a pound. She'd asked, hadn't she? "Ideally you'll be waiting for me in a wedding dress. That would make things simpler." He nodded once and instantly imagined it. "I—"

She put a finger against his mouth, stopping him. "Let me ask you something, genius. Why did you assume that I wouldn't want any of that?"

He blinked. "Because that's what you said. You said—"

"When did I ever tell you that I didn't want to marry you? That I didn't want to have your children and grow old with you? When did I ever tell you that I didn't want to wait?" she all but howled, stomping her foot. "I've been waiting *twelve years!* Where in the hell did you get the idea that I wouldn't wait another *one?* Because I sure as hell never said that."

He was hopelessly confused. "But you said you

didn't want to run the inn, that you were happy with your life."

"I was," she said, her hands framing his face. Her thumbs slid over his cheeks. "I was as happy as I could be considering that I didn't have you."

He nearly melted on the spot he went so weak with relief. "So you'll wait?"

She kissed him. "I will, you fool."

"And you'll marry me?"

"The minute you get back. I'm hopelessly, irrevocably in love with you."

Finn whooped, then lifted her off the ground and spun her around. His chest felt so full he thought it was going to explode. The hole was gone again, plugged up by her. She completed him. Made him whole. "You are?"

She laughed and tears spilled past her lashes. "I am. I told you that you're my Finn. You always have been."

"And when I told you I was going to be gone for eleven months, you were supposed to tell me you'd wait for me."

"I was?"

He smiled sheepishly at her. "I'd hoped."

"How was I supposed to know that's what you wanted me to say?" she asked, her voice climbing. "You haven't given me any hint that you were thinking any of this."

"That's because I didn't think it was fair to ask you to keep sacrificing for me."

"And you thought it was fair to love me and want to spend the rest of your life with me and not tell me that? Dammit, I'm not a mind reader. After we're married, you're going to have to forget about being subtle and just lay it all on the line."

"In future I will not hesitate to tell you everything I am thinking." He smiled. "Even when it's inappropriate."

She chuckled, held him tighter. "I'm counting on it."

"And the inn?" he asked, searching her face. "We don't have to do that if you don't want to, Sunny. I just want to be where you are. We can live in Savannah. Hell, we can live at the North Pole if that's what you want."

"I fell in love with the Sandpiper again while you were here," she admitted, knowing it was the truth. And it was her heritage, one she was proud of. "I'd already decided to move back and let Mom and Dad retire. It's a great place to raise a family."

Traffic whipped by them on the highway and the occasional driver honked a horn. "I want to start one as soon as I get back," he said. "Be ready."

She wrapped her arms around his neck and smiled. "I'll have the chocolate syrup in my purse."

"What?" he teased. "No voodoo priestess and live chicken?"

She chuckled softly and the sound burrowed into his heart. "I love you, Sunny," he murmured. "You know that, right?"

"I do now."

"And you'll write?"

"Every day. I'll email, I'll call, I'll send smoke signals," she teased. "I'm here for you, Finn." She squeezed him. "Know that."

He tipped her lips up for one last farewell kiss, savored the flavor of her on his tongue. "I do," he said, realizing at that moment how important that knowledge was to him.

She was his. *Finally.*

And she'd be waiting.

Epilogue

Two months later...

Looks like we're starting early...
Love, Sunny

CONFUSED BY HER NOTE, Finn held up the small, grainy black-and-white picture that had been included in his care package and wondered what his fiancée had sent him. It looked like a picture of a big bubble with a bean inside. When she'd told him she'd included a surprise in his care package, he'd been waiting anxiously for it to arrive. Unfortunately, if he didn't know what the hell he was looking at, then he could hardly understand the significance, could he? He peered closer, trying to make out exactly what it was he was supposed to be seeing.

Justin Andrews slapped him on the back. "Congratulations, man," he said, smiling. "I didn't know your old lady was expecting."

Finn blinked, feeling suddenly faint, and looked at the little photo again, then read the small print at the bottom that he'd missed before. *Sunny Ledbetter. Gestation 9 wks.*

Looks like we're starting early, she'd said.

A baby. She was having his baby.

He jumped up and whooped loudly, then started shouting at everyone in the barracks. "I'm going to be a father! We're having a baby! A baby! Oh, man!" So much for her being covered, Finn thought. Evidently her birth control had been no match for his virility. He couldn't be happier.

Finn blinked back tears of joy and felt his chest constrict with the strangest, most powerful emotion.

A baby. *Their* baby.

His mom and dad would have been so proud.

Seven months later...

"I'M GOING TO THROTTLE YOU with my bare hands when you get home, Finn O'Conner," Sunny panted into the phone, her voice strangled with pain and irritation.

"Baby, you know you don't mean that," Finn told her, listening to every sound coming from the delivery room. "You love me, remember?"

She howled again, then made a grunting noise. "I'd love you more if you were here so I could knock the hell out of you!" Her voice broke into a little sob. "Why didn't I want an epidural? Why, oh, why did I think I could do this?"

"Because you wanted to be a badass, too, remember? You said you were tough."

"I'm not," she whimpered, breaking his heart with her pain. "I'm a wuss."

He smothered a laugh because he knew she wouldn't appreciate it. Only his Sunny. "You're not a wuss, honey. You're amazing. I love you."

"Shut up," she panted, rallying. "You're not supposed to be nice when I'm mad at you."

"Whatever makes you feel better."

She groaned again and he heard her breathing increase. "Oh, no, here comes another one."

"Push, Sunny," he heard someone say.

"Finn!" she screamed. "I'm going to get you! I'm going to gut you like a fish—"

"The baby's crowning," another voice cried. "One more push, Sunny. You're almost there."

"You can do it, baby," Finn told her, his heart

about to pound right out of his chest. A baby, their baby. He was about to be a father.

Another long growl of pain from Sunny, then an awed silence, then a beautiful healthy cry.

"It's a boy," his soon to be mother-in-law cried.

"I've got a son!" Finn screamed to the room at large and huge cheer erupted around him. "Sunny? Sunny?"

"He's beautiful," she sobbed, her voice tired and reverent. "Oh, Finn, he's so perfect. Our boy. Our baby. I don't h-hate you anymore."

He laughed, spent, wishing with every fiber of his being that he was there with them. *His family.* "I'm glad," he choked out. "I love you."

"You'll meet Cam soon."

"Cam?"

"Cameron Finn O'Conner," she said. "After your dad."

He nodded, unable to speak.

Two months later...

FINN WAS ON THE EDGE of his seat as the plane descended and out of it by the time it taxied to a stop. Though he knew everyone on board was anxious to get off and see their families, he was selfishly pushing his way to the front of the line, determined to be the first one off the plane. He bolted down the steps, his gaze scanning the crowd, and he stilled when he saw them.

She was in a wedding dress, just like he'd asked, but she'd brought the ceremony to him. Sunny was standing under an arbor, her parents next to her, Cam—his son—in her arms. Ferns and flowers and the preacher, it was all there, but everything else sort of drifted out of focus as he ran to her—to them.

His Sunny, his Cam.

"Welcome home, Daddy," she said.

Finn couldn't speak. The words lodged in his throat as he gazed at his son. He was perfect. He had bronze hair and Sunny's mouth and he was, quite simply, the most amazing little boy that ever lived in the entire history of the world. They'd made this little person, this perfect little being. Finn missed his parents even more. They would have been so happy.

"You want to hold him?"

He nodded, his throat tight.

She stroked his cheek, her eyes brimming with unshed tears. "You can't speak?"

He shook his head.

Tears streamed down her face and she smiled at

him. "You're going to have to choke out an 'I do' in a minute, okay?"

He did. And he didn't choke it out. His voice was clear and certain when he said the words. The words that finally told him he was home.

* * * * *

BREAKING
THE RULES

TAWNY
WEBER

Tawny Weber is usually found dreaming up stories in her California home, surrounded by dogs, cats and kids. When she's not writing hot, spicy stories for Mills & Boon® Blaze®, she's shopping for the perfect pair of shoes or drooling over Johnny Depp pictures (when her husband isn't looking, of course). Come by and visit her on the web at www.tawnyweber.com.

To Specialist, James Ramirez. My very own hero.
I couldn't do it without you.

Prologue

SERGEANT FIRST CLASS Maximilian St. James, EOD squad leader, stood at attention at the foot of the hospital bed. Next to him stood the general, also standing ramrod straight. The blistering Afghanistan sun shone through the army medical center window. The sharp scent of antiseptic filled the air.

Specialist Rico Santiago, his leg in traction, returned the general's salute, waiting until the man glanced away before winking at Max.

His face impassive, Max saluted the general and waited for the return salute. As soon as the ranking officer stepped aside for him to pin the Purple Heart on Rico's pajama top, Max rolled his eyes at the look of heroic suffering on his buddy's face.

"Good work, gentlemen," the general concluded, dismissing them both.

Only when the man moved away did Max let himself grin. He tapped Rico's cast and arched his brow as if to say, "Told you so."

"I'd have been fine if you'd presented it," Rico muttered, but Max could tell the guy was seriously proud to have been pinned by a four-star general.

"You deserved a little pomp," Max claimed. He'd made sure his man got it, and had pushed to have Rico brought to the joint theater hospital instead of the closer units. Now, shoulders tense from being at constant attention, Max wished for just a second that they'd stuck with a more low-key hospital.

It had nothing to do with being nervous in the presence of brass. Max had cut his baby teeth on brass.

He'd never had one of his men hospitalized before, though.

He was handling it fine. It wasn't as if he wanted to wince at the sight of the cuts and bruises on Rico's face. The guy's leg all trussed up, with pulleys and contraptions wrapped around it, didn't make his gut clench.

He didn't feel ill whenever he closed his eyes and flashed back to the paralyzing terror of watching the RPG, or rocket-propelled grenade, hit the ground. The dust and flying dirt had made it impossible to see how bad Rico had been hit. For a heartbeat, he'd frozen when the dust cleared and he saw his man lying there on the ground.

Yep, he was handling it all just fine.

Rico was a smart guy, though.

"Dude, quit feeling guilty. It wasn't your fault."

"It was my call to go in and defuse that bomb," Max muttered, giving in to the need to chill by dropping into the chair next to the bed.

"You didn't know we'd be ambushed."

Max shrugged. It should have been a simple bomb detonation. Intel hadn't offered any insurgent warnings. The village had been peaceful with early morning quiet. Standard bomb disarming operation, just like any other day.

Max had assessed the situation and made the call to go in.

It'd been a bad call.

"That grim look on your face is messing up my hero moment here," Rico joked.

"You look pretty in your new jewelry," Max joked, flicking

a finger over the commendation on Rico's chest. "Still, I feel bad leaving you lying here."

"Dude, you'd be going home whether I was busted up or not. Quit being all mama hen and enjoy your leave."

Max smirked, always amused at the hokey folky sayings coming out of a big, macho bruiser like Rico. The man was right, though. Max was due to go stateside in twenty-four hours. It was coming up to the anniversary of his father's death, so whenever possible he took leave to be with his mom on that day.

"But you know…" Rico said, his smile dimming.

Max lost the smirk.

"If you don't mind?"

"Sure, buddy. Anything."

"You're going back to the Bay area, yeah?"

"Yeah." There had been a St. James of *the* St. Jameses on Nob Hill as far back as the 1800s. Sure, the house had been rebuilt after the 1906 earthquake, but the snobbery of the family hadn't changed a bit.

Which meant that while he'd have preferred to spend his month-long leave knocking back tequila with a half dozen bikini-clad hotties on a beach somewhere, that wasn't gonna happen.

Unless orders prevented it, he was expected to spend Februarys at home. Max had learned the rules at his mother's knee. As he'd grown older, he'd learned which ones mattered, which could be ignored and how to bend them all to work in his favor.

"A little favor?"

From the look on Rico's face, a combination of a sheepish grin and the look he got before he pulled one of his notorious pranks, Max figured he'd better hear this standing. He rose slowly, preparing.

"My sister is right outside San Francisco. I told you that, right?" He waited for Max's nod. "She's a peach. A real sweetheart. But she's swimming in the deep end right now, totally out of her element."

Max stood at parade rest, listening to Rico extol the virtues of his little sister, the recently widowed sweet innocent.

"So if you could check on her, I'd appreciate it."

"Just stop in and check on her?" That didn't sound dangerous.

"Well, maybe make sure she's got a handle on her business?"

"Check on her and her business?" Max crossed his arms, eyeing Rico's cast and wondering just how hurt he really was.

"And, you know, make sure any guys sniffing around are worthy."

"Check on her, her business and the men in her life?"

Rico winked. "If you want, you can shovel out the guys. Sophia, she's gorgeous. A real sweetheart. You're gonna love her."

Eyes narrowing, Max rocked back on his heels. "Playing cupid, Santiago?"

"Cupid? Hell, no," Rico said, laughing.

Max relaxed.

"Dude, you take one look at my little sister and you're gonna fall so hard and fast, that flying baby's gonna get whiplash before he can let off a single arrow." Rico levered himself up with difficulty, then slapped Max on the arm. "The two of you? Perfect. Absolutely perfect for each other."

"That bomb rocked your brain? You know I'm not gonna romance your sister. It's against the rules."

"What rules?"

"All the rules. The 'don't date your buddy's sister' rules. The 'don't get seriously involved when you're serving on a dangerous tour overseas' rules. The 'soldiers make lousy husbands' rules." Max arched a brow. "You weren't suggesting I go home and just fool around with your sister, were you?"

Rico moved so fast that the metal bed ground against the cement floor as his traction pulley trapped him in place.

"See, rules." Max nodded, pleased his point was made so easily. "I'll check on your little sister, Santiago. But that's it. Nothing's gonna happen."

Tawny Weber

1

SIS: IT'S CRAZY HERE. Hot, ugly, intense. My kinda place. Still, I miss home. The pictures you sent of the seal pups in Yerba Buena made me smile. But who was that chick with the pink hair? Did her T-shirt really say Blow Me? What kind of people are you running with? You'd better be careful. You know there are jerks out there who'd take advantage of your money, right? Don't trust people unless one of *mis hermanos* checks them out first, okay? Speaking of, I've got a buddy stopping by. He's a good guy and helped me out of a tight spot. He promised to check up on you. Treat him nice. He's the kind of guy you should be thinking about, okay? A stand-up guy with full pockets and real integrity. Think about it.
Love ya, Rico.

Holy cow, Rico was matchmaking from a battle zone. Her brother was certifiable. Sophia Castillo didn't know whether to laugh or cry. A typical reaction when dealing with her family.

She wasn't sure which was worse, though. That he thought he could check up on her? Or the idea that he'd found some guy who had… How'd he put it? Full pockets? As if she'd have the slightest interest in dating at this point in her life, let alone care what was in some guy's pants. So typical, given that none of the men in her family thought she was capable of taking care of herself.

Sophia smiled anyway, though. Even if he was an over-protective, meddling busybody, she was proud of her brother. Bad boy Rico Santiago had finally found his path in life. A member of EOD, the U.S. Army's bomb disposal unit, he was halfway through his 365-day tour in Afghanistan. Risking his life, defending his country. And still bossing his little sister around.

Trying to boss her around, Sophia corrected as the phone rang.

"Esprit de l'Art," she answered, as always loving the sound of the art gallery's name rolling off her tongue.

"Sophia?"

Recognizing her lawyer's voice, Sophia closed her eyes and said a little prayer, then replied, "Olivia, hello. I hope you have some good news for me?"

"Is no news good news?" the other woman asked.

Sophia winced. If Olivia was trying to make jokes, the morning's settlement negotiation hadn't gone well.

"She wouldn't budge?" Even though she'd known it was a long shot, Sophia's stomach still sank into the toes of her sassy red heels. She'd have dropped her head on her desk and let it bounce a few times, but she figured with her luck she'd damage the desk. And she couldn't afford to replace it.

"I'm sorry. Ms. Castillo's lawyer stood firm on their demands. They want you to release all claims to your late husband's estate. They're not willing to negotiate."

It'd been eight months since Sophia's husband of four years had died of a heart attack. The abrupt loss had been a shock. But the reality was, she'd spent the year before he'd died mourning the loss of the man she'd loved after she'd finally realized the charming hero she'd idealistically married only existed in her imagination.

Nineteen years her senior, Joseph Castillo had swept her off her feet. He'd been wealthy, intellectual and polished. Everything Sophia had dreamed about as a poor little girl growing up in a huge family of bossy brothers and a father too busy supporting all of them to pay much notice to his youngest child.

The first year of her marriage had been a fairy tale. Joseph had been wonderful. He'd even bought the gallery she'd loved since childhood for her as a wedding gift. Indulgent and sweet, he'd treated her like a princess. And she'd done everything she could to be worthy of her charming prince. It'd been in their second year of marriage that things had gotten rocky.

To this day, she didn't know if it was because she'd started feeling comfortable enough to start asserting her normal independence, something she'd sidelined in the uniqueness of being taken care of, or if it was Joseph's waning attention as the novelty of his new bride faded. Probably a combination of the two. But things subtly changed. So subtly it'd taken Sophia three years to see the deliberate erosion of her confidence. A master of passive-aggressive power plays, Joseph had wanted her to remain the naively devoted worshiper he'd married and he'd done everything he could to keep her there.

In the end, Sophia had barely recognized herself under the layers of silk, diamonds and obedience.

And she definitely hadn't recognized the man she'd married.

"So what next?" she asked her lawyer, dreading the answer but needing to know. Never again was she going to hide away and hope things would just get better. She'd learned the hard way that sitting with her eyes scrunched closed and her fingers crossed was only good for wrinkles and hand cramps.

"You want it all, she wants it all. So next, we go to trial," Olivia said briskly, as if Sophia having the intimate details of her life publically smeared in court wasn't anything to stress about. "We have an excellent chance of walking away with everything. Joseph's will clearly stated that eighty percent of his estate was to go to you. Despite your stepdaughter's claim that you were going to file for divorce and in so filing, would void the prenup, you didn't actually take any legal steps. Intention isn't fact."

As usual, the thought of divorce sent a feeling of failure washing over Sophia. She'd been brought up to believe that marriage was forever. Despite her family's oh-so-vocal doubts—or maybe because of them—she'd been determined, even when things started to fall apart, to have that idyllic forever.

Part of her had even hoped that the shock of suggesting they end their marriage would somehow push them into fixing things.

Apparently, she'd still been a little naive. But not any longer. Now she had priorities. And priority number one was her gallery.

"What about the money? Can't I access any of my bank accounts? I've been living on what Esprit brings in for the past six months. And given the mess Joseph created last year, it's not bringing in much."

"The joint accounts are all frozen. I've requested an audience with Judge Langley to negotiate. Ms. Castillo refused arbitration, so I might be able to use that as a leverage to get at least a portion of the money released."

Sophia wasn't surprised that her stepdaughter had refused arbitration. Lynn was bitter. Younger than Sophia by only a couple of years, she'd been raised by her mother and taught young to hate everything her father stood for. Except, apparently, his money.

"I need access to my funds if I'm going to keep this business going, Olivia. We have to figure something out. The gallery has a show scheduled next week. It has to be a success."

For so many reasons. Her ego, for one. Years of subtle put-downs and the slow shredding of her confidence, for another. The process had been methodical and clever. Before she'd realized it, she was distanced from her family, cut off from her friends. Her entire world revolved around Joseph.

His opinions. His approval. His guidance.

Her dress was too short. Her lipstick too bright. Her opinions too loud.

And the gallery he'd given her as a wedding gift? She looked around her office, letting the warmth of the space ward away the chills this conversation and her memories were bringing. He'd never let her actually run the gallery. Yes, it was in her name. But he'd thought she should take management classes. Then he'd figured she needed to travel more, see other galleries. He'd explained that she'd learn through watching. So even though she'd technically owned the gallery for four years, until last summer the sum total of her contribution had been choosing hors d'oeuvres for shows and looking pretty.

And she'd sat quietly by while he slowly and surely undermined the gallery, too. She had to turn the business back around. She and the gallery—they were both going to regain their former glory.

She glanced at the pile of bills mocking her from her inbox and sighed. Somehow.

"Olivia, this show's success is vital," Sophia insisted. Actually, she insisted pretty loudly. Not quite at the top of her lungs, but you couldn't say she wasn't passionate about how much she needed this show to work out. Sophia clenched the phone in her fist and took a deep breath, then modulated her tone. "You have to push harder. I don't understand how she can control everything like this. The will clearly stated what was mine and what was Lynn's. How come the judge is giving her this much power?"

Olivia's sigh was so loud, Sophia was surprised it didn't ruffle her hair through the phone.

"Sophia, I'm sorry. Between Ms. Castillo's witness list and documentation, she was able to present a strong enough case that the judge has to consider it."

"In other words, Judge Langley is listening to gossip and rumors."

The rumors that Sophia was a promiscuous money-hungry tramp had started four months ago. If they were to be believed, it was her fault, for everything from the gallery's shift in focus from classy photography to erotic art, to the resulting financial challenges, to Joseph's receding hairline.

"You realize Lynn's probably the one who started those stupid rumors, right?" Sophia pointed out, her fingers tapping in irritation on her spotless desk blotter. "Who else would care what the gallery is showing or how I run it?"

"Regardless of who started the rumors, you need to be aware of the talk and make sure you rise above it. Prove it false. Continue with your plan to restore the gallery to its former focus on photography instead of the erotic art your husband preferred to show. Behave, keep your nose clean, all that stuff. If you do, we'll be fine. Just stay focused and keep a positive attitude."

At this point, Sophia did let her head drop to her desk as she continued to listen to Olivia reiterate again all the ways she should behave before saying goodbye.

It was all she could do not to slam the phone down. God, she was sick of people telling her how to behave. What to do and how to do it. And always, every freaking time, it was supposedly for her own good.

Because, what? She only did things for her own bad?

When did she get to lead her own life? Call her own shots?

"Now, dammit," she said aloud. "It's my life and I have a plan. I'm the one in charge now."

Maybe talking to herself wasn't a part of that plan, but she was considering it a work in progress.

She clicked her mouse, opening a brightly colored goal board on her computer screen. She'd spent the past year reading every self-help book she could find. She searched her soul, delved into her psyche, tiptoed around her inner shadow. And she'd decided that the true path to happiness was through control. Her taking control of her own life, that is.

And now her brother was trying to get her to go out with one of his buddies? Sophia pursed her lips, and even though she knew she was only torturing herself, she clicked open her picture file.

Her mouse went unerringly to the photo Rico had sent her about six months ago. She'd looked at it so often, it was a good thing it was on the computer screen instead of paper, or she'd have worn out the edges. With a click, a group of men filled her screen. Rico's bomb disposal squad. There was her brother in the center, his arms draped over two other guys while another stood just off to the side.

He was dressed the same as the others, a tan T-shirt and fatigues. But he stood out as if he were wearing a tux. Maybe it was his position, a part of the group yet distanced. Or a sign of authority, since he seemed to be in command.

Some men were pure fantasy material. And this guy, Sophia decided with a deep sigh, was a prime example of a U.S. Armed Forces soldier at its finest. A testosterone-loaded weapon in human form. This guy exuded an air of confident sexuality that was so strong in a photograph, Sophia was pretty sure it'd melt her into a puddle of lust if she ever saw him in the flesh. From the curling tips of his damp, dark hair, over the sculpted muscles lovingly covered in the soft tan T-shirt to the hard thighs in khaki fatigues, he was all male.

All sexy, intense, controlled male.

He looked like the kind of guy who knew how to make sex

amazing. The kind who not only put a woman's needs first, but realized them before she did. A man who'd make her feel incredibly wanted.

Desirable, powerful and feminine. Sophia's breath quickened as she imagined his hands. They'd be strong. Hard, yet gentle as he caressed her. He'd explore her body, sending her into a mind-numbing spiral of sexual delight she'd only dreamt of.

Just like she was dreaming now. Sophia's breath shortened, her body tight and taut at the images dancing through her mind.

Realizing she'd done it again, brought herself to the edge of an orgasm fantasizing about a guy she'd probably never meet, who for all she knew was happily married with five kids, she gave a breathless laugh.

He was definitely not the kind of guy Rico would send with instructions to check up on his little sister.

"Yo, Soph," called a voice from down the hall.

Sophia's fingers fumbled, sending the mouse sliding across her desk before she caught it. A quick click closed the file, and its hunky contents.

Her cheeks burning, Sophia lifted her chin and quickly pushed away from the desk and hurried from her office so Gina wouldn't come in. Her little fantasy had been so hot, she was sure there was a cloud of sexual energy floating above her computer.

"Yo, Gina," she answered, smoothing her skirt as she headed toward the back of the storage room. "Did that shipment of frames come in?"

"Yep. That and a few other things."

That tone, with its underlayer of naughty glee, made Sophia frown. "What things?"

"Oh, some this, some that and a really huge…"

When Sophia reached the far side of the storeroom where

they kept shipping supplies and the deliveries were made, her jaw dropped.

"You've got to be kidding."

"The shippers thought they were doing us a favor by uncrating it since it's so heavy. I was watching the floor, so I didn't have a chance to stop them before they took off." Delighted horror filled Gina Mayes's voice. "Isn't it great?"

Sophia couldn't tear her eyes off the mind-bogglingly huge spectacle to spare her assistant a look.

"I've never seen a penis *that* big. It's insane. What am I supposed to do with it?" she mused with a frown, wandering a circle around the statue for a better look. "I mean, sure, it's pretty. Long, hard and smooth. But really…isn't it proof positive that you can have at least four feet too much of a good thing?"

Tilting her head to one side, her dark hair sweeping across her cheek, Sophia tried to figure out why someone would want to create, let alone buy, such phallic glory. She had no clue.

"Men and chocolate, you can't ever have too much when they're good." Gina grinned from the other side of the erect member, her eyes sparkling behind rhinestone encrusted cat's-eye glasses and below a thick brush of magenta bangs. "And this sucker is definitely bigger than the one I got up close and personal with last night."

"Haven't you heard? It's not the size that counts," Sophia quipped, tongue in cheek. "It's how you use it."

"You just know a man made that up." Gina dismissed her words with a flick of her pink feather duster. "Women know size definitely matters. Even in art."

She might have been married four years, held a master's in fine art and owned a gallery that, up until two months ago, specialized in the erotic. But Sophia didn't have enough experience with men to offer more than a weak smile.

There was no arguing that size was a factor with *this* phallic fantasy. Standing at a solid four and a half feet, fully erect, the polished white-veined marble gleamed in the pale morning light shining through the window. It was going to be a total pain in the ass to return.

"Why do people send their work without checking first? I sent out a notice three months ago that we wouldn't be accepting any more erotic pieces. I made it clear we were shifting focus to photography. Not—" she waved her hand again at the huge penis "—this kind of thing. Erotic art is all well and good, but we're not showing it anymore."

Which was a shame, really. Yes, her plan was to return the gallery's focus to photography, as it had been from its inception until Joseph had decided to stir things up a few years back. But damn, that erotic stuff made a lot of money. It'd be worth polishing a four-and-a-half foot penis for a few months if it'd pay some bills.

Behave, Olivia's reminder rang in her head.

"We'll recrate it and call the shippers," Sophia decided with a sigh, scanning the artist's shipping manifest for an email address. "I'll contact this Mita Andress and let her know we're returning her...penis."

"Andress?" Gina asked. "She called last week, wanting to be included in the upcoming show, but I said her work wouldn't fit this exhibit. Pretty ballsy of her to ignore that. Maybe she thought you'd be so wowed, you'd overlook the topic, so to speak." Gina tucked her feather duster into the back of her wide studded leather belt and wrapped her arms around the marble member to tests its weight.

"I might need a little help," she grunted, stepping back to glare at the large piece as if it'd suddenly made a dirty joke and personally offended her. "Maybe Mita didn't ignore you. Maybe this is another one of Lynn's rotten pranks."

Sophia pursed her lips. The other woman had definitely made it her mission since her father's death to create as much trouble in Sophia's life as possible.

But sending a marble penis?

"Maybe," she acknowledged. "But it's just as likely a mistake."

Unable to help herself, Sophia grabbed her ever-present SLR camera out of the loose pocket of her skirt and stepped back to frame the shot. As always, the viewfinder was magic for her. Her objectivity filter. Through it, she saw what was, instead of what she wanted to see.

She let her mind clear, letting the image fill her head instead. White marble against the pitted paneling of the storage room walls. Gina's face grinning under the pink fringe of her bangs, her torn T-shirt and leather a sharp contrast against the smooth, elegant curves of the sculpture.

All she needed was five seconds to frame and snap the shot for her to put Gina's suggestion to rest. There was too much pride, even love, carved into the marble for it to be a prank.

"I'm sure the artist thought we'd love the sculpture and want to include her in the show next week," she decided as she lowered the camera.

"You just like to think the best of people," Gina accused, as if that was a bad thing.

"Not the best," Sophia demurred. She glanced at the photos lining the back hall, studies of light and dark. "I just see the reality."

"Well, obviously some people don't like the new reality," Gina said with a shrug as she gathered the wood, a can of nails and a hammer to start building a new crate. "I wonder how many more people will send us random body art without a contract, wanting to be included in next week's show."

"I guess I should be grateful someone wants to be included," Sophia muttered, holding the long wooden plank so Gina could hammer the L-bracket in place.

Sophia was sure her decision was right, but the lack of enthusiasm from the public, the artists and the photographers was disheartening. It was almost enough to make her doubt her ability to regain Esprit's previous glory.

Not for the first time, she cursed her late husband. He'd taken one of the top photographic art galleries in the San Francisco Bay area and changed its specialty to erotica.

To this day, Sophia didn't know if Joseph's obsession with sexually focused art was homage to the genre, or if it was a crutch for his own lack of talent in that arena.

"What about that von Schilling guy who wanted to show here?" Gina asked as she started building the next crate wall.

Sophia looked past the crate at the photos, barely visible in the showroom. She'd love to have an artist of von Schilling's caliber showing here. But…

"No. He's amazing, a legend, really. But he specializes in nudes. If I show him, it keeps me stuck in the same rut Joseph created." And would lend more weight to Lynn's accusations that Sophia was some kind of sex-obsessed pervert who would run first the gallery, then the rest of the Castillo estate, into the ground. "He'd be incredible, but I need someone else. A totally different direction."

Seeing that Gina had a handle on the construction of the rest of the crate, Sophia stepped away.

"You could put your own photos in the show," Gina muttered between swings of her hammer.

Pretending she hadn't heard the words over the hammering, Sophia wandered over to the door. Her gaze skimmed the short hallway, focusing instead on the main showroom with its glossy wide-planked floors and beveled glass windows. Prisms of light danced softly, the damaging rays weaving a pattern on the floor but not touching the photographs displayed on the walls.

Her photos, in a show.

It'd be the most amazing thing in the world. Her stomach jittered at the idea, a thrill of excitement shivering down her spine at the idea of being in one.

But she knew what she saw when she looked through the

viewfinder at herself. The truth. She was a lover of art, but not brave enough to be an artist. She didn't have the guts to bare her soul through her work.

What she did have, though, was the gallery. Esprit could be her expression of art. She'd spent years apprenticing, so to speak, at Joseph's side. He'd insisted on dangling the gallery like a gold-plated carrot, his last means of controlling his wife once she'd grown a spine.

Right up until he'd had a heart attack on the ninth hole. A familiar mix of sorrow, guilt and a few dregs of anger roiled together in Sophia's stomach.

She started when Gina patted her arm. She'd been so lost in thought, she hadn't noticed the hammer's silence.

"Soph," Gina said, the look on her face making it clear she had a clue where Sophia's mind had wandered. "You okay?"

"I feel fine," Sophia lied. "I just have to get through this month. Get the show set up, start selling art again. That's my priority."

"My priority is sending this magnificent member back to its maker. But I need your help," Gina wiggled her eyebrows, the light glinting off the stainless hoop on the left one. "I'll seal the last wall of the crate after we shove this sucker inside."

"Pushing penises," Sophia snickered with a shake of her head. "Pathetic."

"Admit it," Gina said, her words barely discernible through her giggles. "You'll miss this kind of thing once the gallery is on the straight and narrow."

"Hmm, let me think. A chance to reclaim prestige, acclaim and worldwide admiration? Or the notoriety of being the proud displayer of the world's largest hard-on? Such a choice."

She didn't add that the constant focus on sex was like nails on a chalkboard to her since she wasn't getting any. Torture akin to sending a dieter to work at a Hershey factory.

She joined Gina next to the statue, watching the tiny woman wrap her arms around the marble. She couldn't even reach one hand to the other, the thing was so wide.

"Yum," Gina said, her face pressed against the penis. "On three?"

Sophia kicked off her twice reheeled red patent pumps and hitched up her pencil skirt so she could bend at the knees. Wrapping her arms around the slick, cool stone, she sucked in a breath and, when Gina said, "Now," lifted.

Holy crap, the thing weighed a ton. They couldn't budge it.

"God," she grunted, releasing one arm from the penis to rub her tailbone. "I think I broke my ass."

"This sucker gives new meaning to the term *rock-hard*. Who knew an erection could weigh more than a horse?" No longer amused, Gina scowled at the monstrosity.

"Can I help you, ladies?" The voice was male, it was laughing and it was coming from directly behind her.

Stiffening, Sophia felt the blood drain from her face.

Did anything say professional like two women wrapped around a preposterously proportioned penis?

Could this get any more humiliating? With a quick wince, Sophia pushed her dark hair off her face and, hoping for the best, straightened the collar of her ruffled poet's blouse before turning around.

It only took two seconds for her blood to heat. For her heart to race. Breath catching in her chest, she stared.

It was him. Her fantasy guy. The sexy soldier from Rico's picture. And he was even better live and in person. Cut military-short, his mahogany hair glinted with hints of red. Laughter danced in his deeply, intense melt-her-heart brown eyes as they met hers.

Sophia wet her suddenly parched lips and tried to catch

her breath. His gaze shifted from amusement to masculine appreciation, the look making her stomach jitter. The man was pure, three-dimensional nirvana. The long sleeves of his blue pin-striped button-down shirt couldn't disguise his wide shoulders, his muscled biceps.

He was a dream come to life. And maybe—she pressed her hand against her stomach—just maybe she wasn't ready to try and handle dreams in real life. They were so much safer in pictures.

It was like getting hit with a sexual force field. Towering a good four inches over her five-foot-ten-in-heels self, he exuded power. Charisma. Pure sexual energy.

"Can I have you—I mean, help you?"

TWO WOMEN IN A DIMLY lit room wrapped around an erection that'd do King Kong proud? Struggling against the urge to laugh, Maximilian St. James stepped farther into the storeroom for a better look. He wasn't sure what amused him more—the gorgeous blushing brunette's stammers or the scenario itself.

She was stunning. Golden skin that looked like silk over sharp cheekbones, a high forehead and perfect nose. Her lips were full and lush, making him think of deep, wet kisses. He looked into eyes as pale as her hair was dark, watching confusion, embarrassment and what his ego swore looked like lust stare back at him.

A giggle behind the brunette snagged his attention. He squinted at the sight of the other woman. She was...funky? Was that the right term? A cross between a rainbow-hued Goth princess and a very edgy pixie.

Quite the contrast to the dusky beauty staring at him as if he'd just dropped from outer space. His gaze moved past the women to the huge marble cock they'd been hugging.

Shouldn't they be naked? Maybe chanting or something? Was he a pervert for wishing the brunette, at least, had been?

"Am I interrupting?"

At a narrow-eyed look from the taller woman, the pixie choked back her laugh.

Strong women were so damned sexy.

"We were just…" She trailed off, glancing at the statue. Wrinkling her nose, she just shrugged.

He couldn't stop his lips from twitching, but he did manage to hold back his laughter.

Obviously not as constrained, the pixie snorted. At an arch look from her boss, she excused herself to make a phone call, tossing one last naughty giggle over her shoulder as she left the room.

"I saw you just…" He let the words trail off the way hers had. His lips twitched again. "The offer to help is still open. It looks like you could use a strong back."

A faint wash of color swept over her cheeks. She shifted her stance, stepping away from the statue and crossing her arms in a way that accented her curves beneath her loose jacket. His mouth stopped twitching and started drooling.

It was the first time in weeks that he'd felt something other than bone-deep exhaustion or soul-wearying stress pressing down on his shoulders. Maybe it was the year in the desert. Maybe jet lag after the flight into SFO from Afghanistan. Or maybe she was simply the most stunning woman he'd ever seen.

Despite his exhaustion, Max had been dreading this trip home. If he'd had his way, he'd have spent his month's leave in Europe. In Hawaii. Hell, he'd have stayed in the Middle East if he'd had a choice. But now that he'd met Sophia, he was thinking he should be a little more grateful for family obligations and his promise to Rico.

"I'm Sergeant Maximilian St. James," he said, striding forward to offer his hand. Her slender fingers disappeared in his wide palm. "Your brother is Specialist Santiago, correct? He asked me to stop by."

Her scent, a rich, spicy floral, wrapped around him like

an embrace. Delicious. He breathed deeply and smiled. He didn't know what caused the slight tremor in her fingers. She could be intimidated by his size or be feeling an awareness similar to the one surging through his own system.

Discipline was as much a part of his DNA as his skeletal system. Max might be burned out, but he still knew how to maintain control. At least, on the surface. Beneath, though, he felt as if he'd just been rocked by an exploding bomb at the touch of her slender fingers in his.

"Sophia Castillo?" he asked when she continued to stare at him with those sky-blue eyes, looking like she was absorbing his very essence.

"Yes," she finally said, her voice husky. She cleared her throat and appeared to pull herself together, then offered a proprietor-of-the-gallery-type smile. Friendly but not too familiar. He bet that look sold many a… His eyes went to the statue. Well, whatever she sold in this place. "I'm Sophia Castillo."

"Didn't Rico warn you I'd be stopping by?" He'd figured Rico, in typical big brother matchmaking fashion, had exaggerated his little sister's need for someone to look out for her. He'd gone on and on about how she was all alone now. How she'd never run her own life, let alone the business she'd been left by her late husband. He'd made her sound like a twelve-year-old dropped in NYC with a bus pass and a teddy bear.

Rico's hard sell had put Max on red alert. Guilt and obligation meant he couldn't ignore Rico's request to check on Sophia. But he could avoid his buddy's little romance game. He'd labeled this a simple mission. Get in, do his duty, get out. Or in civilian terms, stop by, say hi, make sure she was handling Rico's news okay, then hit the door.

But now? Judging from the dazed look in her eyes, maybe she could use a little help. And if it gave him an excuse to put off seeing his family for a few minutes, or even hours, so be it.

"Rico mentioned someone might, um, might visit. And I recognize you from your…from a picture Rico sent." Another wave of heat, this time for reasons he didn't understand, washed over her cheeks. "You're in his squadron, aren't you?"

"Squad leader," Max acknowledged, noting the resemblance between his specialist and the woman in front of him. Her hair was a glorious black, falling in long waves over her shoulders and giving her the look of a Spanish princess. Slashing cheekbones, a wide mouth and strongly arched brows all defined a strong face. In contrast, her eyes were a cool sky blue, strikingly Anglo against her Latino features.

As if she just realized it was still there, she slid her hand out of his, then took a quick step backward. She ran her tongue over her full lower lip, glanced at the statue and then back at him. She appeared clueless as what to do next.

Maybe Rico was right. Maybe she really did need someone to look out for her.

"Well, thank you for coming by," she said with a semblance of a smile. "I'd love to show you around but, well, as you can see, I'm a little busy at the moment."

They both looked at the dick. Sophia squared her shoulders.

Max frowned.

"Rico just emailed you today?"

"Yes. Or, at least I just got it today. Sometimes his emails take a while to get through."

"And he said…?"

Brow furrowed, she bit her lip and gave him a long, considering look. Her gaze dropped, for just a second, to where his hands rested in his pants pockets—or maybe a little at the center of the pockets, his ego goaded. Then she gave a tiny shake of the head and told him, "He just said someone from his squad would be stopping by."

"That's it?"

She hesitated.

"He also said you'd helped him out of a tight spot. Knowing Rico, I figure he borrowed money or got in trouble with a local girl's brothers. Our dad always said Rico rolls through life like a bowling ball."

Instead of returning her smile, Max didn't move a muscle. His insides froze. The last time he'd felt like this, he'd been staring down the barrel of an enemy's gun. She didn't know?

In the space of his next breath, he analyzed all available options, mentally cursed his luck and decided to go with a soft-sell version of the truth.

"Rico's fine," he said first.

She frowned.

"He did have a little trouble, but it's all taken care of. He's catching up on a little rest and giving some nurses a bad time."

"Nurses?" Her olive complexion paled as her breath hitched. She clenched her hands and then unclenched them. As if she'd grabbed on to the fear and was letting it go before it overwhelmed her. "He's hurt?"

"He's—"

"Don't tell me he's fine again," she snapped. She didn't look helpless now. Then with a show of control he had to admire, she shook her head, took another deep breath and asked in a calmer tone, "Please. Tell me what happened to Rico."

It was her control, rather than her distress, that had Max stepping forward to offer comfort. It was like stepping from the shadows into a warm puddle of sunlight.

"He injured his leg on a mission." He said it brutally fast, knowing that news like this was better given all at once. "We were heading in to neutralize an explosive in a heavily populated area and there was an ambush. He caught some shrapnel in his leg."

As she blinked back tears, her pale eyes studied him closely. "And?"

He didn't move a muscle, but his insides winced. Wasn't she supposed to be helpless and a little clueless?

"Sergeant? What aren't you telling me?"

"I've given you the pertinent details," he said briskly, automatically falling into command mode. Considering his years of military training, his Nob Hill matriarch of a mother and a father who'd been a three-star general, he could pull on "uptight and reserved" like a second skin. "He was on a mission, he was hurt. He's recuperating and will regain full use of his leg."

And all Max had to do was close his eyes and he could see Rico—his tent mate, the guy he played poker with and shared middle-of-the-night terrors—torn and broken. Pale and dead-looking, with blood pouring from his leg and rocks and debris covering his body. His friend. The man serving under him, who'd followed his orders. His responsibility.

He took a step away from Sophia as if he were stepping away from the memories.

"Was that the tight spot you helped him out of?" she asked, her voice tight, as if she were trying to keep tears from falling.

"I neutralized the insurgent responsible while the others on the squad contained the rest of the dissidents."

"You saved my brother?" Her breath shuddered. Then she stepped toward him, laying her palm on his chest as if touching him would ensure his words were the truth. Max's heartbeat increased, just a beat, at her touch.

God, no. He stiffened in horror that she'd cast him as a savior when he knew damned well if it hadn't been for him, Rico wouldn't have been hurt. Max was shaking his head before she finished asking. "We were just doing our jobs. Both Rico and I. Nobody was playing hero."

"He said you helped him out of a tight spot. He wouldn't have said that if he didn't think it was a big deal."

"It was my job," Max insisted through gritted teeth. Just like it'd been his job to send Rico in the first place. Max's gut constricted, a single drop of sweat making a familiar trail down his spine.

It wasn't his fault. Rationally, he knew that. It was his job to give the orders. Nobody could have anticipated the mission going sour. Rico didn't blame him. The squad didn't blame him. Logic dictated that he shouldn't cast blame, either.

That didn't mean they all weren't wrong.

He glanced down at the long, slender fingers heating his skin through the thin fabric of his shirt. Then he looked into her worry-filled eyes, the lush black fringe of her lashes damp with unshed tears.

Max wanted her to be a little friendlier. But he wasn't willing to use his job, her brother or the hellish realities of war to make it happen. He'd stick with charm, thank you very much. Then he'd know he'd actually deserved the affection he planned on earning.

Affection, he reminded himself, that would fly in the face of the friendship rules he'd reminded Rico of.

Which meant he'd have to step carefully. Bending rules was okay. Breaking them? Something to consider very, very carefully. Not that Max had ever found a woman who had tempted him enough for him to actually go that far. But there was something about the sweet Sophia...

"Look, Rico's fine," Max assured her, putting as much compassion into his tone as he could find. He knew he should step away, disconnect, but he couldn't bring himself to. Not when she was so warm. "He'll spend a few days in the hospital, then a week of R&R. If there were any thanks necessary, he's already offered them. And in return, I promised him a favor."

Max hadn't meant to mention that. It must be the worry

shadowing her eyes that'd wormed it out of him. She'd be a hell of an interrogator. All she'd need to do was look sweet and vulnerable and guys would be tripping over their words to get her to smile.

Then that worry shifted. First she frowned, just a little, then she narrowed her eyes. Just like that, they went from liquid to ice. Max was good at reading people. But as he watched Sophia's face get tight and distant, he couldn't tell if it was irritation or embarrassment. But what did she have to be embarrassed about?

"A favor?" she questioned softly.

"Friends do friends favors," he defended, not sure why he suddenly wished for his bomb suit. "Why's that a problem?"

"No problem. Unless, of course, that favor had anything to do with me."

Smart woman.

"He just asked me to look in on you. Check and see how things were going."

"Rico thinks I need a babysitter? That's it?"

Max's smile spread slowly. "What else could it be?"

"Nothing. Absolutely nothing," she muttered as she stepped back, putting some distance between them.

Immediately missing her scent, Max closed the distance again.

Her eyes narrowed. She took another step back. He took another step forward.

Her eyes narrowed. This time, he knew it was irritation.

"I appreciate the visit. But as you can see, I'm hardly the little girl Rico considers me. I'm fine. I don't need a babysitter."

"I don't mind," Max said with a grin. "Rico would do the same if I had a sister."

"Ha. Rico can't be trusted. If you introduced him to any

woman, as long as she was of age, he wouldn't think twice about seducing her."

Was that like permission? Max's grin grew so wide, it hurt his cheeks.

Sophia blushed. Then she drew her shoulders back and gave an aristocratic tilt of her chin.

"If you're just getting back to the States, I'm sure you have things you want to do," she said, her desire for his departure as blatant as the big ole penis she was standing in front of. "I appreciate you stopping by and bringing the news about Rico."

She offered Max a distant smile. The kind you gave a stranger on the street. Brief and impersonal. He wasn't sure why it annoyed him so much. He'd wanted her to treat him naturally, not to coat their exchange with misplaced gratitude. She obviously thought this was a courtesy visit and was happy to keep it at that.

But he wasn't.

He wanted more.

"Soph?" They both turned, Max squinting a little at the sight of Sophia's assistant. She wasn't any less shocking the second time around. "I talked to the shippers. They'll be here in ten minutes to pick up the crate."

"Ten…?" Sophia puffed out a breath, her gaze bouncing from the other woman to the huge erection and then landing on Max. For just a second, she looked softer. Vulnerable.

Then she pulled herself together and offered her hand to Max to shake goodbye. He took her slender, warm fingers in his and held on. Her eyes widened in a look of heated curiosity. He'd seen that look often enough to know his interest was reciprocated.

Then she pulled her fingers away and stepped back. Apparently *reciprocated* didn't mean *welcomed*.

"I guess I have a penis to pack," Sophia joked. Then she winced and gave him a rueful look. "Or, well, you know what

I mean. I really do appreciate you stopping by and reassuring me in person that Rico's okay."

Max hadn't made Sergeant First Class in the U.S. Armed Forces by being slow, though.

"I'll crate this up for you," he offered with a manly smile. He hoped it didn't show his distaste at handling any penis other than his own. "Then we can get a drink and talk about that favor to Rico."

"I appreciate the offer, but Gina and I can handle things here," she insisted.

Max wasn't sure if she kept protesting out of pride, stubbornness or some weird need to have the statue to herself. But they were all stupid reasons, so he went with what he always did in cases like this. Exactly what he wanted.

Stepping around her, he eyed the polished mahogany base against the floor of the crate. He grabbed the three-sided box and gave it a shake to test for sturdiness. Satisfied, he nodded and turned back to the women.

"This should work fine."

"Of course it'll work fine. Believe it or not, this isn't the first phallic statue we've dealt with," Sophia told him, sounding a little affronted.

The magenta-haired Goth-pixie snickered.

"We'll be fine, but thanks," Sophia continued.

"Why won't you take my help? I'm here and offering myself," he insisted. Then, unable to resist, he added, "C'mon. You know you need me."

Sophia opened her mouth, then pressed her lips tight. A hint of color warmed her cheeks. That look of interest was back, warming her blue eyes. Her gaze traveled the length of his body with a familiarity that made more than his shoulders snap to attention.

And yet, she still refused. What was with this woman?

"Thanks, but—"

"Sophia, we really could use his help. The delivery guy

was laughing when he called. He said it took three of them to uncrate it." The girl's gaze danced behind her cat's-eye frames as she swept her eyes over Max. Her eyes lingered, heated, and then she grinned as she inspected various body parts. He had to stop himself from covering his goods. "He definitely looks…big enough to handle the job."

Max had defused bombs that made him less nervous than the look on the magenta-haired woman's face. Then he noticed the same speculation in Sophia's eyes. As if she were measuring, weighing and wondering just how big he was. Her gaze slid over his body, appreciation warming the sky-blue depths as she assessed what he had to offer.

Max was pretty sure flexing his biceps would be classified as pathetic. He ordered the rest of his body to refrain from flexing, as well. Not that the rest of his body was listening. All its attention was focused on Sophia. The scent of her, the warmth that seemed to radiate from her smile. The curves that made his mouth water as if he was three-days-dehydrated.

"Okay, sure. I guess we do need help," Sophia finally said, making a show of looking at the clock. "Let's get to it, then."

She and Gina ranged on either side of the statue, Gina going into a wrestler's squat. Sophia stepped out of her high heels again before hitching up the slender lines of her skirt so her knees were free of fabric.

Max's body went as hard as freaking marble at the sight.

Knees, for God's sake. He'd been in the desert way too long.

"All we need to do is slide it up to the edge of the crate," she told him. Her hands curved over the gleaming white marble in a smooth caress. He didn't think she was aware that she was running one hand up, then down, as she pushed with the other to test the weight of the statue. "Once it's past the edge, we can wiggle it onto the base until it's all the way in."

Max stared. He could actually feel the heated path his

blood took on its way south to his shorts. He had a vision of
her in that same position, but wrapped around him. Because
God knew, the way she was making him feel, he was pretty
sure his current erection could compete with that man-size
sucker.

"Why don't you two hang on," he suggested, his tone a
little strangled. "Let me try this myself first."

Gina stepped back right away, obviously glad to let him
do the heavy lifting.

"We can help," Sophia stubbornly insisted. "After all, it's
actually our job."

Oh, no. The way he felt right now, watching her keep on
handling that penis—hell, any penis—was going to make
him cry like a baby. Right after he exploded.

Desperate to get it over with, he stepped behind her, gently
slid his hands under hers to release her grip, then grasped
either side of her waist. He lifted. For a tall woman, she didn't
weigh a damned thing. And luckily she was too shocked to
do more than stiffen and gasp when he moved her aside.

"Hey…" Her words trailed off as she watched him unbutton
his cuffs. He shoved his sleeves up to his elbow so he could
get a good grip on the marble.

Max approached the dick the way he'd approach a ticking
bomb—with a great deal of respect, trepidation and determination. His arms couldn't span its girth. For a brief second,
he wondered who the hell had posed for this sucker. Then,
needing that thought as far from his brain as possible, he
started silently reciting detonation codes.

He tilted the statue back toward him, then pushed until it
met the edge of the crate. He angled it just so, then lifted. He
squinted as the room flashed for a second, then, figuring it
was just exertion, grunted and pushed the monster onto the
crate bottom.

Almost there.

His muscles trembled as the marble slipped a little under

his sweaty hands. God, if the guys saw him now, he'd never live this down. That was all the motivation he needed to give it one last shove.

And done.

Not even winded, Max stepped back, dusted his hands together and gave the ladies a triumphant smile. It faded a little when he saw the camera Sophia was tucking into her pocket.

She hadn't, had she?

He narrowed his eyes, trying to read her face. Pure innocence.

Oh, yeah, she had.

He'd just have to get her to delete it. The St. James men were used to getting their way. All he had to do was decide on a strategy. In this situation, he figured a little charming persuasion should do the trick.

"Easy enough," he said, referring to both the crating and the upcoming photo deletion mission.

"Thanks so much. I really do appreciate both the news of Rico, and your help."

Gina grabbed a hammer and a few more boards. Giving him her own smile of gratitude, she went to work packing up the crate.

"Don't you think you owe me at least a drink? As a thank-you?"

She frowned, taking her time sliding her shoes back on as if his request was of monumental concern.

Max wasn't sure whether to be insulted or intrigued by her obvious reluctance to spend any more time with him.

"Sure. We can get a drink. As a thank-you for your help, and to toast my brother," she said finally. "I don't want to take up too much of your time, though. I'm sure you have quite a few better things to do on leave than check up on your squad mate's sister, Sergeant."

"Sophia, we just spent five sweaty minutes together,

wrapped around a mammoth erection," he pointed out, giving her his warmest smile. She blinked twice and sucked in a quick little breath.

"We're practically intimate now. So you might as well call me Max." He loved the way she looked, all flushed and flustered. He wondered if that's how she looked when she made love. "And don't forget to bring that camera."

3

SERGEANT FIRST CLASS Hottie St. James.

He was first-class, all right.

Oh, God. What were the chances that the guy whose photo she'd been dedicating orgasms to would show up in her gallery just when she'd sworn off relationships? Fate, or Rico, had a wicked sense of humor.

Skirting around the temptation to brush against the hard length of his body as Max held open the gallery door, Sophia averted her eyes and held back her sigh. This was crazy. She felt like a schoolgirl whose *Teen Beat* poster had just come to life.

The man was absolutely gorgeous. Even sexier in person than in the photo she'd spent months fantasizing over. He oozed charisma like a gooey caramel-filled chocolate oozed deliciousness.

And she was starving.

For the first time in her life, she wanted to strip a man naked and nibble her way down his body. She, who'd never stripped off so much as a man's shoes.

Sophia almost tripped off the sidewalk imagining what Max might look like naked. She'd spent four years immersed in sexual images, erotic art and, hell, just today had wrapped herself around a four-foot-tall marble cock. And none of it came anywhere close to heating her up, making her want to play out the *Kama Sutra,* like this guy did.

"Slow down," he said, almost making her jump out of her skin when he put a cautioning hand on her forearm. "Gotta watch for cars."

Baffled, she looked up one side of the empty street, then down the other. Cars?

Before she could ask, a motorcycle came around the corner, speeding past from the opposite direction.

"Or motorcycles," he amended with a knowing smirk.

It was that cocky look that punctured her sexually induced bubble. As if he was not only right, but always right. She almost tripped over her feet again as her mind did a quick replay of the last hour. He'd swept in, taken over and she'd… what? Fallen right back into her old habit of letting someone else take over.

She remembered Rico's email. Deep pockets. So not only was Max bossy and domineering, he was rich. Two strikes, right there. And with the lawsuit and swirling rumors of her promiscuity, she definitely couldn't afford to try for three.

Not even for what promised to be, in her limited and in-experienced opinion, the most incredible, intense, wild sex of her life.

No. This was going to be purely a thank-you-and-goodbye drink. She'd be friendly but distant, in a he's-just-her-brother's-friend kind of way. And keep to herself all fantasies about nibbling her way down his chest on her way to paradise.

"Are you sure this isn't too far?" he said as they reached the door of the cantina across the street from the gallery. "We could have sat on that bench there in front of your place and shared a bottle of water."

"Clever," Sophia said, grinning despite her intention to stay aloof. She sailed past him when he held the heavy brass-trimmed door open.

Why couldn't he just be bossy? Did he have to be so freaking cute and charming, too? His picture hadn't said charming, dammit.

Sophia knew that unless a photographer was extremely talented, charisma rarely translated on film. Especially the sergeant's kind. He had a charm that combined clever humor with sexual undercurrents, and that charm promised sensual adventures to anyone willing to hand over control.

Which meant, as usual, Sophia would be missing the sexual satisfaction boat. Because this girl wasn't giving up control ever again.

With that in mind, she called on the hostess skills she'd perfected—the one area Joseph had deemed satisfactory—during her years of marriage.

"This is my treat. A thank-you for all you've done for me and my family," she told him as they stepped into the cool, plant filled foyer of the cantina. "This is a great place. Wonderful ambience, great appetizers and fast service."

"By all means, let's make sure we're served quickly," he agreed, waving his hand to indicate she proceed him. "Dragging out gratitude is such a pain, don't you think?"

A laugh gurgled out before Sophia could control herself. The only thing sexier than those rock-hard biceps he'd shown off when he'd hefted that obscene statue was a wicked sense of humor.

The hostess stepped forward, a pair of gold menus contrasting with her brilliant red blouse and flounced skirt.

"Hi, Carmen. We'd like a table for two," Sophia said after the older woman greeted them.

"Right this way," Carmen invited after giving Max a little leer and then offering Sophia a naughty wink. "I've got the perfect spot."

Oh, no. Her body already in motion, Sophia's feet froze to the floor. She almost fell on her face. The perfect spot. The designated date table.

"Perfect is overrated," she murmured, hurrying to catch up to Carmen. "How about a place by the window instead?"

Carmen frowned, shaking her round, dimpled face. "But the afternoon sun is glaring on that side of the room. The perfect table is shaded. Much more comfortable."

"I like the afternoon sun," Sophia said with a stiff smile, willing the hostess to understand that she didn't want the date table.

"Maybe we could get the drinks to go," Max drawled, obviously getting the message Carmen wasn't. "Avoid these pesky table choices altogether?"

Sophia grinned. Giving up on the unsuccessful subtlety, she tapped Carmen's rounded shoulder and pointed to an empty table that overlooked her gallery. "We'll take that one, okay?"

The hostess's heavy sigh as she seated them spoke volumes. Her inhalation told Sophia just how hot she thought Max was, and her exhalation exclaimed her despair over her friend's poor dating skills.

Sophia gave her own sigh of agreement. Even she couldn't argue that those skills weren't pure crap.

"What can I bring you both?" Carmen asked as they sat on opposite sides of the scarred plank table.

"Whatever dark ale you've got on tap," Max requested.

"Pomegranate margarita, please."

"Mmm-hmm." With that and one last look of frustrated despair for Sophia, she flounced off with a swish of her full red skirt.

A busboy set chips and salsa between them. Sophia nibbled nervously, not sure what to say now. She didn't know how to talk to a man. She knew how to talk to guys, of course. Brothers, fathers, artists. Friends, even.

But sexy men whose photo she'd spent months fantasizing over? Men who confused her, making her want to flirt one second and yell the next? She had to swallow hard to get the fried tortilla past the lump in her throat.

She stared at the tabletop, realizing that she was so totally out of her element here.

"You know," Max drawled after Carmen had set their drinks down and flounced away again, "I don't think I've ever felt so appreciated."

Sophia's fingers clenched the chilly stem of her margarita glass. She lifted her eyes from the frothy red drink to meet Max's dark gaze.

Oh, no. He'd obviously taken her insecurity and nerves as bitchiness. Despite his teasing tone and easy smile, his words cut deep.

"I'm so sorry." Sophia leaned across the table to press her hand to his bare forearm. "You've been nothing but helpful, and I'm being rude. Rico would be shaking his finger in my face if he knew."

Max's laugh lit up his entire face. "He does that to you, too? We rag him about it all the time. Big tough soldier boy, wagging his finger like a nagging granny."

Sophia giggled, her heart softening to hear the affection in his voice for her brother. "He's done it since he was little. We always called him *abuela niño* when he did."

"Granny boy? He must have loved that."

"I do believe that's one of the reasons Rico's so good with his fists," Sophia said with a laugh.

"You said 'we' called him *abuela niño*. Who's 'we'?"

"My older brothers and I. There are seven of us. I'm the youngest, under Rico."

"Seven?" Max's eyes rounded. "Your parents were ambitious."

"It's the only thing my mother ever stood up to my father about. She wanted a little girl and wasn't willing to stop until she had one." Sophia's tone was as bittersweet as her smile.

According to her father, that rare streak of stubbornness had cost her mother her life.

Obviously hearing the underlying pain in her words, Max gave her a searching look, but was gentleman enough not to pry. Instead, he changed the subject. Telling her stories of Rico's funnier mishaps and the practical jokes he'd pulled overseas, he swiftly moved the discussion from pain to laughter. Sophia loved hearing about her rough, tough, kick-ass brother in the words of a man who clearly appreciated Rico's sense of humor, quick temper and fierce pride.

Ten minutes and the contents of her margarita glass later, Sophia had relaxed.

Instead of the aggressive pursuit she'd expected, Max showed gentlemanly restraint with a subtle underlying charm.

"Is it my imagination, or do the figures in that painting look familiar?" he asked as he fished out the last chip from the basket. He offered it to her, and when she shook her head, popped it into his own mouth.

Sophia didn't have to follow his gaze over her shoulder to know what he was referring to. She did have to hide her surprise that he was observant enough to have recognized her and her brothers, though. Especially since the painting was twenty years old.

"No, it's not your imagination," she assured him. "My father used to own this restaurant. When he sold it a few years ago, the new owners asked to keep the decor and art."

He studied the painting, then tossed back the last of his beer. "Dating must have been hell," he decided.

"I beg your pardon?"

"Six older brothers looking out for you? A guy would have to be pretty brave to risk that and ask you out." His words were teasing, but the look he gave her clearly said he was definitely brave enough.

Sophia's stomach tumbled a little. He made her want so much. From him. From herself.

"My brothers were bullies," she confirmed a little breathlessly. "But they're all scattered now and busy with their own lives. These days, nobody vets my dating choices except me."

"Is that so?" The look he gave her was pure flirtation. The giddy, giggly, naughty kind that had her pulling back her shoulders, thrusting out her breasts and fluttering her lashes before she even realized she was responding.

Damn, he was good.

Sophia immediately stopped pulling, thrusting and fluttering.

"But given that I'm not in a dating place in my life," she quickly added, "it doesn't matter. All six of my brothers could be camped out in my gallery watching my every move. They'd be bored to death with the lack of bullying and intimidating opportunities."

"Maybe they'd turn matchmakers instead and find you the perfect guy," he teased, an odd glint in his dark eyes. "Do you think they'd take applications?"

And there it was… Her own personal version of hell. Six over-testosteroned bossy-boys ruining her life. Lurking, judging, taking over. They'd start by telling her how to dress, move on to telling her all the mistakes she was making at the gallery and end with a complete rearrangement of her world.

Her pain must have been evident on her face, because Max suddenly looked stricken.

"Oh, man, I'm sorry," he said quietly, reaching over to warm her hand with his. "That was insensitive of me."

Without thinking, Sophia turned her hand so they were palm to palm. Little tingles of excitement built, swirling from her hand all the way up her arm and down her belly. The palm was an erogenous zone? She was so sexually clueless.

"I forgot that you were recently widowed."

Sophia stared.

Well, shit. Sophia slowly slipped her hand from his. She slid it onto her lap, clenching her fingers together.

She'd forgotten, too.

What was it about Max that made her forget important things?

In the past, she'd have fallen back on her tried-and-true litmus test. She'd have taken his picture. Photos were windows to the soul, showing the real person. No matter how they piled on the mundane disguises, a well-shot photo let her see the true person. Their inner being, so to speak.

It'd been photographs that'd helped her see that her father, a man who ruled his house with an iron fist, was a pussycat inside. Photos had let her see the worry lines carved into his forehead, the responsibility pressing down on his shoulders after he'd lost his wife. The pride in his dark eyes and the love in his rare smile.

Seeing that had made his controlling attitude easier for Sophia to understand. Whereas photos of her late husband had showed an entirely different story. An affable surface, with a streak of mean domination underneath. A warning to watch out for bossy men with charming surfaces.

Like the one sitting across from her.

Her fingers itched for her camera. A waste of time, though. A photo would only confirm what she already knew. The man was pure eye candy, wrapped in a layer of sexual charisma. And underneath all that temptation? He was an alpha leader to the core. The kind of man who issued orders without thought and always expected to be obeyed.

Sophia had never considered herself a sensual woman. She'd even wondered if Joseph was right, that she was a little frigid.

But now? Yes, the sight of Max was a major turn-on. The man was seriously sexy, massively gorgeous. But that was aesthetics. She'd spent years in school viewing equally stunning models, men who turned heads by just walking into a room. But she'd never felt this tug of desire deep in her belly. A spark, a sexual one, that told her that he'd make her feel things she'd never even imagined.

Hands shaking a little at the concept, Sophia lifted her glass, hoping to find a few more comforting drops of tequila.

Was she so insecure in her own strength and independence that she couldn't enjoy a sexy man's company unless he was a wimp who wouldn't threaten her control?

"I'd love to take your picture someday," she blurted out. Her eyes grew round, jumping from his to her empty glass. She hadn't meant to say that aloud.

"More than the one you shot of me back in the gallery?" he teased.

Sophia wrinkled her nose in a self-deprecating little wince. "You saw that, huh?"

"Why'd you think I told you to bring the camera?"

He reached over and made a little gimme motion with his fingers. She laughed, then pulled the camera from her pocket, toggled it to the view option and, after a quick look, pressed her lips together to keep from snorting.

She didn't release the camera, but turned the view screen so he could see the shot of himself in a half squat, hugging the huge white penis.

Max stared, his dark eyes round in horror.

She waited for the explosion.

He burst into laughter.

Heat swirled low in her belly, making her thighs quiver. God, she wanted him.

"Nice job," he complimented, taking the camera to get a closer look. Sophia's fingers itched to grab it back, so she curled them into her palms. The camera was like another limb. She hated being without it.

"I don't know art that well, but you perfectly captured not

just the weight of that marble, but how freaked out I felt. So is that what you show at your gallery? Blackmail shots?"

Sophia laughed as he leaned back in the chair, draping one arm along the back of the seat next to him.

"I doubt there are enough blackmail shots out there to pull together much of a show," she said thoughtfully. "But that would be fun, wouldn't it? It'd probably be a bigger draw than my upcoming romance show."

"Romance?"

Sophia hesitated, so used to her ideas for the gallery being dismissed as soon as she offered them. But Max looked genuinely interested, so she took a deep breath and leaned her elbows on the table.

"Romantic photos, to be precise. Esprit has been…" What? Sinking in depravity? Selling out for the quick buck? Peddling sex instead of art? She went with, "Floundering in its focus for the past few years. I'm hoping this show, my first show since taking over, will get us back on track. We're shifting away from all other formats to focus exclusively on photography."

"Hence turning away the big dick?"

She grinned. "Exactly. Despite Esprit's reputation and history, my late husband thought he'd make more money if he shifted focus to erotic art."

"Reputation and history? Esprit de l'Art," he mused. "I know that name for some reason. Something besides Rico talking about it, I mean."

"Did you grow up locally?"

"San Francisco, born and bred," he confirmed.

"Then you probably have heard of the gallery. Not only was it declared a historic site seventy years ago, as it was one of the buildings that survived the 1906 fire, but it's also made the news for the shows and dignitaries it's drawn over the years. The building itself is owned by the Historical Guild."

"Isn't Esprit one of the most exclusive galleries in Northern California?"

"Yes," she said enthusiastically, thrilled that he'd recognized it. "The gallery started out featuring only California artists and subjects. Pretty soon artists were moving to California for a chance to show here. Until four years ago, its main focus was photography."

"I remember it now," he said. Then he smiled with quick charm. "Are you thinking of showing your own work?"

"No," she said quickly. "My work isn't showworthy."

"But you want to take my picture?" Unspoken, but clear on his face was the question "Why?" She didn't know how to answer him. She didn't think admitting he turned her on and she needed to see him objectively before she gave herself permission to strip naked and straddle his body was an appropriate response.

Especially since it was insane. A woman trying to reclaim—hell, to claim for the first time—control of her life didn't grab the first opportunity to climb all over a man who'd proved in the first five minutes to be just as domineering as her father, her brothers and her ex-husband.

"It's not a big deal," she demurred. The picture wouldn't matter. Because this wasn't going anywhere. She might not be able to control her reaction to the man, but she could damn well control whether she chased after him like a lust-starved groupie.

MAX WASN'T STUPID. THAT offer to take his picture had been an opening. A very brief one, too, since it looked like it'd closed already. Too bad. He'd pose with a whole forest of penises if it meant she'd give him another one of those dreamy wasn't-he-the-best-hero-in-the-world? looks.

"Another drink?" the waitress offered on her way to the bar.

He saw the automatic no on Sophia's lips. Then her pale

eyes met his and she hesitated. Taking advantage of that millisecond, he tilted his head, winked, then offered, "I have some recent pictures of Rico you might enjoy."

"You play dirty," she murmured with a rueful laugh.

"I play to win." The words came easily to his lips, said millions of times over in his life. But now, instead of filling him with inspiration, it just made him tired.

He'd been raised to win. To win and to take care of responsibilities. But lately, he'd felt as if he'd gone a round with a bomb and lost. Maybe it was burnout. Maybe it was the scare of seeing Rico hurt. Maybe it was the letter listing all the things his mother needed him to do when he got home. Either way, he'd been feeling a little rough.

At least, he had until Sophia. She was a refreshing treat. Gorgeous and sweet, with just a hint of sass.

And like any treat, it'd be better if he drew out the enjoyment. So he gave the waitress a smile and, pointing his finger, indicated another round. He shifted his focus back to Sophia and let his smile warm and widen.

"If you look that pensive over a drink, are you going to give yourself wrinkles if I order a plate of appetizers?" Max asked.

"Appetizers?" Sophia frowned.

"It's not that I'm ignoring your hurry-up-and-drink mandate," he assured her. "I'm just hungry. Other than airplane food, I haven't eaten in half a day. Are you going to deny me the pleasure of real, U.S.-made food?"

"You've got an answer for everything, don't you?"

There was something in her voice again. Something cautious and a little chilly. But Max could tell from the reluctant amusement dancing in her eyes that he'd be getting his plate of nachos.

Sophia twisted in her seat and waved her hand to get some attention. The move made her ruffled blouse gape. Just enough to give Max a peek at the golden glory of her full breast and a hint of white lace.

His mouth went dry. The waitress arrived with their drinks and, after a quick look of inquiry, Sophia ordered the large nacho platter. Max could still see her breasts in his mind, though. He imagined sliding his fingers, just the tips, over those lush mounds. Tracing the pristine white lace where it met the silky contrast of her skin. He gulped his beer.

"You said you had pictures of Rico," she reminded him when the waitress brought the food.

Rico.

Hell.

Frowning, Max pulled out his cell phone and punched up the photo application. He kept his eyes on the pictures of his squad, the guys still on the front line depending on him. He bit into a cheese-and-shredded-beef-covered chip and told himself to get over the inappropriate lust.

Rule Number One: You don't go after a buddy's sister, even if he gives you permission, unless you're serious. And serious about sex doesn't count. That's quickly followed by rule number, well, probably Rule Number Seven or Eight if he was being honest. Rule Number Eight, then. Don't hit on vulnerable women.

Sophia being Rico's recently widowed sister made her off-limits according to both rules.

But…

Max had never met a rule he wasn't tempted to challenge.

"Tell me more about the photos you take," he invited, giving her his most charming smile. "Are they nudes?"

Her eye roll didn't quite disguise her amusement.

"Forget I said anything," she instructed. She poked her finger at the camera still on the table between them. Then after briefly sucking on her lower lip and trying to drive him insane, she pulled it toward her and said, "I'll go ahead and get rid of that shot."

Max's hand covered hers before he was aware he'd moved. "Let me get this straight. Not only are you rescinding your offer to take my picture, you're now going to delete the only shot you do have of me?"

Her eyes went smoky blue, sparked by a sudden fire that had flared somewhere inside. Max's body responded to that look as if she'd used it to strip him naked and write dirty suggestions on his bare skin. Instant, flaming passion.

"Why don't we take your camera and a pitcher of those margaritas to go and see what kind of scenarios we can shoot," he said, keeping his tone light, even though he was serious as hell.

Her eyes rounded. The blue depths held a hint of sexual curiosity that made his ego sing. But if he was reading her correctly, there was worry and just a little fear there, too.

God, what was wrong with him? Max felt like a bigger dick than the one they'd crated earlier. He was getting all turned on and seeing sexual innuendo in her look that he knew she didn't intend.

Rico had described her as innocent, despite her marriage. Sweet. And here Max was, horny as hell, ready and willing to take advantage of that sweet innocence.

Whether it was his suggestion or if she'd actually read his thoughts, she slipped her hand and the camera away.

"Like I said, I'm not a professional," she told him. "And while this was lovely and I really enjoyed hearing about Rico, I really need to get back to the gallery."

Taking the rejection in gentlemanly stride, Max nodded. He ignored her insistence on paying the tab, left the waitress a couple of bills and tried to help Sophia from her seat. He was so distracted trying to sort out why he felt so disappointed that he barely noticed her irritation.

He didn't want this to end yet.

All the way across the street, he fought the urge to slip his guiding hand from the small of her back to the curve of her slender waist.

Like any good soldier, he strategized on his feet. He marshaled his arguments, backup plans and contingencies in the sixty seconds it took them to reach the sidewalk in front of the gallery.

He had too much respect for her to use the lonely-soldier-home-on-leave ploy, but he wouldn't hesitate to pull out the Rico card. Yes, he'd love nothing better than to take her away to some secluded rose-covered cottage for a weekend of romance. But he'd settle for dinner. What nonthreatening restaurant should he suggest? The trick would be to keep it light. No scaring her off by hitting hard and horny.

Then she stumbled. His hand shot out, grabbing her around the waist and pulling her tight against his body. She gave a little cry of surprise.

"What're you doing?" she demanded, her words breathless, her eyes huge.

"Saving you from falling." And pressing his luck.

"I don't need..." Her words trailed off as realized how close they were. So close her scent filled his senses. Close enough for him to see the faint sprinkle of freckles on her golden skin.

He could see his own desire mirrored in her pale eyes.

To hell with the rules.

Two steps and they'd reached the side of her building. He backed her up against the bricks, bracketing her body between his and the wall.

Max leaned down and took her mouth. Her sweet, tequila-laced gasp reminded him that taking advantage of a woman who'd been drinking was totally out of line.

Then she gave a little shudder, her breasts shimmying against his chest. She reached up, locked her hands behind his neck and between one breath and the next, she was the one taking his mouth. Her kiss was decadently sweet. Soft. Incredible.

Her tongue traced his lower lip, then his upper. She nibbled, she rubbed. She tempted.

She was driving him insane.

Max groaned. His hands slid down her back, smoothed over her hips. Then, unable to resist, he reached around to cup the delicious curves of her ass. Her delighted little groan brought him to his senses. What the hell was he doing?

"Not here," he murmured, pulling away and trying to find his famed control.

"But here feels so good," she protested, her hands tightening on the back of his neck.

"Inside," he insisted, pulling her arms down and taking her hands.

The passion in her eyes dimmed, replaced by insecurity. She lifted her chin, giving him a look that made him feel as if he'd just kicked a kitten and now she was going to hiss and spit.

"Max, I'm sorry," she started. He didn't have to hear the rest to know she was handing him a rejection. And since he didn't want to hear it anyway, Max interrupted.

"Inside," he repeated, pulling her around to the front of the building. That kiss had been hot enough to melt his shorts. If she was going to boot him to the curb after it, he'd rather it wasn't here on the street, with the hostess grinning at them from the cantina across the street.

Not listening to her sputtering protests, he pulled her through the door.

But once they'd stepped into the gallery, his defenses immediately shifted from lust to protection. His senses on full alert, he squared his shoulders and stepped in front of Sophia to shield her with his body.

"Oh, my God," Sophia breathed, either in shock or because she needed support, her trembling hand clutching the back of his shirt.

"What the hell happened here?" he demanded.

4

SOMEONE HAD MADE DESTRUCTION an art form.

Max wasn't an expert, but it looked to him like it totally clashed with the gallery's decor.

The two tall ficus trees that flanked the door had been shoved over, a messy arc of leaves and dirt dulling the gleaming surface of the hardwood floor. One of the blue velvet settees flanking the walls had been upended, its wooden legs covered in shards of glass from any of the half-dozen broken picture frames that'd crashed to the floor behind it.

In the middle of it all was Sophia's assistant, her face almost the same color as her hair.

"I was in the back with the shippers, then uncrating the frame order. I heard something and came out to this…" She looked shocked, waving ineffectively at the scattered glass, tears pouring down her cheeks. "The bell over the door never rang. I don't know…"

"Call the police," Max ordered.

The pixie started bawling and Sophia trembled against his back.

But neither woman moved toward a phone. Max reached into his pocket for his cell phone.

Dead.

Damn. He hadn't charged it. Given that his mother and uncle were the only ones in the country who'd be contacting him, he'd preferred to not make it easy for them.

A quick glance through the showroom didn't net a phone. "Is the phone in your office?"

"Yes," she responded absently, her focus on the mess that'd once been her beautifully pristine showroom. "I need to clean this up."

At that, her assistant hurried out of the room.

"Don't touch anything until the police get here," he instructed

"I can't just leave it like this." He could hear the despair in her words. She finally stepped around him to face the mess. Max instantly missed her warmth.

The pixie returned with a broom. Sophia went to her, hugging the sniffling woman briefly before taking the broom and murmuring a few comforting words.

"I know it wasn't my fault," Gina said tearfully. "But I still feel horrible. I should have been paying better attention after the last time."

"This has happened before?" Max snapped.

Sophia gripped the handle so tight her knuckles were white, but her look was serenely controlled when she glanced back at Max. "This building's had some problems the past few months. A little graffiti, some vandalism. A few harassing phone calls."

Rico was right. She did need protecting.

"You've notified the landlord, right?"

Sophia sucked in a deep breath. He yanked his gaze from the deliciously tempting curves of her breasts. This was the wrong time to be getting turned on.

"Max, I appreciate your help. But I can handle things here."

"What happened before? What did the police do?" he asked, ignoring her.

"They can't do anything," she repeated. She took the broom back from him. "They've been out for the vandalism and the ugly phone calls. All they can do is write a report. There's no evidence, no witnesses, nothing for them to do anything with."

"Right, but they still need to come out. Why don't you check the rest of the gallery, make sure nothing else was damaged. I'll go call the cops." Before she could snap, Max added, "The sooner it's done, the sooner you can sweep up this mess."

SOPHIA WAS PRETTY SURE smacking Max around the head with her broom was illegal. But it was tempting. Still, just like calling the cops, she knew it would be pointless. With a head as hard as his, he probably wouldn't even notice.

Trying to resist the urge, she pulled her gaze from Max's. The only place to look, though, was at the destruction of her showroom. Her stomach shuddered at the sight.

Sophia forced herself to breathe, blinking fast to keep the burning tears from pouring down her cheeks. She had to clean up. She'd be damned if she'd fall apart.

"Fine. You don't want to check the rest of the gallery, can you point me in the direction of a phone?"

"I told you—"

"Soph?" Gina stood in the marble column-flanked door-way, tracks of mascara streaking her pale face. "I called the police."

Sophia had a brief urge to kick something. Why was it that whenever she tried to assert her independence, someone swooped in and undermined her? And always because they thought it was for her own good.

Did she have some freaking neon sign flashing overhead claiming her incompetence? She glanced back at Max, his sleeves rolled up to show strong arms. Arms that'd been wrapped around her ten minutes ago. She let her gaze wander up those arms to his shoulders, broad and strong. They'd felt muscular, hard, solid under her questing fingers. Her eyes rose, tracing his strong neck, a neck she'd held on to while he'd kissed her.

Her eyes locked on his mouth. Heat swirled low in her belly as she relived the pressure of that mouth. The rich taste of him. The power, passionate and needy, he'd ignited in her body. The way he'd made her think that all the fascination with sex, with erotic delights, was actually warranted.

"Can you show me the rest of the gallery?" Max asked Gina. After a quick glance at Sophia for permission, the girl nodded and led him out of the showroom.

Sophia's hands gripped the broom so tightly, she was surprised the handle didn't splinter. God, this was insane. Her stepdaughter was trying to ruin her life. She had a show coming up next week that needed all her focus. And now her gallery was a mess. And all she could think about was how hot Max St. James was.

The guy was obviously just as detrimental to her sanity as he was to her self-control.

And a part of her didn't care. Closing her eyes, she rested her forehead on her hands where they gripped the broomstick. Maybe she should stop reading self-help books on independence and control and start reading about codependence recovery. Was she the kind of woman who said she wanted to be strong, then sabotaged herself?

Before she could consider that too closely, Max returned. "I checked the back, the offices and other showrooms. This is the extent of the destruction."

His gaze traveled over the dirt-and-glass covered floor until it reached the broom in her hands. His eyes made a slow sweep up her legs, over the curve of her hips, and heated as he noted the flat planes of her belly. She sucked in her tummy and said a quick thanks that she'd turned to Pilates to fight her sexual frustration.

Then his eyes rested on her breasts. Heat washed over her, tingling and warming its way through her system. Her nipples beaded against the soft cotton of her bra, making her ache for more than just his eyes on her. She could picture his hands, large and strong. His fingers circling and petting. His mouth, hot and wet. Her breath quickened. Her body fought against itself, a part of her melting while the rest of her went on high alert. She wanted to curl into the pleasure, and didn't want to miss a single second of the experience.

Her gratitude shifted from her Pilates workouts to the broom in her hands, since it was the only thing holding her upright.

And Max was apparently so sexually intuitive, he knew exactly how she felt.

"Sophia?" His words were low, a sensuous thrum that moved through her welcoming body.

"I don't want this," she whispered. Still, as if working independently from her brain, her body leaned toward him. She could almost feel the hard heat of his chest against her aching nipples, welcomed the imagined pressure, hoped it'd ease the aching heaviness.

"Do you want me to talk you into it?" he asked, his words teasing, but his tone making it clear all it'd take was a nod from her and he'd get to work on the convincing.

Wouldn't it be incredible? All she had to do was let him take control and she'd have what was sure to be the best, most incendiary, sex of her life. And she didn't even have to make the choice. She could just stand here, breathing heavily, and let him take that as complicity.

Talk about seductive.

"Don't mean to interrupt, but did one of you call the police?"

It was like taking an ice-cold public shower. Her lust vaporized in a blast of searing embarrassment. She wanted to kick and scream and throw something almost as much as she wanted to give the cop a hug for his timing.

Max looked like he just wanted to scream and throw things, though. Then he blinked and the look of frustration was gone.

"We've had a break-in," Max offered, stating the obvious as he strode forward to shake hands with the officer. "It appears to be confined to this room, but I'm sure you'll want to check the rest of the building."

Still trying to corral her raging libido, Sophia watched Max handle the cops. He identified himself as a concerned bystander, introducing her as the owner with a wave of his hand. Then he and the cop proceeded to ignore her while they discussed the vandalism. A part of her wanted to scurry off to her office, sink into her couch and let him fix it all.

But she couldn't. She wanted independence, which meant handling things like this herself.

"Officer, I'm the one you need to talk to," she said, stepping forward to interrupt them. "Sergeant St. James was just leaving."

"Sergeant?"

And there they went, off on their male bonding bonanza. Sophia spent the next ten minutes feeling like an interloper as she tried to interject answers, only to have the cop ignore her in favor of Max. Finally, she'd had enough.

"Officer, do you have any further questions for me? No? Then I'm sure you have a lot of serving and protecting to do elsewhere. Me," she said with a stiff smile as she jerked a thumb toward her chest, "I have to clean up my gallery, check the photos closer for damage and get them all rematted and reframed. So if you'll both excuse me."

The policeman nodded, apparently so used to rudeness that he didn't even blink at the abrupt dismissal. He started jotting down a few more notes on his report, then pulled out his card to write something on the back of it.

"Sophia—" Judging by the concern etched on his face, Sophia knew Max was the kind of guy who took helping others seriously. So seriously that he was happy to step right in and take over. Which she didn't need.

"Max, it was wonderful to meet you. Thanks so much for letting me know about Rico." She rushed through her words, suddenly realizing that once the cop left, she wouldn't be safe. From herself, that was. So she needed Max out, too.

"Ma'am, here's my card. The case number is on the back, if you need to contact us."

She took the card and risked her body's rebellion by taking Max's arm with the other hand. Smiling, she pulled Max along as she escorted the cop to the door. It took five minutes and all her powers of persuasion and charm to shoo them both out.

"I'll be in touch," Max said, digging in his heels at the threshold. He gave her a long look, then let his gaze slide over to the side of the building where he'd kissed her. "Soon."

Torn between wanting to make him promise and needing to tell him to stay away, Sophia just shook her head and murmured thanks for the drink before shutting and locking the door.

She'd have sagged against it, but she knew he'd see her clearly through the beveled glass. So she set the broom aside and headed down the hallway.

"Mmm-mmm, you'll have a great time jumping his bones," Gina said, following her into the office.

"Not in this lifetime," Sophia shot back, crossing her office to the little refrigerator in the corner and getting a bottle of water. Then she shook two Advil out of the bottle in her desk drawer.

"Why the hell not?" Gina asked, her tone hitting a new high note. "He's freaking hot."

"Hot or not, I'm not dating him."

Gina crossed her arms over her chest, shifted her hip to one side and gave Sophia her patented are-you-insane? look.

"Look, he was appealing while we were munching on cheese-covered tortilla chips. He's a nice guy and a friend of my brother's. But that's it."

"Nice enough that you let him borrow your lipstick, hmm?" Gina arched her brow.

Heat raced up Sophia's cheeks.

"Okay, fine. So I gave in to the urge to taste." And oh, God, he'd tasted so good. So, so good. "But one taste was enough. Will there ever be another? No way. Did you see the way he just took over? This is my gallery and he wouldn't even let me decide when to call the police."

"In his defense, he wasn't the one who called them," Gina said around the thumbnail she was nibbling.

"It doesn't matter who called. What matters is how Max stepped in and took over. The man didn't listen to a word I said."

"He sure looked like he was listening," Gina said. "He hardly ever took his eyes off you."

Sophia had to force herself not to blush like a schoolgirl. He had stared. A lot. He'd made her feel wanted and sexy and special. He'd also made her feel incompetent and frustrated and useless.

"No," she said, as much for herself as for Gina. "He's too bossy. Sexy charm and a gorgeous body aren't enough to make up for the simple fact that dating him would be a disaster."

"It doesn't have to be forever, Sophia," Gina said in exasperation. "You're not required to hand over your spine along with your underpants."

"Easy for you to say," Sophia muttered. Gina was the kind of girl who put her own needs—especially sexual—front and center in everything she did. Sophia didn't know if it was because of or despite that attitude that she and Gina had become such good friends.

Giving in to the multitude of frustrations that'd been her day, she threw herself on the tapestry couch and pulled a pillow comfortingly against her chest.

"I'm saying just date the guy. Have a good time. Enjoy life. Maybe get a little."

Sophia rolled her eyes as if the idea of getting a little, or a lot, with Max didn't make her thighs melt. Even if he hadn't been brother-approved—which would only give Rico all sorts of pro-interfering ideas—he had too much in common with Joseph. Rich, bossy, charming. Three strikes.

"He's a soldier, isn't he?" Gina asked in a suggestive tone.

"What's that got to do with anything?" Sophia gave in to the lure of comfort and kicked off her heels, tucking her feet up. "I'm not checking the size of his weapon."

"Ha ha. What I'm saying is he's home now on leave, right? That means he's only here for a little while. Temporarily."

Sophia wasn't so tired she didn't immediately get Gina's point. Temporary.

Could she put up with Max's bossiness in exchange for his sexy company if she knew their time together was limited?

Or was that just an excuse to let herself visualize them naked together. His body hard and strong, poised over hers while she trailed one hand over his shoulders and the other down the flat planes of his six-pack.

Naked was good. Finding out what all the fuss about sex was would be even better. But Max St. James? That man was purely bad news for a woman searching for independence.

"Just think about it," Gina ordered. "I'm going to clean the showroom, then head home. I'll check the locks on my way out, though."

Sophia waved her friend away and gave herself another minute to pout.

Then, calling herself a whiner, she rose and went to her computer. She moved her mouse and clicked, pulling up her goal board. Yes, a fabulous and gratifying sexual relationship was typed right there in its purple box. Right next to the box labeled vacation in Greece and the one marked meet Wayne Dyer. All of them were in the uncontrollable column. Dreams, wishes, someday possibilities. The only three purple boxes on a goal board filled with yellow boxes. Yellow boxes were career, business, security. Yellow boxes were things she could control. Purple boxes were things she had no control over.

She sighed, dropping her head against the cushioned leather back of her chair.

So what did she focus on here? Control? Or a man who not only made her forget all of her lessons, but was so bossy he made her brothers look like pushovers?

Nope. There was no choice to make. And since her body was used to being denied pleasure, it shouldn't be too difficult to forgo the promise of passion. It was just a matter of control.

Besides, there was no way he was as good as she was imagining.

"Home so soon, Maximilian?"

"What? No brass band and confetti?" Max returned, stepping around the chilly disapproval of his mother's question at the same time he stepped across the threshold into the world according to St. James.

He handed his duffel bag over to Sterling, the St. James's butler, and returned the man's welcoming smile. He swept his gaze over the opulent foyer, noting that it looked exactly the same as it had a year ago when he'd shipped out. The same as it had ten years ago when he'd graduated high school. The same as it probably had almost three decades ago when his nanny had brought him home from the hospital.

Some things never changed. Speaking of which, he took a deep breath and turned to face the woman standing in the arched dining room doorway.

"Hello, Mother. You look wonderful."

"Do I? It must be the evening light. If you'd bothered to come home directly from the airport, you'd have easily seen all of my worry lines." She didn't step toward him, but did lift her chin so he could kiss her smooth cheek.

"I had some things to take care of." Things that apparently didn't want to be taken care of. Max told himself he'd be crazy to let himself get hurt because he'd been brushed off by a woman he'd only known a few hours. "But I'm home now and you can stop worrying. I'll take care of everything."

"I didn't say I needed anything taken care of, Maximilian. I'm handling my life just fine. I just wish I heard from you more often, even if you only bother to come home once a year."

And yet, it felt as if he'd never left. Max wanted to do an about-face and march right back out the door, then he looked more closely at his mother. She'd aged since he'd last seen her. Tabby St. James's blond hair was still a smooth fall to her chin. As usual, her evening suit was Chanel, her perfume the same and the pearls at her throat and ears heirloom. But there was worry in her dark eyes, a hint of fear and relief as she did a visual inventory. As if she couldn't trust his, or the Army's, assurance that he'd been fine overseas.

It was that look that extinguished Max's ire. She might be the queen of guilt trips, but she did love him. In her way. Since she'd think a hug forward and inappropriate, he laid his hand on her shoulder and gave a light squeeze.

"I had an obligation to attend to," he said, wincing at both the side step and at terming the delicious time he'd spent with Sophia as an obligation. But from the look on her face when he'd left, he was pretty sure she'd use the same term. Or worse. "My cell phone was dead or I'd have called to let you know."

"Well, no matter now." Tabby fluttered her hands in a way that some might take as dismissing the issue, but Max knew it meant she was only shifting it aside for later. "Let's eat before dinner is cold."

And God forbid Tabitha St. James serve anything that was less than perfect. Her dinner rules were etched in granite.

He followed his mother's elegant steps into the dining room, offering the man seated at the head of the table a nod of greeting.

Max took his seat, noting the familiar gleam of his mother's best crystal and china. The food served might change, but the tradition remained the same. He knew the table had been set and waiting since that morning, ready for whenever he arrived. Formality was the rule of thumb for the first meal home. It had been the same when his father was alive.

Max waited until the gazpacho was served before greeting his uncle, the four-star general.

"Sir."

"Sergeant. Eat up, then you can tell me all about your latest adventures."

Yet another tradition. Ever since his father had died nine years back, when the General visited, he sat at the head of the table, taking charge. The man directed the meal like a military campaign. Everyone had a role, with him in charge.

Something Max wouldn't question in the field. But here at his mother's table? He didn't mind stirring things up a little here.

"Not many adventures to share, sir," Max told him, since the ones he knew the General wanted to hear would only give his mom more of those worry lines she liked to complain about.

For the next few minutes, Max shared an upbeat version of his current tour, downplaying the dangers and focusing on the friends and time he spent on base instead of in the field.

"Don't you think it's about time you transfer to a higher profile outfit?" his uncle asked. "I've got connections, some pull with certain people. You can start working your way into a more politically strategic position."

"I prefer to stay with my current assignment, sir. I want to be on the front line doing what I was trained to do. I'm making a difference." Max looked at his soup instead of into his uncle's steely gray eyes and admitted, "What I'm doing matters. One day we save a kid, another a village. The war is ugly. I feel like I'm doing my part to keep it from getting any uglier."

The General leaned back so Sterling could replace his soup with salad, waiting until all the plates had been served before shaking his head.

"You're letting sentiment instead of intellect steer your choices. That's not a good idea, Sergeant."

"They're my choices," Max said without heat. He'd heard different choruses of this same song most of his life. His uncle, just like his father before him, had a specific plan in mind for Max's career. Max wasn't playing by any plans but his own, though.

"Don't be discourteous, Maximilian," his mother said, uttering her first words since they'd sat down to dine. Such was the hierarchy, Max knew. His uncle, like his late father, claimed precedence. If the General hadn't been there, Tabby would have controlled the conversation. As a child, Max had often wondered when his turn would come. Then, when he'd grown older, he'd hoped it never did.

"Darling," his mother continued, "while you're home, I hope you'll find time to socialize. There are many people who'd love to see you again. And I've accepted a number of invitations on your behalf."

"I'm home to help you, Mother. To look over the finances, take the car in for service, make sure the house isn't falling apart," he said, only half teasing. This was his job. Once a year, come home to personally make sure everything was running smoothly. It was how he justified the joy and freedom he felt the rest of the year.

"Your mother's right," the General put in. "Obligations are necessary, of course. But so are building the right connections."

Connections. Both the General and Tabby believed strongly in the power of networking. The most influential people, the correct alliances, the smartest services. Every decision was weighed with an eye for how it'd enhance the St. James name and reputation, from the boarding school Max had been sent to at four to the military school he'd graduated from. His major act of defiance had been to enlist the minute he'd left high school instead of attending West Point.

"We'll see," Max hedged. "Mother's books and the estate take top priority. And I've a number of personal obligations to see to, as well."

He could imagine the look of outrage on Sophia's face if she'd heard him refer to her as an obligation. Hell, he just might tell her so he could enjoy the fireworks. The woman was definitely exciting.

"Don't be silly, darling," Tabby said quickly, as if rushing to stave off an explosion. Since the tension in the room had reached electric proportions, she was probably smart. "I've got Bobby, the gardener's assistant helping me out with all those little jobs, so you'll have plenty of time to socialize."

"You just said you were having problems," the General reminded her tersely. "Over drinks, before Max arrived."

"Well, yes," Tabby said, looking flustered. "But nothing that requires Maximilian's attention. The historical society has an issue with a particular building. We feel the business is too controversial and would like it shut down or moved."

His attention was more on keeping himself from drooling over the rich wine-scented coq au vin Sterling had just set before him than on his mother's comment. His knife and fork were in hand before her words sank in.

"You can do that?" he asked. "Shut down a business because you don't like them?"

"Well, it's not easy, but yes, eventually we can."

Max grimaced. As usual, Tabby didn't take note. Instead she changed topics right back to the list of women she'd lined up for him to date. Dates they both knew Max would avoid. Then her chatter shifted to the upcoming country club winter ball.

That, he wouldn't be able to avoid. Maybe he could convince Sophia to go with him, though. Max recalled the way she'd hustled him out of her gallery and smirked. Right. He was pretty sure she'd just as soon ride naked across the Golden Gate Bridge than date him.

Probably on that marble cock.

5

HER SHORT, APRICOT-TINTED nails tapped an irritated beat on the wood of her desk while Ryan, her insurance agent, droned on over the phone. Sophia stared so hard at her computer screen, her eyes watered and the bright colors of her goal chart bled together.

Every few seconds she made a humming noise to indicate that she was listening.

Five minutes later, she carefully eased the phone from between her ear and her shoulder, gently pressed the Off key and, keeping a pleasant look on her face, swiveled her chair so she could set the phone in its charger.

Across the room, Gina sank deeper into the tapestry couch, chewed off the purple polish on her thumbnail and waited for the explosion.

Sophia pursed her lips as she glanced at the two pages of notes she'd taken during her conversation, then closed her eyes and sucked in a deep breath.

Apparently unable to stand it any longer, Gina asked in a tiny voice, "Are they raising the rates?"

"They're considering it," Sophia acknowledged. "Apparently police reports add to our risk factor."

To say nothing about how they added weight to the ugly

rumors. Olivia had already called this morning to chide Sophia, pointing out that they were supposed to be downplaying the evidence for Lynn, not add to it.

"I shouldn't have called them," Gina said, sounding like she was going to cry. "I just thought…"

"No," Sophia said with a quick shake of her head. "If you hadn't called, Max or I would have."

"I'm sorry."

Sophia shook her head at her assistant, looking so forlorn behind her red and black striped cat's-eye glasses. "Gina, don't worry about it. Seriously. Ryan gave me a list of things I can do to keep the rates from increasing."

"Like?"

"Like…" Sophia stalled for time by looking at the list. She blinked a couple of times to clear her eyes. Most of them were impossible, but Gina didn't have to know that. "Add bars to the front windows. Install cameras and upgrade our security system. Get stronger releases from the artists."

She gave Gina a bright, cheerful smile and flicked her finger at the last item on the list. "And the easiest? Find out who's messing with us and have them arrested. Ryan figures since the graffiti and vandalism have escalated in the past month, it probably has to do with the upcoming show."

"The show?" Gina narrowed heavily lined eyes. "I don't think so. This is personal, if you ask me. Do you think this is all happening because of your money-grubbing slut status?"

"Huh?"

"All those rumors about your competency, about you being a tramp who pushed your husband into focusing on sex statues to make money? They all started after your stepdaughter contested the will, right?"

"Right."

"Now you're changing the focus of the gallery. Eliminating the erotic art it's been known for. You're showing all new

artists. You're trying to bring in a totally different clientele."
Gina talked so fast, her high-pitched words almost tumbled
over themselves on the way out of her mouth. "We both know
that for all Joseph's sex-sells philosophy, the gallery wasn't
doing so well the past couple years. But if you turn it around,
reclaim its former glory, Esprit's going to be huge again. I'll
bet Lynn's furious about that."

Tears blurred Sophia's eyes so fast she didn't even have time
to blink. God, she was tired of this. For eight months she'd
been fighting Lynn for Joseph's estate. She'd struggled with
fear over every damned choice, every freaking decision.

Sniffling, she glanced at her computer screen, her goal
board a blur of colors.

"You're right. She probably is behind it all. But I can't prove
anything. I've told Olivia my suspicions, and she's told the
police. All anyone can do is watch and wait." Sophia clenched
her fists in frustration. Always, it seemed, she was stuck in
the passive role. "Meanwhile, I can't give up. I deserve my
dream, don't I? I'm willing to work for it. To fight for it."

She pushed away from her desk, stepping barefoot toward
the hall where she could see her once again spotlessly beautiful gallery.

"I've wanted this since I was ten. When I helped out at
the cantina, I'd spend my breaks sitting at the table by the
window, wearing my brother's hand-me-downs and watching
the fancy people coming and going through the gallery."

"What was it like? Glamorous? Ritzy? All artsy and bohemian?" Gina asked, anxiety forgotten as she drew her knees
up into story time pose.

"Bohemian?" Sophia laughed, her tears forgotten as she
curled up on the couch next to Gina. "Just how old do you
think I am?"

Gina rolled her eyes and waited.

"It was incredible," Sophia said softly. She stared at the
photos framed on the opposite wall. "The beveled glass win-

dows were like jewels on an elegant lady. In the evening, between the lunch and dinner hours, the sun would hit the brick of the building, turning it the color of a soft rose. It was just so romantic-looking."

She smiled, the memories flooding back. "It was pretty casual during the day, but for shows? Oh, man, it was gorgeous. The women would wear fancy dresses, the men suits. It just screamed class to a girl with dishpan hands and a bowl haircut to match her brothers'."

Gina giggled. With good reason, Sophia knew, since she'd once shared a pitcher of margaritas and childhood pictures with the other woman. She'd been raised by her father and six older brothers; it hadn't been until she'd left for college that she'd learned the finer points of being female. At ten, she'd been just one of the boys.

"My dad used to let me come over once in a while and I'd stare at the photographs. The way they were displayed, the stories they told. I wanted to be a part of this world so badly," Sophia admitted, tracing one finger over the patterned fabric of her sofa. That's why she'd taken up photography. The first time she'd looked through the lens of her dad's old camera, she'd known she'd found her passion. She'd saved for a year to buy her first camera. "I think I saw it as nirvana. A little piece of heaven."

"And you got it, right?" Gina said, sounding unsure.

"In a way. Joseph bought the gallery as a wedding gift. A way for me to have my dream and still keep an eye on my father. This was before he'd sold the cantina."

Sophia remembered how naively thrilled she'd been, believing that Joseph had actually meant that the gallery would be hers.

"So you're going to recreate that world?"

"It's all I ever wanted for the gallery. I mean, c'mon, erotic art? Penises and orgies? That never screamed elegant or classy to me, you know?"

Gina nodded. Sophia had hired her despite Joseph's protests, finding a kindred spirit in the wild younger woman. Gina had been at the gallery for about a year before Joseph had died. She knew firsthand what kind of man he'd been.

"Well, you have to admit that diamond-tipped bust of, well a bust, was pretty elegant."

"Girls with Grills?" Sophia winced, remembering how hard it had been to convince Joseph not to buy it himself. By that time, they'd not only been in separate bedrooms but entirely separate wings of the estate. But still… "Bling does not elegance make."

"I know," Gina gushed. She leaned forward in her best gossip pose, humor glinting in her eyes. "Like the current trend of bedazzling your coochie. Vagazzle. Talk about overkill."

Sophia's laugh gurgled out.

And just like that, all of her stress and anger dissipated. That was one of the things Sophia loved about Gina, her ability to enjoy the absurd in life. And to make Sophia want to do the same.

"Exactly," Sophia agreed enthusiastically, pointing her finger in agreement. "I mean, what's wrong with good old-fashioned girly bits without rhinestones?"

"Nothing, if you ask me," a man's voice offered, laughter lurking behind his words.

Gina jumped so hard, she slid off the couch. Apparently deciding three was a crowd, she stood and hurried out of the room.

Nerves suddenly on full alert, Sophia shivered. All her life, she'd figured lust was the thing of romance novels. Now she found out lust was not only all too real, it could be ignited with just the sound of Max's voice.

Just the man she'd been trying to pretend she didn't want to see. She gave herself five whole seconds—an eternity, in her mind—to gather her control, and to struggle to put her sandals back on. One hand on her stomach to try to calm the

horde of horny butterflies zinging around, she sucked in a
breath, then opened her eyes.

"Sergeant, I didn't hear you come in." She stood, smoothing her skirt and offering a hand that barely trembled. He
looked...delicious. She'd told herself he couldn't be as sexy
as she'd thought. That it'd just been the tequila, the upset over
the vandalism, that'd skewed her perception.

And then she'd spent all night dreaming about him.

"It's Max, remember?" He took her hand in his, subtly
pulling her a little closer. The move doused her passion like a
cold shower. The man was such a control freak; he even took
over the simple greeting.

"Right." She slipped her hand from his and stepped back.
Enough to show she was in control. And almost enough to
keep her knees from melting. "I'm surprised to see you again.
I thought we said our goodbyes yesterday? Or did you have
another message for me from my brother?"

There. She smiled, pleased. That should put him in his
place. Which was out of her reach, clearly marked off-limits
and dangerous.

"The police suggested that your problems are probably
due to a grudge or vendetta. They don't have the personnel
to stake out the gallery," he reminded her. Sophia's smile
faded. "I went ahead and pulled a few strings. Three of the
top private investigative firms in the Bay Area are coming
by this afternoon to talk to you and offer bids."

"What? You...? No way..." She was so shocked at his au-
dacity, she couldn't even finish a sentence. She tried to catch
her breath, sure that when she could breathe again, the spots
would fade from her eyes and she could glare properly.

"You've got to be kidding," she finally sputtered. "What
possessed you to presume such a thing? Do the women in your
world always expect you to shove them aside so you can take
over?"

His friendly look shifted to confusion. She felt bad. She

knew she was taking her own issues out on him. That wasn't fair. He probably didn't mean to be pushy. Here she was jumping all over him—and not in a good way—and he probably thought he was being considerate.

"I wouldn't say I expect women to let me take over," he answered with a puzzled shrug. "At least, no more than the men do. I mean, if I'm the best person for the job, it doesn't matter who steps aside to let me do it, right?"

"Step aside? Best person?" All of her conciliatory intentions flew out the window as his words set fire not only to her issues, but her temper. Before she could grab that control she kept telling herself she wanted, she exploded.

MAX LEANED BACK AGAINST the wall, his eyes narrowed as he watched Sophia rant, her hips swinging with a little Latin flair as she paced the room. She tossed her lush hair, punctuated her accusations with huge arm waves, cussed in both English and Spanish.

She was incredible.

He let her words wash over him, instead letting the delightful view finally calm the churning that'd been making a mess of his gut since the previous night's meal. By dessert, his mother had tried to arrange three dates for him, dumped the company's audit on his shoulders and begged for his help with her little historical society complication.

A complication called Sophia.

If there was one thing he knew, it was that any connection between his mother and a woman he had sexual designs on meant only bad things. Tabby was like the kiss of death to Max's sex life.

A mother's fondest wish, he figured.

"Look," he finally interrupted. "Not that I'm not enjoying the show, but the first guy's going to be here any minute now. Maybe you can yell at me later?"

Sophia stopped pacing so fast he was surprised she didn't

fall off those sexy heels. Strappy sandals today, he noted, in a hot red leather in the exact hue of her toenails. Delicate little toes and smooth arches wrapped in criss-crossing bands. He wanted to slide those shoes off her feet and scatter soft kisses along her delicate ankle. Up her smooth calf. Along the sensitive flesh behind her knee.

He shoved his hands in his pockets, wondering when the hell he'd developed a foot fetish.

"Did you listen to a word I said?" she snapped, the demand in her tone pulling him from his contemplation of how it'd feel to have her toes work their way over his body. "Were you even paying the least bit of attention?"

"Sure," he lied, adding a charming smile to lend weight to his words. "You don't want a P.I. poking into your history or embarrassing you by asking your friends and family nosy questions. Esprit is your business and if you wanted an investigator, you'd hire one yourself. And as for who I think I am, I'm assuming that was rhetorical since we both know I'm the guy your big brother sent to look out for you."

Max's smile slid into a smirk. He couldn't help it. She just looked so cute standing there, her fists on her hips and her mouth working like a fish trying to breathe. After what she'd told him about growing up with her overprotective brothers, he knew brandishing the Rico card was pushing his luck. But hell, he defused bombs for a living. He was used to playing on the edge.

"You're…" She just stared, her hands waving around as if she was trying to grab the right words out of the air.

"A great guy? Yeah," Max said, straightening from the wall and stepping forward until he was a few inches away. Close enough to really appreciate the way anger made her eyes go a deep blue.

And close enough for her to smack him good if he didn't watch his step.

With that in mind, he wiped the grin off his face and

tempered his words as if he were talking to a shock victim. "I'm here to help, okay? I'm not trying to take over or to ignore your authority. I'm just doing what I do, fixing messes before they do damage."

He waited for her to soften.

She squared her shoulders and crossed her arms over her chest.

"I'm sorry. I really am," he offered, trying a different tack. "It sucked seeing your showroom vandalized. You've got a nice, warm place here. Classy and upscale. You've obviously put a lot of time and energy into creating it. I hated seeing how hurt you were when someone screwed it up like that."

Her eyes softened for a second, the blue warming. Max relaxed, wondering if he should push his luck and reach out, brush his fingers over the smooth curve of her cheek. Rub a lock of her silky black hair, trail his palm over her shoulder. God, he really, really needed to touch her.

But first, he'd ask her out. On a real date, not some bullshit obligatory drink.

She wet her mouth, her teeth vividly white against the dusky rose of her lip color. She didn't drop her arms, but he saw some of the stiffness leave her shoulders.

Home free, he thought. He wondered if she'd like to have drinks before dinner, or after.

She leaned closer, her eyes locked on his. Max's pulse jumped, his heart rate spiking.

"I appreciate that you wanted to help," she said. Her words were soft, so soft that he barely caught the underlying fury in her tone. "But I can handle my business myself. I don't need you, or my brother, fixing things for me."

"It's not like I did an end run around you and hired someone. I saw you had a problem. Trying to be a nice guy, I asked around, got a few references and called in a couple favors to get you appointments ASAP."

"I appreciate that you're trying to be a nice guy."

There, maybe she was through with her tantrum and ready to show a little reasonable gratitude.

His smile had barely formed when she stepped forward, closing those last inches between them and poking her finger into his chest.

"But I'd be grateful if instead you'd work on being a nice guy who doesn't try to take over things that are none of his business."

That finger was the last straw. He wrapped his hand around it. She trembled. It was that tiny suggestion of vulnerability that made him look deeper. Past the stubborn set of her shoulders, the pride in her eyes. To the hints of hesitant fear. The way her teeth nibbled on her bottom lip. The slight frown between her brows. And there, in the blue depths of her eyes, the insecurity.

Max didn't understand how a woman this glorious could have an ounce of insecurity. He did know that the sight of it made him crazy.

Unable to resist, he lifted her hand to his lips. His eyes holding hers captive, he nibbled little kisses over the delicate bones of her knuckles.

Her skin was like silk. Her eyes narrowed. He breathed in her scent, letting it wash over him like a caress. His blood heated.

He turned her hand over in his, pressing his mouth to her open palm. Her lips trembled as she sucked in a breath. He scraped his teeth along the soft inside flesh of the finger she'd poked into his chest.

She made the softest, sexiest mewling sound in the back of her throat. His body hardened.

Still holding her eyes, he traced his tongue from the tip of her French manicure, down the slender length of her finger to the crux where her fingers met. Smiling a little, he flicked his tongue there, in the juncture.

Her eyes blurred. She gave a delicate shudder. His dick

pressed painfully against the zipper of his jeans, throbbing in a plea to be set free.

He sucked her finger into his mouth. He slid his tongue along the top, then the sides. Her tiny little moan was all he needed to hear.

Through playing, he lowered her hand from his mouth and pressed it against his racing heart. Before he could shove his own fingers into that thick fall of hair, though, there was a cough in the doorway.

They both froze. Sophia winced then tried to pull her hand away but he held tight.

He wasn't finished, dammit.

"Soph?" Gina broke in uncertainly. "There's a dude in a suit here for you. Said he's a P.I. here about a security consultation."

"Son of a—"

"A suit?" Sophia said dazedly, interrupting Max's oath. She frowned, then puffed out a breath and gave him an arch look. "Interesting timing."

"Isn't it just," he agreed with a rueful laugh. He waited for her to tell the Goth pixie to send the guy away.

Sophia's gaze shifted to his mouth for just a second, then she pressed her lips together and took a deep breath. He almost cried when the move made the silky black fabric of her blouse accentuate her lush curves.

"Tell him I'll be right there," Sophia instructed.

"What?" he yelped.

She slowly pulled her hand away, as if the wrong move could cause an explosion. Her eyes met his. He saw confusion and fear beneath the still flaming passion in her pale gaze.

Before he could assure her that they'd pick up after she was finished with the security contractor, she blinked. When those lush lashes lifted again, her eyes were veiled. Chilly.

He hated how she did that.

"Reschedule," he said softly, unable to stop the words even

though he knew it was one short step beneath begging. If she walked out, there was a damned good chance he'd have to work twice as hard to get back to this point.

"No." She nodded for Gina to go, then gave Max an indecipherable look. "You're the one who insisted I see him, after all. You might consider this a reward for your good deed."

Passion still raging through his system, Max rocked back on his heels and watched her sweep out of the room. He waited until she got to the door and murmured, "But I haven't done the deed with you, yet, sweetheart."

The hitch in her step was barely noticeable. But he grinned when he saw it.

THREE HOURS AFTER HER confrontation with Max, Sophia could still remember the feel of his mouth on her finger. Hot. Wet. Intense. She'd almost melted at his feet. Hell, she was ready to melt at just remembering how it'd felt. Who needed a pulsing shower massage when just the thought of Max's mouth on her finger got her juices flowing?

She'd barely heard the first investigator's questions, with all that passion still swimming through her head. She'd wanted to shove him out the door, flip the locks and rush back to her office to finish what Max had started.

By the second guy's pitch, she'd gone from meltingly horny to irritatedly frustrated. She'd been so busy inventing creative ways to emasculate Max, she hadn't listened to a word this P.I. had said, either.

By the third she'd found Zen. That peaceful place of acceptance, where she could release the anger and lust. It had been a mistake, but it was only a problem if she let it be. As long as she let all thoughts of Max and sex go, she'd be fine. So she'd spent that investigator's pitch time focusing on meditative breathing and images of ice water.

Pretty much all she remembered from the three meetings was that the men all thought her problems were personal, that they probably tied into her upcoming show and that it'd cost her a lot of money she didn't have for them to stake out her gallery, poke through her files and interview potential suspects.

Reaching her office, Sophia wanted nothing more than to kick off her shoes and relax. Before she'd stepped past the threshold, she knew those were impossible dreams.

Well, there went her freaking Zen.

"What're you still doing here?" she blurted out.

"Waiting for you." Max shifted on her couch, angling one arm along the long tapestry back and patting it in invitation. His smile was all charming welcome.

She wanted to throw something again.

And she was deathly afraid that something was herself, right into his arms.

"This entire time?" No man had ever waited for her.

"Most of it. I did run across the street and order some lunch," he said, pointing at the takeout cartons on the little table by the sofa. "I made some phone calls. I took a nap."

"A nap?" Her eyes drifted to the tasseled pillow leaning against the arm of the sofa, its blue silk invitingly indented. The same pillow she often laid her head on while daydreaming. Schoolgirl giddiness made her want to grab it up and hold it to her chest while she giggled.

He'd slept on her pillow.

Crazy. This situation was crazy, and so was she for not telling him to get off her couch, to leave her office and get the hell out of her life.

He was bossy and domineering. He didn't know how to take no for an answer. He was a man for whom the term chain of command was ingrained, with himself at the top of the chain.

He was the sexiest, most incredible man she'd ever met. He brought her to the edge of an orgasm by nibbling on her finger. Her finger, for crying out loud. And she wanted him like she'd never, ever wanted anyone, *anything,* in her life.

"So?" he asked expectantly, leaning back on the sofa and propping the ankle of one leg on the knee of the other.

Could he read her thoughts? Were they that obvious?

"So…?"

"So are you going to eat with me?" he clarified with a charming smile. "Gina said you were wrapping up, so I picked the food up about five minutes ago. It's still hot."

Sophia stood in the doorway, her eyes huge as she nibbled at her bottom lip.

He had no idea how difficult this choice was for her.

If she agreed, it would be to more than just lunch and they both knew it. How much more wasn't clear. But for her, if she opened the door, she wouldn't be able to resist going through it. Max had so many strikes against him. He was rich and bossy, like her late husband. He was handpicked by her brother, and she tried not to encourage her family's interference. He was sexy as hell, gorgeous and charm personified. And he was a danger to her heart. Where she'd thought Joseph was her Prince Charming, Max was easily a warrior knight.

It was like choosing between the temptation of the frying pan or the fire.

And maybe, just maybe, that's all she needed. After all, if she was the only one who realized they were about to have an incendiary, wildly passionate affair, that put her on top. That, and she could use his guaranteed expiration date—he'd be leaving in a month—to keep herself from doing anything too crazy. Like fall for the guy.

She let her gaze roam Max's gorgeous body as he sat, patiently waiting for her answer. From his tidy, military short hair and his laughing brown eyes to the rock-hard breadth of his shoulders. His long, long legs wrapped so lovingly in worn denim. And—call her silly for buying into all the myths, but oh, yeah, baby—his promisingly large feet.

She had a feeling being on top of Max was going to be one helluva ride.

6

SOPHIA PRESSED HER HAND to her stomach, trying to keep the wildly dancing nerves at bay. She couldn't believe she was actually going on a date. Oh, my God, a date.

She was crazy. She was in no position to date right now. She should be focusing on the gallery and the upcoming show, not wondering if she'd get laid.

Despite that, she hadn't been able to say no when Max had invited her to dinner.

"Yowza, hot stuff."

Halfway down the rickety staircase that led from her tiny apartment to the storage room of the gallery, Sophia grinned at Gina.

"You like?"

She reached the bottom step. Then, a little giddy over the evening ahead, she gave a sweeping turn to show off her dress.

It was black. It was shimmery. It was tiny.

It was perfect. From the barely there rhinestone straps to the subtle sheen of the fabric criss-crossing her breasts, to the cut-to-there handkerchief hem that offered teasing glimpses of her thighs when she moved.

It was a dress that said confident sex.

Sophia wanted to giggle. It felt so good to dress up and feel this good.

Her wardrobe over the past half year had consisted of business casual, exercise gear and jeans. None of which screamed sexy date. With no room in her tiny apartment for most of her belongings, she'd left the bulk of her wardrobe at the estate until Joseph's will was settled. Lynn's lawyers had insisted that Sophia vacate the house while the will was in probate. So she'd cleared it with Olivia and gone to the estate to raid her old closet.

"You look fab," Gina exclaimed. "I've seen you dressed up plenty of times for shows, but never so..."

"Sexy?"

Please.

Sophia held her breath.

"Oh, yeah, definitely sexy. Soldier boy isn't going to know what hit him."

"Perfect." The more shell-shocked Max was, the easier it would be for Sophia to hold the upper hand. Since her agreement the previous day to have dinner with him, all she'd been able to think about was him. His smile. His tight butt. His broad shoulders. His laugh. And most of all, his bossy nature.

Her buzzword of the night: control.

"Are you going to sleep with him?"

"Gina!" she gasped.

Her assistant just arched a brow, then dug into the bib pocket of her overalls. With a smirk, she held out a condom.

"Just in case."

Sophia's mouth worked but no words came out. She didn't even know if she was going to sleep with Max. Yes, she wanted to, but that didn't mean she would. Heat warmed her cheeks, caused, no doubt by her suddenly overworked heart. She couldn't take a condom. It was like holding up a sign that said

Horny Woman, Let's Rock. She'd never been that blatant. She'd always been more the please-sweep-me-off-my-feet type.

"C'mon, Soph."

"But… I don't know if I'm going to sleep with him," she admitted, nibbling the gloss off her lower lip.

"It's not like carrying a condom says, 'Let's screw,'" Gina patiently instructed. "No more than having auto insurance says you're going to drive like an idiot. It's, you know, just in case."

Sophia shook her head. No. This was their first date, so no matter how smart insurance might be, nobody was driving tonight. Before she could say anything, though, there was a knock on the side door.

"That's Max," she said, pressing a hand to her stomach. Then she tasted the sweetness of her lipstick on her teeth, worn off from nibbling on her lip. "I have to fix my face. Can you let him in?"

"Sure." Gina offered an encouraging smile and turned to leave.

"Wait!"

She was the one who wanted to take control of her life. Which meant carrying insurance, dammit. Sophia hurried to catch up with the other woman. Not slowing her pace or looking back, Gina held the condom over her shoulder.

Just because she had no plans to drive didn't mean she might not kick a few tires.

And this way, she was making the decision. Any sweeping would be done by her, thank you very much.

Five minutes later, she joined Max and Gina in the showroom. She almost tripped in her Jimmy Choos at the sight of him.

Madre de Dios, the man was gorgeous. As he was half turned away from her, she took a moment to appreciate how well his black slacks cupped his butt, just visible beneath the sport jacket. At her sigh of appreciation, he turned and offered a welcoming smile. His dress shirt was open at the collar, the deep red almost as dark as his slacks. Her heart stuttered a few times as she tried to regain her composure.

"Hello, Max," she said. "You look wonderful."

"I think that's my line," he said with a laugh, stepping forward to take her hand. She wet her lips, glad that her fingers didn't tremble in his, despite the delicious warmth swirling up her arm. Then he lifted her hand to his lips, pressing a soft kiss against her knuckles. Her insides melted into a gooey puddle of lust. "Sophia, you take my breath away."

She stared into his eyes, the chocolate depths assuring her that he was, indeed, as hooked as she was.

Oh, yeah, she realized, watching that lecture in her brain explode in a puff of smoke. This was definitely about right now. And right now was going to feel damned good.

A half hour later, she and Max were surrounded by more romantic lighting, this time from candlelit tables. Sophia followed their host, painfully aware of Max just a couple of steps behind. Watching her butt, she'd noticed.

Should she walk a little stiffer so he didn't think she was enticing him?

Or should she put a little swing in her hips, and hope that made him a little stiffer?

She noticed women left and right were eyeing him, casting warm looks, and one even tried a little finger wiggle. As if Sophia was blind? Risking a quick glance over her shoulder, Sophia noted the appreciation on his face. Not for the women, whom he clearly didn't notice. Nope, his eyes were firmly fixed on her butt.

Yeah. Swing it was.

"What a lovely restaurant," she said, offering her thanks to the waiter as he seated her. "I've seen reviews in the *Chronicle,* but haven't eaten here before. From what I've heard, though, getting a last-minute reservation is harder than getting elected governor."

Max grinned, taking the wine list from the host, then immediately ordering without looking at it. As soon as the host thanked him and left, Max reached across the burgundy tablecloth to take her hand.

"One of my cousins works here," he admitted, playing with her fingers. "I used the family card."

"Nice," she said, laughing a little breathlessly. His touch reminded her of how he'd made her feel the previous day. Pretending her body wasn't melting in his presence, she glanced around. Eying the staff, she wondered which one was his cousin. Guy or gal? "Isn't it nice when family actually comes in handy?"

"Nice, and rare." She glanced back just in time to see an exhausted sort of resignation flash in his eyes. Since she often felt the same when it came to her relatives, she turned her hand to curl her fingers companionably into his. For the first time since he'd walked in on her and the giant penis, she saw him as more than a sexy pain in her ass.

Was his family as much a stressfest for him as hers was for her? Sophia had spent most of her life on a teeter-totter of love versus resentment with her family. Maybe they had something other than lust in common.

She looked at him, all sexy and strong, with that charming grin and glint in his dark eyes. She sighed, glad she'd been brave enough to come tonight.

"What a great table," she murmured, glancing at the view of the city from the wide plateglass window.

"It's all about connections," he said with a shrug.

"Like your connections were handy yesterday afternoon?" she asked, referring to the private investigators who'd paraded through her gallery.

His grin widened. He tried to hide it by lifting her hand to his lips and pressing a kiss on her knuckles, but Sophia caught it despite the lusty surge swirling through her tummy.

"I thought my connections yesterday were put to pretty

good use," he pointed out, arching one brow as he nibbled at her fingertips.

"I think you wasted those men's time, since I can't hire any of them," she told him.

"I wasn't talking about the investigators."

"You're incorrigible," she said, laughing despite herself. Not sure how to handle this weird combination of desire and amusement, she pulled her fingers from his to play with her fork.

She'd agreed to this date in a fog of lust and she was pretty sure, since he'd insisted they have it this evening, that Max knew that. Despite her sexy fantasies, she hadn't been sure the evening would be much more than stilted small talk, a good dinner and maybe another one of those sexy kisses when he walked her to her door.

But now? Now she was pretty sure her lusty hit-and-run was starting to turn into something more. Something a little deeper, a little scarier. Infatuation, she told herself. Nothing to back away from. She could like the guy, admire him for more than his tight butt and gorgeous eyes and still want to jump his bones, right?

Sophia's breath shuddered a little as she contemplated just how great that jumping was going to feel. From the admiring look in his eyes, the jumping was going to feel incredible for both of them.

"YOU LOOK LIKE YOU'RE contemplating the fate of nations," Max teased, wondering what had put that intense look on Sophia's face.

Her eyes met his. The heated curiosity in those blue depths damn near melted his shorts. It was a look that said maybe. His body responded to maybe with definite hardening. His shoulders straightened. His abs flattened. His dick lengthened.

Slow down, he reminded himself. First-date rules meant his dick wouldn't be getting any play tonight.

He wondered how soon they could have a second date.

"It's not the fate of nations I'm considering," she finally responded with a smile that put his resolve to the test. "Much littler fates, actually."

Well, his fate wasn't little, that was for damned sure. Resisting the urge to tell—or offer to show—her, he smiled instead and cast his brain around for some way to cool things down.

"So your family," he said, grasping for a safe topic. "They aren't involved with your gallery?"

Well, it wasn't an ice bath, but there was definitely a little chill at the table now. Her eyes no longer promising the key to sexual nirvana, Sophia leaned back a ways.

"My family isn't crazy about the gallery," she admitted in a tone that was too casual to hide the hurt underneath.

"They don't approve?"

She hesitated, then shrugged. "Let's just say they felt keeping a distance would keep the peace."

"Because you like to run your business your own way?"

"Oh, wouldn't that be sweet," she said, her words low and reverential, as if she were offering up a prayer.

What did she mean by that? And why did she look so sad?

Before he could ask, their waiter arrived with a basket of bread, a tray of dipping oils and his order pad.

Max leaned forward to resume his interrogation... No, the discussion.

"I love this bread. You can always tell a good restaurant by the quality of their bread, don't you think?" she said before he could voice his question. "Had you discovered it before or was it through your cousin that you found it?"

Bread? Was that the best she could do? Max narrowed his eyes, noting her arched brow and closed look. Change of subject it was, then.

"One of the guys in the paratrooper squad grew up in the

area. On his recommendation, I tried it last year when I was home on leave. My cousin getting a job here was just coincidence. One that worked pretty well," Max admitted, "since it got us reservations."

Her smile warmed him. A reward for following topic directions? She dipped a small piece of bread into the basil oil and made a seductive little humming noise when she tasted it. Max almost groaned. The woman was pure sensuality. He couldn't wait to hear the sound she made when he kissed her. Would she moan? Sigh? Give one of those sexy little growls?

To distract himself, he broke off a piece of bread and asked, "So what'd you think of the investigators? Which one will you hire?"

"I told you already, none of them. I appreciate your trying to help, but I'll take care of the gallery myself. Like you said, the police are investigating."

Irritation simmered in his gut. Was she so stubborn she wouldn't hire a professional? What the hell kind of businesswoman did that? Rico had been right when he'd said she needed looking after.

Then he looked past the proud tilt of her chin and saw the worry in her eyes. Maybe she couldn't afford a P.I., which made him a jerk to keep pushing the subject. He wanted to help her, not make her feel bad.

Thankfully the waiter chose that moment to deliver their meals. Max waited until the plates had been settled and she'd had her first bite.

"If there's anything I can do to help..."

"Thanks. But why don't we talk about something besides my business issues," she suggested with a tight smile.

Max considered. He didn't mind pushing if he thought it'd get him what he wanted. But his goal wasn't to piss Sophia off, or to simply get answers. It was to find out who was behind her vandalism problems. He could do that and stay on her good side.

Starting first thing in the morning, he'd simply become her stand-in P.I. He'd hang out, keep an eye on things. He'd ask questions and figure out who was causing problems. And Sophia wouldn't have a clue. Which meant she wouldn't get pissed.

Although the flying sparks might have been fun. He definitely liked the way she stated her mind. It was damned sexy to have someone strong enough to tell him how she liked it. He wondered if she carried that habit into the bedroom.

And how long it'd take him to find out.

"Sure," Max said agreeably. "So who's von Schilling?"

Sophia fumbled her fork. He winced, glad that the spaghetti didn't slide off the tines and land in her lap.

"What do you know about von Schilling?" she accused, her eyes shimmering with suspicion.

"It depends," he said, slicing one of the huge meatballs into quarters and forking up a bite. "If it's Hans von Schilling the photographer, which would make sense given your gallery, then I know a bit. He rose to fame in the sixties with his show chronicling the seedy side of flower power. He ostensibly retired fifteen years ago, becoming a recluse in the past decade."

The candlelight glistened off her lower lip in a very appealing way as her mouth hung open.

"My parents were contemporaries of his," Max explained. Most boys got their first eyeful of naked women sneaking a peek at their dad's *Playboy* stash. At nine, Max had gotten his at one of von Schilling's shows. The man had a way with the naked lady pictures, Max remembered fondly. "My father more than my mother, I think."

She set her fork down. Probably a good idea since her pasta was looking pretty precarious.

"Nice summary," she acknowledged. "But I meant why would you ask me, specifically, about von Schilling?"

"Because his rep called while I was waiting in your office."

Blue eyes huge with shock, her mouth worked. It took her a few tries to find the words, though. "You answered my phone?"

Forking up another meatball, Max shook his head. "Of course not. I listened to the message he left on your machine."

She tapped those sexy fingers on the table, the move shaking her knife against its neighboring spoon in a gentle medley of irritation. Her eyes narrowed in irritation. Why? He hadn't poked through her drawers. He hadn't answered the phone, even though he had a personal history with the caller. And hadn't he just backed down instead of pushing her to hire someone to patrol her building?

None of that came easy for him. But he was a soldier who knew how to assess a situation. And a man wasn't raised by Tabby St. James without learning a thing or two about biding his time and picking his battles when it came to women. So he ate his spaghetti and waited.

He hadn't eaten more than a mouthful before Sophia had enough of the finger-tapping. She pressed those sexy fingers flat on the cloth and leaned toward him.

He prepared himself for the tirade.

"How would you summarize von Schilling's work?" she asked in the same tone one of his squad mates would use asking how he'd assess a ticking bomb.

Even though he had no clue what was going on, Max set his fork down to give her question the attention it deserved.

"Von Schilling. Brilliant composition, a mastery of mood, quirky humor beneath the edgy realism."

She nodded. The huge smile that curved her mouth was so beautiful, he felt as if he'd been hit upside the head. Max had to lean back in his chair to catch his breath. Damn, she was gorgeous.

"He's my hero," she said enthusiastically. "I've studied his work. He sees the soul through the lens of his camera. His photo essay of the European cities was so evocative, it drove me to study in Paris for a year. That's how I started specializing in candid pictures of faces. Not portraits. Portraits are usually masks. Candids give peeks into the soul."

Her eyes shone with a passion that made him wish he could see her visions. She was amazing. There was passion, yes. And that was a total turn-on. But it was the compassion there that really got to him.

"Why aren't you showing your photos?" he asked. He wasn't an art buff, and he'd only seen a couple of snapshots from her camera view window, but they'd looked good to him.

The question shut her down, though. As if watching someone pull the shades on a sunny day, he could see her enthusiasm dim.

"No. My work isn't show-worthy," she dismissed. "Nothing even close to von Schilling's caliber."

"I'll introduce you," Max offered without a clue how he'd pull it off. The guy lived in a fortress in Santa Cruz, and for all Max knew, he hadn't welcomed visitors in years. Would he even remember an old acquaintance's gawking kid? Didn't matter. Max loved the way her eyes had lit up, and he was going to make it happen for her.

"Thanks, but I don't need an introduction," Sophia replied, chopping his white knight impulse off at the knees. "His rep has called the gallery a few times over the past month. From the sound of it, he's willing to meet anytime."

"You don't sound enthusiastic."

"I'm not. I turned down the meeting." As if talking about it ruined her appetite, she wrinkled her nose and set her fork and knife across the plate.

"Why?" Since his plate was all but licked clean, Max laid down his utensils, too, folded his arms along the edge of the table and leaned forward. "You said he's your hero. From the sound of that message, he obviously wants to work with you. What's the problem?"

Her sigh did lovely things to the glittery fabric of her dress. Max's own sigh was pure appreciation as he watched the candlelight.

"While he's delved into a variety of subjects, he specializes in nudes. Women."

Oh, yeah, he nodded fondly. He'd been totally thrilled to discover just that fact. "I remember."

Sophia gave a little roll of her eyes, shaking her head in typical female pity. But she smiled anyway.

"Since taking over the gallery, I've put all my energies into returning the gallery to its pre-erotic days. A show featuring naked woman in compromising positions would be a step in the wrong direction."

Max shifted to attention. "How long had the gallery focused on erotica?"

"Four years."

"Was that a lucrative focus?"

"Haven't you heard? Sex sells." She leaned closer. Her dress was fitted closely, so it didn't gape, more the pity. It did, however, allow the candle to cast a tempting shadow, one he wanted to trace along the silky curve of her breasts. She gave a vampy flutter of her lashes. "Four-foot marble penises, fornicating copper couples, blown glass cli…" She trailed off with a little wince, then shrugged. "Let's just say there's definitely a market."

He grinned. A woman who'd spent four or so years in a gallery that sold naughty bits blushed when discussing them. She was so sweet.

"And you recently shifted focus?" he clarified. "You let all those artists go?"

"I recently returned focus to the gallery's original, historic objective. To feature the best of California photographs and photographers," she explained. "And we don't hire the artists. We show their work on commission. And yes, I've released all of the pieces as their contracts expired."

Just as he'd thought. She was just too close to see the obvious. You'd think the cops would've caught on, though.

"Did you ever think that's where your vandalism might be coming from?" He shifted, resting his arm along the back of his chair, waiting for her praise and gratitude.

Her hair slid like a heavy black silk curtain, covering one sexy shoulder as she tilted her head to the side. Her smile was a little stiffer now. Embarrassed that he'd figured it out so easily? Reassuring her would probably only add to her discomfort, so he waited.

"Actually, I did think of that," she said. Max frowned. Were they on the same page, then? "Gina and I checked into the artists, and all seem to be doing really well. Nobody was hurt by the decision, nobody has any reason to resent the change."

"You're kidding? Nobody's pissed? No one's holding a grudge?"

A shadow flickered in her eyes for a brief second, then she blinked and it was gone.

"I'm sure whoever is behind the vandalism isn't an artist," she assured him.

Max frowned. He thought she was wrong. But he knew he couldn't convince her without getting her pissed off. And pissing Sophia off would definitely ruin his plans for the rest of the evening.

Max struggled with his need to push, to grab hold of her business situation and fix it for her. He could clearly see the challenge in her eyes. If he pushed, she'd push right back. And not in a sexy, pleasurable way.

His two most vital urges battled. The need to fix a problem versus the need to romance a beautiful woman.

"Dessert?"

Max gave the waiter a grateful smile. Good timing. He had no doubt he'd be able to fix Sophia's business issues. But tonight wasn't about that. Tonight was about the two of them.

The two of them, and dessert.

That's what mattered.

He'd fix all her problems tomorrow.

7

"THANKS FOR THE WONDERFUL evening," Sophia told Max as calmly as she could when he opened the passenger door and held out his hand to help her from the sleek black sports car. She was glad for the help, since her knees felt like jelly.

How did women stand this sexual tension stuff? It was making her a nervous wreck.

"I'm glad you enjoyed dinner," he said as he walked her the half-dozen steps from where he'd parked to the polished oak railing of the staircase leading up to her apartment.

They both glanced up at the well-lit landing, the lush dieffenbachia in a wicker basket glinting softly in the lamplight.

"I'd like to see you again," he said, his hand on her arm preventing her from heading up the stairs.

Was this it? Their date was over? But…she had condoms. They couldn't be done yet.

Sophia stared up into his eyes, the amused charm matching his tone of voice. She flushed, her breath catching in her throat at the look in those dark depths.

Definitely desire. Appreciation, respect, amusement. Nice as those were, it was the desire she focused on.

He made her want. Want pleasure, want satisfaction, want

him. Want it all. She could hear Gina's voice, urging her to grab on for the ride. But for all her yearnings to feel those things with Max, she wasn't sure how to handle this. How to ask him.

A part of her wanted to cry because he'd slowed things down enough that her brain could overrule her hormones. Another part of her, the part that had ruled her life for twenty-five years, was grateful. She needed to be careful. To be cautious. To not humiliate herself.

And given her lack of sexual experience, there was a distinct possibility that humiliation could go hand in hand with the naked tangling she'd been imagining.

Just as well to skip it.

"Actually," she said quietly, "I'm going to be really busy for the next week or so. The gallery has a show this weekend and that and the ensuing sales and work will take up most of my time."

"I'd imagine a show takes a great deal of time and energy." He shifted his gaze from her to glance toward the front of the gallery and he nodded agreeably. "But maybe you'll have a spare hour here or there for drinks or lunch?"

The temptation was overwhelming. The same as when her father had promised her a week in Santa Cruz, sans overprotective brothers, if she graduated magna cum laude. Or when Joseph had offered to let her run the gallery as soon as she received her master's in fine art. But neither man had followed through on their promise. Oh, her father had tried, but Diego had followed her to Santa Cruz anyway. And Joseph? He'd never kept promises.

So she'd be crazy to give in to the temptation to see their relationship as...well, a potential relationship and not just an option for hot and wild sex. Wouldn't she?

He was asking her to continue seeing him. To date. To build a relationship. With a man who, yes, turned her on like crazy, but also challenged what mattered most. Her control. Over herself, over her life.

One night, she might be able to handle.

More than an evening of decadent pleasure? She'd have to be crazy. He was overwhelming, and much too much like the other men in her life for her sanity.

Besides, what if she sucked at the pleasure stuff? All she had to go on was her sex life with Joseph. And if that was any measure, she was severely lacking.

Apparently one of Max's myriad skills was the ability to read faces. Noting the regret on hers, he smiled and shrugged.

"Think about it, okay?" He gave one of those guy head nods that spoke volumes. Acceptance, regret and still that lingering desire. Sophia wanted to throw her purse on the ground, kick her feet and have a tantrum. Dammit, couldn't she have the desire without all the baggage?

"I guess this is good night, then," he said, stepping closer, his hand briefly taking hers before moving up her arm to rest on her shoulder. Hearing the regret in his voice, Sophia felt something inside her shift.

"No," she told him, wetting her lips nervously. Terrified excitement buzzed in her ears. A little light-headed, as if she'd just guzzled a magnum of champagne, she reached out to rub the lapel of his jacket between her fingers.

His smile had a hint of wickedness, at war with the sudden caution in his eyes.

"You don't want me to leave?"

"I want you to come up," she said, as close to innuendo as she could get.

"For a drink?" he clarified, stepping closer. Without thinking, Sophia stepped back, her spine plastering itself to the brick wall of her building.

Sophia swallowed hard, then forced herself to meet his eyes. "For the night."

She knew her words had an effect. She was close enough to feel him suck in a surprised breath as his fingers briefly clenched her shoulders. But his charming smile and that mellow look in his eyes didn't change.

Sophia lifted her chin, promising herself that once she got him upstairs, she'd damn well break that control of his. Even if she had to dance on his face to do it.

"You're asking me upstairs…for the night?"

"Yes." Sensing a little gentlemanly reluctance, she bit her lip and took a chance. Reaching out, she tiptoed her fingers up his chest. Then, her eyes locked on his, she slid her fingernails back down in a teasingly erotic caress.

His eyes narrowed.

"And you're asking me upstairs, specifically, for sex," he said slowly, his blunt terms no doubt meant to shock her into… What? Thinking twice?

Instead, the raw words sent a shaft of heat through her. Sophia pressed her thighs tight against each other, the satiny slide of her hose adding an extra punch of delicious pleasure.

"I'm suggesting we go upstairs and keep our minds open to the myriad of possible…positions—" she paused, running her tongue over her bottom lip "—we might find ourselves in."

His heart pounded against her fingertips.

"And, believe me, it pains me to even ask this, but after we see what comes up, shall we say, you expect me to just walk away?"

Her lips twitched at his innuendo. She tilted her head in question, the sensual caress of her own hair sliding over her oversensitized skin adding another layer of pleasure.

"I'm saying that we have an opportunity to enjoy ourselves. And if you're interested in a short visit, then I'd love to chat." She bit her lip. A part of her wanted to promise to spend his entire leave rolling around together naked. But even though she wanted him like crazy, the two main issues remained.

One, he was undoubtedly bad for her. And two, what if she sucked in bed? She'd rather not see him after sunup if that proved to be the case. Better safe than sorry.

"As for tomorrow," she finally said, "we're both busy. You have family commitments. I have a show coming up that needs all my attention. Why put the pressure of promises on either of us?"

His groan was almost silent, but she felt it anyway and grinned.

"I don't know if I can—"

A quick thrill of panic pushed Sophia right out of her comfort zone and into bold sauciness. She let her hand trail down his rock-hard abs, almost groaning herself at the feel of them, over the leather strip of his belt. Then she cupped her palm over his zipper and grinned at the large bulge pressing against her hand.

"Oh, I definitely think you can."

His laugh was a little breathless, a smidge desperate. It was all Sophia needed to hear. She felt more powerful than she'd ever imagined she could. She could climb mountains. Slay dragons. Blow Sergeant Maximilian St. James right here in the alley leading up to her apartment.

Or better, tempt him up those stairs where he'd show her delights she'd spent years wondering about. Did he do all those sexy things she'd read about? Nibble and lick and touch in the ways she'd dreamed of? Did he go down and did he like it? Would he let her try and would she like it?

It was as if a whole new world was right here, throbbing beneath her fingers. She leaned forward, trapping her hand between his heated length and her own body. On tiptoe, her free hand using his shoulder for balance, she pressed her mouth to his.

His lips parted, soft and welcoming. She licked the full-ness, reveling in his taste. Wine, a hint of chocolate and something deeper, darker and ultimately more tempting that was all Max.

She couldn't let him refuse.

Tossing pride aside, for once not waiting for the guy to make the proper move, she took charge. After a quick, gentle nip at his lower lip, she slipped her tongue along his. Swirling and sliding.

He groaned, both hands sliding down her back to cup her butt. Fingers curved into her cheeks, he pulled her closer, lifted her higher.

Their tongues danced, slow at first. She gently sucked his into her mouth. He gave a low groan, his hands convulsing. He slid one in a gentle sweep up her back, curving his fingers behind her neck, cradling her head gently.

And then he got serious. The kiss went from tentative to intense with the stab of his tongue. They dueled. They danced. They delighted each other into going deeper, into wanting more.

It was a dance in which they both led. She tempted, he teased. She moaned, he laughed. His mouth, his hands, his body. She wanted them all.

Sophia had never felt like this. So sexy, so powerful. God, so ready to come.

Wet and throbbing, she rubbed against his throbbing erection, needing something, anything, to relieve the building pressure. His hand shifted, releasing her butt to gather the filmy fabric of her skirt. His fingers warmed her bare skin above the lacy elastic of her stockings.

Sophia moaned her approval, pressing her hand against his chest for support. She shifted, giving thanks to Pilates as she balanced on one leg, wrapping the other around his hard thigh.

"Upstairs," she breathed against his mouth.

He pulled back to stare at her, then closed his eyes as if he were trying to get a grip on his control. Nope, not what she wanted. Desperate to stay in control, and to get her way, she took his hand in hers, pressing it against her aching breast.

His groan was pure surrender.

She slowly slid her leg down his, making sure her heel grazed all the way down his thigh and calf. He gave a little laugh, the helpless kind that sent a shaft of excitement through her ego. He met her eyes with a dark, intense look that promised her the night of her life.

"You're determined to drive me crazy, aren't you?"

"Yes," she confirmed with a wicked smile.

Still holding his hand, she turned and pulled him up the stairs with her. She could feel the warmth of his gaze on her swinging hips as if it was a physical thing. Her knees trembled. Excitement, she told herself. There was nothing to worry about.

She was calling the shots tonight.

She was barely aware of taking her keys out and opening the door. So ingrained were her manners, she was sure she said something to welcome him to her apartment, but for the life of her, she had no clue what it was.

As soon as he closed the door, she pounced. With the living room illuminated only by the porch light dimly shining through the lace curtains, she grabbed Max by his lapels and steered him toward the couch. Once there, all it took was a gentle push to send him lying flat, his grin glinting in the dark room.

Thankful for her floaty skirt, she straddled his body. Palms flat on his belly, she pressed them up the hard planes of his chest and gripped his solidly muscled shoulders.

"Yum," she murmured as she leaned down to brush a soft, open-mouthed kiss over his chin. "I'll bet you're even tastier than dessert."

"I don't know," he said, his hands sliding up her stockings and under the fluttery handkerchief hem of her dress. Sophia shivered at his touch, his fingers making her thighs tingle with desire. "That was a damned good dessert. You might want to do a lot of tasting to compare."

"I'm a dessert expert," she declared, nibbling down his throat and breathing deeply. God, he smelled good. Hot, spicy male. She breathed deep, noting no cologne. Just a hint of soap, shaving cream and Max himself. Delicious.

His shirt was in the way. With nimble fingers, she unbuttoned the crisp cotton. When she reached his belly—and oh, God, who knew bellies could be that toned?—she tugged the fabric from his slacks. He lifted his torso so she could shove his shirt and jacket off his shoulders. Those incredible abs contracted. Sophia whimpered. His body was a work of art. And she had a great appreciation for art.

She needed to touch. To taste. She waited until he'd tossed his shirt and jacket aside before pouncing.

Her thighs gripping his hips, she nibbled her way down his throat again, flicking her fingers over a nipple. He groaned. She flicked again. She ran her tongue over the other nipple, then scraped her nails gently over his belly.

The feeling was incredible. Free reign to enjoy his body, to let herself do, taste, have, anything she wanted. Power mixed with pleasure, both sending tighter swirls of desire deep between her legs.

His hands gripped her thighs, this time a little rougher. She gasped. What was he going to do? Where would he touch? Her heart pounded in anticipation. He curved his fingers over her butt, then continued the upward motion under her dress to her waist.

Getting the hint, Sophia straightened. She reached across her chest, her arm brushing the already aching tips of her breasts as she unhooked, then lowered the side zipper of her dress. She looked down at him, raising her arms in silent command.

Deliciously obedient, he slid his hands higher, pulling the

fabric over her head and tossing it somewhere in the direction of his shirt.

Sophia slowly lowered her arms. Swallowing her nerves, she pretended she wasn't self-conscious of his gaze on her almost-naked body.

"Oh, sweetheart," he breathed, his fingers skimming a heated trail over her shoulder, down her chest and over the lush curve of her breast to swirl a design around her aching nipple. He blazed the same trail down the other side of her chest, this time brushing the tips of his fingers over her hardening tip. Then with both hands, he cupped her heavy breasts in his palms as if paying homage to their weight. She squirmed, hot desire dampening her panties. The move taunted, tormented and brought a hint of relief to her aching body.

Time to kick this into high gear, she decided.

She shimmied down his body, keeping the delicious pressure of his hard thigh between her legs.

Sprinkling hot, wet kisses over his chest, she slid lower, still. Her teeth scraped over the beautiful definition of his abs. Her hands made quick work of his belt, then the snap of his pants.

The point of no return, she knew. And she also was positive she didn't want any returns. So she shoved his pants and boxers lower. She shifted, reluctantly ungripping his thigh with her own, to push the cloth down farther. With a quick move and talented toes, he kicked off his shoes, pants and socks.

Sophia grinned as he arched a brow.

"Impressive," she complimented.

"You ain't seen nothing yet," he promised.

Her eyes dropped to the huge, glistening length of his erection and she sighed. He was right. But she intended to see, touch, taste and experience it all before the night was over.

"Yum," she said again.

One of his hands curved over her back, the other brushed through her hair as she slid down his body again.

She blew on the tip of his dick, smiling at the mercurial response as it gave a little jump. She swirled her tongue over the head. He groaned. She sucked the velvety tip deep into her mouth.

"Uh-uh," he groaned before she could do much more. "We'll be through before we start if you keep that up."

"Keeping it up is your job, isn't it?" she asked with a naughty look.

He laughed, but still pulled her head away from his.

In a masterful move right out of a movie, he gripped her body and flipped their positions so she lay on the couch, the nubby fabric of the couch rough against her bare back. He loomed over her, his hot gaze scanning her body. Then he gave an appreciative hum of pleasure.

"You're gorgeous."

She'd never been called gorgeous before. It was a heady experience.

"Turnabout tasting time," he said in a husky tone, his intention clear on his face.

Sophia giggled. It was wildly inappropriate and would probably piss him off. But she couldn't help it. But Max grinned, his light laugh as much a turn-on as the hand he snaked down her body as if he was making a test run to see which erogenous zone he wanted to taste first.

His fingers brushed her nipple. Sophia sucked in a breath. Apparently that was all he needed to make his decision. He lowered his head, sucking one aching tip into his mouth. The intense power of his mouth on her body sent her spinning on a wave of desire.

"Your bedroom," he muttered, his mouth sliding lower to her naked belly.

"This is it," she gasped.

He pulled his head back to frown at her, giving the large airy studio a quick glance. "Bed?"

"Couch pulls out," she said, shifting her hips to remind him that there were more important matters at hand.

He blinked as if trying to figure out a problem that just wouldn't compute. Then apparently realizing it didn't matter, he shrugged.

"At least we made it to the bed, then," he said before lowering his mouth again. His tongue snaked down to her belly button. His breath warmed the damp silk of her panties. She lifted her hips for him to pull them off. He just grinned and with a quick snap, ripped the fabric from her body.

Her eyes flew open in shock. Sophia swore she actually came a little. Her body constricted, wet and swollen. Her muscles tensed, even as her thighs fell apart to make room for his shoulders.

She shivered when he slid his hands beneath her hips, his fingers caressing her butt, lifting her higher. Anchoring her elbows for leverage, she lifted her head so it rested on the arm of the sofa. She had to watch him. Had to see, to stay in control.

His dark hair was so short, there was barely any tousled evidence that she'd ran her hands through it as he kissed his way down one thigh and then back up the other.

When he reached the crux of her legs, he glanced up and met her eyes. His were glinted with a hunger she'd never seen before. Desperate, wicked, intense. And all for her.

Holding her eyes, he leaned forward and licked the damp juices coating her swollen bud.

She shuddered, her fingers clenching the rounded strength of his shoulders. It was like grabbing rocks. The muscles were so hard, there was no give. Oh, baby, he had an incredible body.

As if he was making a wish, he blew out a puff of air, his

hot breath on her oversensitized flesh making her gasp. Then, apparently through teasing, he went to town.

He tasted her, his lips creating a delicious torment. Sophia dropped her head back, unable to think anymore with all the wild sensations he was showing her.

Intensifying her pleasure, he smoothed his other hand up her torso in a tingling caress. He cupped her breast, his fingers tweaking her nipple as his mouth drove her higher.

He slipped one finger into her. Then two. His fingers swirled, his tongue sipped.

Light exploding behind her eyes, she mewled her pleasure.

Sucking her swollen, aching bud into his mouth, he nipped gently as his fingers speared in, then out. In, then out.

She exploded in a burst of color and pleasure.

"Oh, God," she moaned over and over, her breath coming in pants that burned her throat. Pleasure pounded at her while lights burst behind her closed eyes. Stars. She swore she actually saw stars.

Max pressed a gentle kiss to the swollen bud he'd just tormented before laying his head on her belly and wrapping his arms around her hips in a hug that was both sexy and affectionate at the same time.

Her insides all melted together in a puddle of mind-blowing pleasure, she forced herself to move. This might be the only night she got with Max. She was going to make damned sure it was incredible.

For both of them.

Sliding her legs from under him, she shifted into a sitting position. His eyes heavy with desire, Max fell to the couch in the space she'd left, grabbing her hand to make sure she didn't go far. Lying there on his side, his head propped on his fist, he shook his head in protest.

"Come back," he murmured.

Her eyes traced the hard, delicious length of his body. From his sexy feet—when the hell had feet become sexy?—to the light dusting of hair on his muscled thighs. She swallowed hard when her eyes rested on his jutting erection. That marble statue had nothing on Max. Pure male perfection. She wanted to touch him, taste him again.

She forced her eyes to continue their journey up the drool-worthy planes of his six-pack to the hard span of his chest.

"You're perfect," she said, repeating the compliment back to him. And he was. His body was a work of art. A part of her wished for her camera to preserve this moment. To take it out later to savor. She wanted to know if his beauty was real, if this pleasure was as immense as her mind, and her body, were telling her.

She met his gaze and the need to analyze disappeared. For the first time in her life, she felt like she could trust her own eyes.

"Sophia?"

He sounded so sweet, so concerned. As if he'd picked up on every one of her fears and wanted to put them at ease. As if her emotional needs were just as important as her physical pleasure.

She handed over a tiny piece of her heart in that moment.

Insane. She knew better. She knew he couldn't be a part of her future.

But he was a part of her right now. And she had to believe that their lovemaking would only be that much better for a little love added to it.

Sophia gave him a reassuring smile and stood, crooking her finger to indicate he join her. His sigh was barely perceptible, but his smile didn't waver as he stood to join her.

"We're going to want a lot of room for this," she told him, quickly tossing the cushions aside so she could pull out the sofa bed. As soon as it was open, he grabbed her around the waist and pulled her down.

"Nice," he murmured. He pressed a kiss to her shoulder when they hit the mattress. She smiled and settled into the soft down ticking. She might have to sleep on a sofa bed, but she'd be damned if she'd be uncomfortable.

She'd stolen the feather topper off her bed at the estate.

And while soft was always a good thing, hard was even better. And she wanted Max's hard body beneath her.

With that in mind, she shifted, pressing her hands to his shoulders so he lay flat, his body tan against the pristine white of the sheets.

"Condom," he reminded her as she straddled him.

She reached over, the tip of her breast grazing his chest and sending another zing of pleasure through her as she grabbed her purse from the sofa table. Wasting no moves, she pulled one of the condoms Gina had given her from the tiny case, ripped it open and smoothed it over the hard, tempting length of his erection.

"Now," she told him.

Ranging herself up on her knees, she poised over his body. Needing to prove she could, she waited. One second, then two. Max curved his hands over her thighs, then with a little smile snapped the lace of the stockings she still wore.

She gave him what he wanted. What they both wanted. Slowly, as deliciously slow as she could, she lowered herself onto his straining erection. Hot and wet, she slid down in one swift, easy move.

"Mmm," she moaned. Riding him like the stud he was, she focused on the building pleasure. Each thrust was met with an undulating welcome. God, he felt good.

Pressure built. Passion intensified, an edgy cloud of excitement washing over her. Every fear she'd ever harbored about her sexuality vaporized as she felt the power of Max's desire for her.

Needing more, wanting it all, she took his hands and

pressed them to her aching breasts. His fingers teased, tormented, sending them both higher.

She thrust deeper, her inner walls gripping his dick as if she could milk every drop of pleasure from him.

Max groaned, his body convulsing beneath her. His fingers dug into the soft flesh of her ass. The intensity of his climax destroyed the last of Sophia's control. She threw back her head, her orgasm exploding through her. Panting, mewling and shuddering, she felt the pleasure in every atom of her being.

Spent and exhausted, she dropped. Her thighs slid flat against the mattress as her head hit his chest.

"You're right," he said eventually, his words a little breathless rumble against her ear.

"Right?" She didn't even know where she'd found the energy to speak. She was wrung empty.

"That was better than dessert."

She laughed, a soft giggle of delight, as she curled into his arms and drifted off to sleep, feeling smug and happy. She'd not only had the best sex of her life, she'd proved that she could have it, stay in control and still make the guy smile like he'd won the world's greatest orgasm sweepstakes.

It was only temporary, but it felt pretty damned good.

8

"WAIT A MINUTE," MAX said, his jacket in one hand, a cooling piece of toast in the other. "What's the deal?"

He'd been lucky to get his damn slacks zipped before Sophia had started making shooing motions to push him toward the front door.

"I have a crazy day and really need to get started," she was saying, looking a little crazy herself. Her hair had that wild, sex-all-night look going and her bare face was gorgeous in the morning light. But the look in her eyes was edgy. Determined. He could have handled that. But underneath was a hint of vulnerability that he wasn't sure what to do with.

So he let her herd him toward the door.

"I'll pick you up for dinner around six," he told her, leaning in for a kiss.

Her lips went soft and sweet under his. His hands were full, but he angled his body to trap her between him and the wall. She felt so damn good.

Then she pulled her mouth from his and slid free.

"Dinner? Um, no. I'm supposed to be getting a shipment in this evening. With the show next weekend, I'm going to be really busy."

His ego refused to believe she was giving him the brush-off. They'd been too good together. So she was afraid of something. Max narrowed his eyes. "Really busy, huh?"

She dropped her gaze and nodded. Then she flipped the locks and opened the front door. "I had a great time last night, though."

A lesser man might doubt those words in the face of the bum's rush she was giving him. But Max knew she'd enjoyed every second of their lovemaking.

"What's the deal?" he asked.

She sucked on her bottom lip. He almost groaned. Then she shrugged and gave him what he guessed was supposed to be a tough look. "I had fun, Max. A lot of fun. But you're a guaranteed distraction. I need to focus, okay? Why don't I call you when things shake loose?"

Max frowned. Her decision would give him the space to deal with his mother's mile-long to-do list, and for a little investigating into the gallery's issues. But that wouldn't take much time, especially not at night.

Still, he let her push him out the door. Then he planted one more kiss on her, watching her melt against the doorjamb.

"Pretty sure that's supposed to be my line, sweetheart," he told her, grinning as she tried to focus through the haze of desire blurring her eyes. Yeah, she might be doing the pushing, but he was the one in control. "That means I'll need to come up with a different one. I'll let you know what it is."

FIVE DAYS AND SIX VERY long, restless nights later, Sophia pressed her hand to her stomach, trying to calm the wildly dancing butterflies. Her first show as sole proprietor of Esprit de l'Art was in half an hour and she wanted to throw up.

What a week. Between trying to garner any form of publicity, and handling the caterers and the artists, she'd wondered at times if she'd pull it off. Preparation for the show had been crazy.

Just crazy enough to keep her from obsessing over Max

Her thighs trembled, the tiny bud between them throbbing in remembered pleasure.

Every freaking time she thought of the man, her body went into a sexual meltdown. She had to get hold of herself. She rolled her eyes, remembering that getting hold of herself the night before in an attempt to relieve a little tension obviously hadn't dulled her desire.

It was a testament to her control that she'd managed to keep herself from diving for a phone and dialing Max's number.

She paced the length of her office to try to shake off a little anxiety. Show nerves, she assured herself. The simmering doubts had nothing to do with her pushing Max away.

Sure, maybe she was a little surprised that he'd backed off. After all, that'd been some pretty incredible sex, if she did say so herself. Explosively hot, orgasmically wild. And she'd offered him some toast, a bowl of fruit and a goodbye wave the next morning. She'd been afraid if she'd taken the time to scramble an egg, she'd have begged him to stay and take over her life.

But you'd think he'd have argued over his dismissal. Tried to change her mind. Maybe called a few times or dropped in to convince her to go another round of pleasure.

But had he? She barely restrained herself from kicking the couch in frustration. Nope, he'd done exactly what she wanted. Left her alone.

"The caterers are all set and the string ensemble arc tuning up. You ready?" Gina asked from the doorway. Dressed in her version of conservative, black Doc Martens, a knee-length black tulle ballet skirt and a black leather corset, the other woman was bouncing on her toes.

"Sure. You okay? You seem a little nervous," Sophia said, her own anxiety tripling when she saw the unflappable Gina all on edge.

Maybe she should have worn black, too? Or in keeping with the black-and-white theme of the photographs being shown tonight, white to contrast with her assistant? She smoothed the rich red jacquard of her sheath nervously then grabbed her camera and joined the other woman in the hall. She couldn't wait to make a photo record of this evening.

"Anticipating," Gina corrected, adjusting her rhinestone-embellished glasses with a twitch of her finger. "I mean, we're shooting for a higher class of clientele tonight. Before, all I had to worry about was someone cornering me in the hallway and trying to cop a feel so he could compare me with one of the sculptures of naked lady bits."

Some of her own nerves melting in amusement, Sophia laughed.

"Oh, yeah, I had a few of those myself. Joseph always thought it was a great joke," she recalled, wrinkling her nose at the memory. Her late husband had never gone for the knight in shining armor persona. Instead he'd chide her if she was too abrupt in slapping down the idiots who hit on her. After all, he'd claimed, it was bad form to discourage sales. Not that he'd have used his wife to make a sale. He hadn't been slimy. Just oblivious.

Unlike Max, who was so hyperaware of her every mood, it was as if he was linked into her brain. She shivered as she remembered waking in the middle of the night wrapped in Max's arms, feeling sore and a little sticky. Just as the fantasy of her, Max and a bath flashed through her mind, he'd murmured a naughty suggestion that'd included bubbles, a shower massage and his tongue.

Max was anything but oblivious.

"Soph?"

Sophia forced herself to focus on now. She could obsess over Max and his magic mouth later.

"I knew how to handle the jerks and their innuendos. But this—" Gina waved her hand at the caterers arranging canapés on silver trays in the smaller showroom "—this is fancy.

These people will want to talk art. The subtleties of lighting instead of fornication. Creative vision instead of fellatio."

"Color and composition instead of methodologies of ménage a trois?" Sophia asked, snapping a picture while Gina's nervousness drained into laughter.

"Yes," Gina giggled, still bouncing. A second later, her giggles ceased and she winced. "What if I mess something up, Soph? Are you sure you wouldn't rather one of the part-timers fill in? I can keep things smooth in the background and Danny can assist tonight."

Danny was an art student and the gallery's part-time employee. "I don't need an expert tonight, Gina. I need a friend. You'll do great. Bring any technical questions to me if you have to, but I'm sure you can handle anything that comes your way."

At first Gina just stared, her eyes buggy behind those crazy glasses. Then, with a deep breath, she tucked a stray hair, orange tonight, into her black velvet headband and finally nodded.

With a deep breath of her own, and one last fleeting thought to how nice it'd be if Max were there with her, Sophia pulled back her shoulders and led the way to the front showroom.

An hour later, her nerves were a thing of the past. They'd drowned in misery and despair. She'd been right about Gina being able to handle any questions. Where's the sexy stuff? and Is this crap really fish eggs? were about the toughest queries of the night.

She'd thought she saw Max at one point, just catching a glimpse of broad shoulders and a sexy butt, but she'd obviously been mistaken. If he'd been there, he'd have said something to her.

"Danny wants to know if he should go home," Gina whispered. "I told him to wait another hour, things are bound to pick up after eight."

Sophia's shoulders slumped. Given that staff and catering

outnumbered guests four to one, cutting Danny loose was probably smart. No point paying wages when she wasn't going to be making any money.

"I don't get it," she said, not even attempting to lower her voice. Why bother? She and Gina were the only ones other than the musicians in the main showroom. "I mean, I know we didn't have much press. But still, there should be more guests. We've had this show planned for months. We sent mailings, we put an ad in the art section of the paper. We've had spur-of-the-moment, completely unpromoted shows that were better attended than this."

"Do you think it's the changes?" Gina ventured.

It took all of Sophia's willpower to keep her lower lip from drooping. She didn't want it to be. Dammit, this show was supposed to be a validation.

"I used the mailing list and contacts from when we bought the gallery. I edited our current list, targeting people who'd bought non-penis-focused art at any point. I…" She trailed off, throwing her hands in the air. Frustration wound so tight in her belly, she felt like screaming. She paced the room. "I did everything I could think of."

"Maybe you just need to accept that there's nothing else you could have done," Gina consoled.

Accept it? Wasn't it enough that she had no control over her finances, over her life, over her freaking out-of-control lusting thoughts of Max? Now she was supposed to accept that she had no control over the gallery, too?

Screw that.

Before she could dig into a full-blown temper tantrum, a large limousine pulled up to the curb out front. As if it were a flagship of some kind, another half dozen cars followed, all pulling around the side to the parking lot.

Sophia had spent her married years learning to live with money, so she had no problem recognizing it when it came waltzing through her front doors.

"Holy cannoli," Gina breathed. "It's like the cavalry just arrived decked out in diamonds and fur."

And credit cards. Sophia almost cried, she was so excited.

"Do the rounds, make sure the caterer serves fresh food and have the musicians play a little softer until everyone gets comfortable," she ordered. Shoulders back, she plastered on her most persuasive smile and strode forward to greet her rescuers.

Five minutes later, she wanted to dance through the showroom. There were at least two dozen people here now. Many she recognized as patrons who'd visited during the gallery's nonerotic heyday. Not nearly as large a crowd that attended Esprit's recent shows, but better than the single person who'd come through the previous hour.

Ten minutes later, she was more confused than giddy.

"Any interest?" she asked Gina quietly as they passed through the archway between the large and small showrooms.

"A lot of looky-loos, but no bites."

Sophia licked her lips, looked at the crowd and puffed out a breath. Then she forced herself to ask, "Are they saying anything...well, weird?"

Gina frowned.

"Compared to offers to paint my breasts in dayglo? Nope. One thing's kinda funny, though," she said slowly. "They all seem to know—"

"Max," Sophia said at the same time Gina did.

As if their duet were an incantation, he suddenly appeared in the doorway. Dressed in a dark suit, a black open-necked dress shirt and a sexy smile, he looked gorgeous.

"How'd he know we were sucking?" Gina wondered.

Maybe she really had seen him earlier. Brows furrowing, Sophia gestured for Gina to do the rounds, then strode forward to meet her questionable fairy godfather.

"Max." She'd greeted everyone else with a handshake, but she was afraid she'd melt into a puddle of lust at his touch. So she kept her hands, with her palms itching to feel him, at her sides.

"Sophia," he greeted in equal gravity, humor lurking in his dark eyes.

Despite his friendly ease, she could feel the desire pouring off him in waves. She'd never had a man want her like Max did. Never felt so feminine and sexy and wanted. It was like being in an explosion of hot need. She couldn't think of anything better than giving in to that need.

"I didn't expect to see you here," she murmured, barely aware of what she said. As long as it wasn't *Please strip naked so I can straddle your body* it probably didn't matter.

"I wanted to make sure everything came together for you."

All she heard was making sure she came. She was sure that wasn't what he'd actually said, though.

"I beg your pardon?"

"The show," he said, stepping a little closer. Sophia breathed deep his warm scent. "I wanted to be here to see a gallery show, to make sure everything went okay. And I wanted to see you and didn't figure you'd toss me out of a public event."

His smile was pure charm. His eyes were pure heat. His body, wrapped in a black suit, was pure temptation.

Then his words finally sank in.

"Why wouldn't everything go okay?" she asked, starting to frown.

As if sensing the change in her, Max tilted his head and waited. Probably all that bomb training had given him ultra-sensitive perceptive powers.

"Why do all these people seem to know you?" she asked slowly, trying to fit all the puzzle pieces together. "Did you come by earlier?"

"Don't you think I'd have said hello if I had?" he side-stepped.

She narrowed her eyes. "And these people?"

"They look like they're enjoying the photos," he mused, glancing at the people milling about. He nodded to a couple negotiating with Gina, who was bouncing on her toes again. "And buying."

"What's going on?" Sophia demanded. "Did you have anything to do with our sudden rush of patrons?"

Max gave her a long look. She'd seen that look before. It was one of those how-much-does-she-really-need-to-know looks. Her father used that look. All of her brothers used that look. Joseph hadn't even bothered with that look after the first year of their marriage.

Anger churned in Sophia's belly, masking the lust. Oh, the lust was still there. She couldn't be within five feet of Max without wanting to see him naked. But now she had an overwhelming urge to throw things at him. While he was naked.

"Actually I might have had a little to do with it. I had to escort my mother to a country club dinner this evening and mentioned the show to a few people," he explained with a shrug. "It looks like they were interested, huh?"

"You just happened to mention it?" she asked, her frown fading to a furrow between her brows.

"Yeah. I thought I'd seen a lot of their names on your mailing list when I was hanging out in your office last week," he said, grinning when she narrowed her eyes again at his admission of snooping. "I don't get why they seemed clueless about the show, but I figured you'd wanted them here and I could give them a nudge to attend."

"I sent invitations. Unless they all moved without a forwarding address, they shouldn't be clueless."

He shook his head. "Nobody I spoke with had received an invitation."

Nonplussed, she just stared. She wasn't used to men actually explaining their motivations.

The anger was still there. But now it was scattered, with no specific focus. What had happened to the invitations she'd sent, then? Was it only the high society segment of her mailing list that hadn't received them? Or everyone?

"Mrs. Castillo?"

Sophia reluctantly tore her gaze from Max's, took a deep breath and turned to face the caterer.

"Yes, Becca?" Forcing herself to focus, her frown deepened. The usually unflappable blond caterer looked as if she wanted to cry.

"Um, we have a little problem."

Sophia gave Max a look, but he didn't move away. She took Becca's arm and pulled her to the side. Max followed. She didn't bother rolling her eyes.

"What's wrong?"

"I was doing rounds with the canapés and Juliet was bringing in ice from the truck. We were doing our jobs. We weren't being lax or careless or anything," Becca insisted, blinking back tears.

Sophia's stomach slid into the toes of her pumps. "And?"

"Someone got into the food. They dumped the crackers into the shrimp, poured the chocolate syrup over the ham bites and the stuffed mushrooms are floating in the ice chest filled with all the champagne."

It took Sophia a solid five seconds to decipher her words. Since they were said in such a rush, they all tumbled over themselves.

It took her another five to blink the black mist of panic from her eyes.

"All the food?"

"And the champagne," Becca confirmed, a tear tracking down her cheek.

A quick glance confirmed that her gallery was still filled

with fancy dressed patrons with no-limit credit cards and a taste for being served champagne and shrimp.

It was all she could do not to start crying along with Becca. Sophia puffed out a breath and without thinking about it, slid her gaze to Max.

His frown was a scary thing. It was also oddly reassuring. As if it gave her permission to be pissed instead of bawling like a baby deprived of its binky.

With the anger came clear thinking. She had a gallery full of rich people whose money she wanted. To get that money, she had to make them feel relaxed and happy. Which meant feeding them.

"Becca, is there any food left in your van? Any more champagne? Or wine? Or soda even?"

"A couple bottles of champagne, a brick of cheese but no crackers, a tray of veggies and some petit fours left over from the baby shower we catered this afternoon." The blonde hesitated, then added, "We still have a box of the penis pops and some frozen soft pretzel busts from the last show."

Sophia grimaced and shook her head.

Despite growing up in the kitchen of her father's restaurant, Sophia's cooking expertise started and ended with canned soup, bagged salad and microwavable meals.

"I'll run across the street to the cantina," Max offered. "Send around the veggies, cakes and champagne while I get some appetizer trays ordered."

Becca's wince made it clear her catering menu wasn't geared toward Mexican finger food, but she nodded and hurried out of the room.

Torn between independence and the need to salvage the evening, Sophia hesitated. Then, realizing she was being an idiot, she laid her hand on his arm. "Thank you."

His smile was slow and melting. He lifted her hand, brushed a kiss over her knuckles and murmured, "You can thank me later."

Oh, baby! It took her thirty seconds to catch her breath and force her legs to move. She did her hostess gig, charming her way through the crowd and enjoying every second of what was—thanks to Max—shaping up to be a fabulous show. Within a quarter of an hour, Becca's staff was circulating with appetizers—because really, nobody could call empanadas an hors d'oeuvre—trays. Sophia watched anxiously, but everyone who tried it seemed to enjoy the food.

And then Max was back at her side and the last of her tension seeped from her shoulders and spine.

"Hi," she murmured, smiling up at him. "Do you do this knight-in-shining-armor role very often?"

"Do you like it?" he asked softly, reaching out to rub his index finger over her shoulder. Such a simple move melted her insides.

"Sophia?"

She reluctantly pulled her gaze from Max's. "Yes, Danny?"

"There's a customer who'd like to speak with you about the Redwood series."

"I'll be right there." She looked back at Max, relieved to see him already nodding.

"Go make a sale," he said. "I'll work the room."

Grateful for his help and his support, she smiled. Then, knowing what she was offering, she stepped closer and brushed her lips, just a tiny kiss, against his. "Thanks."

Sophia was halfway to the hall when she heard the scream.

A bony, lace-encased woman wearing enough diamonds to buy a small country screamed again, falling onto the velvet settee and drawing her knees up to her chest.

Sophia ran forward, Max right beside her. Gina came scurrying toward them, one hand holding a sales receipt, her other covering her mouth and nose.

Before they could ask her what happened, the room gushed

people. They just sort of poured out, hands over mouths and nose as they rushed for the door.

The front door. Escaping.

"No," Sophia moaned, reaching out as if she could grab them all back. Or at least their credit cards.

Shoulders sagging, she arched a brow at Gina.

"Skunk" was Gina's muffled response.

Sophia would have dropped to the floor if Max hadn't leaned in and wrapped his arm around her shoulders.

"How the hell..."

Max's growl worked as well as if he'd taken her by the shoulders and shaken her. Sophia battled back the panic, sucked in a breath and tried to remember the rules of control. She was pretty sure *do something* was somewhere on the list.

"Gina, see if anyone's left in the gallery and, if so, try and charm them into buying something."

"What're you going to do?" Gina mumbled from behind her hand.

Sophia wrinkled her nose. "The skunk didn't spray, did it? I don't smell anything."

"Not yet."

"Then I'm going to get it out before it does something to ruin the upholstery."

"I can take care of this, Sophia," Max offered, his hand on her shoulder as if he was trying to steer her in the opposite direction as the skunk.

"It's my gallery," was all Sophia said.

As she'd expected, Max stayed at her side as they crossed under the arch and into the smaller showroom. Despite her expectations, though, he didn't try to push her aside and take over.

He didn't have to. She skidded to a halt in the doorway.

It was a disaster. Broken champagne glasses, food all over

the floor, one of the huge ficus plants overturned and dirt scattered everywhere.

Sitting there, in the middle of her red plush velvet settee with rosewood trim was a very large skunk, eating a canapé.

"Shit," Max breathed, taking in the mess with a quick look before wrapping one arm around her and pulling her close. His arms were safe, secure. She turned into him. His chest a warm haven.

The sweet move almost melted her heart.

For just a second, Sophia let herself be weak. She let him hold her, drew in his strength as if it had healing powers.

All she wanted to do was lean in. To let him take over. Obviously she was doing a lousy job of things, so why not hand over the reins.

"Soph?"

Defeated, Sophia glanced around Max's shoulder with dull eyes.

"Everybody left," Gina said quietly. "I called animal control to pick up the skunk."

"I need a break," Sophia murmured, pulling out of Max's arms. She instantly wanted to burrow back again and hide.

She glanced at the mess again and winced. Yeah, she definitely needed a break. Maybe a long one.

Shaking her head at Gina's questioning look, she slowly made her way back to her office and shut the door. She didn't even have the energy to turn the lock. Instead, the two steps feeling like two miles, she walked over to the couch and collapsed.

God, what a disaster.

MAX FINISHED HIS INSPECTION of the gallery. He'd talked to everyone, from the catering crew to Gina to the crowd at the cantina across the street to see if anyone had seen anything. Nada.

He checked with Jorge, the cantina busboy he'd hired last Wednesday to watch the gallery when he couldn't. Jorge had seen a motorcycle drive by and pause in front of the gallery, but it hadn't parked. Max remembered seeing a motorcycle the day he'd first met Sophia, the day the gallery had been trashed. He'd bet it was the same bike.

But other than Danny, who'd seen a guy with dark hair dressed in a catering jacket—in contrast to Becca's assistants, who were all women—there wasn't much else to go on.

He didn't need much to know that this was a personal vendetta against Sophia, though. And he was going to make sure whatever it was stopped.

But first he had to make sure Sophia was okay. He headed for her office. A year of watching untold degrees of pain, suffering and misery had molded a hard shell around his heart. He needed that shell. And damn if he didn't feel it melting away a little at the sight of her sitting at her desk. With her head in her hands and the luxurious curtain of silky black hair falling over her face, she looked defeated.

"Sophia?" he said quietly, afraid if he crossed the threshold he'd push her over the edge.

She shifted so her fists supported her chin instead of her forehead. Her eyes drooped a little at the sides, matching the heaviness of her mouth. It physically hurt to see her so unhappy.

He wanted to take care of her. He wanted to wrap her in his arms, tuck her away someplace quiet and fix this mess so she could get back to making her dream come true.

Rico would have applauded that idea. Hell, he'd practically said as much in the email Max had received that morning.

Sophia's independent streak is a PITA, amigo. It's easier to work around her, keep her distracted while you do the heavy lifting. She's not much muscle-wise and needs someone to take care of her.

Max was pretty sure that Sophia would take her not-much muscles and use them to kick her brother's ass if she ever read that email.

And his if he tried that kind of crap on her. So instead of doing the end run he'd prefer, Max steeled his heart and forced himself to add to her stress load.

"The cops are here," he said.

"Can you deal with them?" she asked quietly. "I'm really not up to it."

He almost turned heel to do just that, then stopped. She'd damn near ripped his head off when he'd tried to deal with her business last week. He thought of Rico's note again and with a sigh shook his head.

"It's your place," he told her. "You're the one in charge. Not me."

Her shrug said she didn't give a damn.

Max's frown intensified.

"You're not going to let them win, are you?" he asked quietly, needing to see something out of her besides defeat. God, where was her anger, her fighting spirit? She couldn't have used it all up on him.

"Them?"

"Someone's screwing with you. Deliberately trying to run you out of business." He glanced around the office, inwardly winced because he knew he was risking the best sex he'd ever had, and said, "Are you going to give up on the gallery the same as you bailed on your photography? Don't you have any guts? Or are you, what's the term Rico uses? *El pollo loco?*"

Her eyes narrowed.

"A crazy chicken? You think I'm bailing?" Her voice hitched. "You think just because my big brother appointed you my protector, suddenly you're the expert on my life?"

"Nope." He tucked his hands in his pockets and rocked back on his heels, forcing himself not to smile. "I'm the guy who thought you were a savvy businesswoman who knew what she wanted and had a plan to get it. But then, maybe I was wrong."

Her jaw worked. Her eyes sizzled. Lust speared through Max like lightning. He wondered how long they had before the cops came back here looking for her. Probably not long enough for what his body was craving.

She shoved away from the desk so hard her chair hit the wall. Fists clenched at the sides of her pretty red dress, she stomped around the desk.

Definitely not enough time to soothe her out of her tantrum. He was treading on thin ice but he couldn't stop his grin.

"I'll deal with you later," she said with a glare as she swept around him, all princess to peasant. "After I've spoken with the police."

"I can't wait," he murmured, watching the delicious swing of her hips as she stormed off. Then he rescued her chair and settled in behind her desk.

But he was the one who'd be dealing. Only it'd be some comfort and soothing. And, once Sophia was feeling less stressed and upset, maybe they could find other ways to relax.

Max thought of the bag he'd left in the backseat of his car. Bubble bath, candles, the docking station for his iPod. All he needed to set a soothing scene.

And in the meantime? Time to do a little investigating. Starting by poking through the gallery's files.

9

HER BODY WARM, LAX AND well-loved, Sophia slowly made her way to the surface of consciousness. She tingled all over. While she was finishing with the police, Max had talked Gina into letting him into her apartment, where he had filled her bathroom with candlelight, music and hot, frothy bubbles. Then he'd seduced her into forgetting all her woes.

Eyes still closed, she sighed and stretched. She didn't get far. Her toes skimmed a hair-dusted leg and her butt wiggled against a very hard male body.

She gave a sleepy frown, her fingers tracing the arm that lay across her waist. The hand at the end of that arm slid up, cupping the heavy warmth of her breast.

Her frown faded as the fingers worked magic on the tip of her breast. Swirling, tweaking, flicking. She gasped. Heat swept down her body, pooling wet and sticky between her legs.

She shifted her hips, smiling at the hard length of desire pressing against her. She wasn't the only one feeling the love here.

Her hair was swept aside.

She clenched her thighs, all her girly bits trembling at the sensation. Who knew the back of the neck was an erogenous zone? Then again, who knew there was a direct line to her G-spot when Max touched her?

"Mmm, I feel good," she said in a sleepy murmur. She loved what he was doing, but needed more. She wanted to play, too. Sophia turned in his arms, giving Max a warm smile and practically purred. "I really like your plan for working off stress."

"Bottled-up stress is a health hazard," Max assured her, his mouth tracing whisper soft kisses along her jaw and down the sensitive skin of her throat. "You need to release it before it causes problems."

"You definitely offered a lot of releases last night," she said with a breathless laugh.

"You up for another?" he asked. His smile said sex, but his sleep-rumpled cuteness made her want to hug him close and giggle. He was just…amazing.

His mouth moved lower so his soft kisses were now focused on the tips of her breast. She heard the rustle of foil, then felt his fingers warm between her legs. Testing, teasing, readying her for the ride.

Before she could do more than sigh with pleasure, he slid into her. Gentle and sweet, just like the kisses warming her throat. Sophia's breath shuddered as they rocked together. Max shifted so his eyes could hold hers. She wanted to blink, to look away, but knew he'd stop the delicious dance if she did. While he'd happily do anything, absolutely anything, she wanted, Max insisted on real intimacy with their lovemaking. It added a scary layer of tenderness and honesty to the passion.

He shifted higher. She wrapped her legs around his waist, resting her weight on her arms as he rose to his knees and stared down at her body. For a brief second, he dropped his eyes to watch their bodies slide together. Sophia followed his gaze. Four years of erotic exposure had taught her that she was a bit of a prude, so she expected to have to hide her ick reaction. Instead, though, the sight of their bodies joining made her gasp.

Sexy, hot, intense. Her heart pounded. Passion intensified. Her eyes met Max's again. His hands gripped the soft flesh of her butt, holding her in place as he pumped, in and out. The heat intensified, swirling tighter. Her body tensed. His eyes darkened.

She panted, her entire being focused on reaching higher. Climbing. Grasping. Her eyes glazed, her brain shut off as her body took over. Max plunged. Sophia exploded.

The climax was so strong, so wild, it shook her whole body. She shuddered, her thighs squeezing tight. Max tensed. She forced her eyes open, needing to see him fall over the edge. Deeper. Harder. Over and over. Then, his head thrown back, he came with a loud growl of delight. His climax sent Sophia over the edge once again.

Oh, yeah. He was definitely amazing.

Ten minutes later, sated and starving, Sophia wrapped herself in one of the blankets they'd kicked to the floor and headed for the kitchen.

"Toast, dry cereal or toaster waffles?" she asked as she skirted around the short counter that separated the kitchen from the rest of the apartment.

"Breakfast of Champions," he teased.

Her shoulders tightened and her stomach tightened. Self-doubts she'd worked hard to overcome suddenly wagged their judging fingers. She should have good food to offer a guest. She should have man food. She should know how to cook it, or at least have thought to get up and have it delivered.

An apology on her lips, Sophia glanced back at Max, who hadn't bothered with a blanket, but lounged on the bed, half sitting with his arms behind his head and with a look of total satisfaction on his face.

That was not a man who was looking for an apology. Unable to help herself, she grabbed her camera off the counter and snapped a picture before Max could react.

"I also have fat-free yogurt, a spotty banana and some leftover chocolate cake," she offered with a grin.

He gave a good-natured grimace.

"Sweetheart, I spent the past year on MREs—meals ready-to-eat. I'm not picky. If you want a fancy breakfast, we can get dressed and I'll take you out," he offered. "Or we can stay naked and lick toast crumbs off each other. Totally your call."

She wordlessly dropped bread in the toaster. Then, feeling adventurous—who wouldn't after eight, count 'em, baby, orgasms and a whole new understanding of the number sixty-nine—she scooped yogurt into two bowls and sliced the banana over them. She opened the cupboard and pulled out a can of almonds and sprinkled a few over the bananas.

"This'd probably be better if I'd chopped the almonds," she told Max as she loaded the bowls and toasted bread onto the tray she usually ate dinner on. "But I don't have a sharp knife."

He shifted so she could set the tray in the middle of the bed. "Can I ask a personal question?" he asked around a mouthful of toast.

"You had me bent over the bathroom sink last night," Sophia teased, spooning up some yogurt. "I think we're way beyond personal, don't you think?"

"Why do you live so spartanly? You have a low-end apartment furnished with less than most college kids move out with, and a ten-year-old car."

Her teasing smile fell away. Sophia looked around the apartment. It wasn't as luxurious as the estate in which she'd spent her married life, or as comfortable as the home she'd grown up in. But it was hers. Her very first place of her own.

"I like it here," she said, her tone a little defensive.

He just arched a brow.

"And it's all I can afford," she admitted. There was no shame in being poor, Sophia knew. She'd grown up borderline poor. The cantina and raising seven kids had gobbled up every penny her father made.

"I thought Castillo was pretty well off," Max asked with a frown. "And the gallery isn't chump change."

He winced after he'd asked, as if he was a little worried he'd stepped over a line. Sophia considered that for a second. He'd seen her naked. He'd had her every way there was, at least in her limited knowledge, to have a body. He'd held her after the nightmare that was supposed to be a showing at the gallery. And he'd let her call all the shots the previous night, from talking to the cops to handling the help to who cleaned up what. He understood her enough to know she needed that. A man had to really, *really* care to understand a woman that well.

Nope. No lines between them.

"Joseph's daughter contested the will. She's laid claim to everything except the gallery, which is in my name outright."

"And you let her?" he asked incredulously.

Maybe there were lines after all. Sophia lifted her chin and tightened the blanket, suddenly very aware and very irritated by her nakedness.

"It's not so much a matter of letting her as not being able to stop her."

He frowned, sliding from the bed to tug on his jeans, commando-style, and carried the tray across to the kitchen counter. Her mouth drooled. She'd just seen him in his full glory and the sight of the man in unzipped jeans and a bare chest made her wish she knew what really kinky sex was so she could do it to him.

It took her a few seconds to realize he'd returned to the side of the bed and was staring at her, one brow raised and a questioning look on his face.

"I take it you don't get along with your stepdaughter?"

"Not even a little bit."

"Did you ever consider that she might be the one behind all of your problems?"

Sophia rolled her eyes. "Are you trying to piss me off?"

Max stared for a second, then nodded. "Of course you've considered it."

"Lynn is an indulged, selfish, spoiled brat with major entitlement issues. But she's also very confident that she'll win the lawsuit. Why would she bother to mess with the gallery?"

"Maybe to hurt you?"

Sophia shrugged. "Lynn wouldn't think twice about trying to hurt me. And ruin the gallery? She'd love nothing more."

"Have you told the police?"

"The police. My lawyer. Gina," Sophia confirmed. "But suspecting, even wanting, it to be her doesn't make it fact. As far as I know, as anyone knows, she hasn't done anything."

"This is why you should have hired the P.I.'s," Max murmured.

Sophia clenched her jaw. Then Max smoothed his hand along her shoulder. Down her arm, then back up, so his fingers brushed the insides of her breast where the sheet didn't cover them.

Irritation at his suggestion melted under the onslaught of lust. She sighed.

"I can't afford to hire an investigator," she admitted. "Maybe, if last night's show had done well, I could have considered it. But now? It's out of the question."

She tensed a little, waiting for him to offer money or some other humiliating resolution to her woes. She couldn't accept, and he'd argue and push, then they'd fight. Then everything would be ruined. She had to force herself not to climb off the bed and prepare to stand her ground.

"Have you considered a compromise?" he asked absently,

his eyes focused on her body and the amount of skin he was systematically revealing with his sneaky fingers.

That wasn't an offer. Nor was it pushy. She blinked a couple of times, trying to figure out what he was up to.

But she couldn't think when he was touching her like that.

"Huh?" she asked, barely following his words now that the sheet had been teased aside to expose one breast. He was barely touching her, his finger a whisper. But his eyes caressed, enticed. Wet heat pooled between her legs and she swallowed hard.

"Compromise," he said, leaning forward to blow gently, making her nipple pucker in response. "You want the gallery to focus on photographs. The kink drew a big audience and made money. Show erotic photos."

"Like von Schilling's?" she murmured, her breath coming in short little pants.

"The guy sounded like he really wanted to show here," Max pointed out. He flicked her nipple with his tongue, making desire spear through her body like lightning.

"No," she said, lying back and drawing him with her. She held his head to her breast, loving the feeling of his mouth working her nipple. She wrapped one leg around his thigh, the abrasive feel of denim against her swollen bud making her whimper. "That'd be a step backward."

Max skimmed his hand beneath the sheet, teasing little trails of fire everywhere he touched. His fingers dipped into her wet heat, soothing and enticing with each stroke.

He shifted his weight, sucking her other nipple through the sheet, the wet fabric adding another layer of delight. Then he slid down, his breath sending shivers through her as he skimmed his tongue along her torso and belly.

"Compromise, sweetheart. Sometimes you gotta pull out a little before you drive it home," he said before he settled between her legs and took her into his mouth and exploded all thoughts of the gallery into tiny pieces.

"I STILL THINK YOU SHOULD call von Schilling," Max advised for the hundredth time as he pulled into his mother's driveway.

He and Sophia had spent the past week together, in and out of bed. The in-bed Sophia was great. She was amazing. Sweet, sexy and adventurous. The out-of-bed woman was a little more challenging. She was smart, sexy and adventurous there, too. But unlike in bed, she wasn't willing to let him be on top.

Ever.

It was enough to give a guy a complex.

The only thing—besides the incredible sex—keeping his ego propped up was playing secret investigator when Sophia wasn't paying attention. He hadn't found anything, but he was pretty sure he'd tapped the vandal. He hadn't made the guy's face, but that motorcycle had been back three times, its license plate covered in mud. He'd slow down, notice Max, then speed off.

"And I think we should have a naked lunch at my apartment," Sophia decided after a quick glance at the fancy-ass Nob Hill property. Max wasn't sure, but he thought she gave a little shudder. Probably she wasn't comfy with the snobby upper crust. He could relate.

"How about naked dessert?" he compromised, offering his most charming smile. His ego, among other things, swelled a little when she got that dazed do-me look in her eyes.

"I can't do naked dessert if lunch gives me a nervous stomach," Sophia warned, her smile a little shaky. "I shouldn't have taken the afternoon off, anyway. The gallery needs me."

"I need you," Max said as he reached over and took her hand, lifting it to his mouth and brushing a kiss over her softly scented, silky skin. "And I already told you, pull in von Schilling, a couple other photographers that specialize in sexy and do a show. Voilà, all your problems are solved."

When she tugged her hands from his and offered an impatient roll of her pretty blue eyes, Max briefly wished he were back in Afghanistan where people actually obeyed his orders without question or argument.

"I told you, it's in the gallery's best interest that I stick with the plan," she said for the hundredth time. What she'd never explained, though, was *why* it was in the gallery's best interest. "Now change the subject, please and tell me why I have to have lunch with you."

"You're here to protect me," he said, only partially teasing.

"I'm here to protect the big bad bomb defuser from his mama?"

Max grinned, flicking off the engine and leaning over to give her a kiss. "Exactly."

Her smile faded as fast as it came. He recognized the look on her face when she glanced at the house. Dread.

"What's wrong? You lived in similar overblown luxury when you were married, right?" he teased, wanting—needing—to put her at ease. After all, things would be tense enough inside. No point in her being all stressed out before the soup course.

"I did, but as I was often reminded, I never quite fit in," she said with a one-shouldered shrug and a half smile.

Not for the first time, Max wished her ex-husband had lived long enough for her to divorce him. Then he'd still be around to get his sorry ass kicked like he deserved. Over the course of the past week, Sophia had told him enough—and not told him even more—to let him know that the old guy had been a first-class jerk, emotionally abusive and totally unappreciative.

When he'd asked Sophia why she'd married him, she'd given this sad sort of smile and said he was her Prince Charming.

Whatever the hell that meant.

"I probably should have warned you," he started. "My family is…difficult."

"I have six overprotective brothers and a hardheaded father. You don't think I can handle this?" she asked, one brow arched. The look in her beautiful blue eyes was both confident and vulnerable.

Max didn't know how to answer. He wasn't even sure he could handle this. But it was the only way to stem the flow of his mother's nagging him to date Tabby-approved women. Under normal circumstances, his mother was interfering and pushy, but she still loved her son and wanted him to be happy. Lately, though, she'd been antsy and snappy. She was obsessed with her historical society vendetta against that building.

He glanced at the wide doors and had his hand on the ignition key before he realized it.

"Running away?" Sophia asked. Her words were teasing, but her look was hopeful.

He really wanted to.

But years of training, from both the military and his family—not that there was really much difference—came to the forefront. Max sighed, then offered her a smile as he pulled the keys from the steering column and opened the driver's door.

He was around the car and opening Sophia's door before she'd gathered her purse.

"Remember this morning?" he asked as she took his hand to exit the car.

An appealing blush washed her cheeks and she gave him a questioning glance. "You mean this morning on my desk?"

"Exactly." He tucked her hand into the crook of his and held it there, as much to force himself up the stairs as to keep her from running. "If you stick it out through this meal, I promise that again for dessert."

Her eyes glowed with wicked amusement and her mouth

made an oh. Before she could respond, though, Sterling opened the door.

"Sergeant," the butler greeted.

Max greeted the older man with a smile, noting the questioning look Sophia slanted his way. He probably should have warned her that while it looked like a home, in reality they were eating at a very fancy, very upscale military base.

He could only hope the brass skipped this particular meal.

"Your mother and uncle are entertaining the rest of the guests in the parlor," Sterling instructed.

So much for that wish. God, he hoped his mother and uncle didn't act like snobs with Sophia. They were so obsessed with status and connections, sometimes they could come off as... well, as assholes if they didn't think someone measured up.

As usual, though, Max kept his feelings to himself and, taking Sophia's hand in his, drew her down the hallway.

Thirty minutes later, they all sat down to eat. Max assured himself that the afternoon wasn't any different than approaching a live bomb with a civilian to protect.

He was courageous, skilled and unwavering in his determination to defuse the potential explosion.

Which meant they had an eighty-percent chance of survival.

"I'm sorry the Gaskins and the Lorimars couldn't stay to eat," Tabby said as she took her seat and waved a hand at Sterling to begin serving. "They are off to the Museum of Modern Art for the afternoon. I think it'd be fun to join them at the ballet this evening, though, don't you?"

"Waste of time," the General muttered as he stabbed a forkful of the salad that'd just been set in front of him. "Ballet is second only to opera in things I'd rather be shot than do."

Silently echoing an agreement, Max noticed Sophia pressing her lips together to keep from smiling.

"But you like art, right, General?" Max prodded. He

figured the old man could be an ally in his campaign to save Sophia's business. If Max played it right, the General would do all the convincing he, himself, hadn't been able to.

"Some art can be good."

"Photography?"

"Pictures are better than that crap they call art. Twisted metal, splashes of paint on a wall. Who comes up with that crap?"

Sophia had said very little all afternoon, mostly smiling, nodding and staying unobtrusive. He saw her fingers twitch a few times, though. The same way they often did right before she grabbed a camera. He wondered if it was artistic curiosity or simply a defense mechanism.

"Weren't you and Dad pretty tight with a photographer once upon a time?" Max asked his mom. He knew the answer already, but the game had to be played the right way if he was going to win.

"No," Tabby snapped. Everyone stopped eating to stare. Max frowned as a hint of color seeped into his mother's face, but before he could figure out what'd bothered her, the General cleared his throat.

"Marshall and I knew one," he offered, frowning at the past as if he were trying to gather the memory together. "Not sure if Tabby here ever met him, though. Van something."

Max's mother opened her mouth as if to correct her brother-in-law, then closed it and viciously stabbed a piece of arugula. Sophia frowned, giving Max an arch look. Confused by the undercurrents, but still undaunted, he sipped his lemon water and smiled.

"Right," Max said. "I remember Dad buying a few of his photos. Aren't they hanging in the library or something?"

Max wasn't sure why his mother was glaring at her plate. Sophia's glare was easy to understand, though. And it didn't bode well for his naked dessert plans.

Maybe it was time to change the subject. Before he could,

though, his uncle leaned back from his empty plate so it could be cleared and tapped his fingers on the table.

"If I recall, he was pretty damn famous," the General mused. "Eccentric, too. Those artist types always are. He sold pictures all over the world, traveled more than I did in my first tour of duty, and refused to show at any place except this obscure little hole in the wall here in the city. I went to a few shows with Marshall. He was a…what do you call it, Tabby? Patron or something."

Sophia's frown had faded. She smiled her thanks when Sterling cleared her plate and asked, "He didn't show anywhere else? I'd think with that level of fame, he could command top showings anywhere in the country."

"Right, he could," the General agreed, his gaze fixed on his plate as he carved into his steak. "He had a thing with the owner. Signed a lifelong exclusive."

"Lifelong?" Sophia asked. "Doesn't that mean as long as the owner has the gallery?"

"Nah. As long as the picture place is still at that location." The General laughed, shaking his head. "Guy must've signed that contract in the seventies. All that free love and freer dope got to him, if you ask me. Nothing a stint in the service wouldn't have fixed. But he never served."

Sophia leaned forward, obviously surprised at the news of the exclusive. "This photographer, is it von Schilling by any chance?"

The General shrugged, scooping up some potatoes. "Something like that. Marshall paid more attention than I did. He was stationed here at the time. I was over in Germany."

Max could see Sophia's mind working. Obviously she'd never seen this contract, but it could only work in her favor. He made a mental note to tell her to push for a higher commission since they had von Schilling in a corner.

Obviously finished with the polite chit chat, the General turned his attention toward Max. "Now, I've got some good news, Sergeant. I've made a few calls, pulled a few strings. I've found a stateside post for you. One with enough prestige and potential to set you up quite nicely."

Sophia's eyes rounded, her gaze bouncing between the two men while Max's mother continued to silently eat her salad-only lunch.

"Perhaps this is something we should discuss later," Max suggested, amusement fading as his almost-victory began to fizzle. Irritation surged at the interference, well-meaning though he knew it was.

"This post won't be open for long, Max. We need to get the orders written, get things moving immediately."

"We have a guest," Max pointed out tightly.

"Charles, this isn't the time."

Sophia's gaze bounced around the table.

"Bull pucky," the General said with a hearty laugh, waving away both Max and his mother's protest. "If the girl is interested in you, she'd be glad to hear you're sticking around."

"My leave is up in two weeks," Max said, his tone calm.

"Which is why we need to get you reassigned right away."

"I don't want to be reassigned," Max stated, leaning forward and staring straight at his uncle.

"You'd question orders?"

"I'd question nepotistic interference in my career," Max said, at attention even though he was seated. Familiar frustration pounded through him. All of his training meant he took orders from his superiors. He accepted that in the field. When he was on duty, he never questioned a command, no matter how much he might personally disagree. But here? At his mother's table? Because his uncle was brass and wearing his freaking uniform, Max was expected to silently follow along.

"It's my job to oversee your career."

"No, sir," Max denied, using every bit of control at his

disposal to keep his tone level and emotionless. "I'm not under your direct command. I appreciate your advice, but I prefer to stay where I'm currently stationed."

Max's uncle sat stock-still, his stare a lethal weapon. Max felt Sophia's tension radiating off her like a heat wave. His mother, used to these skirmishes at mealtimes, signaled Sterling to bring her a drink.

Regret washed over him for bringing Sophia into this mess. He reached under the table to take her hand and squeeze it in silent apology.

Before he could let go, he felt her take a deep breath. Out of the corner of his eye he caught the movement as she knocked her ice water across the table.

"Oh, my gosh," she exclaimed, jumping up and shaking the fabric of her now soaked skirt. "I'm so sorry. I'm a total klutz, obviously."

Tabby jumped up, using her napkin to try and stem the pool of water. The General rolled his eyes. Max's lips twitched.

Before anyone could say anything, though, she continued. "I hate to be a bother, but I'm going to be miserably uncomfortable in this wet dress. Would you all mind terribly if Max rushes me home?"

His uncle's frown was rivaled only by the patent relief on Tabby's face. Sophia continued to babble apologies and thanks all the way out of the room, glancing back only once to make sure Max was following.

By the time they reached his car, Max's grin was full-fledged and he was laughing out loud.

"Subtle," he complimented her as she slid into the passenger seat.

"Hey," she said when he took his place behind the steering wheel, "now can we focus on what really matters? Didn't you promise me a naked dessert?"

10

FLIPPING THROUGH THE MAIL, Sophia tried to remember the blissful pleasure she'd woken up to, with Max doing naughtily delicious things to her body. But with each envelope, her mood sank deeper.

Bill, bill, bill, letter from Rico, bill, letter from her attorney, bill.

This sucked. She'd rather be back at Max's mother's being treated like a hooker with open sores. Between Tabby—and what the hell kind of name was that?—and her horrified chilly looks, and the General—what the hell kind of name was that, did the man sleep with his combat boots on?—and his overbearing attitude, that had definitely been the most miserable lunch she'd ever experienced. And to discover von Schilling had an exclusive contract with Esprit? Now that had been a shock.

And still it'd be preferable to this morning.

She might as well face it. The gallery was sinking fast. The most exciting thing that'd happened at her big show was a skunk attending. She'd sold nothing in the past week. Artists were pulling their work.

At this rate, she'd lose the gallery before summer.

She sank into her desk chair and threw the mail, half of

it unread, onto her desk so it scattered in an angry fan of envelopes. The movement jostled her computer mouse, pulling her computer out of hibernation.

On the screen, mocking her, was her goals chart. Bright colored rectangles, each filled with an unachieved goal.

At least she could highlight the purple box with its dream of having a fabulous and fulfilling sex life. Who knew, the one goal she'd been sure was a pipedream was the only one she'd achieve.

No wonderful career. No returning the gallery to its former glory. No proving she was savvy, strong and in control. The only time she was on top these days was when she had Max stretched out beneath her.

Too bad finally finding the key to great sex couldn't solve all the rest of her problems.

Heart heavy and confidence skimming the floor, Sophia found her fingers moving of their own volition. They slid the mouse arrow over to the photo file and opened the pictures she'd taken of Max. Other than highlighting them in the upload box on her computer, she hadn't once looked at them. What was the point?

Pictures were windows to the soul. A snapshot of the inner self. Without the force of his commanding—albeit charming—personality, she'd see what was underneath all that sexy sizzle. It'd be one of two things.

She'd either see that he wasn't what she thought—and she'd be heartbroken—

Or she'd see that he was everything she'd ever dreamed of—and she'd be terrified.

Because Max wasn't sticking around.

Oh, sure, at first his being a sexy soldier boy who'd be heading back overseas had been one of the things in his favor. After a lifetime of men bossing her around, the idea of having one who had a defined deadline, who'd head back to his job defusing bombs and saving the world, held a lot of appeal. There was a freedom in opening her life, her body, to a man like that.

The plan had been to have a great time, with the built-in relationship deadline keeping her from opening her heart.

She poked her finger at the ugly splay of envelopes on her desk and sneered. Apparently all of her plans equally sucked.

Still…

Her heart pounded a heavy beat in her chest, so loud she could feel it all the way to the tips of her hair. No matter, she had to look.

Two quick clicks and she'd pulled up the slideshow of Max's pictures. The first one had her laughing aloud. There he was, hot and sexy soldier boy, wrapped around a marble cock almost as tall as he was. His muscles bulged beneath the cotton of his shirt. Muscles she had since spent delightful hours stroking and enjoying. Sophia clicked the plus key and zoomed in on Max's face. Sexy, focused on lifting the heavy marble. His mouth was set. His jaw determined. She zoomed in more, and there, his eyes laughed. Amused delight, both at the situation, at Sophia and at himself.

She smiled a little. For such a driven man, Max always seemed to find a way to enjoy himself.

She clicked through a few more pictures, stopping at one where Max was naked. The shot was only his head and shoulders, but since he'd been spread out on her sheets, she knew he'd been completely bare right down to his sexy toes. The look on his face made her thighs tremble.

Pure sex. Those amused eyes promised a good time. The half smile had a satisfied tilt to it, speaking well of the intense passion they'd shared right before she'd grabbed her camera.

Sophia zoomed in on Max's face and tried to push past the desire and focus on what she saw.

Honesty. Pride. Intelligence. Amusement and desire. A hint of stubborn determination.

And love.

Her eyes burned. She pressed her lips together, and, trying to focus, blinked away the moisture.

He hadn't said anything about love. He'd barely said anything about like. They didn't talk about those things. No mention of a relationship, no hint of the future. Max wasn't going to make promises, and he definitely wasn't going to corner her into making any.

Which was exactly what she wanted.

And yet...there was that love. Real, intense, accepting. She stood toe to toe with him, sometimes arguing just for the sake of proving she had a spine, and he didn't leave. He just watched, sometimes he yelled back, always he helped her defuse. And he still cared.

He tried to point out a smarter way to do business, and she ignored him. He suggested ways for her to fight for her inheritance, and she told him to mind his own business. He took her to meet his family, and she dumped water on the priceless furnishings. He listened to her plans for the future, her pie-in-the-sky hopes for the gallery. He'd even coaxed out of her the deep, hidden dream of being a professional photographer.

All the while, he wore that charming smile and made her feel great about herself. He might have rolled his eyes and stalked off a few times when she refused to listen, but he'd never made her feel stupid. Never, ever made her feel less than capable, less than in full control.

Except, of course, in bed. There he'd taught her that giving up control brought both of them more pleasure.

No man in her life had ever looked at her, really looked at he real her, and accepted what they saw.

"Soph?"

She swiped a tear from her cheek and looked at the door-vay. Gina, in her ripped stovepipe jeans and Metallica T-shirt, tood with a worried look on her face.

"What's up?" Sophia asked. That it would be something ᵇad was inevitable. Everything lately had been bad. At least, when it came to the gallery.

"Special delivery."

"Another penis?"

Looking like she didn't know whether she should give ᵇophia a hug, run out for chocolate or ignore the tears, Gina inally settled for a grin. "I wish. Nope. A letter. It looks le-ᵍal."

Sophia's stomach jittered. "Lynn must be upping the ᵍame."

"Maybe it's time to kick her where it hurts?" Gina said, ᵘnconsciously echoing Max's argument.

"She can afford harder boots than I can," Sophia said. It vasn't defeat, she told herself. She wasn't being a wimp by ᶰot fighting. She was choosing her priorities and ensuring she ᵃchieved them. That was control. Not cowardice.

And maybe if she recited that a few million times, she'd ᵃctually believe it. Because obviously she wasn't doing much ᵒf a job at convincing anyone else.

A case in point was standing in front of her. Gina opened ᴴer mouth to argue, then gave a grimace that reached all the vay to her eyes, half-hidden behind the huge seventies-style, ᵇug-eyed glasses she wore today. Then she set the eight-by-ten ᶰvelope on Sophia's desk.

"Lynn may have harder boots, but you have a better aim," ᵍina replied.

Sophia could see the frustration in the other woman's eyes.

She knew Gina, like Max, wanted her to find a way to fight Lynn. They didn't care that Olivia, Sophia's lawyer, was adamant that the gallery—and Sophia—stay away from anything controversial. Especially with the settlement conference coming up in a week. Olivia had just argued two days before that as long as Sophia stayed the course, she was proving all those rumors false, which would go over well with the judge.

It was as if her hands were tied. Yes, she supposedly finally had control over her own life. But she couldn't use it.

"I'm running across the street to get lunch," Gina told her. "Want to watch the front or should I lock the door?"

A month ago, neither of them would have considered locking the door. But after all the vandalism and problems, it was now second-nature.

"I'll come out," Sophia said. She skirted the desk, ignoring the envelope. The lousy news would still be there after she'd had her chili relleno.

"WHAT THE FUCK?"

Max glared at the letter. He wanted to wad it into a ball and throw it across the room. He wanted to rip it to shreds and stomp it into the cement floor. Even better, he wanted to punch the man responsible for it in the face.

Years of military training kept him in check, though.

He sucked in a breath, then met the eyes of the man behind the desk in front of him. The man who'd had the unfortunate task of delivering the letter. Apparently some things, while not better, still demanded that personal touch.

"Colonel, I'd like to formally protest this reassignment," he said, the letter at his side now as he stood at attention. He wasn't in uniform. He wasn't on duty. It didn't matter. He was a soldier in the presence of his superior.

"St. James, I understand your frustration. Truth be told, don't want to lose you from EOD. You're a fine leader. You'r a credit to your squad, to your company and to your family's history of service."

"Permission to speak freely, sir?"

"Permission granted."

Max relaxed into parade rest and looked at the man sitting behind the beat-up metal desk. The Oakland Army Base didn't lend itself to fancy or frills. Neither did Colonel Gilden. Like most brass in the area, Max knew the older man through his father and uncle. He also knew the guy was honest, by the book and known for doing whatever it took to take care of his men.

Max wondered how far that'd go.

"Sir, my uncle is pulling strings."

"That's obvious, Sergeant. One of my men is pulled out of combat and put on fluff duty at the Pentagon. Doesn't take Sherlock Holmes to figure out someone's playing politics."

"This isn't what I want, sir. I requested EOD for a reason. I'm good at it, my squad is solid. My record stands."

"Then you had no part in this request for special treatment?"

"No, sir."

"Does General St. James know you're against this move?"

"Yes, sir." Max hesitated, torn between loyalty to his family and loyalty to his uniform. The uniform won. "My uncle sees my career as a stepping stone to bigger things. His feeling is that three generations of military service would look really good on a political bumper sticker."

Gilden winced. "Damn politicians."

"Exactly, sir."

"Be that as it may, your uncle outranks us both, Sergeant."

"This is clearly nepotism and backroom negotiating, sir. There has to be a way around it. Can't I lodge a formal complaint?"

"If it ever got through the red tape, it could get ugly."

Max stared at his feet. Even out of uniform, he wore boots. Solid, black, bulky. Made for defense. For standing on his own two feet. He'd be damned if he'd be railroaded.

What choice did he have, though? The Colonel was right. Lodging a complaint through official channels would get ugly. Lodging an argument over the dinner table was useless. Max knew from long experience that people in his family believed in the chain of command. They issued commands, others followed. In other words, the General didn't listen to anyone.

So…what? He was stuck?

"Can you talk to your uncle?"

Max shook his head. He'd already made himself clear. That his uncle had done this, despite Max's protest, indicated that he felt the discussion was over.

"My ETS is up in two months, sir," Max said swallowing the bile in his throat and taking a deep breath. ETS meant his term of service was finished. He'd signed on for another two years, but he'd be damned if he'd spend them playing toy soldier. "If I can't do my duty on the line, I'd prefer to step down. My papers guaranteed overseas service. If this reassignment isn't pulled, I'll file breach of contract."

Gilden rocked back in a creaky wooden chair and stared over steepled fingers.

"You'd walk instead of taking this transfer?"

Max hesitated. He'd never wanted to be anything other than a soldier. To serve his country. In Afghanistan, with his squad, he made a difference. Playing babysitter to a bunch of suits in uniform wasn't what he'd signed on for.

But serving was all he'd ever known. Ten years he'd been in the Army. He'd planned to retire a soldier, not to walk away defeated. But he'd choose defeat over dishonor. And taking a fluff job while his men, his friends, put their lives on the line was absolute dishonor.

"Yes, sir. I'd choose to walk."

WHILE SHE WAITED FOR GINA to bring back lunch, Sophia walked through the gallery. There was a couple in the smaller showroom, admiring the winery studies. The older man in the main showroom lounged on the settee, ostensibly looking at the black-and-white display of spring flowers. From the occasional snore, it was obviously afternoon nap time.

Unable to help herself, she slipped the camera from her pocket and snapped a picture. From behind, so his face was obscured, but his slouched position, chin on chest, made it clear he was cutting z's. "Art Soothes," she'd call it.

Smiling, Sophia was halfway through the next room before she realized she'd started naming her photos. As if someday, she'd actually put them in a show. She wasn't sure how she felt about ambition growing stronger than her fear of failure.

Maybe she had more confidence because Max liked her work. He'd insisted on seeing actual prints, claiming he couldn't tell diddly on the tiny view screen. So she'd printed a few of her favorites. Not any of the photos of him, of course. But one of the Golden Gate on a foggy morning, a couple of floral studies. Like her, his favorite had been the shot she'd taken of her family the morning before Rico had gone overseas. Using a timer, she'd squeezed into the shot at the last minute. Her father had been seated in his favorite recliner, with his sons ranging all around him and Sophia curled at his feet.

Max had been impressed with how strong each personality had come through in just a photo. Rico's wildness, Carlos' humor, Ben's thoughtfulness. Most of all, her father's pride.

Sophia was used to using her photos for clarity, to see to the heart of people or situations. She'd never thought that they'd provide that same gift to others.

So the idea of others seeing her work? Of deeming it worthy art? She wasn't quite there, yet.

But…maybe someday.

Which was safe, she assured herself. Someday was a nice, murky time way off in the future with no pressure.

Grinning at her own self-justification, she waved to Gina as the other woman came through the back with lunch, setting Sophia's on her desk for later.

"Go ahead and eat," she told her assistant. "I'll cover the front until you're done.

Twenty minutes and four additional pictures later, Sophia returned to her office. She was much less depressed now. So what if things weren't quite where she wanted them yet? And yes, Max was leaving, but not tomorrow. They had a couple of weeks together. She was sure that a few more bouts of wild, hair-tangling sex and she'd be over this silly idea of falling in love.

She had to be. Her priority was the gallery. First, pulling it out of this mess, then working hard to make it the success she'd always dreamed of. After that, maybe she'd start thinking about other things.

Like letting that dream of being a photographer out of hiding. And falling in love.

Both equally terrifying.

Filled with a calm that she knew perfectly well was hiding the heartbreak underneath, Sophia unwrapped her salad, tore off a piece of tortilla and nibbled.

Then, fortified and ready to tackle the letter Gina had brought in earlier, she slit open the envelope and pulled out the papers. Yep, more legal crap.

She skimmed the cover letter. The tortilla fell from her numb fingers.

What the hell?

Horrified, she read the letter. The Historical Guild of Northern California was insisting that Esprit vacate the premises or they'd take legal action to sell the building. Since they, in effect, owned it and were only leasing it long-term—

freaking century should count for something, shouldn't it?—
they were within their rights, the letter stated.

She had the phone in hand and had dialed Olivia before
she realized she'd moved. Ten minutes later, her shock had
faded into stunned horror.

"What do you mean, they have documentation? How can
someone document a lie?" she demanded.

"What they have is a case file of what the Historical Guild
feels is a breach of confidence," Olivia, who'd received her
own special delivery letter, replied. "Obviously whoever had
started those rumors about your sex addiction sent them doc-
umented evidence of what they see as the gallery's focus
on offensive fetishes. In the Guild's opinion the gallery isn't
supportive of their vision and policy."

"It all comes down to the gallery showing erotic art instead
of photographs?" Which had been going on for four freaking
years. So why now? Sophia ground her teeth together. Because
of Lynn, obviously.

"Yes."

"But I didn't do that. Joseph did. And we've stopped." Sophia rolled her eyes at her whiny tone. Way to stand up and
take control of her life. By sniveling like a three-year-old.

"What can I do?" she asked before Olivia could say anything. "How can I keep the gallery?"

In the long pause, Sophia could almost hear Olivia lining
up and discarding options.

Finally she sighed. "You're not going to like it."

"Just tell me," Sophia insisted with a sigh.

"Negotiate with Ms. Castillo. Split the estate so you can
access enough funds to purchase the building outright."

Automatic refusal was on the tip of Sophia's tongue. She
swallowed it back with an effort.

"I'll work up a list of suggestions," Olivia continued, obviously sensing Sophia's struggles. "I have notes on the specifics

your stepdaughter was especially adamant about. Perhaps we can find a middle ground. I'll get back to you in the next few days with suggestions."

Sophia made some sort of grunt that must have passed as agreement, because Olivia hung up. It took Sophia a while longer to unclench her fingers from the phone.

She hadn't lost the gallery.

She could buy it.

All she had to do was come up with a whole lot of money in the next ninety days.

"DOES IT ALL LOOK OKAY?" Sophia asked Max the next afternoon as she set out a tray of cookies and a bowl of sugared nuts on the small sofa table in her office. She was expecting von Schilling any time now.

Max didn't know which made him hungrier—the sugar glistening off the chunky peanut butter cookies, or the sight of Sophia bending over, her black skirt stretched temptingly over her hips.

He knew which he wanted more. But he was pretty sure lusting after Sophia's body was fogging up his clear head. He knew damn well that she needed help. She was over her head and going down for the third time. There had to be some way he could save her from drowning.

"Who's trying to shut you down, again?" he asked, hoping he'd heard her wrong.

"The Historical Guild of Northern California," she said, barely paying him any notice as she busied herself with the silver tea service.

The name didn't help. California was full of do-gooder clubs and historical societies. His mother served on a million of them. He remembered his first night home and her talking about a problem her gang was having with some building or other.

Could she have meant Esprit? No. Of course not. She wouldn't do something so underhanded. Tabby would have the decency to confront the business owner and give her a chance to make things right. Wouldn't she?

His shoulder blades twinged from the recent stab wounds in his back he'd recently incurred from his uncle. Maybe that underhanded, as-long-as-I-get-my-way-I-don't-care-how-I-screw-you habit was contagious.

Hell, he was guilty of it himself. He thought of the money he'd handed over to the busboy across the street to watch the gallery building and the online snooping he'd done on Lynn Castillo. He'd even planned to drive up to Tahoe, where she lived, and confront her in person. But his career suddenly crumbling yesterday had got in the way of that scheme.

But the things he'd done, they'd been to help Sophia. He only had her best interest at heart.

"I wish you'd let me lend you the money so you can just buy the building," he offered again. He didn't even have to wait for her to shake her head to know what her response would be.

He didn't know if her independence was sweet or stubborn.

Probably both.

"That's kind of you, but no. I couldn't. I'll make this happen myself," Sophia insisted. She gave Max a determined smile and claimed, "One way or another, I'll work it out."

His jaw worked as he tried to keep from telling her that one way or another wasn't good enough. Even though she'd finally given in and decided to do a show with von Schilling, it was going to take more than one show to bring in enough money to buy the building.

Unable to do anything else, Max grabbed her hand and tugged so she tumbled into his arms. Soft meets hard.

Hand behind her neck, he pulled her down for a kiss. Her

lips were magic, sending a shaft of heat straight through his body. His tongue slipped between her teeth, tasting, teasing and tempting. His ego, among other things, soared when her body went lax, her breasts pressing tight against his chest.

Mmm. She was delicious. He wanted to lose himself in her arms. To let all the worries and decisions fade in the face of such hot temptation. He wanted to explore all the sexy possibilities she was offering.

She slowly pulled her lips away from his and gave his chest a pat, then levered herself to her feet.

She checked the coffeepot and the hot water for tea for the fourth time. "You don't have to stick around, you know. I can handle this meeting on my own."

"The guy's a perv," Max pointed out. "He takes pictures of naked women. Maybe I'd be jealous leaving him alone with you."

"Maybe you should be," Sophia teased.

"After all," she continued, "he's seen it all. Done it all. And recorded it all on film."

Max nodded, getting up to swipe a cookie off the tray. He wandered the room for a few minutes, then dropped to the couch again.

Picking up on his restless stress, Sophia stopped fussing around the office. She sat next to him and rubbed a comforting hand over his knee. "What's going on?"

"Nothing." At least, nothing he planned to talk about until he'd figured out his new career. And made sure Sophia wanted him around. He took a bite of the cookie. Mmm, good. Almost as tasty as Sophia herself.

"Are you sure?" She frowned, her blue eyes shining with concern. "I know I've been a little obsessed with my own problems today, but you really do seem off-kilter. Maybe later, we can get dinner and talk. If you don't have something else to do, of course."

He winced, the peanut butter cookie turning to dust in his mouth. He had absolutely nothing to do. At twenty-eight, his career about to go up in flames, his family was sure to disown him when they found out his plan, and he didn't know if the woman he loved wanted him to stick around past the end of the month.

A chilly terror moved through his body. He ignored it, as always, pushing emotion aside. A man didn't survive defusing bombs if he let emotions in. He'd deal with all of his problems later, after he'd fixed things for Sophia.

After all, ladies should always come first.

"Dinner sounds great," he finally told her. "I'm all yours, babe."

11

Sophia took a deep breath, not sure why the idea of Max being all hers made her stomach a knotted mess. Maybe because he looked so miserable about it?

Worried, she watched the impatience roll off him like an early morning San Francisco fog. She wanted to help. She really did. But she had enough experience with stubborn men to know he'd tell her when he wanted and not a second sooner.

Unless maybe she asked naked. Something to try later. Sophia gave a happy little sigh, knowing that image would get her through this afternoon.

Sophia tried not to chew her lipstick off, but, man, she was nervous. Von Schilling was her hero. The man was a photographic genius. And she was going to meet him. Meet him and discuss his show in her gallery.

She hurried to her desk to reapply her ruined lipstick.

"Mr. von Schilling," she said half an hour later. She forced herself to offer the plate of cookies to the man seated on the tapestry couch instead of throwing it at his head like she wanted. "I don't understand. Why did you contact me if you didn't want to do a show?"

"Hans, please," the gray-haired septuagenarian insisted.

"And what do I want with a show? Things like that, they belong in the material world. I'm old. I've disavowed the material world in search of a higher spiritual realm. I have no need for adulation and groveling."

"You have need of money, though," muttered the woman sitting next to him.

There were four people sitting in Sophia's office—herself and Hans, one of the most celebrated photographers of his decade, Max, who was silently watching from behind her desk, and Lily, von Schilling's daughter.

Lily was beige. Beige hair, beige skin, beige clothes. She sort of faded into the tapestry fabric of the couch. Her father, on the other hand, seemed to suck in all the light and color from the space around him. Long and lanky, he looked like the crooked man from that kid's poem. Knees and elbows poked out at odd angles, not softened at all by his loose hemp pants and shirt, both held together with drawstrings. He'd obviously never left his hippie days behind.

And then there she was, all prepared to graciously accept von Schilling's request to do a show, then flex her negotiating muscles by getting him to agree to a higher commission. Smart move when she'd thought he was desperate to show and she was his only option.

Now? Now she had a guy who didn't want to do a show she really didn't want to give. And now she had to talk him into it? Sophia gave Max a desperate look, but he just shrugged, his expression as baffled as hers.

"Why are you disavowing the material world?" she asked, more to buy time to figure out how to rescue this situation than because she cared.

"I no longer need physical constraints. I have closed the book on that phase of my life," he declared, his tone echoing eerily through the room. Like one of those TV psychics she remembered watching as a child at one in the morning when she'd snuck out of bed for a snack. "The constant focus on outside demands creates a ripple in my chi."

"Right," Lily said, finally speaking up. "But don't forget that Guru Wolfdragon said you can't move forward until all of the baggage of the past is released."

Wolfdragon? Sophia mouthed to Lily. The younger woman rolled her eyes and sighed, then in a subtle gesture out of Hans's line of sight, rubbed her thumb and forefinger together.

Ahhh, Wolfdragon must be from the Guru school of con artists.

"The photos are baggage?" Sophia guessed. And from the look on Lily's face, she was worrying a little that the baggage might end up a donation to the guru's retirement fund.

"They tie me to the past," Hans declared. "I no longer live there and am ready to move on."

"Okay, so you want to move on." Baffled, Sophia stared at the two of them. "But if you don't want to exhibit your photographs at Esprit, why has someone been calling weekly, nagging me to do a show?"

Sophia wanted so badly to rub her forehead and try to massage away the ache there. From what he'd said so far, Hans had spent most of the seventies stoned and never recovered. He'd walked away from his art, claiming the stress of photography was at odds with his Zen.

More likely, his daughter had cut off his dope supply and insisted he get clean.

"Hans is going to do this show," Lily broke in, her voice quiet, but firm. "His various…hobbies have sunk him in debt. His financial advisor suggested he sell off all those photos that are gathering dust in the attic. He won't sell direct to the public, though. He claims it's against his artist ethics."

"Plebeians." Hans dismissed her around a mouthful of cookie.

His daughter ignored him, continuing in her soft, almost

nothing voice. "This will be his final show. The goal is to sell his entire body of work. His contract with Esprit de l'Art requires that he show them here."

Sophia glanced over at Max, who was leaning back in her desk chair reading the contract. He met her eyes and nodded, then gave a slight head tilt toward the calendar hanging on the wall next to him.

A reminder, she knew, that the only way the show would be held at the gallery was if they did it next week before word got out that the building was being sold.

Sophia didn't bother freaking out. There wasn't time. If she did this show right, and von Schilling was serious about this being his final show, a huge thing since it would be his first in twenty years, then she stood to make enough for a solid down payment on the building.

Her gallery, and her future, lay in the hands of a man wearing embroidered silk bedroom slippers and beads in his goatee.

"I'll be happy to host the show," she heard herself say. "But we'll have to have it the weekend of the fourteenth."

"That soon? Isn't it a holiday?"

"That's the only weekend I have available," she claimed. "And I think tying the show in with the romance and glamour of Valentine's Day will be a wonderful promotional tool."

"SO WHAT'RE YOU DOING for Valentine's Day?" Gina asked as she uncrated yet another stunning framed black-and-white photo. This one of a topless cabaret dancer, one leg stretched to amazing lengths as she bent over a wooden spindle-back chair. "Hot plans for the most romantic holiday of the year?"

"I'm working on Valentine's, same as you," Sophia said.

Exhausted, she shoved the long swing of hair off her face and leaned back on her heels. It was casual night in the back of the gallery with she and Gina both in jeans. Gina's were shredded every which way, held together with band pins, while her own were pure stonewashed comfort.

After her meeting with the von Schillings two days before, she'd called in every favor, used every contact she had to push a promotional blitz like none other. She'd even recruited Max, giving him free rein to contact his country club cronies, his mother's ladies' club grand dames and any and all military personnel who might want to see some naked pictures.

Screw glamour and dignity. She'd pulled out Joseph's show playbook to use as a template. It'd worked plenty of times in the past, and even if she didn't like it, she knew it'd work now.

"A hugely successful gallery show, with promotion guaranteed from three newspapers, a magazine and a local TV crew," she muttered, unwrapping the paper from yet another half-naked dancer. "You know, ole Hans must've been tight with all the clubs here in the seventies. He's got cabaret, he's got ballet, he's got girls in go-go boots dancing in cages. And he got them all to take their tops off."

"Dude had a boob fetish," Gina agreed, her gaze skimming the twenty framed photos they'd already uncrated and leaned against the walls. "And quit changing the subject."

"I didn't. I told you my plans." Then, because her calves were killing her, Sophia gave up all semblance of dignity and dropped flat to sit on her butt. She tilted her head, squinting at the six-photo series of a go-go dancer, trying to figure out what it was about the images that were nagging at the back of her brain.

"You could be doing the romantic thing after the show," Gina pointed out. "I am. I'm having midnight drinks and dinner with Art of Defiance."

Sophia's gaze cut to the rock band pins keeping her assistant's jeans from unraveling. "Which member?"

"The whole band." Gina waited for Sophia to pick her jaw up off her chest before giggling. "I'm their greeter girl for the after-party. Handing out carnations, Hershey's kisses, that kind of thing. I might get lucky, though, and the guitarist will ask me out."

"That sounds…romantic?"

"No," Gina corrected with a happy shrug. "That sounds like sex. Which I hope you'll be getting, along with something really romantic for Valentine's. Hearts, flowers, chocolate. Bling is always good, too."

"All I'm getting is sex," Sophia assured Gina. Despite the fact that she and Max had spent almost every waking minute together the past week, she had no illusions that she'd be receiving red roses, nuts and chews or anything glittery. Unless, of course, any of those came with her goodbye hug. Max was scheduled to leave the Wednesday after the show. Heading back overseas where he'd face down bombs and bad guys.

Not a bad thing, given how important she knew serving the country was to him. But still, part of her wished it was a temporary goodbye instead of forever.

Blinking away the tears, she focused on rubbing a non-existent smudge off her jeans. Since when was an incredible sex life something to cry about? She had what she wanted. So what if she'd fallen in love with Max? Everything had a price. Apparently, the cost of the best sex of her life was a broken heart. It was worth it.

It had to be.

"The show will be romantic enough," she eventually said. She ignored the long, worried look Gina gave her and hurried on. "Don't you think it's clever to tie the holiday in by calling it Ode to Love? It's my attempt at de-eroticizing the displays."

"You don't really consider these erotic, do you?" a voice said from the doorway.

Gina giggled and offered Max a little finger wiggle, while Sophia just shrugged, leaning back against a crate and letting her eyes take in the man standing in front of her. He just kept looking better.

He still wouldn't tell her what was bothering him. He claimed it wasn't anything important. But he had a look in his eyes, half sad, half furious, that made her heart ache.

"I think I'm getting immune to erotic," she told him with a smile, hoping to cheer him up. "You've ruined my prudish side."

"Nah. I'm sure it'd resurface pretty fast if someone tried to plunk another four-foot dick in the middle of one of your shows."

"Only if it had Christmas lights wrapped around it," Sophia teased. Max's smile flashed. He reached down and took her hand, pulling her to her feet.

"We're going to take a break," he told Gina as he wrapped an arm around Sophia's shoulder.

"It won't be a long break," she told Gina, curving her own arm around Max's back. He was hard, warm and smelled wonderful next to her. Whenever she was this close, she just wanted to eat him up.

"My apartment?" she murmured quietly.

"Your office would be better," he decided, steering her down the hallway. Sophia frowned. The office meant no sex. At least, it usually meant no sex. There had been a couple of times...

"What's up?" she asked him when he closed the door and released her.

"How's the show coming along?" he asked.

Sophia narrowed her eyes. He had something else on his mind, but she was willing to play along. "We're doing pretty well. Von Schilling's got enough inventory for an entire show on his own, but we're pulling in a couple other photographers anyway to balance his with some less controversial displays."

"But you've got a pretty good handle on it all?" He stood

there, rocking back on his heels and looking as casual as ever. But she had the feeling he was mentally pacing.

"I think so," she said slowly. Not that she had a clue how to deal with her vandal. The creep had hit twice in as many days. Once spray-painting trash on the back door, then this morning calling the paper to put in an ad stating the cancellation of the show. Luckily Sophia had spent so much time on the phone with the editor of the lifestyle section that he'd called her to confirm before running it.

Had Max figured something out? Was that why he looked so serious and stressed? Or was it because he hadn't?

"Are you arranging for security so there isn't a repeat of the last show?" he asked.

"I…" The man knew her panty size and what flavor body oil she liked. He'd held her hand while she fell apart, listened to her dreams. And he knew damn well the state of her bank account. So why was she embarrassed to tell him she was too broke to afford security for the show?

"Will you let me take care of this for you?" he asked quietly. "I'll call in a few favors, get a few guys I know who're on leave to stand around and look tough. Low cost, no long-term commitment."

Sophia bit her lip. She needed this. She knew she did, and Max had made it as palatable as possible. There was a fine line between stubborn pride and idiocy. She might toe that line regularly, but she wasn't going to jump over it.

"I'd appreciate that," she told him, stepping closer so she could wrap her arms around him. His hands soothed a comforting path up and down her back and she let herself relax. Eyes closed, her ear against his heart, she listened to the steady beat.

What would she do without him?

"I've taken care of a few other things, too," he said, his voice a low rumble. "Some of mine. Some of yours."

Not sure why she suddenly felt like a scary cloud of gloom

had drifted into the room, Sophia slowly pulled back and looked into his face.

No smile in his eyes. The grim set of his jaw.

"This doesn't sound good." She stepped out of his arms and leaned against her desk. The look on his face made her think she was going to need the extra support.

"No, it's all good," he assured her. He shoved his hands in the front pockets of his jeans, the move emphasizing another good thing, which was how happy he'd been to have her in his arms.

Telling herself not to get distracted, Sophia crossed her arms over her chest, arched one brow and waited.

"First off, I received a change of orders," he told her. Sophia's breath caught in her throat as she noted the fury lurking in his dark eyes. "I was reassigned stateside."

Her heart leaped in joy. He wasn't leaving the country? She could still see him. Then she remembered the look on his face when his uncle had suggested a change in orders.

"I didn't think there was much call for EOD stateside," she said slowly.

"There isn't. If I'd taken the assignment, I'd have served at the Pentagon."

"If?" She actually heard the giddy bubbles of joy popping over her head.

"I refused."

"I didn't know you could do that."

"Under most circumstances, no," he acknowledged. "But I'd already termed out. My re-up contract specified EOD service in a battle zone."

She forced herself to only show calm interest, but her nerves were jumping like water on a burning skillet.

"I've notified legal that unless they correct this breach of contract, I'll be leaving the service." His words were emotionless. His face was expressionless.

And Sophia could clearly see he was miserable.

How could she be thrilled in the face of such horrible pain? But it wasn't as if she'd messed up his orders, right? She hadn't encouraged or pushed him to leave the service. Hell, she'd never once said a word about it.

She hadn't mentioned the terror felt by those left behind when someone they loved was in battle.

She'd even managed to keep herself from begging him to promise her a future, when she knew from Rico that pressure like that only made service more difficult.

So why did she feel guilty?

Maybe because while she hadn't done any of those things, she'd definitely thought about them.

"I'd think the Army would be more meticulous in their assignments," she said quietly, trying to figure out what was beneath the surface of his anger.

His stare was lethal. The anger wasn't directed at her, but in those few moments it occurred to Sophia that he knew her inside out. Max knew her dreams, her goals, her fears. He knew what she wanted and what stood in her way.

And she knew almost nothing about him.

Unable to stand it any longer, Sophia pushed way from the desk. She wanted to pace, but didn't think he needed the added stress.

"The Army isn't behind this problem," he admitted. "This is direct nepotistic interference."

It only took her about three seconds to figure that out. "No way. Your uncle?"

"Exactly."

Stunned, she dropped into the wingbacked chair and stared.

"Are you going to let him get away with this?"

"There is no getting involved. The chain of command is clear."

Sophia stared. Far be it from her to tell someone how to

get pissed off. But, holy cow, shouldn't he be doing something here?

She started to ask what his uncle had said, then stopped herself. She opened her mouth to ask what he'd do now if he wasn't going back to Afghanistan. Then she pressed her lips together. Her heart screamed at her to hurry up and nail down the details on their future together. Did they have one? How would this affect it? Them? Were they a them if they weren't temporary?

Her brain spun. Her stomach churned. Her nerves were shot, so she gave in to the need for comfort and pulled her knees up to her chest and wrapped her arms around her legs.

Why wasn't he saying anything else?

"You said you'd taken care of some things?" she murmured, needing a distraction to give her time to collect herself. "Was this the 'yours' part?"

"Yes," he said, nodding and shifting his stance.

"And the mine part would be?"

He paused, looking like he was gathering his thoughts, then shifting gears. He walked over to the desk and, in the same spot she'd stood a few minutes before, leaned against it and crossed one ankle over the other.

"The yours part is I've solved some of your gallery problems."

"You what?"

"I've had someone watching the gallery and we've—"

"Wait," she interrupted. "You've had someone watching my building?"

"Right," he said with a nod. "The culprit rides a motorcycle I have a partial plate number and talked to the police."

Before he could say anything else, Sophia held up her hand. She shook her head, trying to clear the buzzing from her ears.

"You did what?"

"Look, the police have a lead now. We can talk about that later. The important thing here is that you want to keep the gallery and make it a success, your vision of success." He paused. She guessed he was waiting for her to agree, so she nodded.

"In order for the gallery to be that vision, you have to come up with the money to buy the gallery."

He paused again. This time she didn't humor him with a nod. Instead she stared, waiting.

"You need money. You need a great deal of money and luckily you have a direct line to it. I just cleared things out of the way so you can use that line to reel it in."

"You took out a loan?" she guessed with a frown. He'd better not have after she'd told him she wouldn't borrow money from him. But if he was staying, and they were a couple, maybe down the road they'd be more like partners. Him the silent partner with the money, of course, and her the vocal partner in charge.

"I hired an attorney," he corrected her. "He's the biggest shark in the Bay area and after reviewing your case, he's sure he can win it before the building is put up for sale."

"But Olivia is already negotiating a settlement," she said blankly.

"You shouldn't have to settle for half. It's all yours and you should fight for it."

Sophia saw black spots in front of her eyes. The room swam in a greasy wave of fury, making her ill it was so intense.

"Let me get this straight," she said quietly, trying to keep her tone even. "First you found a lead to who is behind the vandalism but didn't bother to tell me you were even looking. And then you went behind my back and hired an attorney? Filled him in on the details, the private details, of my situation? You paid his retainer out of your own pocket. A pocket that's now going to need to hold tight to its pennies since you're out of work."

"My career isn't the issue here," he told her, his words a little tight. As if he'd caught on to her anger and was feeling defensive. As well he should. She wanted to hit him over the head with something, so defensive was smart on his part.

"Your career isn't the issue? Why do you get to decide that?" she demanded. "You poke your fingers all through my career. What makes you so special that yours is off-limits?"

"Mine isn't in danger like yours is," he said, biting the words off as if they tasted nasty. Which, considering she could see the angry awareness in his dark eyes, she figured they must.

"Really?" She knew it wasn't fair to throw his destroyed career back in his face. She knew he was hurt and upset and feeling betrayed. But dammit, so was she.

Maybe if the *her* news hadn't come so close on the heels of the *his* news, she'd have been able to control herself. She'd had a whole three minutes of happiness and hope for a future together before he'd proven to her that there was no chance in hell they'd last beyond today.

She surged to her feet and started pacing.

"Because I could have sworn your career had just blown itself all to bits, Sergeant," she tossed over her shoulder. His wince didn't make her feel any better. If anything, being a bitch just made her feel angrier.

"How dare you," she snapped, the rope on her control fraying with each step. "Who the hell do you think you are?"

"I'm the man who cares about you and wants to make sure you get what you want, dammit."

"You?" she retorted. "You can't even stand up to your own uncle and save your own dream career. So what gives you the right to decide what's necessary to save mine?"

For a second she thought she'd gone too far. His entire body froze. His glare made her want to hide under her desk. She waited for him to yell. To throw something. Nerves jittering she shifted away from the chair in case he decided that'd be the best missile to send flying across the room.

But Max did none of those things. His glare faded to ice. He pushed away from the desk, his eyes locked on hers.

Then, without another word, he walked out the door.

She wished he'd thrown the chair.

12

MAX STORMED INTO HIS mother's house, letting the heavy door slam behind him with a loud boom. Like a bomb detonating. How apt, he thought. After all, his entire life was exploding around him.

"Maximilian, what is wrong with you?" his mother demanded, halfway down the stairs, glaring at him like he'd just pulled a gun on her. Or spilled wine on her carpet.

"Did you know Uncle Charles pulled strings and had me assigned stateside?" he demanded.

From the look on her face and the infinitesimal shrug, it was clear his mother had known perfectly well what her brother-in-law had done.

"He had no right," Max said. "Neither did you. What the hell is with you people that you think you can sneak around behind people's backs and screw them over?"

"Watch your language, Maximilian."

"Or…what? You'll destroy my career?"

Shit. Max shoved his hand through his hair and ground his teeth. Son of a bitch. He hadn't meant to say anything about that. Confrontations were futile in his family. The men clammed up in stubborn silence and Tabby melted into a puddle of tears when the yelling started. In Max's experience confrontations never led to resolutions. It was like trying to talk to the fanatic who just got a charge out of detonating a bomb.

Pointless.

"I can't believe you're taking that attitude after all we've done for you," Tabby said. Typically, her words were accompanied by a teary-eyed sniff. "Your career is our business. Your father and I had a plan. When he died, your uncle stepped in to ensure the completion of that plan."

She led the way into the parlor, stopping just short of swiping the back of her hand over her forehead to declare herself the queen of the martyrs.

"Dad might have wanted me to do things his way, but he understood when I didn't," Max said, standing in the doorway.

Well, that stopped the waterworks. Tabby turned, jutting out her chin. She hated talking about his father. Apparently this family was all about holding things in and manipulating behind one another's back.

"When he wanted me to go to West Point and I enlisted instead, he was angry but he understood. Then he wanted me in communications. I trained in EOD."

"He worried about you."

"But he understood."

Tabby's jaw worked, then she gave a slow nod. "He did. And he was proud of you."

"Then why can't you be proud, too? Why would you ruin what I've worked so hard for?"

His mother stared for a long, drawn-out moment. Then she shook her head. "It's for your own good, Maximilian. You are too close to the situation to be objective."

"Too close to my own life?" he asked incredulously. "You've got to be kidding."

"Your uncle has already made arrangements. There's no point arguing about it," she said quietly. Then, as if she was afraid of what he'd say next, she made a show of looking at her watch. "I have to run, Maximilian. I have a meeting with my, um, with a friend… An employee. With, well, a lunch thing. We'll discuss this later, shall we?"

And with that confusing announcement, that was that. Stunned, Max just stood there as she swept from the room.

He strode into the parlor and dropped onto the couch. Everything he was so pissed about—the manipulations, the arrogant decisions *for his own good,* the lack of respect toward his choices—he'd been doing the exact same thing to Sophia. Just like everyone else in her life had. And yet, she'd found a way around it.

Maybe once he'd made it up to her, she'd help him figure out how to fix this mess.

Two days later, Max strode through the doors of Esprit and stopped, stunned.

"Holy shit," he muttered.

It was incredible. Instead of a huge, empty—albeit elegantly empty—expanse of polished wood flooring, white walls and a few framed photographs lined up like soldiers in formation, the room was filled. Filled with color, with motion, with imagery. Framed photos still lined the walls, but at varying heights that drew the eye. Rather than a bare floor, there were easels strewn in what looked like a strategic pattern to move people through the room toward the back. Candles were lit in wall sconces he'd never noticed before, and sweet-scented flowers burst from round vases in wooden pillars. The red velvet settees were still there, but next to each was a small table. Probably to set drinks or food on, he imagined.

"What do ya think?"

He'd been so focused on the room he hadn't noticed Gin come in. Max turned. He stared. He blinked a couple of times, then shook his head. Even if he had noticed, he wouldn't have realized it was her until he'd heard her voice.

"I think it's very different," he said, his brain trying to take in what his eyes were seeing. Gina was…normal. Smooth black—and only black—hair, tucked neatly back in a lacy headband. Minimal makeup, wire-rimmed glasses and a simple black dress without a rip, tear or pin anywhere. Sure, she still had metal glinting off her face and her shoes looked like something Frankenstein might wear. But all in all, she looked normal.

He didn't understand.

"Why's everything so…"

"Uptight?" Gina offered when he hesitated.

Max grinned, not wanting to put his foot any further in hot water by agreeing.

The smile was enough for Gina, though. She went into her gameshow hostess routine, waving her arms and using a snooty tone. "The Ode to Love show will not only be featured on the evening news, there will be reporters of all sorts, reviewers and a guest list that reads like the who's who of Northern California. Rumor has it even the governor has been invited."

"Rumor?"

"Yep, a rumor started by me when I slipped his invite into that big blue mailbox up the street."

"Sophia really pulled out all the stops."

Gina looked around and nodded. "She said this is her last chance. It's the show she's always wanted to give, but was saving for the right artist."

"I guess right's subjective when you're on the edge of a cliff."

Gina wrinkled her nose. "Actually, this exhibit is amazing. If you get past the nipples, it's some of the best photography I've ever seen."

Max wanted to ask how much she'd actually seen to make that judgment, but he didn't want to have to deal with two pissed-off women tonight. Sophia herself was going to be difficult enough.

Then he looked at the pictures. Actually looked past the pomp and décor.

"Damn," he breathed. Gina was right. They were stunning. The play of light against shadow. The pictures all told a story, some subtle, some harsh. One photo in particular caught his attention. An elderly woman holding a toddler. The contrast of the woman's skin, wrinkled and spotted, against the pure unblemished sweetness of the little girl's was moving. But what really told the story were the eyes. The same shape, and even though the photo was black-and-white, Max was sure they were the same color. There was a touching continuity in the photo. A reminder that life circled.

"These are Tristan DeLaSandro's photos," Gina told him. "He's one of the artists Soph's been wanting to bring in. He's got some erotic stuff, too. It's in the back two rooms with von Schilling's work."

"Is von Schilling's this good?"

Gina nodded. Before she could say anything, they heard the rat-a-tat-tat of high heels from the hallway.

Sophia.

Max turned to face her. Gina scurried away.

Sophia stopped just inside the arched doorway, one hand on the wall as if to steady herself.

"What're you doing here?" she asked, her tone more breathless than confrontational. Good. He was tired of confrontations.

"I told you I'd handle security for this evening's event," he reminded her quietly. Did her eyes dim a little or was it just wishful thinking on his part?

The sight of Sophia in another of those sexy little black dresses made him want to drool. This one had wide straps that crossed over her shoulders and breasts, a glittery sort of belt that made her waist look tiny and a skirt short enough that he could get his hand up without her worrying about wrinkles. She'd paired it with a pair of sexy little black strappy sandals and black hose that had a seam up the back. He'd spent half his teenage years and all of his adult life fantasizing about stockings like that.

He wondered for a second if she'd known he was coming, and somehow tapped into his deepest sexual desire and worn them just to torture him. Given how angry she'd been when they'd last spoken, he wouldn't put it past her.

"What do you need to set up the security for the evening?" she asked calmly. He could see the hurt in her eyes. Knowing he'd put it there made him ill.

He'd make it up to her, though. Just as soon as this evening was finished.

"A couple of buddies will be here within the half hour. We'll mingle, guard and generally make sure nobody lets loose their pet skunk. You do your thing," he told her reassuringly. "We'll make sure everything's secure."

Sophia gave a cute little wrinkle of her nose, looking doubtful. "Can you do this without being obvious?"

Max gave her a long stare. "The guys will be in fatigues and wearing guns, but they promised not to wear camo face paint, so they should fit in fine."

Her lips twitched. Max's shoulders relaxed a little. At least she hadn't lost her sense of humor. "They'll be dressed in suits?"

"Just like me," he said with a raised brow. Her eyes skimmed his body, light and quick. As if she were afraid if her gaze lingered anywhere too long, he'd get all turned on and grab her.

She was smart that way.

"Fine. Coordinate with Gina," she said, turning on that sexy little high-heeled sandal and walking away.

Max rocked back on his heels and considered. She looked as delicious from the back as she did from the front.

But he needed to keep in mind that the back, just like the front, was off-limits.

When she reached the arch leading to the hallway, she shot a long, considering look over her shoulder. He had no idea what the look meant. He had no intention of finding out.

But damned if she didn't get him rock-hard with just the flick of those long eyelashes of hers.

SOPHIA MOVED THROUGH the gallery with a friendly smile, playing the ultimate hostess. Guests with food and drinks, check. Happy faces and the occasional laugh, check. A comment here, an observation there about the photos, double check. It was all going great.

Von Schilling hadn't been willing to come to the show. Apparently public events *harshed his mellow*. But the other three photographers featured were all in attendance, charming the patrons into buying their work and, in Tristan's case, into a few trysts in the hallway.

She should be ecstatic. It was going even better than she'd hoped. Instead, though, she felt like screaming. It was like being in a pinball game. She was ricocheting from room to room, always looking over her shoulder to make sure she stayed away from Max.

She could barely concentrate. Every time she saw him, she pictured him naked. Then, just as her body started to heat up, she'd remember how he'd totally overstepped her boundaries and hired that attorney and anger would chill her right down. If this kept up, she was going to catch a cold from the constant body temperature changes.

"Excuse me?"

Sophia almost jumped out of her heels.

"Sorry. Didn't mean to startle you," the elderly man said. He had one of the show brochures in his hand and, she noticed with a tingle of excitement, had circled quite a few of the featured photos. "I'd like to make a purchase."

"Of course," she told him, almost purring as she looked at the list he handed her. "Right this way."

Ten minutes later, it was all Sophia could do not to dance across the polished floor while singing "Money." What a fabulous night.

And because she was feeling so good and wanted to keep this great feeling, she decided this was the perfect time to tell Max to take his platoon of canapé-munching security wannabes and head on down the road.

Shoulders back, chin up and determination in place, she scanned the room. There, at the far end by the arched doorway she caught sight of a dark-haired man. She didn't need to see through the crowd to be sure it was Max. The heat curling in her stomach assured her it was.

She'd taken two steps when something caught her eye.

Oh, God, not again.

A movement across the room caught her eye. Max. Frowning, he gave her a long stare. Then he scanned the room, immediately honing in on the skunk curled up under the red velvet settee. Pepé Le Pew all tuckered out and napping.

Nobody else seemed to see it, though.

How could they not? It was lying there snoring, for crying out loud. Maybe because it was black-and-white, like the pictures?

Sophia looked at Max again, her eyes pleading. She was so close. The show was going so well, halfway through the evening without a hitch. They'd sold a third of von Schilling's inventory already, along with a large number of the other artists' work. Her commission would soon be enough for a down payment on the building. Not that she'd figured out how she'd get an actual loan or anything.

One step at a time, she figured.

First the down payment. Then collateral. Then a loan.

Only now she'd shuffled *Get the skunk the hell out of here* to the top of her list.

Max had apparently gotten her silent message. He gave her a nod and jerked his chin toward the doorway. Sophia pressed her lips together, then nodded.

Stepping into the room, she raised her voice so the dozen people milling about the room could hear her. "Ladies, gentlemen, if you'd join me in the main gallery, we'll be..." What? A dozen pairs of eyes stared at her, asking the same question that was ricocheting through her mind. She caught sight of Tristan DeLaSandro. Sexy as hell, he lounged against the wall with the look of a man who wasn't worried about a thing.

"We'll be joining one of our guest artists, Tristan DeLaSandro, who will be happy to answer any questions about his work." She wondered why nobody seemed to hear the hysteria in her voice.

Tristan was inches away. Tall, dark and all bad-boy artist, he had a half smirk on his face. Sophia cringed, waiting to get blasted.

"Nice distraction from the skunk," he murmured before continuing into the larger gallery. A few seconds later, she heard the soft timbre of his voice, then laughter as he entertained the crowd.

Max waited until the room emptied before slowly, carefully approaching the skunk. Sophia's mouth went dry. Both nerves and desire worked through her system. She knew this was a serious situation. A skunk spraying would ruin the event—and the photographs. But, oh, baby, watching Max work was like watching a sexy ballet.

He probably looked like this when he defused a bomb. All intent and focused, like a cat stalking its prey. He stopped at one of the easels and slipped a flat cardboard box from behind the display. With quick, soundless moves, he folded it together, stepped silently toward the settee.

Sophia held her breath, both in anticipation and in self-defense. The skunk didn't move when he dropped the box over its head.

Her hands pressed tight against her mouth, she watched him slowly, carefully slide the box onto its side. He closed the flaps and gently lifted it.

Still no noise from the box. And, thankfully, no stink. Before Max could take another step, one of his friends brushed past Sophia and took the box. She and Max watched him hurry through the arch. Sophia wanted to follow him, to make sure it didn't spray in the back room and that, please, oh, please, he didn't let it out by the building.

But her knees were too shaky for her to even attempt to walk.

Instead, she gave Max a horrified look.

"I thought you were securing the building," she whispered.

"All the doors are covered," he told her. "The only way that skunk got in here is if some woman carried it in her purse."

She wanted to dismiss that as ridiculous, but she knew better. Who the hell carried a purse big enough for a skunk, though? And more important, who hated her enough to cart a stink bomb under her armpit into a public place?

"St. James."

Together, they turned. One of Max's friends gestured them to the back room. Heart sinking, Sophia forced her feet to move. Max pressed one hand on the small of her back and she almost whimpered and threw herself into his arms.

"What's ruined?" she asked when she reached the storeroom where the caterer and staff had gathered.

"Nothing," Becca assured her. "The food's fine, the wine's fine. Nobody's messed with it."

"Someone sure tried, though," the big blond friend of Max's said. His haircut said he was military. His huge shoulders said he was a force to be reckoned with. It was the grin on his face that Sophia couldn't read, though.

"What happened?" Max asked, curving his arm around Sophia's shoulder. She didn't know if the move had been deliberate or habit. She didn't care. She shifted closer, needing his warmth and strength.

"Someone got into the catering truck and loosened the parking brake," Becca said, her lips white and trembling. "It hit the lamppost, and while everyone ran out to check it, somebody dumped the trays of canapés and fruit on the floor."

"Man or woman?" Max asked.

"Woman," Becca and Blondie answered.

"Back up food?" Sophia asked.

"Across the street in the cantina's kitchen," Becca confirmed. "I've already sent someone to get it."

Before anyone could say anything else, Gina popped her head in. "Soph?"

"In a second," Sophia said impatiently.

"Um, now would be better."

She glanced at Gina, noted the red splotches on her assistant's pale cheeks and how huge her eyes looked behind her boring glasses.

"What happened?" she said, ducking out from beneath Max's arm and hurrying over. She followed Gina into the hall where they wouldn't be overheard. The heat warming her back assured her that Max had followed.

"Someone called a tow company. There are eight trucks out there trying to tow patrons' cars away. Apparently they were told the exact ones to take."

"The most expensive," Max guessed.

Gina nodded. "I convinced them to leave, but just as the last one pulled away, a different company's tow fleet showed up."

Max cursed. He moved toward the door but before he could take a second step, Sophia grabbed his jacket. She was afraid if he left her, the building would collapse or something.

"Can you send one of the other guys?" she asked quietly.

He gave her a long look, then unclenched her fingers from

his jacket and held her hand. "Gina, find Allen. He's on duty in the main gallery. Wearing a butt-ugly tie with fish on it. Have him deal with the tow trucks. I'll get someone else to cover the front room."

Gina nodded and hurried out. Sophia gave him a grateful look. Before she could throw herself into his arms, though, another harbinger of doom called out.

"St. James, Louie sent me to find you," a huge man said in a gruff voice.

Sophia gulped. Like Max and the rest of the security team, he was dressed in a suit and tie. But unlike Max, who looked sexy and urbane, or the blonde, who looked like a buffed surfer going to church, this guy looked like The Hulk on his way to court. He had no neck, so the tie looked like it was hanging from his chin.

"What's up?" Max asked. She could feel the tension radiating off him, but his words were calm. She glanced at him. His face was calm, too.

She felt some of the tension draining from her own body.

"Someone tried to start a fire," The Hulk said.

The tension came back with a vengeance and brought a whole slew of terror with it.

"It's out. Some woman lit a trash can back in the office. Louie doused it with a pitcher of ice water before it caught hold."

"Oh, God." Sophia twisted her hands together. Her mouth went dry and spitless.

"Did he see who did it?"

"Yeah," the guy told Max. "He walked in on her. While he was watering she tried to run."

"And?"

"He grabbed her. Dumped another pitcher over her head when she kicked him. He's holding off calling the cops until you decide what to do with her."

"Where is she?" Max and Sophia asked together.

"Locked in the office bathroom."

"Take care of things," Max ordered.

Sophia didn't bother to protest his taking over. She was so grateful to have him here, she'd have curled up on the floor and cried if he hadn't taken charge.

Needing his strength, she slipped her hand into his and hurried along the hallway one step behind him.

"I thought I had it all handled," she said quietly, her words almost a whisper. "I did everything I could think of to make the show a success."

"And it is a success," Max pointed out. "We're just making sure it stays that way."

As they passed through the arches toward the hall that led to her office and the bathrooms, Sophia shot a quick glance at the showrooms. A few dozen people were milling through, talking, sipping champagne and enjoying the show. She saw Gina, clipboard in hand. Taking orders, Sophia knew.

A skunk, an attempted catering catastrophe and a fire. And they were still buying.

She'd celebrate later. After she'd thrown up.

They went into her office and stepped over to the closed bathroom door someone was pounding on. Max accepted the key from the guy standing guard. He gave a nod and the guy left, closing the door behind him. She could see his shadow against the etched glass of the door as he stood, arms crossed and his back to them. Ensuring privacy, Sophia realized.

Privacy was good.

"Ready?" Max said, holding up the key.

13

"WHAT IF IT'S LYNN?" Sophia winced. She hadn't meant to say that aloud. She knew the woman hated her. But to have to see proof, face-to-face, made her a little ill.

"Then we have her arrested."

Dread moved through her stomach like greasy smoke. She took a deep breath, trying to banish the sick feeling.

The pounding on the bathroom door continued.

They kept right on ignoring it.

Overwhelmed, Sophia closed her eyes and dropped her forehead against Max's chest. His arms encircled her, pulling her tight against him. She felt safe. Safe and loved. Breathing in his warm male scent, she realized that half of loving someone was trusting them. She'd been so afraid of giving up control, she'd refused to see the obvious. That Max was a man she could trust. With her life, with her business, with her heart.

"I need you," she finally admitted, lifting her head to meet his eyes. "I know I can deal with this. That's the important thing, right? That I can handle it on my own. That doesn't mean I have to be all stubborn and independent, though. I want you there…just for support."

Sophia waited for the roof to cave in. For Max to crow

in triumph or give her a condescending smile, as if he'd just been waiting for permission to run her life.

She got neither. Instead, he gave her a tight hug and whispered against her hair, "Sweetie, I'm here for you. Just for support."

She smiled against his chest, warmth and contentment like she'd never felt before centering her. Maybe, so busy trying to prove she could do it all by herself, she'd blown chances to let people show her that they believed in her.

Then she thought back to Joseph's passive-aggressive attacks and her brothers all-out bullying bossiness.

Nope. Max was just special.

"Ready?" he asked after a few seconds.

Sophia took a deep breath and stepped out of the safe haven of his arms. Whoever was on the other side of the door had added kicking to their pounding. Sophia winced. She'd rather stay wrapped around Max permanently, but she knew she had to face this head-on.

"Ready," she told him.

Max inserted the key into the shaking door.

He motioned her back, just in case Lynn came out swinging, she figured.

And he turned the knob.

The door swung open.

Sophia gasped. Her knees turned to jelly and her jaw hit her chest.

"What the…" Max growled.

"Oh, my God," Sophia breathed, dropping onto her tapestry couch when her knees gave away. "This is some kind of a joke, right?"

"Mom?" Max said, stunned.

FIVE MINUTES LATER, SOPHIA paced her office, tugging at her hair just in case it relieved a little of the pressure on her brain. "But… I don't understand."

"What's to understand? Insanity is beyond comprehension," Max muttered through clenched teeth.

Finally unable to deny the truth, Sophia threw her hands in the air and exclaimed, "Your mother is a vandal? The dame of Nob Hill? Mrs. General St. James, the committee queen?"

"I'm going to have to have her locked up," Max said, pacing opposite her and muttering. "Psychiatric evaluations. Therapy. House arrest. The press. Oh, hell, the press. This is going to be a nightmare."

"Going to be a nightmare?" Sophia exclaimed. "It's been a nightmare for the past two months. I can't believe this. She can't be responsible. Not all along. Can she? I didn't even know she was at the gallery tonight, for crying out loud."

Max shook his head, holding his palms up in a who-the-hell-knows move. Then he twirled his finger around his ear in the classic cuckoo sign.

"I'm standing right here, you know," Tabby stated in a snippy tone. She gave them both an icy glare. Her arms were wrapped around her chest like a straight jacket. Apt, Sophia figured, since she was apparently crazy.

"Since you're sitting here," Max growled, "how about you tell us what the hell is going on."

"I won't be talked to in that manner, Maximilian." His mother gave him a chilly look and lifted her chin. Faint color warmed cheeks still damp from the ice water deluge.

Class, Sophia realized. This was class. The woman's perfect hair was dripping down her back, she had tiny chunks of ice cube melting on her shoulder and she'd been caught trying to set fire to Sophia's bathroom. And she still looked as if she'd have a servant beheaded if the cold cucumber sandwiches weren't cut into perfect circles.

"What's going on, Mother?"

Apparently that manner of speaking was more acceptable to Mrs. St. James. She nodded and, after a brief glance at her options, sat in one of the leather wingbacked chairs. Sophia wondered if that was a courtesy so her wet self didn't ruin the upholstery, or if it was because nothing else was deemed worthy.

"The fire, the food, the vandalism. Was that all you?" Sophia asked Tabby, her head still reeling in shock.

"I had to stop the show," Tabby explained, looking at Sophia instead of her son. "I couldn't let…"

Sophia frowned. Couldn't let what? Before she could push, Max butted in.

"A skunk, Mother? Where the hell did you get a skunk? How did you get it in here? Twice?"

"SANALT."

"Huh?"

"What?" Max asked at the same time.

"Stinky Animals Need A lot of Love, Too. It's one of the groups the Ladies Club supports. I just drop by their shelter and check out one of the destunk skunks. The skunk's name is Andrew."

"That stinky little thing is named Andrew?"

"They don't spray, so they barely stink." Tabby gave Sophia a horrified look. "You don't think I'd risk carrying a fully loaded one, do you? No, these are more like kitty cats. They're litter-box trained, sweet and cuddly. Very good pets, actually."

"Pets?" Sophia repeated faintly.

"You use someone's pets as a threat," Max said, his voice strong and sure. Strong and sure enough to make both women wince. "You trashed Sophia's place, ruined her show and are now hauling skunks in your purse?"

"Oh, Maximilian, calm down. Of course I didn't do all of that." Tabby waved her perfectly manicured hand and confessed, "Bobby, the gardener's assistant, did most of the dirty work for me. Which is why my roses look so poor this year to be honest. He's been so busy with this little side job."

Sophia shook her heard, trying to get rid of the buzzing in her ears. Roses? Really?

It was like being dropped into bizzaro land.

Next thing she knew, Tabby would break out in song and dance on the coffee table. It wouldn't surprise her one bit, either.

Dance.

Sophia caught her breath. No way.

She lifted her head and squinted at Tabby. Was it possible?

"Wait a minute," Sophia said slowly. Max gave her a questioning look but she wasn't paying any attention to him. She tried to pretend she was looking through a camera's viewfinder. Snap, she imagined.

Yep, and there it was.

"I know what's going on," she breathed, shock rocking through her system.

Max's mother narrowed her eyes, one disdainful brow arched as if she were calling Sophia a liar. Then she looked closer. She blanched, her face the same gray as the muted black-and-white photo behind her head.

"No, you don't," she dismissed. But her voice was shaky and she looked scared.

"What's the deal?" Max asked, directing his question to Sophia.

She gave him a long, considering look. "Maybe this would be easier if you waited in the hall."

Tabby nodded.

Max clamped his arms over his chest and stared.

Sigh. Sophia knew she shouldn't feel sorry for the woman who'd gone out of her way to cause so many problems. But now that she understood why. Kinda.

"You're the cage girl, aren't you?" she asked quietly.

Tabby burst into tears. Not ladylike and contained tears. Big, gulping sobs. As if the shell she'd carefully crafted had cracked and suddenly everything was gushing out. If she'd shown as much of her stuff as Tabby had in those pictures, Sophia figured she'd crack, too.

She grabbed a box of tissues and pressed it into the older woman's hand. Then, already wincing, she looked at Max.

He looked like a bomb had just exploded in his face.

MAX STARED, HORRIFIED. What should he do? Panic gripped his stomach. He stood, sat, then stood again. Should he go to her? Get a doctor? Run?

He liked the idea of running.

"What the hell is a cage girl?" he heard himself ask. Whatever it was, he was sure he'd regret finding out.

His mother cried harder. He winced, sinking down in the chair and wishing someone would throw an explosive into the room. At least he'd have something less dangerous that he'd know how to handle.

Sophia sighed, then apparently unable to watch the drama any longer, got up and moved over to sit next to his mother. She wrapped an arm around Tabby's shoulder and the older woman sank into her chest, bawling as if someone had told her she was broke.

"Sergeant?"

Max glanced at the door.

"Just wanted to let you know everything's under control out here. Louie said the skunk is in the back room drinking milk. The food and drinks are being served again. No sign of an accomplice. Do you want the cops called?"

Hell, no, he didn't want to call the police on his mother. The words were on the tip of his tongue, but he stopped. He slanted a look at Sophia. Her pale eyes stared back. Waiting.

"Ask Ms. Castillo," he said. "It's her call whether we call the police or not."

Tabby howled louder.

Sophia glared.

"What?" he asked. "I thought you didn't want me interfering in your life or poking my nose in your business."

"Don't be mean," she said, now giving his mother's back a soothing pat. "No, of course we won't need the police."

She stopped and bit her lip. Max could see the battle between wisdom and compassion going on behind that pretty face. Finally she said, "Unless someone else is involved. If there are any more threats or problems, I want the cops and my lawyer called."

Tabby shook her head, leaving a black smear on Sophia's shoulder. Max winced.

"No, no," his mother said in a small voice. "No threats. Nothing else."

Max waited for Louie to close the door behind him, then he dropped his head into his hands.

Sophia was right. Who was he to tell her how to fix her problems? He was the root of all of her problems.

"I don't understand what's going on," he said, finally raising his head to stare at the two women who'd apparently bonded. His mother and his girlfriend. All cozied up, buddy-buddy and giving him fish-eyed stares as if he was the bad guy here.

"Von Schilling's show includes a few photos of your mother," Sophia said.

Max frowned. "No, it doesn't. Those are all…"

Horrified, he broke off and stared.

First at Sophia.

Then at his mother.

Then at a spot on the wall behind them both where he hoped the blank space would cover the images in his brain.

"Oh, God." Max closed his eyes. The images wouldn't fade. He didn't know which one of those photographs had been of his mother. He didn't want to know.

His eyes popped open.

"This is the project you mentioned? The business you

thought was too controversial? You sicced the Historical Guild on Sophia?" he accused.

"What?" Sophia exclaimed. "Your mother's behind that?"

She pulled back to glare at Tabby. Then she and Max both grimaced at the sight of his mother's face, all swollen and blotchy. Mascara ran in streaks to her chin and her lips were white as she pressed them together to try to hold back sobs.

Sophia sighed, then pulled her arms tight again. Max's heart did a little flip-flop.

"You should have told me," she hissed.

"Why are you holding her so tight?" he countered.

She tried to glare, but he could see there was no heat behind it. Then she rolled her eyes and pulled back so Tabby had to look at her.

"You're going to convince the Historical Guild not to sell this building," she told his mother. "You owe me that."

Tabby nodded without hesitation.

"In exchange, I'll pull your photos from the display."

Tabby started bawling again.

Max just stared, baffled. He'd been prepared to bring in an attorney. To fight his own mother to protect Sophia's interests. And just like that, she'd taken care of it all by herself.

Max knew he should be glad. Thrilled and proud. But all he felt was a defeated sense of uselessness. Sophia had solved her problems with the gallery vandal. His mother had solved her apparent problems of her, oh, God, nudie shots. And him? He'd started out without any and now his entire life was a problem.

Needing air, he murmured something about letting the women figure things out together. He barely noticed Sophia wave him out of the room as he left.

MAX DIDN'T KNOW HOW HE found himself on the cement stoop in front of the plain one-story military house. He had no clue what he was doing here. It was pointless.

But while he'd always worked his way around confrontations, he'd never backed down from anything. Or anyone.

He glanced at the small brass plate next to the doorbell. General C. St. James. The lights were on, so he knew his uncle was home. That wasn't why he was hesitating.

Suicide missions done in the name of useless heroics had always pissed him off. And yet, here he was.

Ordering himself to get it over with, he rapped on the door. It took his uncle a minute to open it, then, after a frown, the older man silently stood aside to welcome Max into the house.

"Well, this is a surprise. What can I do for you?" the General asked after they were both seated in the den.

Max had to give the old guy credit. He was a strategist right down to his toenails. After his silent welcome, he'd bypassed the comfy living room with its welcoming fire and led the way down the hall, seated himself in the position of command behind his desk and waved Max into the leather seat opposite him.

"I'd like you to rescind the Personal Change of Status," Max said, getting right to the point.

"Request denied."

Exactly what he'd expected. Max raised one eyebrow and rested his hands on the studded arms of the chair. Nothing showed on his face. He'd just been schooled by the two most important women in his life about what it really meant to fight for something, and he'd be damned if he'd fail.

"I won't serve at some cushy job while we're at war," Max calmly stated. "Not while men are overseas risking their lives."

For a brief second, he saw a glimpse of pride in his uncle's eyes. But then he blinked and the stoic command was back in place.

"You have no choice," the General corrected. "Orders have been issued. You'll follow them."

"I do have a choice. And if these orders were for the good of anything other than your own personal agenda, I would follow them. But they don't benefit me, they don't benefit my unit and they don't benefit my country."

"Are you questioning my authority?"

"As my superior, no," Max said, knowing he was walking a very fine line. The road to family loyalty only went one way with his uncle. "But as your nephew, I'm saying you've crossed the line."

The General stared, his face blank. For a second, Max hoped he'd gotten through. Maybe the old guy would finally accept that Max was a good soldier, a credit to his uniform and, dammit, an adult who could make his own career choices.

Then the General shook his head. "The order stands."

Max's gut tightened. But he didn't hesitate before replying. "I'll ETS and leave the service."

"Bullshit."

"I've already informed Colonel Gilden that I was leaving."

"You signed reenlistment papers."

"I signed a contract that specified that I'd serve overseas in EOD. Unless you rescind this PCS, the Army is in breach of contract. I might have to serve the last month of my duty in Washington, but then I walk away. Honorable discharge."

His eyes locked with his uncle's. Neither man blinked, neither looked away. And Max knew that was it. He was out of the Army.

SOPHIA WAVED AWAY THE last of the cleaning crew and said good-night to Gina. Then, with a deep sigh, she locked the front door. She left the back unlocked, though. Max had to come back eventually, right? She thought of the roses and chocolates in her office and smiled. She had an early Valentine's celebration planned when he did.

She was equal parts exhausted and exhilarated. Since the two emotions didn't mix well, she felt a little woozy. The night had been seriously overwhelming.

But it was Valentine's weekend. And despite the weirdness of it all, her problems were solved. Well, mostly solved.

Before she could consider the ones that were left, Max walked through the back hallway. Joy filled her as she hurried forward to wrap her arms around his waist. She settled her face against his chest and gave a deep sigh.

"There you are," she murmured.

"You shouldn't be so quick to hug me," he said, stepping back just a little.

"Why? Did you bring Andrew the skunk back with you?" she teased. Then she got a good look at his face. He looked... stressed. "What's up? Where did you go?"

"I...had some things to deal with."

Sophia waited.

Max grimaced. "I just came back to apologize. I can't believe I didn't realize it was my mother. I tracked down the motorcycle. It belongs to one of the gardeners."

He paused. As if he were waiting for her to blow up at him or something. Sophia frowned and shrugged. "Apparently he moonlights."

"Be serious, Sophia. It was right there under my nose the whole time, and I didn't catch on. I almost let your big night be ruined."

"No way—" she started to say. But Max, apparently juiced up on guilt, interrupted her.

"I'm responsible," he said, his chin jutting out.

She was still puzzled, but now Sophia was getting pissed, too. Why was he ruining their cuddlefest?

"You've got to be kidding," she said incredulously. "How do you figure this is all about you?"

"I'm the one who pushed you to do the show with von Schilling," he said coldly. His tone was worthy of that big high society house he'd grown up in. Rigid, uptight and distant. "I'm the one who was supposed to provide security for the show and make sure nothing happened. And it was my mother who not only almost ruined your show, but who has spent the past month vandalizing your gallery, tried to evict you and destroy your business."

Sophia sucked in a deep breath.

"So let me get this straight," she said. "You're taking credit for the state of my career?"

The icy mask cracked. Brows furrowed, he gave a little shake of his head. "No. I'm taking the blame for its destruction."

"But I'm the one who made the choices I did. Your mother made her choices. Why can't *we* have the blame?"

"Because I should have stopped it, of course."

"Oh, fine. You win. You're so freaking bright, the universe should revolve around you instead of the sun. There's just no reasoning with you." Sophia threw her hands in the air. "It's all your responsibility. Obviously you don't believe I'm capable of running my own life when you can do it so much better for me. Which of my many problems will you solve next?"

He just stared at her. His soldier face. Blank, stoic, detached.

"There's only one that I see. And I've already solved it," he said. His words were even, his tone soft and quiet.

"You solved it, did you?" she asked, just as quietly. Hers wasn't a soothing tone, though. Nope, she just sounded bitchy. Sophia wanted to cry. She didn't want to sound bitchy. She wanted to sound romantic, sweet. To curl up in his lap and tell him how glad she was the problems were over, to give him big sloppy kisses, then start planning the rest of their lives—or at least their next few months—together.

"I did solve it, yes." The corner of his mouth twitched with the hint of a humorless smile and he shrugged.

"Care to fill me in?"

"I talked to my uncle. I told him how I felt. I made it clear that if he didn't step out of my career, I'd be leaving the service."

"You confronted him?" She should be glad, shouldn't she? He'd stood up for his career. For something he loved. And he was thanking her for pushing him to do it.

But she didn't feel glad. She felt scared.

"I met with him. We settled things. He'll stay out of my career from now on."

"What are you saying?" she asked. She knew. She'd known from the beginning but she'd let herself hope. She'd let her heart dream out loud that secret little hope she hadn't even admitted to herself when she'd pretended to be happy he'd be leaving at the end of the month.

Then, when he'd told her he was staying, she'd actually believed it could work. She'd have made him happy enough if he'd stayed. But how selfish was it to expect someone you loved to settle for enough?

"My original orders were reissued. I'm going back to Afghanistan. I leave Wednesday."

Sophia licked her lips, trying to find the words. Any words. Her mine was blank, engulfed in pain.

"I'll come see you before I leave," he murmured, reaching out to slide his hand through the heavy fall of her hair.

"No," she whispered, blinking fast. She wasn't going to fall into a puddle of mush and make him feel guilty. She wasn't going to mess with his head or try to make him second-guess his decision. "I'm going to be busy this next week. Despite the problems, the show was a huge success. We've got a series of smaller events all week. I'll be tied up here and need to focus. On business. On negotiating with your mother."

On learning to survive without him.

"This doesn't have to be goodbye," he said, even though his tone said he knew it was. "If you'd like, we can—"

"No," she exclaimed before he could finish the suggestion. She took a deep breath, then shook her head.

"No," she repeated, more calmly. "You know the rules. No baggage when you return to duty. Rico told me about that." He winced, but she shook her head. She didn't want him to feel bad. That was its own form of baggage and she'd be damned if she'd send him back to war lugging it with him.

"Max, it's fine. You're doing what you're meant to. And we knew we only had a short time. We made the most of it. It was a wonderful month, but now it's over."

Just like she'd intended. Wow, look at that. She'd made a plan, seen it through and got exactly what she'd said she wanted. And now he needed to leave before she started crying.

"Be safe," she said quietly.

She stood on tiptoe, brushing a soft kiss over his lips. His hands clenched her shoulders. Max gave her a long look. She could see the arguments in his eyes. Which meant he could probably see the pain in hers.

Then, finally, he nodded.

And he turned to leave.

She waited until the door closed behind him.

Just in case, she waited a few seconds more.

See. She was in complete control.

And then, unable to stand any longer, she threw herself on the couch and gave in to the tears.

14

THE NEXT MORNING, SOPHIA had cleaned the gallery and was now tallying sales. She had to keep re-adding, though, because the number on the calculator seemed too big to be real.

"I'm surprised you didn't use these photographs in the negotiations," Tabby said. She stood next to Sophia in the storeroom, wrapping the half-dozen framed photos of her wild cage times in innocuous brown paper. "If you pushed hard enough, I'd have probably bought you the building to keep these out of sight."

"Isn't it bad for negotiations to give that kind of information away?" Sophia asked, shoving aside the adding machine—was that number really right?—to help wrap one of the framed photos.

"Oh, no. We already made the deal and you won't go back on your agreement."

Sophia considered that and sighed. Yeah, Tabby was right.

"It worked out okay," she said with a shrug. "I got what I wanted."

Sort of. Now that the looming threat of being evicted was off her shoulders, Sophia didn't really know what she wanted.

Success, of course. But in what way? In the normal way—return the gallery to the old format and keep the boobs out of it? Or in the holy crap way—she'd made a lot of money last night and those photos really weren't porn?

"Why'd you do these photos?" Sophia asked, the words out of her mouth before she could stop them. Then, because she'd already put her foot in it, she continued, "I mean, I understand why you wanted to get them back. But why'd you pose in the first place?"

Tabby paused. She looked across the table with dark, intense eyes she'd passed on to her son and considered. She was back to society matron today. Her hair perfectly coiffed, her clothes dry and sedate. But there was a wicked light in her eyes that Sophia kind of liked. It made her more real.

"I guess I thought it was a good idea at the time," Tabby finally said. "I'd had a pretty sheltered upbringing and was free for the first time. Out on my own, independent, determined to make my mark."

They both glanced at the triple-matted photo framed in dark walnut. Her hair had been a waterfall, hanging straight and heavy to her hips. Thigh-high white patent leather boots a barely-cover-the-essentials skirt whose fringe screamed shimmy. Peeking through all that hair was a perky rack like only a twenty-year-old could claim.

"And this was your mark?"

"It was one of them." Tabby gave a little smile and folded the paper, hiding her mark. "But then I met Marshall and realized that he wouldn't be comfortable with that. I had a choice. Continue with my little rebellion, or return to the life I'd grown up in, create a future and make my mark in other ways."

"So you gave up your dreams to get your man?" Sophia surmised.

"Goodness, you're making this into a much bigger deal than it actually was."

This from a woman who'd smuggled a skunk in her purse.

"I've made a point not to interfere in my son's life. He's got enough of that from his father's side of the family, after all. But I'm going to make a tiny exception right now and suggest that you and Maximilian sit down and talk to each other. I'm sure whatever the problem is, you can solve it if you want to."

"I doubt it," Sophia muttered. She'd let Max go for his own good. So she wouldn't—couldn't—do anything to solve the misery engulfing her.

"I know why he's so stubborn," Tabby said, folding the brown construction paper neatly over another framed photo. "But why are you?"

Emotionally numb, Sophia just stared.

"Maximilian was raised with expectations. He was told from the time he started walking what his life was going to be. My husband had huge plans for his son." Tabby paused her wrapping, lost in memories for a moment. Then she shrugged. "Some people would have rebelled and walked away from having their entire life outlined for them before they were out of diapers. Luckily, Max loved the Army. He'd never wanted to be anything but a soldier."

"So he fell right in line with what his daddy wanted."

"Oh, no," Tabby protested, holding out a length of twine and eyeing it before wrapping it around the wrapped frame. "Max was a smart one. He got what he wanted on his terms, not his father's. He's always been determined to go his own way. I expect that's one of the things he found so attractive about you. That independence."

Not attractive enough to want to continue a relationship with her, though. Sophia tried to stop her lower lip from trembling. She'd promised herself she was through crying, dammit.

"I didn't mean to upset you," Tabby said, sounding sincere

despite the stiffness of her words. "To be honest, while at first I thought the relationship might be serious, now I realize it's anything but."

Sophia heard the condemnation in those snooty words.

"How can we have a relationship thousands of miles apart?" Sophia asked, wiping at the tears streaming down her cheeks.

"It's doable, as I well know." Tabby arched a brow and gave Sophia a piercing look. "Of course, it doesn't matter since you're perfectly willing to let him go? You had all the means right there at your fingertips to make him stay but you refused to use them."

"You mean emotionally blackmail him into giving up his career?" Sophia glared. Did the woman never learn? Hadn't last night showed her that manipulation and sneaking around never paid?

"Don't be silly. You wouldn't ask him to give up his career any more than he'd ask you. That's not love, after all." Tabby added her last package to the stack on the hand truck and then gave Sophia a stern, penetrating look at odds with her fluffy society looks. "Or, well, I guess it's not love, anyway, is it. At least not on your part."

Shock was the only thing that kept Sophia from protesting.

Tabby shifted the hand truck into travel mode. "To quote my daddy, 'Until you step up to the plate and swing, you're just pretending to play the game.' In other words, you obviously didn't care as much as you claim, now, did you?"

Stunned, Sophia let her go.

Apparently it was time to put away the martyr wear and go get her man.

Before she could, the phone rang. She glanced at the caller ID. "Hi, Olivia. What's the news?"

"THIS IS NICE."

Sophia turned from her contemplation of the ocean and gave a shaky smile. She loved the estate, especially the gardens and this view. She was so glad to be able to share them with Max.

"I didn't think you'd come."

"You asked me to, so here I am," he said as he stepped farther into the garden. Her breath caught at the sight of him.

He was in uniform. God, he was gorgeous. He was always sexy, no matter what he was or wasn't wearing. But seeing him in uniform almost gave her a heart attack. Desire curled deep in her belly. Her nipples tightened and heat pooled between her legs. She wanted to check her chin for drool.

"I love this spot," she said, stalling. She had so much to say, so much on the line. And she was terrified. "It always makes me think of romance."

"Is that why you called me? You wanted a romantic goodbye?" He sounded both shocked and a little angry. She couldn't blame him, considering how she'd blown off his suggestion that they try to keep their relationship alive long distance.

"No. I didn't want to leave things ugly between us. What we have is too special for me to let you leave without telling you…" She couldn't do it. The words choked in her throat. Black spots danced in front of her eyes. She gulped and sidestepped. "Without telling you what I've done."

"What did you do?" he asked, a little half smile playing on his lips.

"I made a deal with your mother, the photographs of her in return for the Historical Guild not selling the building. And she's going to help me with some promotion for the gallery. The exhibit was such a success, I realize it'd be stupid not to show nudes. Tasteful ones, at least. And apparently, the nude photos only pose a problem for your mother if she's in them," she told him. His wince made her smile.

When he didn't say anything, though, she kept babbling. "I heard from my attorney yesterday, too. Lynn's agreed to settle. The battle over Joseph's will is over."

She tried to remember that incredible feeling of triumph

when Olivia had called to tell her they'd waved the white flag. But she couldn't get past the frayed knots of nerves in her belly.

Then Max's grin flashed, instantly relaxing her. Sophia automatically smiled back.

"Did you get everything?" he asked.

Sophia wrinkled her nose. "I got everything I really wanted. This estate, my jewelry, the cash holdings. She gets the business and stocks."

"That's great." He reached out and wrapped one arm around her shoulder, pulling Sophia close and giving her a quick kiss.

"Congratulations. Your life is exactly what you wanted now," he told her. "You've settled the will. Your gallery is both successful and safe. And you've reclaimed your life."

He reached out and slid one hand over the heavy fall of her hair and arched a brow. "What's next?"

She'd rehearsed what she wanted to say. She'd written it down, polished it and memorized it as if it were a part in a play. She'd figured it'd give her control over the discussion.

But her mind was blank.

"I love you," she said.

"I love you, too."

Their kiss was gentle and sweet, making Sophia's heart sing and her toes tingle. Slowly, Max pulled back to look into her eyes.

"I didn't want to love you," he confessed. "I wanted to be able to walk away. Hopefully set the memory of you aside so you weren't in my way."

Her brows shot up. He grimaced.

"Not like that." He paused, trying to find the words. "All my life, I've felt penned in by rules. My family's rules. Uncle Sam's rules. Hell, even my own rules. I accept them all, and understand their value. But sometimes I just have to break one. Like seeing you. I knew you could make me break my number one rule, but being with you was worth the risk. But a part of me was afraid you'd put strings on me and do what my uncle failed to—make me take the easy career path and end my respect for what I was doing."

He stopped, watching her face. Sophia couldn't believe his fears were the exact same ones she had herself. Different, but the same.

"I'd never want to hold you back," she said softly.

"I know. I finally realized that. You pushed me to confront my uncle, to fight for my station. You cared enough about what mattered to me to let me pursue it."

"Like I said," she told him, "I love you."

His smile flashed just before he took her mouth. His lips seduced, sweet and sexy as they moved softly over hers. He pulled her closer, so her breasts pressed against the stiff fabric of his jacket. His medals poked her shoulder, adding an oddly erotic element to the kiss. Sophia melted into him. Their tongues slid together in a familiar dance of passion.

"I want to marry you," he said quietly, drawing back just enough to look into her eyes.

Sophia's heart raced. Oh, yes, she wanted to yell. She wanted to dance around the garden and clap and laugh with joy. But she couldn't.

"I can't marry you," she said quietly, holding tight to his hands so he wouldn't step away.

He frowned and shifted. Not away, but enough so that they were no longer plastered together.

"Is it because my mother vandalized your gallery and tried to ruin your business?" he asked. Sophia had to smile at the grim resignation in his tone because beneath it she heard the exasperated love.

"Of course not. I actually understand why she did it. And she's more than made up for any problems she caused by hosting the series of Friends of Esprit Gallery luncheons. Who knew high society was so interested in naked breasts?"

Max's smile flashed, but just as quickly it was gone.

"Then the fact that she'd posed with her naked breasts isn't the problem?"

She had to give him credit. He barely cringed as he said the words. She figured it was his military training. The man faced live bombs; he wasn't about to back away from his mama's wild past.

"No. Like I said, I understand why she tried to hide it, but I also understand what it's like to be seduced into letting go of all inhibitions."

"Right," he muttered, obviously more comfortable with his mother having her inhibitions intact. Then he shrugged it off, obviously not wanting it in his brain. "If it's none of that, then what is it?"

Sophia licked her lips, sitting on the edge of the fountain and trying to gather her nerve.

"Here's the thing," she started.

Max shook his head.

"Nope. I don't want to hear about the thing," he insisted. But he was smiling.

"The thing is, I love you."

He reached out to pull her into his arms, but Sophia shook her head.

"I love you. But I'm not ready to take that step. I'm afraid."

"Of marrying a soldier?"

"No," she insisted, jumping to her feet then and pressing her palms against his chest in assurance. "Oh, no. You were a soldier when I fell in love with you. I know your job is scary. It's dangerous and hellish and it means you're away for long periods of time. But I knew that when I fell in love with you."

"Then what's the problem?"

Sophia sucked in a deep breath. "I'm afraid of losing myself. You're a strong man. You know what you want. You've got a plan and you know where your life is going."

Max frowned, shaking his head in confusion. "So? You're a strong woman. You've got a gallery and you know what you want for it, right?"

"Yes. But it's not enough." She looked over his shoulder at the adobe estate, still amazed that she had her home back. Not because she'd suddenly gotten brave, but because Max had pushed her off the cliff. "I need to figure out where my life is going. Once I know, I can share it with you."

"Does this involve other men?"

"No!" she exclaimed, horrified.

"Then go for it."

She laughed. "Just like that?"

"Sure. I want you to be happy. I can't think of anything you'd do that I couldn't support."

She took a deep breath, then blurted, "I want to be a photographer."

"Are you planning an exposé of men's anatomy?" he asked.

"Eww."

"Then, again, why wouldn't I support you? You're a fabulous photographer from what I've seen. Whatever you need, just tell me. You want me to do security at your shows, I'm there. You want me to drive you to remote mountains so you can take shots of wildflowers, just say so. You want me to do nothing and stay out of it, I'll try my best. This is your dream, sweetheart. You're calling the shots."

She didn't know what to say. She couldn't think of a single reason. So she hugged him instead.

Not for the support, although that was amazing. But because he hadn't even blinked at the concept of her being a photographer. He'd met famous ones. He'd been a part of a quarter-million-dollar exhibit this past weekend. And he believed in her so much that he didn't question that she'd fit all of that.

It made her brave enough to continue.

"I want to be with you," she told him. "I want to give us a chance. But like you said, I need to do this on my own. I need to know I'm strong enough to marry you."

She held her breath. She'd taken more risks in the past week than she'd taken in her entire life. But this one scared her the most.

"I want to travel and take pictures," she admitted. "There's so much I want to see and do. So much I want to learn about myself. I'd visit you if you'd let me, but I don't want to promise anything until we're both sure."

Max was silent at first. Sophia's stomach tilted toward her toes. He puffed out a breath, then leaned his forehead on hers and closed his eyes. Then he pulled back and gave her a look of such intense love, her eyes stung. No, she wasn't going to get all emotional here. She was going to stay in control.

"You need this time?" he said. "Then take it. I'm in the war zone for a year. I'm sure I'll be stationed stateside after, unless you'd rather I request something else."

"You're willing to wait for me?" she asked, knowing tears were leaking down her cheeks but unable to stop crying. At least she'd learned from Tabby to wear waterproof mascara.

"Sweetheart," he said, lifting both her hands to his mouth and pressing a kiss on her knuckles, "I'd be waiting anyway. I'll do it better if I know you're happy until I get back."

Epilogue

Two years later

"ARE YOU SURE THIS ISN'T too cliché?" Sophia asked, her voice shaky with nerves. "It's like Saint Valentine went crazy."

Silver hearts and red roses. Chocolate and champagne. Love and romance. It was almost too perfect.

Tabby smoothed her hand over the heavy white satin of Sophia's skirt with a giddy sort of smile. The kind inspired by a proud mother or a woman who'd already downed half a magnum of champagne. Or in this case, both.

"It's perfect," the older woman declared. "You're perfect. In that dress. For this day. And most of all, for my Maximilian."

My Maximilian, Sophia silently corrected.

Who knew they'd actually make such a crazy relationship work, let alone work so well it'd flourish into a three-tiered cake and flower girl?

Max had completed his tour overseas with Sophia flying off to some exotic locales to meet him for a few days here, a week there. They'd written. They'd talked on the phone. They'd discovered that the rush of lust and excitement that'd launched their relationship was solid and lasting and real.

And today, they would promise to spend the rest of their lives together.

She'd risked it all. And she'd gotten everything she ever dreamed of in return. Both in love and in her career. While she traveled, Tabby and Gina ran the gallery, which was a surprisingly perfect pairing. On a roll with her success, Sophia had nagged von Schilling into mentoring her. It'd taken her a year to get past her insecurities. But Max had been there for her, totally believing in her. Then last month, her shots of the women in Afghanistan had won an award.

Sophia stepped into the hallway and took her father's arm. His kiss on her cheek, the music and cheers as she walked down the aisle were all a distant blur.

There were hearts and flowers decorating the garden and she knew Rico was standing as best man. But all she saw was Max, there in his black tuxedo, waiting for her at the altar.

In her mind's eye, she snapped a picture of this moment. Of their future together. She wouldn't need to analyze it, though.

She knew it was going to be amazing.

* * * * *